Unexpected Hawaiian Love Story

Unexpected Hawaiian Love Story

by CJ Johnson

Unexpected Hawaiian Love Story by CJ Johnson

www.novelstokeep.com
Email: Novelstokeep@gmail.com

eBook ISBN: 978-1-64953-528-3
Paperback ISBN: 978-1-64953-527-6

Printed in United States of America.

Dedication

To my daughter, Tami Wellman. She took her first steps in Australia, entered kindergarten in Africa, became a soccer star in Hawaii, and has remained a faithful daughter through the highs and lows of life's journey.

Acknowledgments

I could not produce a publishable novel without the dedication of editors and faithful friends that read the drafts. Of the many that assisted me, I wish to thank Stacey (www.fiverr.com/grammargal) for the final edit, plus editing suggestions by David Burson and Michelle Johnson-Wang.

Chapter 1

*T*he East-West Center Christmas party was in full swing when Alex Silverton arrived from the adjacent University of Hawaii campus. Uncomfortable with large parties, he headed to the pupu (appetizer) table covered with platters of holiday cookies, sushi rolls, fresh pineapple, and local vegetables. As he reached for a broccoli crown, his fingers touched another's, and he jerked his hand away. Looking up, he gazed across the table into the emerald eyes of a lithesome woman with red hair cascading to her shoulders, framing delicate features lightly brushed with freckles.

"You like broccoli too?" *God, what a dumb question.*

She smiled—her eyes locked on his. Before he could say something intelligent, she was gone like a mirage. He scanned the crowd searching for the red hair as he absentmindedly dipped his broccoli into wasabi. Moments later, his mouth and nose burning, he rushed to the punch bowl and gulped down two cups.

"Alex, glad to see you could make it."

Bob Taylor was silver-haired and although only five-seven and slight in build, had an outsized deep voice. He was a senior

1

fellow at the East-West Center, and they had coauthored a journal article on volcanism in Circum-Pacific countries.

"Bob, quite a party. Thanks for the invitation."

They chatted briefly about plans for the holidays. Ever the matchmaker, Bob suggested Alex ask out Eva Hirschfeld from the English Department. Alex forced a smile and said he'd think about it.

Bob chuckled, "I know what that means. Anyway, now that you're here, I want to introduce you to Kelsey O'Connor, a promising grad student from UC Berkeley who's here on a fellowship to study the impacts of natural disasters on Pacific Island economies."

"Kelsey," he called out in a booming voice.

Alex swallowed hard as the tall redhead emerged from the crowd and walked directly toward them, her hips swaying just enough to distract his eyes from her face.

"Kelsey, Dr. Silverton is the person I told you was an expert on volcanism in the Pacific."

She offered her hand and quipped, "Our fingers met over the broccoli."

Bob had a quizzical expression, and Alex clarified her peculiar comment. "At the pupu table we both reached for the broccoli at the same time."

Bob laughed. "Well, I'll leave you two to sort out who gets the broccoli. Sorry to dash, but I've got to pick up my son from Punahou."

Bob left, leaving the two facing each other. Alex struggled to think of something witty and engaging to say as Kelsey tucked wayward strands behind her ear. *I better stay safe.* "Bob told me you need assistance regarding volcanism and its risks to Pacific Island nations."

"Yes, Dr. Taylor said he'd introduce me to you but wasn't sure you would come to the Christmas party. I wasn't expecting to meet you over broccoli. May be serendipity. I thought it might be you, as you've obviously come directly from your laboratory. You're in a khaki shirt, and everyone else is wearing aloha clothing."

"I decided to come at the last minute because Bob had mentioned there was someone he wanted me to meet. I'll be pleased to help you, but I only know about volcanism in the Pacific region and not much about other risk factors facing island countries."

"Dr. Silverton, I spent three months visiting Pacific Island countries collecting information for my dissertation, and I'm filling in details with experts like you. My chapter on geological risks to Pacific Island countries is weak, and any help you can give me will be greatly appreciated."

"When do you want to get started?"

She tapped the side of her plastic glass as she glanced around the room. "I've met the people I want to meet here, so if you're available now, maybe we could go someplace quieter to discuss my research?"

"Sure. We could go to my office on campus, though it's pretty cluttered, or a nearby coffeehouse in Manoa Valley."

"A coffee would be great, and if we walk, I can find it again since I walk or take the bus everywhere."

He showed Kelsey the well-traveled university student path along Manoa Stream past Mid-Pacific Institute and along a narrow street lined with plantation-style homes surrounded by a profusion of tropical flowers and fragrances. When they passed a plumeria tree in full bloom and a fan of flowers on the pavement, Kelsey paused to collect pink blossoms.

"Planning to make a lei?"

"They're for my daughter, Nadia."

"You have a daughter?" he said, his voice a higher pitch.

She smiled as she zipped her backpack. "Yes, and I'm single if you're wondering why I'm not wearing a ring."

"I suppose you have a significant other to help with Nadia while you're doing research?"

Kelsey stopped walking and turned to Alex. "Dr. Silverton, why are you asking such personal questions?"

"Sorry, it's none of my business."

She nodded. "My mother's here over the Christmas break. After she leaves, I'll organize my schedule around Nadia's school."

Better not further raise her ire with personal questions. "We're almost there. Just a block along Woodlawn Drive, and we'll be at Manoa Market Place, where my favorite coffeehouse is located."

Coffee Manoa was set back in the middle of the complex, facing a congested parking lot with large shade trees. "This is a popular hangout for university students and professors. What do you want to drink?"

"A cappuccino." Kelsey reached for her wallet.

"Kelsey, it's on me."

"Dr. Silverton, I insist on paying." She handed him a ten-dollar bill.

He frowned. "Okay, but I prefer that you call me Alex."

Kelsey grabbed the only available table on the sidewalk, while Alex went inside for their drinks. To Kelsey, Coffee Manoa didn't appear special compared to the funky coffeehouses around the UC Berkeley campus.

Alex returned with foam-topped cappuccinos dusted with chocolate powder. The pattern in the foam was of a five-petal plumeria flower. "Bet you've never tasted one with this flavor?"

She took a sip and then her tongue flicked over her foamy upper lip. "Delicious. A little like hazelnut but smoother, like a touch of fragrant honey was added."

"It's macadamia nut flavored coffee, only found in Hawaii. It also makes delightful iced coffees when cold brewed. If you look straight out into the parking lot, you'll see just cars— nothing to write home about. But raise your gaze, and you get a view of the emerald-green Ko'olau Mountains at the back of Manoa Valley."

"Alex, they're breathtaking!"

"The jagged Ko'olau peaks snag the clouds, keeping this side sunny year-round. On most mornings, you can see ribbon waterfalls at the back of Manoa Valley, and when the sun is at the right angle, the falls appear as silvery strands of tinsel, and the pièce de résistance is when a perfect rainbow arches over the valley."

Kelsey leaned back in her chair. "You read those lines somewhere? Geologists don't use such prose. The geologists I've met speak and write in technical jargon only understood by other geologists."

Alex chucked. "Well, for your information, I wrote a novel and have over two dozen rejection slips in my desk drawer to prove it."

"What's it about?"

"A Shangri-La hidden in the Himalaya Mountains. The idea was on my mind since I was a teen and read the novel *Lost Horizon* by James Hilton. I discovered there were Buddhist legends about a hidden mythical kingdom called Shambhala. After doing projects in both Nepal and Tibet, I wrote a story about a Shangri-La that would be plausible in the twentieth century. I attempted to make the novel believable from a scientific perspective, then sent queries out to twenty-seven literary agents, with visions of a best seller. The rejection slips came back fast and furious, so I'm sticking to geology. Anyway, you're not here to learn about my naïve attempts to become a novelist."

"Yes, but I'm impressed that you wrote a novel." She set down her cup. "Alex, where should I start in assessing risks to islands from volcanic activity in the Pacific?"

"For starters, most volcanic activity is along the so-called Ring of Fire that circles the Pacific Ocean and has more than 350 volcanoes. The islands at greatest risk are Japan, the Philippines, Papua New Guinea, Indonesia, and the Solomon Islands. The largest risk is from tsunamis caused by earthquakes below the seabed. No island in the Pacific, including Hawaii, is safe from tsunamis, that have the potential to kill tens of thousands of people. So I suggest the threat from major tsunamis, although rare, should be emphasized in your dissertation."

Alex paused and scratched his chin. "You really need to talk to Dr. Thomas Chandler, director of the Disaster Preparedness Office. They recently completed a study of island risks from volcanic eruptions and earthquakes in the Pacific, and he is a much better source of data than me. I'll be pleased to give you an introduction to Dr. Chandler."

"Sounds almost too good to be true. I don't know how I can repay you."

"You could accept my dinner invitation."

"I thought university faculty weren't allowed to date students."

Alex nodded. "Faculty can't date students in their classes or anyone they're advising or have any control over. None of those criteria apply to my asking you out to dinner."

"Thank you, but it would be a date, and I don't have space in my life for possible romantic complications. I'm here to complete the research on my dissertation and nothing more."

"I understand. I do find you interesting."

"Interesting or sexy?"

"Hmm. As we're not having dinner together, it's a moot question."

They were the last to leave when Teresa closed Coffee Manoa at 10:00 p.m. They followed the dimly lit road under streetlights to an even darker trail along the Manoa Stream. Kelsey took out a small flashlight and handed it to Alex, then tucked her hand under his arm. "I'm afraid of the dark, particularly in unfamiliar places like this."

He liked her closeness and the bumping of their hips as they walked. *Does she feel the same way?* When they reached his car, she let go and stepped away. She gave him directions to an older home at the base of Diamond Head, two blocks from Waikiki Beach. "I'm staying in an apartment under the house. Thanks for your advice."

"Mind if I walk you to the door?"

"I can find my way from here."

"Umm, any chance I could show you some of the sights on Oahu this weekend?"

"Remember, my mother's staying with me, and I give my spare time to my daughter."

"Bring your mother and daughter, and we'll all go snorkeling at Hanauma Bay."

"Nadia's afraid of putting her face in the water, and she's never snorkeled."

"A better reason to come, so I can teach her."

"We don't have snorkeling equipment."

"I have extra snorkeling gear, and if they don't fit, we can rent them at Hanauma Bay. Be ready at seven thirty tomorrow morning, and we'll stop for coffee and pastries on the way."

"You're really persistent." She hesitated. "Okay, but it's not a date—understand?"

"Absolutely. We'll have lots of fun."

Dora was curled up on the couch when Kelsey stepped inside. "Meet any deliciously handsome bachelors at the Christmas party?"

"Moooom! Why do you always ask the same question? You know I'm not looking!"

Dora bookmarked her novel and patted the cushion beside her. "Sit and tell me all about the party. You must have met some interesting people."

Kelsey sat next to her mother, kicked off her shoes, and rubbed her ankles. "I should know better than to wear new shoes to a party."

"They're muddy. I thought the Christmas Party was inside."

Mom's so nosey. "I met a professor that can help me with my research. After the party, we walked to his favorite coffeehouse for coffee and a chat."

"Until ten forty-five p.m.?"

"We had a lot to talk about."

"Is he single and eligible?"

"Mom! You're infuriating! I've told you a hundred times that I'm not looking for a man, and let's face it—how many handsome, eligible professors would be interested in a thirty-one-year-old freckle-faced woman with a child?"

"Honey, when I was dating your father, he spent an entire evening counting and kissing the freckles on my body. It's been thirty-three years and he's still counting."

"I'll never meet a man as romantic as Dad. Did Nadia give you any trouble?"

"She never does." Dora unzipped the back of Kelsey's dress. "Do you know what Nadia prayed for tonight?"

"The presents she wants for Christmas?"

"No. She prayed that you would find her a daddy and make the family whole."

Kelsey stepped out of her dress and hung it in the closet, then stood gazing at her motley collection of dresses—some older than Nadia. Dora massaged Kelsey's shoulders as she tilted her head back, her hair cascading over her mother's hands. "That feels so good."

"Is he interested?"

"Uh-huh."

"What's he like?"

"He's really tall and faintly resembles Clint Eastwood in the movie *The Bridges of Madison County*. He came straight to the Christmas party wearing a khaki shirt and was fine talking about his research interests but awkward when he got around to asking me out to dinner."

"Wonderful! You accepted?"

"I turned him down. I'm not looking, and he's not my type."

"So . . . no chemistry?"

Kelsey stiffened as she straightened the clothes in the closet. "It's been so long since I had those feelings, and I'm not sure they'll come back again."

"You'll never find out if you chase away every man that shows an interest in you. I'd like to meet this mystery professor."

"You will tomorrow. He insisted on taking all of us to Hanauma Bay to snorkel. I want your promise that you won't say anything to embarrass me."

"Sweetie, you know I wouldn't do that."

Chapter 2

*S*aturday was Alex's opportunity to make up for his awkward performance with Kelsey at the Christmas party and Coffee Manoa. He was nervous, knowing he would be scrutinized by two women and a child. Kelsey's mother, Dora, would probably want her to begin dating eligible men. But Kelsey's seven-year-old daughter could either be the gateway to her heart or a poison pill. If Nadia saw him as a threat, then she would sabotage any chance of a romance taking root. Teaching Nadia to snorkel would win him points from everyone, but if it was a bad experience, he would be blamed for frightening her.

Alex sorted through his drawer of faded T-shirts and took out the one of the Great Barrier Reef. The print of a coral reef teeming with colorful fish, including two small black-and-white-banded clownfish, was perfect for the outing.

When Alex pulled up in front of Kelsey's place, Nadia was lugging a large beach bag up the narrow flagstone steps at the side of the house. He popped open the trunk, then walked over to assist.

"Hi! You must be Nadia," he said cheerfully. "Your mother told me all about you. I'm Alex, and I'm gonna teach you how to snorkel. It's really easy."

"I can't snorkel," she replied tersely.

"That's no problem. I promise you'll be snorkeling and having fun in no time."

"I kind of want to learn, but I'm afraid to put my face in the water."

"With a facemask on, your face doesn't even touch the water, and you'll see more colorful fish than you can count. I will be right next to you and promise to keep you safe."

Nadia grinned. "I'll try."

Kelsey and her mother appeared at the top of the stairs. "Good morning. I see you've already met Nadia."

"Mom, Alex promised to teach me to snorkel, and I don't even have to get my face wet."

"Nadia, you must call him Mr. Silverton."

Alex was struck by the resemblance between Kelsey and her mother—the intense green eyes, red hair, and sprays of freckles. While Kelsey's red hair was natural, her mother's was probably enhanced in a beauty salon. Nadia was a scaled-down model of the women, with dimpled cheeks and a bouncier walk.

"Kelsey, I see where you get your good looks."

She pursed her lips at the comment she'd heard since she was a teen. *You're not fooling me with your attempt to ingratiate yourself with my mother.*

Dora stepped forward with a generous smile as she extended her hand. "Dr. Silverton, it's a pleasure to meet you. Kelsey told me you're going to help with her research on volcanoes." Her fingers glided into Alex's hand with purpose.

"Mrs. O'Connor, I'm pleased to have the opportunity to take all of you to my favorite snorkeling spot on Oahu, and also one of the most picturesque beaches in the Hawaiian Islands."

Still holding his hand, she said, "Please call me Dora."

"With pleasure, and call me Alex."

Kelsey frowned. *You'd think* they're *going on a first date.*

Nadia scrambled into the rear seat with her grandmother, and Kelsey joined Alex in the front. He took the longer and slower Diamond Head Road around the iconic volcano then along tree-lined Kahala Avenue past posh beach-side homes that sold for more than $20 million. Alex pointed out that all beaches in Hawaii were public, so everyone could enjoy them and their priceless views.

"Anyone up for a coffee and hot chocolate with lots of whipped cream plus fresh pastries?"

"Can I have a glazed donut too?"

"Sure, if it's okay with your mother."

"Do I have a choice?"

Dora spoke up. "I really would like a coffee, but I insist on paying."

"But you're my guests today," Alex said cheerfully.

"It's the least we can do for taking us snorkeling on your day off."

Starbucks was at the front entrance of the upscale Kahala Mall. Alex and Nadia were the only ones wearing T-shirts and shorts among the older and wealthier clientele. Kelsey grabbed the only unoccupied table while the others stood in line.

Nadia was beaming as she carried a glazed donut to the table, while Alex and Dora brought the drinks and warm blueberry scones.

"Nadia, before you ask, you can't dip your donut in my coffee."

"Humph." Nadia stuck out her lower lip and shifted her chair closer to Alex.

Alex struggled to keep from chuckling. "Kelsey, why don't you check out the Starbucks mugs with Hawaiian motifs and pick out one for your dad?"

As soon as Kelsey and Dora stepped away from the table, Alex moved his cup closer to Nadia. "You can dip your donut in my coffee, but be quick."

Nadia couldn't control her giggles when Kelsey and Dora returned. Kelsey immediately discovered their ruse as she looked at the telltale trail of coffee spots on the table and soggy bits of donut in Alex's cup.

"Nadia, I told you not to dip your donut in the coffee."

"Mommy, you said not to dip it in *your* coffee, and Mr. Silverton doesn't mind."

"Kelsey, I confess I told her it was okay. I do it all the time, and it makes my coffee sweeter."

"What am I going to do when you're both in cahoots?"

"Mommy, what does *cahoots* mean?"

"You two conspired against me."

"What does *conspired* mean?"

"Nadia, that's enough. Eat your donut, and no more dunking in anyone's coffee."

Dora slowly stirred her coffee as she observed the playful banter. Kelsey needed a man that could make her laugh, and Alex was off to a good start. "Kelsey told me you study volcanoes. What got you interested in such an unusual profession?"

"Most kids like to collect rocks but lose interest when they grow up. I didn't. After my undergraduate degree in geology at UC Santa Barbara, I joined the Peace Corps and spent two years in Papua New Guinea. There I witnessed a volcano erupt, lighting up the night sky and raining ash down on the village where I was staying. I suppose it was an epiphany, as I knew instantly that I would study volcanology in graduate school."

Kelsey turned from wiping up Nadia's coffee spots. "I planned to visit PNG during my research, but the grant money ran out. I've read that there are over eight hundred languages spoken and there may still be small groups of people with no contact with the outside world."

"That was true until World War II, but today, some contact has been made with every village. I hitched a ride in a mining company helicopter into the remote interior of the main island of New Guinea and met native men in traditional dress with curved boar's tusks through the nose and wearing penis gourds."

"Mr. Silverton, is a penis gourd a necklace?"

Alex looked at Kelsey. "That's one for you to handle."

"Well, Native people use different materials from the jungle to make clothes and cover themselves, and a gourd is sometimes tied at the waist."

"Kind of like a skirt?" Nadia replied.

"Umm, yes."

"Were you scared?"

"A little because we couldn't understand each other. But the scariest thing was when I had to deliver a baby. The mother was so happy that she named the boy Alex." He pulled out a photo of himself holding the newborn baby.

"You look really happy."

"More relieved than happy that the baby was okay. Part of my Peace Corps training was how to deliver a baby in an emergency, something I didn't expect to use. It's exhilarating to hear a newborn cry for the first time."

The Hanauma Bay parking lot was nearly full when they arrived at nine twenty and parked at the overflow parking lot.

Alex opened the trunk and handed beach bags to Kelsey and her mother, then a plastic ABC Store bag to Nadia. "This is just for you."

She peeked inside. "It's a kid's snorkeling set."

"You need proper equipment to enjoy snorkeling."

Kelsey frowned. "Alex, you said we would rent snorkeling gear at Hanauma Bay."

"Yes, but it's much easier to learn to snorkel if Nadia's face mask fits properly and doesn't leak, and now she can snorkel off Waikiki Beach."

Kelsey looked in the bag. "Where did you buy these so early in the morning?"

"My secret, and they're my gift to Nadia, but you'll have to rent your own," he teased.

Dora cut in. "My granddaughter will never forget your special gift."

"I'm sure I can learn to snorkel with my very own mask, snorkel, and pink fins."

Kelsey slowly shook her head. "I suppose it's okay."

"Yay!" Nadia yelped as she pranced around on tiptoes.

Midway across the tree-studded lawn, a family of mongooses tumbled from a clump of bushes and bounded across to a hedge of red hibiscus and disappeared.

"Mr. Silverton, what are those cute animals?"

"There're mongooses that were brought to Hawaii by sugarcane plantation owners to control the rats, but the mongooses also liked birds' eggs and were a major factor in wiping out half of the more than fifty native species of birds."

"So they're not so nice?"

They stopped at the overlook to take photos of the horseshoe-shaped bay filled with coral and tropical fish and trimmed with a crescent of golden sand dotted with coconut palms.

"The bay is what remains of a volcanic crater with the seaward side washed away and is ideal for snorkeling. Most of what you'll see is actually a dead coral reef overgrown by coralline algae. That large keyhole-shaped blue area in the coral is perfect for beginner snorkelers. The water's smooth, and there are hundreds of fish to see. Beyond the barrier reef is where the large coral heads exist, but it is for more advanced swimmers."

Nadia skipped ahead as they walked down the steeply dipping roadway to the beach. "Nadia, be careful and look out for the trolly," Alex called out.

Dora whispered to Kelsey, "For a single guy, he's pretty kid-savvy."

"Mom, Alex is just trying to weasel into my heart."

"And what's so bad about that?"

"Because I'm not ready."

"Honey, it's been seven years."

Kelsey didn't reply as she hurried ahead of her mother.

The beach was already checkered with beach towels and grass mats, so Dora and Nadia were left to find a spot while Alex and Kelsey rented snorkeling gear. They returned to find Dora sitting on a beach mat watching Nadia waist-deep in the ocean trying to put on her face mask. Kelsey hurried into the water to help her daughter, while Alex slipped out of his T-shirt and shorts.

Waist-deep, Nadia leaned over but jerked her head up as soon as the facemask touched the water. "I can't do it," she wailed.

"How do you know if you won't even try!" Kelsey snapped.

Alex wadded in. "Kelsey, mind if I help?"

"She's all yours!" Kelsey stomped out of the water.

"Nadia, your mom's cute when her dander's up. Let's show her how easy it is to snorkel." He carefully adjusted the rubber straps while explaining what he was doing, then pushed strands of hair from her face and fitted the mask, then demonstrated how she should put the snorkel mouthpiece in her mouth. "Now start breathing normally and keep breathing as you lean over and just touch the water with your face mask, and then raise your head and tell me what you saw."

Nadia did as she was told and quickly jerked up her head. "I saw a fish right by my fins!"

"Great, the hard part is over. Now, look a little longer before lifting your head."

Kelsey sat beside her mother. "Nadia won't listen to me, but look at her; she does whatever Alex says."

They stood up as Alex and Nadia snorkeled away from shore, holding hands as they followed the edge of the keyhole out to where waves were breaking over the reef, before turning back.

"He's quite a guy," Dora said.

"He's infuriating. He struts into our lives and gets all the attention from Nadia with a cheap snorkeling set, and now she's swimming all over with him! I'm not falling for his ploy to win Nadia's heart and get me into bed."

Dora fluffed out her hair and adjusted her sunglasses. "Maybe Alex is just what you and Nadia need."

"Mom, you're impossible!"

A half-hour later, Nadia kicked off her fins and dashed across the beach. "Mom, snorkeling is the most fun thing in the whole world! It's even better than riding the pony at the fair, and Alex and I saw a zillion fish and a ferocious-looking spotted eel."

"Weren't you a little scared?"

"Oh no . . . not with Alex."

"Nadia, you must call him Mr. Silverton."

Nadia glanced at Alex, who winked. "Sure, Mom, what-ever you say."

Alex turned to Kelsey. "It's your turn. Are you a good swimmer?"

"Yes, I was on my high school swim team."

"Good. I have something to show you."

They snorkeled along the edge of the keyhole, then south-west across the shallow coral to the narrow channel through the reef where the current was strong. Between wave surges, they swam through the channel into the best areas for live cor-als on Oahu. The water was clearer and deeper, with a profu-sion of fish encircling large *bombies* (coral heads) rising from the sandy seafloor. A school of over a hundred canary-yellow tangs swam past, while below, a large green sea turtle grazed on sea algae. Alex took Kelsey's hand and led her into deeper water above massive lobe and finger corals that covered large patches of the seafloor. A school of pennant butterflyfish passed to their left, and below, a two-foot-long iridescent-blue parrotfish was biting off chunks of coral that it ingested along with the nutritious algae.

Alex pointed to an odd shaped and patterned fish and mumbled through his mouthpiece, "*Humuhumu-nukunuku-ā-pua'a.*" Kelsey didn't understand what he was trying to say but thought the cartoonish-looking fish was cute.

An hour later as they staggered back onto the beach, Alex explained that the *humuhumu-nukunuku-ā-pua'a* was the offi-cial State of Hawaii fish and was sometimes called a Picasso triggerfish because of its unusual shape and bizarre pattern.

"Alex, I'm so glad you brought us here. It's the most fun I've had since I came to Hawaii. Here there's breathtaking beauty both above and under the water. Mom, you've got to try snorkeling! You'll love it."

Kelsey picked up a towel and turned toward Alex as she dried off, her eyes taking in his lanky, tanned, muscular body, something he didn't get from sitting in an office. Alex slowly dried his chest as he gazed at the shapely body an arm's length away. Her blue-and-black one-piece swimsuit clung to her body like paint, sucking his breath away.

Dora observed the exchange of gazes with a knowing smile. "Kelsey, before I go snorkeling with Nadia, I need to put sunscreen on you, or you'll turn to a lobster. Your shoulders are already pink."

Kelsey spread her towel on a beach mat and flopped on her stomach. Dora knelt and deftly slipped the straps off her daughter's shoulders and squirted sunscreen on her back. Kelsey closed her eyes and began to purr as her mother smeared the lotion on her back. Dora looked up at Alex, put her finger to her lips, and handed him the bottle. Nadia covered her mouth with both hands to suppress her giggles as she watched Alex take her grandmother's place.

Kelsey instantly detected the stronger fingers that did more than gently spread lotion over her body. She struggled to muffle her feelings as his fingers massaged her thighs, then relief as his hands worked their way down to her feet. The respite from his titillating fingers was momentary as he caressed the sensitive soles of her feet and probed between her toes, causing her to shudder.

"Stop!" Kelsey yelled as she flipped over and sat up, hugging her knees to her chest. "You have no right to touch me like that!"

"I was just giving you—"

"Don't try to deny what you were doing. I didn't like it one bit!"

Alex sighed as he snapped the cap closed on the sunscreen. "I think I'll take a walk."

"Good! Make it a long one."

He walked aimlessly along the beach a few feet above the gently lapping surf, the happy chatter of the beach crowd silenced by his troubled thoughts. Kelsey was right. It was more than rubbing lotion on her, as he'd hoped it would awaken romantic feelings toward him. *This time I blew it big-time.*

He had just reached the dark volcanic boulders near the end of the crescent beach when he heard his name called. He turned to see Nadia waving her arms as she ran toward him.

"Nadia . . . something wrong?"

"No, I was wondering if you would help me build a sandcastle? Mommy's in a bad mood and doesn't want to do anything."

"Sure, I'd love to."

Nadia took his hand and led him along the beach to where another girl and father were building a sandcastle at the water's edge. "Do you think we can build one as big as that girl's?"

"We'll build a bigger one."

They feverishly dug and piled sand until Alex's fingertips were sore. Nadia's excitement and giggles assuaged his embarrassment over the debacle with Kelsey. As they nudged ahead of the competition, Nadia excitedly jumped around, patting down the wet sand Alex threw onto the castle. Neither saw Kelsey approach to snap a photo.

"*Daddy*, we're winning!" Nadia squealed.

Kelsey gasped, spun around, and hurried back to where her mother was sitting, and stomped on the sand. "I'm so angry at Alex, I want to scream!"

"What happened?"

"Everything! Nadia just called Alex *daddy*, and I won't stand for it!"

"Honey, we both know how badly Nadia wants to have a father, and Alex is the first man, other than her grandfather, to give her special attention. What's wrong with letting her pretend for a day?"

"That's not all!" She dropped to her knees, scooped up a fistful of sand, and threw it down. "You should have asked me before letting him rub lotion on me."

"I thought it was a good way to break the ice. Did he touch you inappropriately?"

"Boy did he! He didn't just do my shoulders and back but rubbed lotion all over my thighs and legs and on the soles of my feet and even between my toes."

"So, what's the problem?"

"I don't like a man I just met yesterday rubbing his hands all over my body."

Dora took Kelsey's hands and kissed them, then gazed into her eyes. "He sparked feelings that you've been suppressing for too long. Now you know there's chemistry between you two. Give him another chance before deciding whether to chase him off. Look how happy he's made Nadia."

Kelsey took another handful of sand and let it sieve between her fingers. "Mom, he's too smooth, and that's what got me into trouble the first time."

"You were in love, and it didn't work out, and you're blessed with a beautiful daughter. Last night you told me he was awkward, and now he's too smooth. Seems to me that you've found a man that's smart, handsome, interested in a woman with a daughter, plus makes your heartbeat faster. I just might ask Alex to rub lotion on me."

"Mom! I'm serious!"

"Honey, so am I. Now come snorkeling with me."

They walked over to Nadia and Alex. "Nadia, are you okay? I'm going snorkeling with your mom."

"Yep, I'm fine. Alex . . . I mean Mr. Silverton is going to show me some special green sand."

Alex and Nadia walked to the far end of the beach where there was a band of greenish sand at the base of the cliff. He scooped up a handful and poured it into Nadia's palm. "These green crystals weathered out of the volcanic cliff. About half of the sand is made of green olivine crystals that were formed deep down in the earth. In my car I've got a hand lens that geologists call a *loupe*. You can use it to examine the green crystals."

She looked closely at the sand. "I see lots of green sparkles. Are they valuable?"

"They aren't valuable like diamonds, but some larger crystals are used in jewelry that's sold in Hawaii. Rocks and minerals are like books written in a special language that only a geologist can read. They tell how a rock was made, how old it is, and often where it came from. We know the volcanic rocks around Hanauma Bay are quite young at only thirty-five thousand years old."

"That's so cool. You know all about rocks?"

"I liked rocks, so I studied geology in college."

"Can you teach me how to read rocks?"

"I can teach you a little, but you'll have to study geology in college to learn to really read rocks."

"I want to take these crystals back to show my mom and grandmother."

Alex found a crushed plastic cup and pushed out the sides, and Nadia filled it with green sand. She carefully held the cup in two hands as they walked back along the beach. "Mommy will be surprised about our discovery."

They only had to wait a few minutes before Kelsey and Dora returned from snorkeling—both with oval red rings on their cheeks from their face masks. Alex was nervous, hoping Kelsey had calmed down after her angry outburst.

"Mommy, look what we discovered!"

Kelsey took the cup and looked in. "Dirty sand?"

Nadia giggled. "No, they're olivine crystals from deep under the earth."

"Really?"

"Yes, and rocks tell stories that geologists can read."

"Sounds like you've been talking to a geologist."

Nadia giggled. "Mom, you know Mr. Silverton's a geologist."

Dora spoke up. "How about we discuss the wonders of geology over lunch. Snorkeling has made me really hungry. Alex, is there a casual place close by?"

"There's a pretty good Chinese take-out in Hawaii Kai about a five-minute drive from here, and we can eat at outdoor tables overlooking the marina. There might be a long line, as it's popular with the beach crowd."

After refreshing showers on the beach and a change into dry clothes, Nadia and her grandmother walked ahead up the steep road chiseled into the side of the crater, while Kelsey walked behind with Alex.

"Alex, I kind of overreacted. You need to understand that we've just met, and I'm not ready to be touched like that. I haven't had a serious relationship since I was pregnant with Nadia eight years ago. I meant it when I told you my priorities are caring for Nadia and finishing my PhD."

"So, Kelsey, what do you propose?"

"A friendship. We enjoyed snorkeling . . . and I apologize for screaming at you."

"Apology accepted, and I'm sorry I upset you down at the beach."

As Alex had warned, there was a line leading out of the door of the Chinese take-out. Dora remained outside, waiting for a table on the terrace overlooking the lagoon, while the others stood in line. Kelsey was shaking her head when they exited the take-out restaurant with Alex carrying four Styrofoam lunch boxes. "Alex, you're going to make all of us fat."

"The meal's not complete without bubble tea." He slipped into the adjacent tea shop and reappeared with four iced teas in clear plastic cups with fat straws. "I got mango-guava bubble teas."

Nadia took her drink in both hands. "Mr. Silverton, what are the marble things at the bottom of my drink?"

"Tapioca balls that you can suck up with your fat straw. Try one. You'll love them."

She moved her straw around and sucked one up, and cautiously chewed. "They're yummy." Then she proceeded to suck up every one at the bottom of her drink, then turned to her grandmother's bubble tea.

Chatting was mostly replaced with smacking lips as they ate the lemon chicken, spicy eggplant, deep-fried tofu, and shrimp dumplings. Nadia followed Alex's lead and tried chopsticks. Her lack of skill was a delight for the hungry calico cat at her feet.

Across the lagoon, a sailing instructor was teaching a class how to sail. One by one, the novice sailors maneuvered their sunfishes into the gentle breeze, and away they sailed. Alex mused, *after having been becalmed for so long, is there a chance of putting a romantic breeze into Kelsey's sails?*

Chapter 3

*A*lex knew that when a woman said, "Let's just be friends," she was saying romance was not in the cards. He had female friends that he occasionally asked to dinner, a movie, or a play, and neither had expectations of more. While he had hoped for more in the relationship with Kelsey, it was Nadia that had touched him deeply when she called him daddy as they built a sandcastle. It was an easy decision to try to give Nadia a special Hawaiian Christmas.

Snowy landscapes and crackling fireplaces were not part of the Christmas holiday season, but the friendly Hawaiian spirit was at its finest in December. It started with the arrival of a shipment of evergreen trees in the first week of December that would sell out within four or five days.

Waikiki and the Ala Moana Shopping Center were adorned with Christmas decorations along with free stage performances adapted to the tropics. At the Ala Moana Shopping Center, hula dancers performed Christmas carols as Santa arrived on a surfboard as white soap flakes fluttered from the third floor. Nadia sat cross-legged in front of the stage and screamed along with other children when the Christmas Grinch tried to steal Santa's gifts.

Honolulu Hale, where the mayor's offices were located, was converted to a winter wonderland with sixty Christmas trees entered in the annual competition for the best tree and decorations. Nadia was enthralled with the miniature villages on display, especially the one with ice skaters twirling around on a mirror for a frozen lake.

Kelsey appeared to enjoy the family outings, solidifying the romance-free friendship. Dora was more affectionate toward Alex, often slipping her hand under his arm as they walked. When he asked if he could take them to a special Christmas breakfast, Kelsey declined, saying it was family time to be spent at home. Dora interjected that she would be leaving soon and preferred a special breakfast in Waikiki, and they could open presents on Christmas Eve. Kelsey warned Alex not to buy any expensive gifts, even for Nadia.

Alex bought an inexpensive boogie board, then spent almost as much having her name painted on it in flowery letters. For Dora, who loved cooking, he bought a cookbook of Hawaiian recipes. A present for Kelsey was a challenge. He couldn't buy jewelry for just a friend and finally sought advice on a meaningful book at Barnes & Noble. The middle-aged woman at the desk asked if the recipient was a significant other. When he replied that unfortunately she was just a friend, she suggested *Romancing Waikiki*, a novel with twenty-one love stories set in Waikiki. She assured him that they were not shallow plots and had meaningful messages that might resonate with a special friend.

Nadia and Dora gushed at their presents, while Kelsey was more reserved, reading the back cover, then thanking Alex before setting it aside. Alex received a hard-bound edition of *The Diamond Hunters* by Wilbur Smith, and a note from Kelsey:

"Alex, let me know when you find a volcano with diamonds."
Alex chuckled. "I'll have to go to Africa to find diamond kimberlites."

Nadia chirped, "Mommy, I want to go to Africa to see wild animals."

Alex was up at five o'clock preparing the special breakfast, then picked them up at six-thirty as the starry sky was being replaced by shades of blue. "Mele Kalikimaka," he said as he jumped out to open his car doors. Alex had given a hint of their destination by telling everyone to wear shorts and flip-flops.

"Where are you taking us for our special breakfast?" asked Kelsey.

"You'll have to wait and see."

As he turned into the Ala Moana Beach Park, Nadia asked, "Aren't we going to breakfast first?"

"We're having a special breakfast on Magic Island."

"But there's no boat to take us to the island."

"Nadia, we're on Magic Island. It's actually a man-made peninsula that extends into the ocean where we'll have the best views of Waikiki Beach."

Alex carried the ice chest while the others helped with the bags and thermos bottles. They followed the curvy path to the tip of the peninsula and spread out an old blanket on the grass near the rock-sheltered lagoon. Alex served the breakfast on disposable holiday plates and matching cups. He had prepared omelets stuffed with shiitake mushrooms and cheese, with sliced Portuguese sausage and flaky biscuits on the side. The fruit plate of watermelon, strawberries, and pineapple spears was a hit with Nadia. In addition to the Kona coffee and hot chocolate, Alex brought a bottle of champagne wrapped in a

27

paper bag. While consumption of alcohol was illegal in parks, the police didn't bother anyone as long as the bottles were concealed and there was no drunken behavior.

Alex offered the toast. "Christmas is most exciting when there are children near to fill the air with giggles and laughter. Thank you, Nadia, for just being a kid." He gazed into Kelsey's eyes. "Next year will bring major changes for you as you complete your PhD and move on to the next stage in life. And, Kelsey, you're so lucky to have Dora for a mother. She gives me a glimpse into how gracefully you will age."

Dora's smile was genuine, while Kelsey's was reserved. *You can't fool me with your ploy to worm your way into my heart through Nadia and my mother.*

Dora returned to California in early January, leaving Kelsey without a babysitter, and she adjusted her research schedule to be home when Nadia returned from school. Kelsey appeared fine with outings that centered on activities for Nadia, and Alex didn't push for more. He was aware that Kelsey was using Nadia as a buffer to avoid any pretense of a romantic relationship. Nadia had become the de facto chaperone.

February brought the annual high waves to the North Shore of Oahu, and Kelsey accepted Alex's offer to take them to watch the International Surfing Competition. They made good time on H1 and H2 Freeways as far as Wahiawa. Then traffic slowed to ten miles an hour on the narrow two-lane Hawaii 99. Nadia's patience ran out, and she began complaining that she was hot and thirsty.

"Anyone up to stopping in Hale'iwa for the tastiest shave ice on Oahu?"

"Me!" yelled Nadia. "Is it far?"

"It's only a few minutes away." He turned onto Highway 83 and down the main street of Hale'iwa—the laid-back historic village that retained the façade of a bygone era with its single-story, weathered wooden buildings and wood-planked porches fronting boutique stores and cafés. On the left was Matsumoto's, which had served shave ice since 1951 and had established itself as the place to go on Oahu for shave ice infused with local fruit flavors.

Alex pulled in between a dusty pickup with oversized tires and a new Acura. Nadia joined Alex in the double line of people snaking out the front door and along the wooden porch. The line moved steadily, and Nadia oohed at the colorful shave ice cones that people carried out the door.

"Why are snow cones called shave ice in Hawaii?"

"Shave ice is much finer—like fresh snow—plus you have tropical flavors only available in Hawaii."

A white stretch limousine was double-parked in front with a demure-appearing Japanese bride peering out the window. Her just-minted husband stood in line, his white tuxedo and red carnation boutonniere in stark contrast to the others in shorts, T-shirts, and flip-flops. Ten minutes later as they exited onto the porch, Nadia stumbled, and her shave ice splattered on the floor. Tears gushed from her eyes as Alex squatted to clean up. "Nadia, you can have mine."

"I don't want yours," she sobbed.

"Dat okay, sweet *keiki* (child). I take care of eva-ting." The Hawaiian woman filled the doorway as she entered the building and moved to the front of the line.

The woman making shave ice greeted her. "Auntie Nani."

Minutes later she returned with a rainbow-striped shave ice in an extra-large plastic cone. "What's your name, sweetie?"

"Nadia," she replied as she wiped her eyes and took the cone. "Thank you."

The benches behind Matsumoto's were filled, and Kelsey didn't want to risk having Nadia spill her shave ice in Alex's car. They stood for only a moment before the Hawaiian woman called out, "Nadia, come sit with my Lilly and Malia."

The two girls near Nadia's age made a space between them, and within minutes were chatting and giggling as they shared their cones.

"Children make friends so easily, but I don't. Alex, you're my only friend in Hawaii."

"I'm glad. But you need more than friendships for you and Nadia."

Kelsey shrugged as she jabbed the straw several times into the shave ice. *Last time I skipped the friendship step, I got pregnant, and I'm not doing that again.*

"Nadia's a priceless daughter."

"Yes, but the past seven years would have been so much easier if my Scottish beau had meant what he said when he said, 'I'll love you forever.'"

Nadia's new friends gave her hugs, and the older one tucked a flower behind Nadia's ear. She waved as the girls scrambled into the back of the dented pickup with oversized wheels—then they were gone.

Traffic was stop-and-go along Kamehameha Highway to Sunset Beach where the surfing competition was being held. The best surfers from around the world were competing on twenty-five-foot waves, guaranteeing heavy traffic and little parking. They parked several blocks away from the crowded beach, and Nadia watched surfers from atop Alex's shoulders. There were breathtaking spills sending surfboards spiraling above the waves like jumping spinner dolphins. Men on jet skis raced out to rescue dethroned surfers, performing breathtaking maneuvers to snatch surfers from the waves.

"Alex . . . why would anyone want to do such scary stuff?" asked Nadia.

"Good question. I suppose for the satisfaction of achieving something requiring great skill, and for a few lucky surfers, money and fame. A surfer told me that nothing is more thrilling than riding a perfect wave. I'll show you how to ride small waves with your new boogie board."

After an hour in the sun, Nadia went into her dying of thirst and hunger routine as she clutched her neck with both hands and staggered on the beach.

"Nadia, if you can hold off starvation for ten minutes, I know a tropical valley with ice-cold drinks and hamburgers and french fries."

Waimea Valley Park was set back a mile from picturesque Waimea Beach and a world away from crowded tourist sites. Occupied by Hawaiians for five centuries, the narrow valley was a botanical garden cloaked in massive tropical trees, hundreds of rare plant species, and a profusion of colorful flowers. Inside the entrance was a take-out cafe and gift shop. Nadia wanted a hamburger, french fries, and Coke, while Kelsey and Alex had mahimahi sandwiches. The picnic tables on the raised terrace overlooked a manicured lawn with peacocks that strutted about, periodically stopping to display their crowd-pleasing feathers in blue-and-green iridescent fans. A peacock hopped onto the terrace and was rewarded with bits of Nadia's hamburger bun.

Alex's Hawaiian driver's license got the discounted *kamaʻāina* (local) rate to enter the half-mile-long park. A private one-lane paved road followed Waimea Stream to the waterfalls and small lake at the back of the park. They strolled along the sinuous road past massive monkeypod and kukui nut trees, thick stands of bamboo, ferns, and floral patches of cobalt, red, yellow, and white flowers.

There were sublime reminders of the early Hawaiians that once occupied the valley—a rough stone *heiau* (temple), a stone *hale iwi* (house of bones dating before Western contact), a *kauhale* (reconstructed thatched living site for a chief or priest), plus several Hawaiians giving lectures on the history of their culture and the valley. Nadia was drawn to a semicircle of children sitting around a Hawaiian woman making flower leis.

"Mommy, can I make a lei?"

"Of course."

Auntie Lani, as the children called her, was draped in a tent-like, blue-and-white floral muumuu that spread out around her, giving her a noble appearance. Her generous smile and soft, hypnotic voice kept the keikis entranced as they strung flowers into leis.

Alex whispered to Kelsey, "Without the welcoming culture of Hawaiians, Hawaii would be just another tropical tourist destination fleecing tourists out of their money. I'm amazed that Hawaiians have been able to preserve their friendly aloha spirit despite the explosion of tourism in the islands. The woman that so quickly came to Nadia's aid when she dropped her shave ice is an example of what makes Hawaii special."

Nadia finished her plumeria lei and after a hug from Auntie Lani, joined Alex and Kelsey. "Mommy, I know all about leis. Did you know that leis can even make sick people well and can bring peace between warriors?" She waved her finger. "And you must respect anything made with ti leaves, like hula skirts, and not throw them in the trash, or you will have bad luck. Even with a lei, when it's all wilted, you should untie the string and scatter the flowers in the sea."

"You learned all that while making a lei?"

"Yes, Auntie Lani is a hundred percent Hawaiian and went to a special school just for Hawaiians."

32

Alex added, "She must have gone to Kamehameha School, a private school reserved for the best students with Hawaiian blood. It has had many distinguished graduates that went on to attend elite universities on the mainland."

Nadia kicked up her feet and giggled as she swung between Alex and her mother, the thread that drew them closer. Nadia let go and dashed ahead toward the squeals of children and melody of cascading water. At the bridge over the Kamananui Stream, they could see the waterfalls and the children bobbing in the pond below the falls.

"Mommy, can I swim?"

"Alex, do you think it's safe?"

"Pretty safe. It says in the brochure the pond's deep and cold, so one of us needs to swim with Nadia."

"Alex, I'm a little tired, so I'll watch you two."

Nadia hesitated knee-deep in the jade-green water. "It's really cold."

Moments later she yelped when Alex grabbed her hand and pulled her into the water. Kelsey, her expression pensive as she watched the two swim together over to the falls. She mused, *He's what Nadia needs, but the timing's all wrong. I've got to finish my dissertation first, and he's a little too perfect and must be hiding something.* Kelsey watched the two duck under the waterfalls; then as they turned back toward shore, Nadia wrapped her arms around Alex's neck and clung tightly. Kelsey bit her lower lip as she felt a twinge of jealousy.

Nadia became irritable when they were delayed almost an hour by an overturned truck on Highway 99. "I'm so hot, I'm dying," she moaned.

"How about an icy pineapple treat?"

"Anything cold—pleeeaaase?"

Alex pulled into the large parking lot in front of the touristy Dole Plantation. He led them inside the main building, past rows of tourist trinkets, to a long line waiting in front of the Dole Whip counter. Kelsey sat at an outdoor table while Alex and Nadia waited in line for the soft-serve pineapple cones— Nadia declaring she liked hers better than the shave ice cone.

As they exited the front door, an Asian woman called out. "Young lady, if you're under twelve, you can pick out an oyster with a pearl inside for the special price of $4.99."

Nadia blushed and stood taller as she replied, "I'm almost eight." Nadia looked at the bowl of oysters and the sign—cultured pearls—$8.99. "Mommy, can I pick out a pearl oyster? They're only four dollars."

"Nadia, if you get a pearl, then you'll need a necklace and pendent, and that will cost too much."

"Kelsey, it's something Nadia will keep forever and will make this day memorable. I want to buy her a pearl and necklace."

Nadia tugged on her mother's arm as she looked up with her big doe eyes. "I never had a real pearl."

"Why do you two always put me in a box? Okay, but just a silver chain and nothing expensive."

"Goodie!" Nadia leaned over the bowl of oysters in saltwater. "How do I know which one has the nicest pearl?"

"The new shipment of oysters has smaller pearls, but there is one from the previous shipment that no one picked because it was irregular-shaped, and I'm sure it will have a bigger pearl. Can you find it?"

Nadia pointed to a rough, asymmetrical one. "Is it that one?"

"You have good eyes." The woman handed Nadia wooden tongs and told her to place it on the wooden block. "Now, Nadia, I need you to say a special Hawaiian chant with me and tap the shell three times with the tongs."

Nadia's expression was serious as she repeated the woman's words, and several people gathered to watch as the shell was pried open. Nadia bit her lip as the gelatinous, grayish insides came into view. The woman had a practiced routine, expressing doubt as she probed the oyster, then gasping as a shiny pearl popped free. "Oh my gosh! A rare pink pearl." She carefully wiped it and placed it in Nadia's palm.

"Mommy, it's the prettiest pearl I've ever seen."

The woman pulled out a tray of necklaces and pendants and said, "There's a 15 percent discount on the silver necklaces and pendants, but 30 percent off the gold ones."

Kelsey quickly capitulated when Alex pointed to a gold necklace with a small pendant. Minutes after Alex pulled back onto the highway, Nadia was asleep in the backseat—her hand clutching her necklace with a pink pearl set in a turtle's shell pendant. Kelsey looked back at her daughter, then briefly stroked the nape of Alex's neck, before pulling her hand away.

The touch of her fingers gave Alex a fuzzy feeling in his stomach. *Maybe this is a sign of more to come.*

Chapter 4

*T*he hoped-for uptick in the relationship after the trip to the North Shore didn't come, and after almost a month, Alex was feeling increasingly uneasy about the stalled relationship. The day trips with Kelsey and Nadia were enjoyable, but there had been no time alone with Kelsey, and she seemed to like it that way.

Alex was thirty-seven, and although his biological clock wasn't sending the warning signals women experienced, he was anxious to find a marriageable partner. The women of interest from high school and university days were married, and the couple of times he'd gone to singles bars, he'd felt like a fish out of water. On his last visit, one of his students spotted him and said with a sardonic tone, "Dr. Silverton, what are *you* doing here?" He gave an awkward reply, then gulped his drink and quickly left.

Alex found that long, warm showers reduced tension and gave him inspiration to solve problems. As he adjusted the water temperature, his thoughts turned to Lora, who had showed him creative ways to comingle in the shower. He recalled joking that she could write a book on 101 fun ways for couples to shower together. Lora, a psychiatrist specializing in marital sex and abuse problems, would know what to do about Kelsey. It was time to get professional advice.

"Dr. Daniels speaking. How may I help you?"

"Lora, it's Alex."

"Alex, where have you been hiding? Haven't heard from you since the masked Halloween party and our unmasking at your place. Are you calling for advice, or a dinner and a romp between the sheets?"

Alex had dated Lora Daniels, a twice-divorced, attractive, witty blonde before they mutually agreed that a path to marriage wasn't in the cards. She didn't want children and preferred an open marriage that wasn't acceptable to Alex. They had, however, remained good friends and enjoyed occasional dinner dates and sex.

"Lora, I need some advice about a woman."

"I suspected a woman was the reason I hadn't heard from you. Girlfriend, or did you do something stupid like get married?"

"It's about a woman that I'm attracted to, but I'm at an impasse in the relationship."

"I'm listening."

"I met Kelsey last December at an East-West Center Christmas party. She's never been married but has a cute, precocious seven-year-old daughter, Nadia. Over the past two months we've had enjoyable outings to the beach and family dinners, and Nadia likes me more than her mother does. My problem is there's friendship but no romance—not even a meaningful goodnight kiss."

"You really want my advice?"

"That's why I'm calling."

"Toss the cold fish back in the ocean and meet me at my place."

"Lora, this is important. I need your *professional* advice."

"Yeah, I know. It's been a tough week for me. I had a client that was severely beaten by her husband; then a woman that overdosed trying to commit suicide; and this morning, a pregnant sixteen-year-old that ran away from abusive parents. Alex, if your problem can wait until tomorrow morning, we can meet at Honolulu Coffee in the Moana Hotel, and you can buy me an espresso and decadent chocolate croissant."

"Thanks, Lora. I knew you'd help."

Lora was sitting next to the open window overlooking Kalakaua Avenue when he entered twenty minutes late. "Sorry, I stopped by the office, and a student called, and—"

"Save the excuses. You call for a free consultation, then stiff me for a drink and pastry."

When he leaned over to give her a peck on the cheek, she pulled him in for a lip-locking smooch. Releasing her grip, she sat back and handed him her cup. "After you get me another espresso, you can tell me about this woman that's giving you wet dreams."

Lora was on her cellphone when he returned with the drinks and a pumpkin chia muffin. "I'm tied up with another client for the next hour, so go straight to the safe house, and I'll meet you there at ten thirty." She turned off her phone and dropped it in her large handbag. "Okay, you've got forty-five minutes, so start with a little background about your heart-throb."

"I'm not sure I know the full story."

"No one ever does."

"As I mentioned yesterday, I met Kelsey at the East-West Center Christmas party. She's from UC Berkeley and has a fellowship to do research on the risks of natural disasters among the Pacific Island countries. She wanted my advice on threats posed by volcanoes."

"I thought university faculty were forbidden from getting romantically involved with their students."

"True, but she's not technically my student, and I sent her to work with another expert that can be more helpful to her research."

Lora smirked. "Which freed you to pursue your romantic interests."

"It just worked out that way. Anyway, she's never been married, and her problems go back to when she did research in the Galapagos Islands and fell in love with a man from Scotland. After returning to the States, she discovered she was pregnant, but her Scottish beau wanted nothing to do with matrimony or parenthood and offered to split the costs of an abortion.

"She refused to have an abortion and moved in with her parents, and they helped care for their granddaughter while Kelsey finished her master's degree. Three years later, she began working on her PhD, and that brought her to Hawaii on an East-West Center fellowship to fill in the gaps in her research. She knows about my romantic interest and has made it clear more than once that her research comes first, and she doesn't want any male entanglements. I suspect her distrust of men goes back to the disastrous outcome of her romance in the Galapagos Islands. You're a psychiatrist and better than me at ferreting out people's hang-ups. We've had enjoyable outings with Nadia, but no real dates. I'm not sure if it's worth trying to juice up the relationship or if I should throw in the towel and move on."

"So, the chemistry is only on your side?"

"Not totally. On an outing to Hanauma Bay, I used the technique you showed me of applying lotion to your body. I did her shoulders, back, and legs. Then when I got to her feet and toes, she jumped up and screamed at me."

Lora toyed with an earring, a devilish smile on her face as she poked her bare foot up his pant leg. "You're turning me on."

"Lora, I'm serious."

"So am I."

He moved his leg away, and she frowned impishly and nibbled at her pastry, her tongue flicking out to lick crumbs from her lips. "Sounds like your massage had the intended effect and that frightened her. I would need a few sessions with Kelsey to know what's really going on in her pretty little brain. Two options immediately come to mind. Accept that she doesn't want a romantic relationship and move on. There's no shortage of smart, attractive women out there that are good bets for wedding bells. Or you can continue being a tour guide and daddy stand-in, hoping a romance ignites. You already know this. You called because you want to know how to dial-up the relationship from platonic to romantic."

"Yes, and is it worth it?"

"Perhaps not. But you won't know for sure without having a real date. Ask her out on a date without the little chaperone, and I'm not talking about a dinner at California Pizza Kitchen or Moose McGillycuddy's. Women want a suitor to treat them like a princess, at least on special occasions. Choose a classy, upscale restaurant like La Mer, the Orchids, or Morimoto Waikiki, lay on a triple pikake jasmine lei, and don't fumble the wine selection. Check out the menu and wine list in advance, and for God's sake, don't talk about geology. Listen to her and show empathy—women love seeing the soft side of men. Talking about rocks may turn on a geologist, but they're a poison pill to a romantic evening."

"Spruce up your bachelor's pad—clean sheets on the bed, clothes off the floor, toilet seat clean and down, and scented candles. After the meal, suggest a tasty dessert at your house. If she accepts, let nature take its course. Oh yes, surreptitiously find out when her period is and give those dates a wide berth. If she turns down your offer, call me."

Alex leaned back in his chair. "I don't know if I can remember every detail."

She leaned over and ran her fingernails across his palm. "You can do a dry run with me."

"Lora, I really appreciate your advice. I owe you more than a coffee."

"You can mail me a check to assuage your guilt. Alex, beyond getting into Princess Kelsey's pants, is she someone that can hold your interest after the hot romance fades?"

"I think so. We're both interested in the Pacific Islands and have similar social and political leanings. We love the ocean and enjoy reading and travel. Most important to Kelsey may be whether I'll be a good father for Nadia, and I think I get high marks in that area. I didn't want to move on without trying one last time. Lora, thanks for your advice."

"Enough chitchat. I've got more serious cases to attend to, like wife beatings and worse." She stood up, straightened her dress, and leaned into Alex with a lingering kiss. She stopped at the door and said loud enough for everyone to hear. "I hope she dumps you. I'll leave my porch light on and the keys under the doormat."

Alex smiled as he watched her merge into the tourist crowd along Kalakaua Avenue. *She's outrageous in the way she talks, but her heart's in the right place, and she gave me what I needed—no-nonsense advice.*

Chapter 5

*T*he choice of a fine-dining restaurant was easy—the Orchids in the Halekulani Hotel. Alex had marveled at the romantic setting while having sunset cocktails in the adjacent House Without a Key. Taking Lora's advice, he drove to the Halekulani Hotel to check out the menu and wine. The smartly dressed maître d' appeared aloof as he approached the reception desk at the Orchids, adding to his nervousness.

"May I help you?" asked the maître d', his French accent distinctive.

"I would like to book a table for two this Friday evening, preferably at seven."

"That will be quite difficult, as we're heavily booked on Friday and Saturday evenings for the next three weeks. I can check for any cancellations."

"Please do. It's important."

He flipped through the reservation book, then smiled. "You're lucky. There was a cancellation a half hour ago for Friday evening at seven. Your name?"

"Alex Silverton. I work at UH."

An immediate smile. "My son's attending UH. Are you a professor?"

"Yes, in the Geology Department."

"First time at the Orchids?"

"Yes, I have a special date and want to impress her."

"Dr. Silverton, you selected the right place. Would you like dinner and wine suggestions?"

"Yes, that is greatly appreciated. I want her to have a memorable meal accompanied by a nice wine, but not too expensive."

"Not a problem. A favorite among regulars is Kendall-Jackson's Vintner's Reserve Chardonnay that pairs well with our seafood entrees and is an excellent value. It will not disappoint you or break your wallet. And for the main course, the chef's two signature seafood dishes are delectable."

Before leaving the Halekulani, he made a 6:00 p.m. reservation at the adjacent House Without a Key so they could have cocktails and pupus on the terrace while watching the sunset hula show.

Alex was prepared for Kelsey's excuse that she didn't have a trusted babysitter. "You must have at least one special dinner while in Hawaii. I've lined up a reliable female graduate student to watch Nadia, and I'll pay. Her father's a professor at UH and a friend."

"Um, Alex, I'll check with my neighbor's teenage daughter and get back to you this evening." She called back within an hour. "Alex, Nancy's available Friday night until ten thirty."

Alex pretended to be pleased, but returning Kelsey home so early squelched any possibility of bringing her to his home for dessert and perhaps more. He carefully prepared for the date, even buying an expensive Tori Richards aloha shirt, washed his Honda, and cleaned his place just in case there was a last-minute change.

He arrived a few minutes early and was stunned when Kelsey opened the door, wearing a shimmering cream silk blouse with pearl buttons that matched her earrings, and a gold-trimmed, Thai-silk skirt that hugged her figure.

"Kelsey, you look gorgeous!" He slipped the pikake lei over her head, careful not to mess up her hair, and gave her a light kiss on the cheek. Her intoxicating perfume made his knees weak.

As they drove northwest on Ala Wai Boulevard, Kelsey gazed at the canal that separated Waikiki from the adjacent neighborhoods. Alex explained that Waikiki was once a swamp and the canal diverted water from the Manoa and Palolo Streams from flooding Waikiki, but his mind was on the woman beside him, not on a canal.

"Alex, the canal reminds me of a moat around a forbidden kingdom."

"I never thought of it that way. But it's true the Ala Wai Canal separates the vibrant kingdom of Waikiki from quieter residential Honolulu."

He pulled in front of the Halekulani Hotel, stopping behind a shiny black Jaguar. A tall blond slithered from the luxury automobile and tucked her hand under the arm of a balding man three inches shorter and a quarter century older. Her coiffured hair was pulled back to reveal large pear-shaped diamonds dangling from each ear and a one-inch-wide choker of diamonds.

"She's right out of a Hollywood glamour magazine," Kelsey gushed.

"Looks to me like a high-maintenance woman with dollar signs for eyes. I'm having dinner with a woman with both beauty and substance."

Kelsey smiled. *I like that line, even if contrived.*

They paused at the elegant pool with a giant orchid pattern on the bottom made from more than a million glass tiles in various shades of blue. They were early enough to get seating near the low stage on the outdoor terrace of the House Without a Key.

"Kelsey, we'll have drinks and pupus while watching Kanoe Miller perform hulas accompanied by a trio of singers. Then after sunset, we'll move to the Orchids over there for dinner."

"Sounds delightful. I've read that the House Without a Key is where movie stars and other famous people come for sunset drinks. I wanted to come here before leaving Hawaii, but with Nadia, it wasn't realistic."

"You won't see many professors here, Alex chuckled."

"Their loss," replied Kelsey.

She was cautious about sashimi after a bad experience at Fisherman's Wharf in San Francisco but relented when Alex assured her that Halekulani served the freshest quality sashimi in the islands. "If you don't love the first morsel, I'll order another pupu."

The thin slices of sashimi were presented artfully, and Alex carefully mixed soy sauce with hot wasabi using his chopsticks. He deftly picked up a thin slice of the ruby-pink ahi and swished it in the sauce and offered it to Kelsey. She cautiously took the sliver of sashimi and closed her eyes for several seconds . . . then the hoped-for smile.

"Wow, I think I've just had a taste of heaven," she purred, then took a sip of her mai tai. At first it was chitchat about the day and Nadia. Then Kelsey began to reveal her personal feelings and dreams, including the desire to marry after graduate school—her eyes locked on his for a few moments. Alex reached across the low cocktail table and lightly stroked the back of her hand as she discussed her struggles in raising a child alone.

The sun had dipped below the horizon, leaving pink frosted clouds as they strolled to the Orchids Restaurant—open on the front and the side facing the House Without a Key. The maître d' greeted him with a welcoming smile. "Dr. Silverton, nice to see you again. We have reserved a special table for you."

The unexpected greeting and reserved table soothed Alex's anxiety. Their table was in the front left corner with views of Diamond Head on the left and the Pacific Ocean in front. The coiffured blond looked their way, her eyes narrowed as she wondered how this pedestrian-appearing couple that had arrived in a Honda got the best seat in the house.

The waiter presented them with menus and reviewed the chef's specials, noting the fish came directly from the fishing boats that afternoon.

"Thank you. We need a few minutes to peruse the menu."

"Of course, Dr. Silverton." Then he moved on to another table.

"Alex, I need some help. All the seafood entrees are tempting."

"I suggest either of the chef's signature dishes—macadamia nut–crusted mahimahi or the opah with black-truffle sauce. If you like, we can order both and share?"

The sommelier appeared with the wine list in an oversized, black leather folder. Again, Alex was greeted as if he was a regular and after briefly looking at the wine list, ordered a bottle of Kendall-Jackson Vintner's Reserve Chardonnay.

"Excellent choice. A perfect selection for Hawaii with hints of tropical fruit that will pair nicely with your entrees."

Kelsey stared at Alex after the sommelier turned away. "You must come here often."

"Not really," he answered truthfully. He mused, *Sometimes less said is better.*

As they neared the end of the meal and bottle of wine, Kelsey reached over and took Alex's hand. "Before this evening, my most memorable meal was after high school graduation when my girlfriend's parents took three of us to a fancy seafood restaurant in Sausalito overlooking San Francisco Bay. The lights reflecting off the bay were magical, and we talked about our dream places for a honeymoon. Anne wanted to go to Paris, and Kathleen dreamed of a moonlight gondola ride in Venice, but I wanted to honeymoon in Hawaii. I'm the only one that made it, but minus a husband."

It was exactly ten-thirty when he pulled up in front of Kelsey's place. Kelsey clutched her small purse in her lap. "Alex, why don't you walk the babysitter home, then return for a nightcap at my place?"

Am I dreaming? "I'd love to have a nightcap with you."

She held his hand as they walked down the concrete stairs on the side of the house to her place. Then Alex escorted the babysitter home. When he returned, the rear door was open, leaving just the unlocked screen door. He could see an open bottle of Courvoisier on the table and two water glasses.

"Knock-knock," he said.

"Come in," she said, her voice low and seductive.

Inside, he paused before sitting next to Kelsey on the couch. She poured several drams of the golden liquid into each glass and handed one to him. She surprised him by not offering a toast before gulping hers down, then setting the empty glass on the coffee table. She snuggled closer, her hair brushing his neck as he took in the intoxicating fragrance of her scent.

He gently nuzzled her hair, then softly kissed her ear lobe, her cheek, then lingered at her lips. Encouraged, he kissed her chin, then descended down her slender neck to the first button of her satin blouse. Her faint moans were reassuring as his fingers unfastened a pearl button and his lips touched the edge of her lacy bra. Fingers unfastened a second button, and his tongue flicked between her bra cups as his hand slipped around to her back to unclip her bra.

Suddenly, Kelsey's body stiffened, and she screamed, shoving him away. "You're just like Colin! It's all about sex!"

Stunned, he shook his head. "Kelsey, it's not like that. I'm not him," his voice pleading as he stood.

"Oh really!" Kelsey snapped as she jumped up. "Isn't this what you really want?" Pearl buttons popped from her blouse, bouncing across the glass-topped coffee table as she ripped it open, and she yanked up her bra. "Have a good look because you'll never see them again."

Alex's eyes were on Kelsey's angry face as he got up, then hurried to the door and out of her life.

"Mommy, why are you yelling?" Nadia said as she opened the bedroom door.

"It's nothing, honey." Kelsey turned away as she pulled her bra into place and wrapped her blouse across her chest before facing her daughter.

Alex was dazed and depressed as he drove home. *How could such a perfect evening disintegrate into a total disaster?*

I thought I was reading her cues of encouragement, but then she exploded. He entered his home, slammed the door, kicked off his shoes, and took a beer from the refrigerator and guzzled it. The phone rang, but he ignored it, discarding his clothes as he headed to the shower. It rang again as he adjusted the shower. "Kelsey, I don't want to talk to you," he muttered angrily as he stepped into the shower. Minutes later, the shrill ring again.

"Damnit, I'm not in the mood to talk to you now or ever again," he blurted out as if she was standing in the shower. The phone rang a fourth time, and he threw down his bar of soap, grabbed a towel, and stomped to the phone. "I don't want to—"

"Mommy's crying, and I don't know what to do. Pleeaase talk to her. I'm afraid mommy will hurt herself."

Alex took a deep breath. "Yes, honey, put her on." He could hear Nadia begging her mother to come to the phone, then a long silence.

"Alex, I'm too upset to talk now," she said in a shaky voice.

"You must think about Nadia. You're frightening her. She doesn't understand."

"Alex, I need help. I can't get past Colin. It should have nothing to do with you, but it does."

"Kelsey, you need counseling. I know a psychologist who can help. If you want, we can meet tomorrow morning after Nadia goes to school? No conditions."

"Okay . . . where?"

"Starbucks at the corner of Kalakaua and Kapahulu. It's only a short walk from your place. How about, say eleven?"

"Okay. It will give me time to pull myself together."

Alex wasn't sure meeting Kelsey was a good idea, but for Nadia, it was worth a try. He drove to Ala Moana Shopping Center and was at the door of Macy's when it opened at ten. The saleswoman listened to his description of the blouse, then led him to a rack of identical ones in different sizes. He guessed her size but left the receipt inside the box so she could exchange it.

Kelsey was sitting at the window facing Kalakaua Avenue when he arrived. "Waiting long?"

"I came early to give me time to compose my thoughts. I'm buying the drinks."

Alex nodded and smiled. "An iced coffee with two shots of hazelnut."

She returned with two iced coffees.

"Thanks." He swirled his drink and sipped.

The ice rattled noisily in the plastic cup as she nervously stirred before looking into Alex's face. "I had an unforgettable dinner with you last night, and thought I was ready for more, but when you reached around to unclip my bra, you became Colin, the man who abandoned me when I needed him most. It sounds crazy, but it was him that I reacted against. It may be too late, but I'm truly sorry. Alex, I'm not sure where things can go from here."

Is Kelsey offering a new start to our relationship? He pulled the gift-wrapped package from the Macy's bag and set it on the table. "My peace offering."

"Alex, I'm the one that owes you something."

"You just did."

She ran her fingers over the package and unfastened the red satin ribbon, then lifted the glossy cardboard lid. She ran her fingers over the satin blouse. Then, as she raised her head, he saw the teardrops on her glasses.

Chapter 6

*K*elsey took his suggestion and had three therapy sessions with Lora Daniels, before calling to invite Alex to an Italian dinner at her place. Alex was both anxious and hopeful when he arrived with a bottle of Chianti, a loaf of french bread, and a Polly Pocket toy for Nadia.

Kelsey greeted him with a warm hug, then told him to stay out of the kitchen while she prepared the meal with Nadia's help. He enjoyed watching the mother-daughter interactions with Kesey tasting her daughter's salad dressing and Nadia giving her opinion on the spaghetti sauce.

Kelsey started the meal with a toast—Nadia's glass filled with grape juice and Kelsey wishing for fairer skies ahead. The only mishap was when a meatball escaped Nadia's plate. Alex entertained them with stories about adventures on uninhabited volcanic islands in the South Pacific.

"Did you find any pirate treasures?" clamored Nadia.

"No. Most pirate treasures of gold and jewels are recovered from sunken ships in the Caribbean. The treasures in the Pacific are the occasional rare shell on beaches and porcelain dishes and bowls on sunken Chinese ships in the South China

Sea. I did find the wreckage of a World War II American fighter plane in the jungle with the pilot still inside."

"A skeleton?"

"Yes. I retrieved the pilot's metal dog tags that identify him and sent them and the location to the military's Missing in Action Office in Honolulu."

"So there's no use looking for buried treasure in Hawaii?" sighed Nadia.

Alex speared a meatball with his fork and held it up. "I have read stories of pirate treasures buried on Oahu, but none have ever been found. But there's a chance of finding a rare shell, like the multicolored sunrise shell, once worn by Hawaiian royalty. Thousands of people walk on the Oahu beaches, so there's little chance of finding anything of value. There are two tiny uninhabited islands about a mile off of Lanikai Beach on the other side of Oahu. We could rent a kayak and paddle out to the Mokuluas, called the Moks by the locals, and pretend we're lost on an uninhabited island. Few people go there, and you might find an unusual shell or something that drifted all the way across the Pacific from Asia."

"Mommy, can we go? That will be so much fun."

"Do I have a choice?"

Alex suggested they go during a weekday when they were more likely to have the island all to themselves. It was a forty-five-minute drive over the Ko'olau Mountains to Kailua, where they rented a two-person kayak a block from Kailua Beach. Nadia was small enough to ride in the middle. From Kailua Beach it was two miles to the cone-shaped remnants of a larger volcano off of nearby Lanikai Beach.

They launched their kayak where the Kaelepulu Canal entered the ocean at Kailua Beach. After a wobbly start, Kelsey picked up the rhythm as they paddled across the smooth water. Nadia sat in the middle humming to herself as she trailed her fingers in the ocean. Ten minutes from the beach, they passed Flat Island, a desolate coral islet appropriately named. As they rounded the point separating Kailua from Lanikai Beach, the Moks came into view—appearing to float on the ocean. Below the ocean's surface, scattered coral heads gradually coalesced into expansive coral gardens that stretched most of the way to the Moks. Nadia slipped on her face mask and leaned over the side, then jerked her head up.

"Wow! Mommy, there are pretty fish everywhere!" She ducked her face back into the water.

"Alex, you've introduced Nadia to the wonders of the underwater world and maybe set her on a course to become a marine biologist."

"Maybe. Kelsey, the barrier reef, a mile offshore, provides a wide shallow area that's ideal for coral growth and hosts millions of mostly smaller tropical fish, turtles, and an occasional eel. The calm water on most mornings becomes choppy in the afternoons when the winds pick up. The tricky part will be landing on the small beach without flipping our kayak."

"Why would we tip over? The ocean's smooth."

"The waves sweep around the tiny islands from both sides and crash together in front of the beach, sending water six feet straight up. The key is to time our landing between the colliding waves, so we won't be flipped. Nadia if we tip over, swim directly to shore, and Kelsey and I will handle the kayak."

They paused twenty-five yards from the beach, waiting for the wavefronts to crash together, then paddled hard and reached the beach upright. Nadia threw up her arms and cheered as Alex jumped out and pulled the kayak high on the beach.

"There's a secluded spot for a picnic on the other side of the island, and it's a good place to spot dolphins."

Alex led the way, stopping to lift Nadia over a ledge. The narrow footpath led to a rock shelf a few feet above the ocean where waves had thrown sand and pebbles and carved out two bathtub-sized tide pools.

"Mommy, can I go into the little pools of water?"

"Alex, anything dangerous in the tide pools?"

"No, and the water's warm, and maybe she can catch a goby."

Nadia climbed into the larger of the two shallow tide pools and splashed the warm water over herself. "It's as warm as my bath at home. Why is the water so warm?"

"The water is only replenished at high tide when the waves splash into the tidepools, and the black volcanic rocks soak up the sun and warm the water."

"Alex, you know so many interesting spots for Nadia to enjoy and are so patient in answering her questions."

"I suggested coming here for you too."

"I know."

"Alex!" Nadia screamed. "A little black fish jumped out of my pool and hopped over to the next one!"

"That's a goby. They use their fins to hop between tide-pools, an adaptation that helps them survive in small tidepools that often dry out."

Nadia jumped out of the water, shaking drops over them. "Alex, I need something to try to catch a goby."

"You can use one of the plastic cups we brought, but you'll have to be quick to catch one."

Nadia squealed as she chased gobies, while Alex and Kelsey laid out the lunch of roasted chicken, carrot sticks, clam dip, and potato chips.

"Nadia, time to give the gobies a rest and have lunch."

"Mommy, I'm not hungry. I need to catch a goby."

"They'll be waiting until after lunch."

Alex and Kelsey chuckled as they watched Nadia devour a drumstick and a handful of crushed potato chips.

"Nadia, how about going on a treasure hunt after lunch?"

"Yes, this is where I would bury a treasure if I was a pirate."

"Nadia, sometimes interesting things wash up on the beaches. First, let's check out the far side of the island to see if any rare shells were tossed up on the ledges. Stay close to me, as big waves can wash you off the rocks."

Alex held Nadia's hand as they climbed around to the rugged east-facing side of the island, where they spotted a clutch of shells in a crevasse, but unreachable from their ledge. They returned to the beach to find their backpacks tied to the kayak with bungee cords and Kelsey sitting on a beach towel.

"What'cha find?"

"Mommy, we saw a bunch of shells, but we couldn't reach them. Now I'm going to search this beach."

"Nadia, we can't stay long because the wind has come up and the water's getting choppy. Best place to look is the far end of the beach where the sand is coarser and you'll have a better chance of finding a nice shell. You can use one of the paddles as a shovel."

While Nadia searched for treasure, Alex smeared sunblock on Kelsey's shoulders and face. "Alex, it's hard to imagine this secluded spot less than a mile offshore from the crowded Oahu."

"I found something," Nadia yelled as she ran toward them.

"You couldn't have found a treasure already."

"I found a bottle that looks really old." She handed Alex a green bottle heavily encrusted with calcareous algae and barnacles. "It was just sticking out of the sand. I didn't even have to dig or anything."

"Must have been uncovered by last week's storm and high waves." Alex held the bottle up and turned it in the sunlight. "There's something inside, but I can't tell whether it's the dried contents or a *pirate's* map!"

"Alex, now you're delusional," said Kelsey.

Alex grinned. "Okay, there's no pirate map inside, but it's been floating in the ocean for a long time and might be valuable, and maybe it has a message inside. Long ago, people came to Hawaii on ocean liners and sometimes tossed bottles with messages inside into the sea. Nadia, we'll clean your bottle and see what's inside as soon as we get home."

Nadia frowned. "Okay, but an old bottle is not nearly as exciting as a real pirate's treasure map."

The stiff afternoon breeze had turned the water choppy as they launched their kayak. Nadia sat in the middle clutching her treasure bottle. They mistimed the colliding waves that turned their kayak sideways, and it was Kelsey's quick action that prevented them from flipping over.

"Kelsey, where did you learn that maneuver?"

"I took a kayaking trip down the Colorado River and after a few spills was hooked on whitewater kayaking. Two years later, I was leading groups on whitewater kayaking trips, where we had to dance our kayaks between sharp boulders to keep from spills."

The rough water and wind slowed progress, adding an extra half hour to the return trip. Nadia raced up the beach with her bottle, while Alex and Kelsey dragged the kayak onto the sand and flopped down in the shade of an ironwood tree.

After turning in their kayak and lifejackets, Alex took the Pali Highway that snaked up the steep eastern side of the Koʻolaus and through the two tunnels to the sunnier and dryer western side of the island.

Kelsey had dozed off when Alex took a sharp right into a canopied world of giant trees, their leafy branches splintering the sunlight on the pavement. Crowding the side of the road were plants with elephant-ear-sized leaves, bamboo, and ropy roots dangling from muscular banyan trees.

"Can I swing on the long roots like Tarzan?"

"I don't see why not." Alex pulled over to the side of the road. "Be quiet so you don't wake your mother." Alex lifted Nadia so she could grab a hanging root, then pushed her. "I'm Tarzan!" she squealed.

Kelsey was still asleep when Alex pulled into the parking lot at the Pali Lookout. He put his finger to his mouth as he carefully opened the door, leaving the window down to let in fresh air. Nadia skipped along holding Alex's hand as they approached the near-vertical cliff (*pali*). He lifted Nadia so she could see over the pali.

"It's straight down! Hold me tight."

He pointed out Kailua Bay where they had launched their kayak, and to the left, Kāneʻohe Bay. "Those irregular white patches in the aquamarine water are shallow coral reefs and sandbars. "There's one called the Sand Bar that appears for a few hours at low tide and is where people kayak or sail to for picnics."

A strong wind gust billowed skirts, and wide-brimmed hats took flight. Nadia scampered after the hats, catching one before it fluttered into a tree. She returned it to an elderly Japanese woman. Nadia shook her head when the woman offered a dollar.

"Nadia, that was the right thing to do. You did it without expecting payment, and that's the best kind of charity."

Kelsey was still asleep when they returned to their car and didn't wake up until Alex pulled up in front of their place and Nadia shook her mother's shoulder.

"Mommy, we're home, and Alex is going to open my treasure bottle."

Alex spread a newspaper on Kelsey's dining table. "Kelsey, do you have a chisel?"

"No, but I have a screwdriver."

Nadia hovered over the table as Alex chipped away at the thick calcareous crust with a screwdriver.

"Don't break my treasure bottle."

A few white flakes fell onto the table; then the neck of the bottle shattered. "Dammit," Alex muttered, and Nadia groaned.

"Sorry, Nadia."

She sniffled. "My treasure bottle's broken."

"Nadia, something's rolled up inside. Kelsey, do you have a pair of needle-nose pliers?"

"No, but I've got tweezers." Kelsey carefully extracted the rolled yellowed paper wrapped in a sheet of wax paper. Time had welded the sheets together, and Alex warmed them over the stove. Alex carefully unrolled the fragile paper and flattened it under a sheet of glass. The letter had been written in pencil and not ink and was still quite legible.

May 6, 1942

Dear Marge,

I watched you waving as our ship left Pearl Harbor, and kept looking back, even after I couldn't make out anyone. Then the islands grew smaller and finally just a smudge on the horizon. I'm afraid and don't know where we're going, but am sure we'll soon be fighting the Japs. I hope I'll be brave in battle, but am anxious. I never imagined I might have to kill someone.

Last night I had a nightmare that my ship was sunk and you never knew my final thoughts about my love for you and our baby, so I'm sending two letters, one by military mail and one in a bottle. I have no idea where or when the bottle will drift ashore, but it gives me peace of mind that no matter what happens, my message of love is coming to you.

I want you to know how much I already love our baby that will be born while I'm away at war. Please tell our baby how much I love him or her, and always remember that I love you more than words can ever say.

Love forever,
Johnny

WHOEVER FINDS THIS LETTER IN A BOTTLE, PLEASE SEND IT TO:

Marge Newton
1426 Irwin lane
Apple Valley, California

"That's so sad," Kelsey said. "What if Marge never heard from Johnny?"

"One way to find out. Give her a call."

"But it's so long ago. She's probably moved and may be deceased."

Alex handed Kelsey his cell phone. There was only one listing—a Linda Newton in Apple Valley. A woman answered on the third ring. "I'm searching for a Marge Newton and hoping you know her."

"She's my mother. Why are you calling?"

"This probably sounds strange, but my daughter found a bottle with a letter in it for her."

"Is this some kind of prank?"

"Not at all. My name's Kelsey O'Connor, and my daughter, Nadia, found a bottle on the beach in Hawaii that contained a letter written in 1942 to Marge Newton and signed Johnny. Your address is on the letter with a request for the person that found the letter in a bottle to send it to Marge Newton. The letter is very fragile, so we're not sure what to do next."

"My mother Marge is under hospice care and in the final stages of Alzheimer's. She just dozed off and is only awake for two or three hours a day. She never heard from Johnny, as his ship was sunk shortly after entering the conflict in the Western Pacific. She was devastated and devoted her life to raising me, and never remarried. My mother was pregnant when my parents married in Hawaii two days before his departure. Recently she has been telling me that her Johnny is coming home soon. Mother is expected to pass away any day. I'll try to wake her. It would be nice if you read the letter to her?"

"Not a problem. I'll have my friend Alex read it."

It was several minutes before Linda could get her mother to the phone. "Hello, is this my Johnny calling?"

"I'm Alex Silverton. I have a letter from your Johnny that I want to read to you. He read the letter, pausing as he struggled to control his emotions. When he finished, he could hear her raspy breathing, then a long pause. "Johnny, I've been waiting a long time for you to call. Our daughter, Linda, is all grown up now. She has your blue eyes. Please come home soon. I love you."

"Hello, this is Linda. That was wonderful how you read the letter. I'll tell Mom that Johnny will be meeting her soon, and that's true, as we believe in heaven. Please send the letter so I can keep it in the family album next to their wedding photo. Bless you for calling."

After Alex hung up, he leaned over and hugged Nadia. "You gave Johnny's wife something worth more than a pirate's treasure."

Chapter 7

*K*elsey was walking Nadia home from school when her cell phone chimed. "Hello."

"Kelsey, do you recognize my voice?"

"No."

"Prom night. Full moon on a knoll covered in tall wild grass that made you sneeze."

"Mark Trent! How did you get my number?"

"Megan Silva. She was at last year's high school reunion. She told me you had a research fellowship in Hawaii and you're still single."

"Mommy, who are you talking to?"

"A friend from high school is on the phone. Mark, where are you calling from?"

"I'm on an overnight stopover in Honolulu and hoping you'll be free for drinks and dinner so we can catch up on our lives."

"I would like that, but I'm not carefree and single. I have a seven-year-old daughter and I'm seeing someone. Do you still want to meet?"

"Absolutely. I've thought about you often and wondered how you were doing."

"I doubt that. You never called me once after high school. Anyway, give me an hour to see if my babysitter is available. Mind if I ask the guy I'm dating to join us?"

"Kelsey, there's nothing more boring than sitting through an evening listening to two people jabbering about the juvenile things they did in high school. Um . . . does he know about our tryst after the senior prom?"

"No, he doesn't! And for your information, at that time, I thought it was more than a prom-night fling."

"It meant a lot to me too."

"So why didn't you contact me as you promised?"

"I was an immature eighteen-year-old. I'll explain everything when we get together. Are you in a serious relationship with wedding bells in the future?"

"Way too early to know. He's comfortable to be with, but I'm cautious, as I still have a dissertation to finish and don't want to repeat my past mistake. Anyway, I need to check on a babysitter and will get back to you. When and where do you want to meet?"

"Mommy, what was the *mistake* you said on the phone?"

"Big ears. You're too young to understand."

"Humph."

Kelsey was nervous as she called Alex to tell him she was meeting a high school classmate for drinks and dinner and was relieved that he encouraged her to have a good time, and even offered to drive her. The babysitter wasn't available, so Kelsey arranged for Nadia to spend the night with her girlfriend.

As Kelsey prepared to meet Mark, she thought back to the friends she had in high school. Most classmates had been with her since kindergarten and had written thoughtful messages in her senior yearbook, usually ending in the words, "Let's keep in touch," but that was the last time she heard from them.

Mark Trent had seemed to be the heartthrob of half the girls in their senior class. He was almost too handsome, and the high school's star football player. It started when Kelsey stumbled and dropped her books, and Mark bent down to pick them up. She was surprised when he asked her to the Christmas dance and treated her like a princess. By the spring they were going steady and would often go to the top of a small hill and lie among wildflowers and talk about backpacking together across Europe—Paris, the Swiss Alps, Venice, and the Greek Islands, then end up making out. In the moonlight on the knoll after the senior prom, she lost her virginity, and Mark made promises that were never kept. A simple letter to say that he had moved on would have been much better than silence as if that night had never happened.

She hesitated, then slipped into her nicest dress—the one with the slit up the side—and put on a generous amount of her favorite perfume along with red lip gloss. She wanted Mark to see what he had missed, and mused in front of her mirror. *You had your chance, and I'm not interested in a relationship with you.* Yet there was a part of her that wanted to know if the embers that she thought flickered out long ago were still smoldering. The thoughts made her feel like she was cheating on Alex. In any case, she wouldn't let anything romantic go beyond drinks and dinner.

Kelsey remembered Mark's ambitions to study international finance and jet around the world putting together major oil and gas projects but had doubted he'd stick to a rigorous university program. The truth was about to be revealed.

The most vexing question was why he had dropped her without a single letter or even a call to explain. Megan Silva had said she'd heard a rumor that a woman in college had accused him of date rape, but the case was quietly dropped. Megan spread gossip like a wildfire, and Kelsey hoped the rumor was false. It wasn't a topic she would bring up.

There was a cooling Kona breeze as she walked from her Diamond Head apartment along Kalakaua Avenue past coconut palms and stately banyan trees into central Waikiki. At the entrance to the Reef View Hotel, she paused to check her makeup.

"Kelsey O'Connor!"

She shoved the mirror into her purse and looked up. Looming from the crowd was Mark—bigger than life with his big blue eyes and wavy tawny hair that had made her body tingle in high school. He was as handsome as she remembered, with a stippling of whiskers that gave him the masculine appearance of a male model. His meaty six-foot frame rippled with muscles that threatened to split the sleeves of his Thai silk shirt. His hair was swept back over his ears, with locks tumbling across his tanned forehead. His high cheekbones and chiseled jaw added a noble look, and nestled among the curls of his chest hair was the gold cross she remembered toying with as they lay together on the grassy knoll in high school.

"Kelsey, you're absolutely stunning." He moved quickly to sweep her into the air with an embrace that took her breath away. His masculine cologne stirred memories of the fateful prom night, yet there was a difference. She was no longer a star-struck teenage girl in a coming-of-age romance. She had a child and a career ahead of her and was in the early stages of dating a man with promise.

When he set her down, she stepped back. "Mark, you're still the charmer."

"Just a natural response to your beauty. I never should have let you slip away. I was young and immature and needed to find out who I was and what to do with my life."

"And have you?" Kelsey calmly asked—her eyes locked on his.

"I made mistakes, but what I want in life is best discussed over cocktails and dinner." He led her into the popular cocktail lounge crowded with mostly young singles, where they waited twenty minutes to get a beachside table. Mark ordered the drinks, and Kelsey selected the shrimp-roll pupu platter.

She plucked her miniature umbrella from the fruity mai tai and twirled it between her fingers. "So, Mark, did you go into international finance as planned?"

"I met a girl and foolishly jumped into marriage, then dropped out of college when she got pregnant and we needed money. Our marriage failed two years later, and a year and a half later she was married to Bobby Woodburn from high school. I entered a community college and got an associate's degree in marketing and eventually got into international sales of high-end luggage, which allows me to travel to Asia and continue my hobby photographing ancient temples. The frequent trips haven't given me much time to settle down and start a family."

"Maybe marriage isn't for you."

"I keep looking for someone like you."

Kelsey studied Mark's face. *I wonder how often you've used that line?*

The braised tiger shrimp and spring rolls arrived along with sweet and spicy Thai dipping sauce. Mark dipped a crispy roll into the sauce while Kelsey squeezed a lemon wedge over the plump crustaceans. Holding one to her lips, she studied the face of the man from her past.

"You're still as flattering as you were in high school."

"I can't help it. Seeing you brings back wonderful memories. But, Kelsey, you don't sound like the girl that was thinking about college, marriage, and kids, in that order. Do you mind if I ask what happened?" For the first time since they had met, Mark appeared serious.

"I was studying marine biology at UC San Diego when I was offered a summer internship at the Darwin Research Center in the Galapagos Islands. I met a charming, adventurous graduate student from Scotland, and two weeks after returning to the States, I discovered I was pregnant. Fatherhood was not on his agenda, and he conveniently disappeared. It has been a struggle raising a child, taking courses, and working, and that has left little time or energy for developing a serious relationship. My parents have been very helpful with Nadia, but they have their own life to live."

"How about the man you're dating now?"

"Great guy so far, but as I said, I'm taking it slow, so too early to say where it will lead. Trusting a man enough to have intimacy is a challenge."

"So you're not sleeping with him?"

"Umm, he's understanding, not like you were."

"Kelsey, we were just teens, and it meant a lot to me."

"Everyone remembers the first time, but it's different now with so much at stake."

"Kelsey, are you seeing a therapist to work out your relationship issues?"

"I've recently been seeing a therapist to work through my intimacy issues." She gulped down her mai tai.

"Maybe I can help you with your intimacy problems."

"I bet you can! No thanks."

"In Asia, women take a harmless herbal pill to relax tensions and enhance intimacy."

"Mark, I'm not in Asia, and I prefer a therapist."

"Just trying to be helpful." He changed the subject and updated Kelsey on classmates he'd met at the reunion. Twilight merged into night, and instead of moving to the restaurant, he ordered another round of mai tais and a mixed pupu platter.

The second mai tai seemed especially strong. "Mark, I'm getting quite dizzy and need to go home. Could you call a taxi?"

"Sure, but please take a few minutes to see my collection of temple photos and pick out one for a keepsake."

"Ah, I guess so."

By the time they reached his sixth-floor room, her head was spinning, and he had to hold her up.

Kelsey was awakened by a police siren. Disoriented, she gazed into the darkness broken by a dim glow from the partially open balcony door. *This isn't my bed—my home.* Kelsey groped for the bedside light switch, then stumbled out of bed, falling to her knees as she gathered pieces of her clothing. The cloud of confusion dissipated as the evening's events crystalized, then went blank when she entered the elevator with Mark Trent.

The balcony door slid open, and Mark sauntered in and nonchalantly reclined into a stuffed chair, his robe falling open to reveal his nakedness—his grin mocking her. "No need to rush home."

Clothes clutched to her breasts, she screamed, "You bastard! You drugged and raped me!"

"Kelsey, no one forced you to come to my room and jump into my bed. I gave you just what you needed. You should be thanking me." He smirked. "It would have been much better if you'd been awake and lucid."

"I should have believed the rumors about you and never agreed to meet you!"

He lit a cigarette and puffed out smoke donuts as he watched her hurriedly dress. As she stumbled to the door, he twirled her panties around his index finger. "Forget something?"

"Go fuck yourself!" she screamed, and bolted from the room and slammed the door.

The concerned taxi driver asked if she needed help down the steps to her home.

The following morning, Nadia shook her mother. "Mommy, I have to go to school."

"Honey, I don't feel good. Call Stacy's mommy and see if she'll take you to school."

Nadia tried to take care of her mother but was overwhelmed. She answered her mother's cell phone calls—repeatedly telling Alex her mommy didn't want to speak to him. When Kelsey neglected to say whether she was meeting a male or female classmate, he had suspected it might be an old flame from high school but wasn't jealous at the time. But her refusal to answer his calls caused him to wonder if the meeting had reignited romantic feelings.

On the fifth day, he could wait no longer when he heard Nadia sniffling on the phone. He drove to Kelsey's place and knocked on the door, ready to accept the truth that it was over between them but not willing to remain in limbo—not knowing. "Nadia, I need to see your mother!" His voice was demanding.

Nadia slowly opened the door. Her normally neat braids were gone, and her T-shirt was spotted with ketchup. Tears welled up in her eyes. "Mommy told me to tell you to go away."

"Nadia, I'm here to help. I'm not leaving until I have a talk with your mother."

Nadia looked down at the floor. "She won't talk to anyone."

"Nadia, are you okay?"

Tears spilled from her eyes, and she didn't pull away when Alex wrapped his arms around her. "Whatever's going on, I will help, and I won't leave until you're both okay."

She held onto him as he stepped inside. The front room was a mess with clothes overflowing from a plastic laundry basket and McDonald's bags on the coffee table. The kitchen was worse, with a stench coming from the sink half full of greenish-gray water.

"The garbage disposal doesn't work, and Mommy won't let me cook alone. I've been going to McDonald's until yesterday, but there's no more money in Mommy's wallet."

He checked the disposal and retrieved a fork with twisted prongs, then knelt under the sink and pushed the red reset button, and the disposal hummed as the putrid water swirled down the drain.

"I'm sorry, I dropped a fork down the disposal"

"Nadia, I've done that too. But never put your hand into the disposal. as it might start. Now I need to talk to your mom."

"She's in her room, but she won't answer."

Alex knocked. "Kelsey, I'm here to help you, and I'm not leaving until we have a talk and I'm sure Nadia's okay."

"Go away," came a raspy voice. "I'm okay."

Nadia clung to Alex's arm. "Don't leave. Mommy's not okay."

"I know, honey." He opened the door, catching a whiff of the stale, musty air. Kelsey turned over, her back to Alex. More

McDonald's bags were on the side table, along with french fries scattered on the floor like pick-up sticks.

He sat on the bed and massaged her shoulder, then gently began untangling her matted hair. "Kelsey, I don't know what happened or if everything is over between us, but you need help, and I'm not leaving until you get it." Nadia hopped on the bed, her small hands helping to untangle her mother's hair.

Kelsey moaned and rolled over—her lips parched, with puffy half-moon shadows below her emerald eyes. Alex lifted strands of red hair from her face and tucked them behind her ear. Kelsey slowly pulled herself into a sitting position, her nightgown spotted with coffee and remnants of McDonald's meals.

"I'm so incredibly stupid, humiliated, and depressed."

"Kelsey, I really want to help you."

"You won't after you hear what happened."

"Whatever happened or whether there's a future with us, I love you." He lifted her hand to his lips.

"Alex, you shouldn't say that before knowing what happened."

"I know someone hurt you, and Nadia and I are very worried about you. So whatever you feel about me, I'm not leaving until you and Nadia get help."

"Nadia, honey, I need to talk to Alex alone."

"Okay, Mommy." She kissed her cheek, then scurried out of the room, quietly closing the door.

Kelsey fidgeted, picking at her cuticles. "Mark Trent, my boyfriend in high school, was the one who took my virginity after our senior prom. When he went off to college, he didn't even bother to send me a single letter, so I knew there would be no future with us. He was the one who called me and asked me for cocktails and dinner. After the second mai tai, I became quite dizzy and asked him to get me a taxi. He asked me to stop by his room to see his photos of ancient temples and to pick one as a keepsake. I agreed and fell for the oldest trick in the book. You know the line: 'Come to my room to see my etchings.' All I remember is getting into the elevator. I woke up in Mark's bed, my clothes on the floor. He must have drugged me, then had sex with me, as I was sore. I can't describe the humiliation. I wanted to die."

Alex pulled Kesey against his chest. "I'm so sorry for you. Have you reported Mark to the police?"

"No. I went to his room voluntarily, and it would be his word against mine, and the case would be dismissed. And then there would be the humiliation of it getting into the newspaper! Nadia would find out, and classmates would tease her. Nadia is the only thing that kept me from running away and maybe doing something awful. She's been doing her best to take care of me."

Alex leaned in and kissed her lips before she quickly pulled back. "I'm awful. I haven't bathed or brushed my teeth in a week."

He chuckled. "That was de rigueur when I worked for two months in the Australian Outback. Sometimes I brushed my teeth with beer!"

A slight smile. "What do we do now?"

"Kelsey, a shower wouldn't hurt. Then we'll go for a special breakfast at the Hau Tree in the Kaimana Beach Hotel. It's only a ten-minute walk from here. After breakfast, we can talk about the next step."

"I don't feel like going out."

"You need to get some fresh air, and neither of you has had a decent meal in a week."

Alex and Nadia were washing dishes when Kelsey emerged from the bedroom wearing a simple floral skirt and a white blouse. Nadia held their hands—the bridge between them—as they walked across Kapiʻolani Park to the Kaimana Beach Hotel.

They were seated under the low branches of a hau tree a few feet from Sans Souci Beach. The waiter had a look of disbelief when Nadia ordered a full stack of buttermilk pancakes topped with strawberries, and hot chocolate with whipped cream. Kelsey ordered a mushroom-and-cheese omelet with Portuguese sausage and a papaya, while Alex settled for a bagel with cream cheese and Kona coffee.

He kept the conversation on lighthearted topics and possible outings they might do in the weeks ahead. Nadia perked up and said she wanted to see a real volcano, and Alex said they could all go to the Big Island and see hot lava flowing into the sea. Kelsey said she had to catch up on her research, and then they could discuss a trip.

Nadia crossed her arms over her chest and frowned. "That means no."

Chapter 8

*A*lex fought back the anger and sickening feelings he had every time he thought about what Mark Trent had done to Kelsey. He hoped it hadn't ruined his chances of developing an intimate relationship with Kelsey. Alex got her to return to Lora Daniels for counseling, and he followed Lora's suggestion to take a more Buddhist, empathic approach to Kelsey.

Their relationship was in a holding pattern for several weeks, then came the call from Kelsey.

"Alex, I have a favor to ask."

"Sure. How can I help?"

"Nadia wants to write about volcanoes for her school science fair, and I'm sure she chose volcanoes because of you. Would you have some spare time to help her this weekend?"

"I'm flying to the Big Island this weekend to check on a grad student's research on Kīlauea volcano. "How about you and Nadia joining me? Then she can have firsthand experience studying a volcano."

"I can't afford that and won't accept your charity."

"I have two extra flight coupons to the Big Island that will soon expire." It wasn't true, as the coupons were good for nine more months, but this was an opportunity he didn't want to miss.

"I need to discuss it with Nadia." Minutes later, as Nadia screamed in the background, Kelsey agreed to the trip.

Nadia's nose was pressed to the window as she watched the Hawaiian Islands slowly pass, each framed by the cobalt-blue sea. Thirty-five minutes into the flight, Alex pointed to two shimmering-white flying saucer–like features in the distance. "Nadia, do you know what those are?"

"Streaky clouds?"

"Good guess. They're the snow-covered peaks of Mauna Loa and Mauna Kea, the tallest mountains in the world if you measure the height from the seafloor."

"There's snow in Hawaii?"

"Yes, at almost fourteen thousand feet above sea level, the temperature is below freezing, so it's possible to build a snowman in the morning and a sandcastle on the beach in the afternoon."

"Cool. Can we do that?"

"We don't have time on this trip. Maybe we can come back another time."

"Mommy, can we stay a little longer?"

"Nadia, you should be happy that Alex is bringing us on this trip and not ask for more."

"I know, and I really want to look into a volcano."

They stepped from their plane into the humid, ginger-laced air and squawking mynahs at the Hilo Airport. Alex upgraded the rental car to a convertible and turned up Highway 11 for the forty-minute drive up the side of Mauna Loa Volcano. Nadia's and Kelsey's hair danced in the wind as they drove to the tiny community of artists and B&Bs nestled in the rainforest, minutes from the entrance to Volcanoes National Park. He followed the treehouse-shaped signs down a short gravel road to a plantation-style house nestled among ohia trees and giant *hāpu'u* ferns.

Popping gravel signaled their arrival, and a barrel-chested man emerged onto the wide veranda of a plantation-style home, fringed in bird-of-paradise flowers. He wore a classic Hawaiian shirt patterned with hula dancers and surfers, and a broad-brimmed hat of woven pandanus leaves with a headband of pheasant feathers.

"Aloha, folks. I'm Jim Reed." He bounded across the stepping stones and warmly shook Kelsey's and Alex's hands, then squatted to take Nadia's. "Missy, our cat, Koa, is all alone in the treehouse and would love to have you pet her."

"You have a real treehouse!" shrieked Nadia.

"Sure do, and it's reserved for children." He pointed to a thatched hut among the branches of an ohia tree to the left of the main house. "I built it for my daughter. Be careful on the steps, and Koa loves treats." He pulled a small bag of cat treats from his pocket and handed it to Nadia. "Now, skedaddle."

He turned to Alex and Kelsey. "Your timing is perfect, as we had a cancellation and I've upgraded you to the honeymoon suite at no extra charge."

Kelsey grimaced as Jim grabbed her bag and headed into the house, followed by Alex with the second carry-on bag. Their *Male'ana* (wedding) suite was in the rear, past the *Ānuenue* (rainbow) and *Pu'uhonua* (place of refuge) rooms. It was tastefully decorated in rare koa furniture—the centerpiece, a canopied bed with hanging white orchids on each of the four pillars. Sliding french doors opened to a small private balcony with a jacuzzi.

Kelsey, whispered to Alex, "This won't work."

"Let me take care of it." He turned to Jim. "Is there a bed for Nadia?"

"The couch has a hideaway bed for your daughter. Better yet, if it's okay with you and your daughter, she can sleep in the treehouse with Koa."

"This is so much more than we expected. We'll talk to Nadia about sleeping in the treehouse and let you know," said Alex.

As soon as Jim left, Kelsey lamented, "Alex, this is not what we agreed. You know we're not sleeping together."

"I know. You'll sleep in the canopied bed, and I'll sleep in the hideaway bed. I'm sure Nadia will love sleeping in the treehouse with Koa. Problem solved."

"Okay, but the jacuzzi is out, as I didn't bring a swimsuit."

"Neither did I, but I'm not going to pass up the opportunity to soak in our own private jacuzzi. You can turn out the lights and look the other way." He chuckled.

She smiled at Alex's attempt at humor and lay back on the canopied bed. "Well, I suppose the arrangement can work. I need to see the treehouse before letting Nadia sleep there overnight."

They climbed the treehouse stairs and knocked on the door. "Can we come in?"

"Yes, but don't scare Koa."

Nadia was sitting cross-legged on the child's bed with Koa curled up in her lap. It was furnished with children's furniture with a small teapot and cups on the table. A framed picture of a *hapa* girl about Nadia's age was on the wall with an engraved plaque underneath: In Memory of Leilani.

"Mr. Reed said you can sleep here if you want."

Nadia screamed, and Koa bounded from her lap. "Mommy! This is what I always wanted."

They took Jim's suggestion and stopped for take-out lunches at the Kīlauea General Store before entering Hawaii Volcanoes National Park. Inside the entrance of the five hundred-square-mile park was the historic Volcano House that began as a thatched building in 1846. Rebuilt and updated several times, it had hosted countless dignitaries going back to Mark Twain's visit in 1866. Perched on the lip of the three-mile-wide Kīlauea Caldera, the hotel provided a 150-degree view of the surreal moonscape of buckled black lava flows across the floor of the caldera. After viewing the expansive Kīlauea Caldera in 1866, Mark Twain wrote, "Here was room for the imagination to work!"

Nadia was hungry, so they ate their boxed lunches on the empty hotel terrace, while inside, the restaurant was packed with visitors from the tour buses.

Standing at the overlook, Alex pointed out the volcanic features. "The smoke and steam you see billowing up in the distance are from Halemaʻumaʻu Crater."

"Alex, why is Kīlauea called a caldera and Hale-ma-uma-u a crater?"

"Calderas are bigger volcanic craters." He pointed. "See the hikers walking across the caldera floor."

"I'm just a little girl and can't walk all the way across to the smoking crater."

"We'll take the road around the caldera to the Halemaʻumaʻu Crater parking lot. Then it's a short walk to the crater's edge where we can look down into the witch's brew of bubbling lava. But first, we have to finish our lunches."

Watching from the bushes were little eyes, and as Kelsey began to lay out the boxed lunches, sparrows flittered down around their table, pausing to tilt their heads to watch for crumbs. Nadia made the first offering with a corner of her sandwich, and more birds swooped down and encircled her chair.

"What's the pretty pink-and-gray bird watching from the branches?"

"Nadia, it's a Hawaiian honeycreeper. At one time, there were more than fifty species of Honeycreepers that ranged in color from drab brown to scarlet red and canary yellow. But two-thirds were wiped out after the introduction of mongooses, rats, and diseases."

"Honeycreeper is a funny name."

"Watch how they hop among the branches—kind of like they're creeping in the bushes."

"I see. I hope we see a red one."

"Best chance is around the Thurston Lava Tube where there's a dense patch of rainforest. We'll stop there after visiting the Halemaʻumaʻu Crater."

Their first stop was at the Sulfur Banks, a two-minute drive from Volcano House. As they approached the steamy fumaroles, Nadia frowned and held her nose. "This place smells like rotten eggs."

"You're right. The sulfur mixed with steam smells like rotten eggs, and you can see the yellowish-green sulfur coating on the rocks near the vents."

They didn't stay for more than a couple of minutes before driving on to the Halemaʻumaʻu Crater. From the parking lot, they took the short trail toward the clouds of sulfurous smoke and steam belching from the crater. From the overlook, they gazed down into the bubbling, belching lake of molten lava.

"Wow! A real volcano. What if it erupts while we're standing so close? Won't the lava burn us up?"

"Yes, at 2,200 degrees Fahrenheit, we'd be toast. Don't worry; there are seismographs on the side of the caldera that detect tiny vibrations to warn geologists when Pele's getting restless, so there's plenty of time to warn tourists to leave."

"Whose Pele?"

"According to Hawaiians, Pele is the goddess of fire and volcanoes and must be respected.

"Is Pele real?"

"To scientists, it's a myth, but many Hawaiians still believe it is important to respect Pele and perform ceremonies to honor goddess Pele. Those stones we saw stacked like snowmen along the trail with ferns between the rocks are offerings to Pele and called *ahu*."

"I don't get it. If it's just a myth, why do people believe it?"

Alex shrugged and looked at Kelsey. "Can you help?"

"Alex, now you know the challenges of raising an inquisitive young girl. Sweety, traditions and beliefs of Pacific Island people are about respecting the land, the volcanoes, the ocean, and all living things on the land and in the ocean. For centuries, native islanders have had rules to not use up all the resources on the land and in the sea and to respect the power of volcanoes. With the notable exception of Easter Island, Pacific Islanders were good conservationists, before Europeans arrived to exploit the limited resources."

"Mommy, I see. We're studying about conservation in school, and to not waste so much. But I still don't understand why people worship volcanoes."

Kelsey turned to Alex. "Okay, volcano expert. What do you think?"

"Nadia, think of it this way. The Hawaiians respected the power of volcanoes and to stay away when lots of steam was coming out, and that was a good thing."

The shadows were long, and the tour buses were gone when they arrived at the trailhead of the Thurston Lava Tube. The footpath descended into a mist-shrouded rainforest of giant ferns and ohia trees with red pom-pom-like tufted flowers. Honeycreepers flitted amid the verdant foliage, adding flashes of scarlet and saffron to the primeval setting.

Nadia clutched Alex's hand as they paused at the dark cavernous cave opening. "I'm a little afraid that those long twisty vines hanging over the spooky entrance will grab me."

"The only thing that might grab you is me. Grrr. It's perfectly safe, and our flashlight will push away the darkness." Inside the entrance, they were bathed in cool air and silence broken only by the melodic sounds of water dripping into puddles.

Alex handed the flashlight to Nadia. "Describe what you see."

Holding the flashlight in both hands, Nadia moved the light beam over the lava wall. "Umm, it looks like melted chocolate flowed through the tunnel."

"Good analogy. Can you tell which direction the lava flowed?"

"I see streaks but can't tell the direction."

Alex showed her how to recognize the flow around protruding rocks where the long tail pointed in the direction of the flow.

"I didn't realize I was going on a trip with two geologists," Kelsey chortled.

"Mommy, Alex is teaching me so much about volcanoes that I'm sure I'll win a ribbon at the school science project."

Alex put his hand on Nadia's shoulder. "You're a winner by trying your best."

"A diplomatic answer," Kelsey said.

"Mommy, what does *diplomatic* mean?"

"Diplomatic is giving an answer that pleases everyone."

"Mommy, is that like when I ask for something in front of your friends, and you smile and say we'll discuss it later?"

Kelsey sighed. "Enough questions. Time to start thinking about dinner."

"There aren't many choices around here. There's of course the restaurant at Volcano House and Kīlauea Lodge."

"I have a better idea," said Nadia. "We can pretend we're on a deserted island and buy some fruit and vegetables and eat in my treehouse."

Alex grinned. "That's a great idea! We can stop at the Kīlauea General Store and pick up the kinds of food we'd find on a deserted island."

Nadia took the lead in the store, picking out fruit she imagined people on a deserted island would eat—a coconut, papaya, and finger bananas. Alex added *poke*—a mixture of diced morsels of raw ahi tuna, chopped tomatoes, lime juice, sea salt, and a dash of soy sauce and ginger flakes. The Hawaiian cashier heard Nadia talking about the meal in a treehouse and added a half pint of *poi* to their bag. "Must have *ono poi* with da meal. Eat with these two fingers. My treat."

Koa jumped from the bed and purred as she brushed against Nadia's leg and was rewarded with morsels of *poke*. Alex used the saw blade on his Swiss knife to cut the top off the coconut, so they could sip the clear coconut milk. Then he demonstrated to Nadia how to scrape out the soft young coconut meat with a spoon. Banana leaves were used as plates, and they ate with their fingers.

Nadia's last words as Kelsey tucked her into bed were, "I wish we could stay here forever."

Alex and Kelsey walked silently back to their room, neither knowing what to say—anxious about the night together. Kelsey opened her suitcase and took out her pajamas and toiletries.

"Kelsey, I'm going to soak in the jacuzzi. You're welcome to join me."

"Alex, remember, I didn't bring a swimsuit."

"Just wear your jogging shorts and a T-shirt and turn off the lanai light."

"I'm really tired and think I'll just go to bed."

"I understand."

She tried not to notice as he stripped down to his boxer shorts, took the bottle of champagne from the small refrigerator and two flutes, and walked out to the jacuzzi.

He's trying to tempt me.

Alex sat submerged to his chest in the bubbling jacuzzi, gazing into the darkness. He didn't move when the porch light was flicked off, nor when she slid in beside him. The champagne cork popped and disappeared into the darkness. Their fingers touched as he handed her a flute of bubbly.

"Alex, I was worried that Nadia would quickly be bored looking at lava rocks, but you brought them to life for Nadia and me."

"Kelsey, I enjoyed every minute of the day." The ping of their glasses was as pure as the cheeps of rare birds in the rainforest. She moved closer and laid her head on his shoulder—her hair tickling his neck.

He turned, nuzzling her hair, and cautiously took her hand.

"Mommy, Mommy," came the muffled voice.

"I'm coming," Kelsey called out. She gulped her champagne and handed the glass to Alex as she stepped from the jacuzzi. Kelsey flicked on the lights revealing her wet T-shirt clinging to her chest. She glanced toward Alex before hurrying to open the door. Nadia jumped into her arms. "What happened?"

"I had a bad dream. I want to sleep with you."

"Of course." Kelsey hugged her daughter.

"Mommy, you're all wet."

"I was in the jacuzzi."

Alex stepped inside—a towel wrapped around his waist. "Nadia, are you okay?"

"I had a scary nightmare and want to sleep with Mommy."

He gave a furtive glance at Kelsey. "You'll like the canopied princess bed."

After Nadia drifted off to sleep, Kelsey whispered to Alex, "Sorry."

Chapter 9

*M*ommy, Alex, wake up. I smell food, and my stomach's growling."

Kelsey sat up and stretched. "Alex, how was the hideaway bed?"

"Lonely."

"Why were you lonely?" chirped Nadia. "We were all together in one room."

Nadia raced ahead to their breakfast table on the corner of the veranda with a view of the treehouse. The sun filtered through a giant *ohia* tree, casting a soft mottled pattern over the veranda. Nadia's chatter attracted a fourth guest. Koa appeared in the door of the treehouse, stretched out its front paws, then padded down the steps.

"Aloha," said Jim's wife as she glided across the polished veranda floor. Her ample figure and rich Polynesian complexion were reminiscent of Paul Gauguin's paintings of Tahitian women. She wore a bright, palm-frond-patterned muumuu, accented by ebony hair trailing to her waist, and a scarlet hibiscus flower behind her right ear, signifying she was married.

"Welcome to our patch of paradise. Call me Lani. This morning, we're serving sweet papaya from our garden, Kīlauea coffee grown on a small plantation near here, and warm scones with ohelo berry preserves. The ohelo berries come from small bushes high on the slopes of the Kīlauea volcano. We also have your choice of eggs prepared to order, and for the young lady, may I suggest hot cocoa with lots of mini-marshmallows."

"Oh, yes. I love yummy marshmallows in my hot chocolate."

Lani disappeared into the house, and Nadia lifted Koa onto her lap. "Sorry that I didn't stay with you last night." She looked at her mother. "Aren't you glad I came to sleep with you last night?"

Kelsey gave an enigmatic smile. "Nadia, you ensured a good night's sleep for everyone."

Nadia caressed her purring feline. "Koa, I'll sleep with you tonight."

Jim and Lani prepared lunch and dinner baskets along with an ice chest of drinks. Lani was overly attentive to Nadia and even helped her buckle up in the backseat of the car. "You remind me of our daughter when she was your age." Before closing the car door, she gave Nadia a packet of *li hing mui*. "My daughter loved these sweet-and-salty preserved plums."

"Please thank her for letting me stay in her treehouse."

"I'm sure she's happy you're staying in her treehouse."
Lani quickly turned away, and her husband put his arm around
her waist as they slowly walked back to the house.

"Mommy, why was Lani smiling with tears in her eyes?"

"Sometimes grown-ups are happy and sad at that same
time."

"I don't understand."

"You're not a grown-up."

They turned left at the park entrance and in less than ten
minutes reached the turnoff to the Chain of Craters Road. The
two-lane road was etched into a broad lava flow that stretched
nineteen miles down to the sea. "Nadia, we're driving on basalt
that was once a river of fiery lava flowing from the Kīlauea
Volcano down to the sea."

"Alex, it's not very pretty—just black rocks and no grass
or trees."

"Nadia, there's a lot of hidden beauty that I'll show you,
like *'aʻā* and *pāhoehoe* lava and lovely Pele's hair growing out
of the lava."

"I don't understand. How can a rock grow hair?"

"You'll get to see for yourself."

Kelsey and Nadia soon lost interest in the miles of monot-
onous lava on both sides of the road, but not Alex, who saw
pages of geologic history. Twenty minutes passed. Then, in the
distance, an isolated grove of trees appeared to be growing in
the middle of the desolate lava flow.

"Alex, how can trees be growing out of rocks?"

"Nadia, let's find out why." He turned off on a bumpy track
across the lava past a sign: Official Vehicles Only.

"Are you sure we won't get into trouble?" Kelsey asked.

"I have a permit to drive off the main road and collect rock specimens." They stopped at the edge of a grove of trees about twenty-five yards wide. "Nadia, these isolated islands of land in the lava flows are called *kīpukas*, and I want you to figure out why the lava flowed around it. Now describe the patterns of the lava."

"Hmm, the lava kind of looks like Mommy's chocolate brownie mix when she pours it into a pan."

"Good analogy. The ropy textured lava is called *pahoehoe*, which can be smooth or braided like black hair. Do you see any other textures?"

She wrinkled her nose. "There's a jumble of jagged lava rocks piled up in front of the island that looks like the burnt brownies you baked for me."

"But you said they tasted good?"

"Mommy told me to say that so I wouldn't hurt your feelings."

Alex laughed. "I shouldn't have asked. The blocky lava is *'a'ā,* and it moved slowly because it was less liquid than pahoehoe lava. Now go over and look closely at the jumble of lava and see if you can figure out why this little island exists."

As Nadia scampered over the rocks, Kelsey said, "Alex, you really know how to keep Nadia's interests high, by always challenging her to figure things out."

"Just make it a game, like a treasure hunt. Too often parents answer children's questions, rather than challenging them to solve them. Getting them started early will help them later in life."

Kelsey fixed her gaze on Alex. *I hope he's not playing a game with me.*

Nadia came running back, scrambling over slabs of lava. "I think I know why the lava went around the island. The slow-moving lava that looks like burnt brownies piled up at the front of the island, and the speedy lava had to go around the island."

Alex grinned and nodded. "Smarty-pants."

"Now, let's see if we can find some Pele's hair." Nadia followed Alex as he looked in crevices in the lava, where they discovered tiny ferns, insects, and a lizard that scurried away. "Nadia, even in this harsh landscape, life is beginning to emerge. All the Hawaiian Islands began as lifeless volcanic rocks, then migratory birds left seeds, and over thousands of years, vegetation took hold and helped break down rocks to produce soil. Around 1,600 years ago, Polynesians from the Marquesan Islands brought food plants and domesticated animals to Hawaii, including taro, coconuts, bananas, sweet potatoes, pigs, dogs, and chickens."

Nadia followed Alex as he climbed over slabs of lava, peering between the crevices and showing her the lichen and tiny ferns that existed inches below the hot, barren surface.

"Alex, is that Pele's hair?" Nadia pointed into a crevice.

Alex knelt and peered at her discovery. "You have sharp eyes. Those bristling needles are made of volcanic glass and are fragile, so don't touch. You won't find Pele's hair along tourist paths, as people can't resist the temptation to touch the delicate spines."

"This is so much more interesting than my science class at school."

"Nadia, you need to take pictures of everything you see and write down your observations, including the location, date, and time in your notebook."

"Why is the time of day important?"

"Good question. Sometimes I get my pictures and descriptions mixed up, and knowing the date and time helps me remember when and where I took a photo. Also, the angle of the sun and lighting conditions can change the way things look in photos."

Alex sat beside Kelsey as they watched Nadia taking pictures and writing in her school notebook. "You've really sparked Nadia's interest."

Alex gazed into Kelsey's eyes. "Have I sparked your interest?"

"In rocks . . . not so much." Then her enigmatic smile became less mysterious.

Near the end of the Chain of Craters Road, Alex turned off at marker 16 to the Pu'u Loa Petroglyphs site where over twenty-three thousand early Hawaiian petroglyphs existed. From the parking lot, they followed a 0.7-mile trail across lava, then a raised wooden boardwalk that circled the petroglyphs carved on smooth pahoehoe lava.

Although Alex had seen hundreds of petroglyphs, it was Kelsey that was most knowledgeable, having taken a course at UC Berkeley on Pacific Island petroglyphs. She pointed out aspects of Hawaiian life depicted in the stylized etchings of sailing canoes, fish, spears, moon, and stick figures.

"Mommy, what are the round circles with dots in the middle?"

"They're especially important. This was a sacred place to Hawaiians for generations, and fathers brought their infants' umbilical cords as an offering to the gods to ensure long lives. The circle represents the spot where the umbilical cord was buried. While most ancient Hawaiian beliefs had no basis in science, like most religions, they allowed the religious leaders—in the case of Hawaiians, their chiefs—the authority to maintain order and control over their people. So Hawaiian beliefs had both good and bad aspects."

It was twilight when they reached the parking area for tourists that had come to watch the nightly fireworks display caused by molten lava flowing into the sea. People stood shoulder to shoulder along the rope barrier that kept them far back from the river of lava plunging into the ocean.

"I can't see a thing," Nadia whined as she stood on tiptoes. "Alex, what do you suggest?"

"Kelsey, a grad student is supposed to meet us here."

"Dr. Silverton."

Alex and Kelsey turned toward a wiry man trotting toward them, dressed in khaki clothes with the National Parks emblems on his shoulders.

"Hank, I was worried that you couldn't make it."

"I was delayed by a group of visitors that drove into a restricted area and got stuck. They blamed me for not having a bigger sign warning that the road was closed to tourists."

"Kelsey, Hank Collins is completing his PhD in volcanology at the University of Hawaii and working part-time as a park ranger. He's agreed to take us to a better vantage point for viewing nature's fireworks."

Hank squatted and introduced himself to Nadia. "I've been interested in volcanoes since I was your age. I think you'll enjoy the show that Pele will put on tonight. Do you have any questions?"

"Um, what do park rangers do besides keeping tourists from going where they shouldn't?"

"Our main responsibility is to keep tourists safe, and second, to ensure they don't damage any geological features or take rocks from the park. Native Hawaiians believe people who take away rocks will have bad luck. At the visitor center we have a display of lava rocks mailed back by visitors that had bad luck after taking away rocks."

"Does taking a rock really bring bad luck?"

"No, but the display of rocks that have been returned and notes accompanying the rocks discourages other tourists from taking away rocks. Now follow me, and I'll take you to a better viewing spot."

Hank led them past the roped-off area and a hundred yards closer to the lava flow. "I can't stay. I see four people that have wandered past the rope barrier. I'll return and meet you at around nine. Enjoy the show." Hank turned and bounded away as agile as a mountain goat over the volcanic rubble.

They ate *huli-huli* chicken and Maui taro chips with clam dip and sipped sauvignon blanc, as darkness smudged out the last traces of blue. The darkness provided the backdrop to a fiery display that lit up the sky with canon-like missiles of glowing lava bombs arcing above the swirling steam clouds and lighting the sky. Over the next hour they watched thousands of yellow, orange, and red lava bombs fanning out above the violent clash between the two thousand-degree river of molten lava and the ocean.

Nadia's excited shrieks gradually gave way to yawns, and by the time Alex spotted Hank's bobbing light coming their way, Nadia was slumped asleep in Kelsey's arms.

"Sorry I'm late. I had to give first aid to a woman that tripped and skinned her knee. Nothing serious."

Nadia remained asleep as Alex carried her back to the car and during the drive to their B&B. "Nadia, we're home. Tonight, you can sleep with Koa in the treehouse."

"Mommy, I want to sleep in your cozy princess bed."

"Yes, sweety." She shrugged as she looked at Alex.

Before sunrise, Alex quietly slipped away to meet his graduate student at the Volcano House to have coffee and discuss her research. Cassandra was completing her dissertation on the chemistry variations in lava that could explain why Hawaiian volcanic eruptions are not dangerously explosive like those of the volcanoes along the West Coast of the Americas. Cassandra had grown up in Olympia, Washington, and watched the Mount St. Helena eruption in 1980 from her backyard. While frightening, the childhood experience eventually led her into geology to better understand the causes of volcanic eruptions.

Alex returned late in the morning to find Kelsey and Nadia in the treehouse having a tea party. He stood for several minutes at the base of the stairs listening to the mother-daughter chatter. He mused, *Kelsey's given her heart to Nadia, but is there space for me?* He climbed the stairs and knocked. "Is this an all-girls tea party?"

Nadia giggled, and Kelsey said, "We saved a cup for you."

Chapter 10

*A*s soon as they arrived home on Sunday afternoon, Nadia started on the poster for her science project. With a few suggestions from Alex, she painted Kīlauea Volcano, leaving spaces around the edge for photos showing examples of 'a'ā and pahoehoe lava and two blurry photos of the fireworks display. She didn't win the science contest but was delighted to get an A for her class presentation and have her poster put on the art wall at the entrance to her school.

Alex had hoped Kelsey's flicker of romantic interest on the Big Island trip would continue after their return, but it was not to be. She plunged back into her research and took on additional work when she accepted an invitation to speak at an East-West Center conference on Pacific Island Challenges. Their occasional meal together was centered around her research and Nadia, ending with perfunctory hugs and light cheek kisses.

Alex was in his university office grading papers when the phone rang. *Probably an anxious student.* "Hello, Silverton speaking."

"Alex, do you remember Arovo Island?"

The French accent and salacious tone were unmistakable. "Nicolette Richet! How could I ever forget spending four days in your room without lights when a typhoon swept through Papua New Guinea." After the storm flooded his room, he had found more than shelter in Nicolette's room. Nicolette was the UN coordinator of the conference on disaster preparedness in the South Pacific, and Alex was a speaker. Most attendees were evacuated by tugboat back to Bougainville Island before the typhoon struck, but Alex, Nicolette, and four others decided to ride out the storm on the tiny island in their twenty-room resort. Nicolette, a tall, curvaceous, thirty-two-year-old woman with luxurious black hair, had more than survival on her mind, and by the second night, only one bed had been necessary.

"Nicolette, are you still with the UN?"

"Yes, I'm director of their natural disaster program for island economies."

"Congratulations on your promotion."

"Thanks. Alex, I'm on a stopover on my way to Tahiti and Fiji and hoping you're free for dinner?"

"Absolutely. Where're you staying?"

"At the Hilton Waikiki Beach in the Rainbow Tower with a great view of Waikiki that I'd like to show you."

"Nicolette, I'm seeing someone."

"Too bad . . . I have vivid memories of our little South Pacific tryst."

"Me too. How about sunset drinks and dinner at your hotel?"

"I'd like to get away from the center of Waikiki. Maybe a place with an ocean view that has fresh fish dishes prepared with island herbs."

"Kinkaid's is a local favorite for their macadamia nut–crusted mahimahi, and it overlooks Honolulu Harbor. How about meeting you at the Hilton reception at six forty-five, and we'll drive to Ward Warehouse a few minutes away?"

"Sure you don't want to meet at my room to see the view?"

"I'm tempted but will have to pass this time."

"I suppose the only way to get you to my room would be to whip up a typhoon."

"There are no typhoons in the forecast."

Alex left Kelsey a message that he was going to dinner with a friend from the UN and would be by Saturday morning to help Nadia with her project on Hawaiian beach sands. Kelsey didn't check her messages before rushing out with Nadia to buy a gift on the way to a birthday party at the Spaghetti Factory adjacent to Kincaid's. They were just leaving the party when Nadia tugged on her mother's arm.

"Mommy, is that Alex with a pretty woman?"

Kelsey froze as she watched the fashionably dressed female at Alex's side, his arm snuggly around her waist as they strolled into Kincaid's. Kelsey froze, then pulled Nadia closer.

"Honey, she's, ah, probably a colleague from the university."

"But, Mommy, Alex doesn't put his arm around you like that."

Nadia clung to her mother's arm as they hurried back to their car. Kelsey struggled to make small talk as they drove home, yet Nadia sensed something was wrong. As Kelsey tucked her daughter into bed she said, "I'm tired tonight, so I won't be reading you a bedtime story."

"Mommy, is Alex going to leave us?"

"I don't know."

She closed the door to the bedroom and walked to the kitchen cupboard and took out the cognac and a water glass. Her hand shook as she splashed the golden liquid into the glass, then chugged it down. Slumping onto the couch, she lay back, eyes closed. *what should I do?* Alex had become a surrogate father to Nadia, and she got tingling feelings when they kissed, even though she kept her lips closed . . . afraid to give encouragement. *I had the perfect opportunity in the wedding suite on the Big Island, and stupidly didn't insist that Nadia spend the second night in the treehouse.*

He was jarred awake by loud knocking and rolled over and groped for the light switch. The bedside clock read 1:17 a.m. *Who would be at my door at this ungodly hour? Must be Nicolette. I told her a romantic tryst was out of the question.* He flung open the front door, his robe loosely tied, ready to rebuff Nicolette.

"Kelsey! What are you doing here?" She was struggling to hold her sleeping daughter.

He scooped Nadia from her arms. "Is Nadia sick?"

"Alex . . . is she here?"

"What are you talking about?"

"I saw you going into Kincaid's with her last night."

"Oh . . . that was Nicolette Richet. She's head of the UN's natural disaster program. It was just a dinner with an old friend."

"You were holding her very close for just a friend."

Alex grimaced. "Um, we had a little fling a few years ago. I can explain after I put Nadia to bed."

As Alex tucked Nadia into bed, she opened her eyes and threw her arms tightly around his neck. "Don't leave us? We need you."

"I don't want to leave you or your mother. Now go to sleep."

She pulled him closer and kissed his scratchy chin, then fell back on her pillow. He held her hand as she drifted off to sleep. Kelsey wasn't in the living room, and the front door was ajar. He hurried to the door. *Where did she go?* "Kelsey, come back, please?"

"I'm here." Her voice was soft . . . different . . . tentative.

He cautiously pushed open the bedroom door and entered. The side-table light was on, casting just enough light to make out her clothing neatly folded on a chair. She was sitting on the side of the bed, her hands behind her back. Moments later, Kelsey's lacy red bra fell away from her breasts.

"Kelsey, are you sure you want to do this?"

"I don't want to lose you."

"Kelsey, I love you, but I'm afraid you can't get over your past."

"Tonight, when I saw you with that woman, I thought I had lost the man that had patiently built a bridge to my heart and is the father Nadia desperately needs."

Alex slowly undressed . . . anxious after waiting so long . . . not wanting to frighten Kelsey again. His lips and caresses were tentative, like the soft voice that had called him into the bedroom. Kelsey took his hands, touching his fingers to her lips, then slowly guided them over her body. She whispered the three words he had waited so long to hear. His hormones screamed, "Faster," while his mind warned to pace his desires with hers. When she pressed against him and her fingernails trailed down his back, he was overwhelmed by passion, and his attempts to pace his lovemaking lost. Later, when they embraced again, he was able to match his lovemaking to the resonance of Kelsey's heart.

It was almost 4:00 a.m. when they entered the shower lined with special tiles from Bora Bora. As the warm spray washed the sweat from their bodies, Alex guided a bar of soap over her. When the bar slipped from his hand and skittered across the shower floor, he slid to his knees, the spray dancing off his shoulders as she braced herself against the shower wall. When steam dissipated as the water turned cold, she turned off the faucet. Alex remained kneeling with his head tilted back, hair dripping over his face as he took her hands in his. "Kelsey, I love you and Nadia with all my heart, and my life will be complete if you'll marry me. I promise to be a faithful husband and the best father I can for Nadia."

Kelsey hadn't come to Alex's home expecting a marriage proposal, especially in a shower, yet the answer came without trepidation. "Yes." And she knelt and embraced him—the flood of tears invisible on their wet faces.

As they dried each other, Alex commented on the Bora Bora imprint on her back.

"And who pushed me against the wall?"

"Wake up, sleepyheads."

Alex rolled over and opened one eye, smiled, and nudged Kelsey. "Honey, Nadia's brought us breakfast."

She slowly opened her eyes, stretched her arms, and yawned. "I had a wonderful dream."

Alex kissed her. "It wasn't a dream."

"Does it still seem real?"

"One hundred percent!"

Nadia knocked lightly on their bedroom door.

"Nadia. Just a moment."

"Mommy, I made toast and coffee for you two. The toast is a little burnt and I wasn't sure how many spoons of coffee to put in the coffee maker."

Kelsey pulled a sheet up to her neck as the door opened. "Nadia, sweety, you're so thoughtful."

Nadia had a perspicacious smile as she placed the tray on the bedside table. "I'm going back into the living room to watch cartoons." At the door, she gave a furtive glance and a smile, and then she quietly closed the door.

Alex added sugar and creamer to a cup and handed it to Kelsey. "She knows a lot more about the birds and bees than I did at her age."

"She wants you to become her father. I found a drawing under her pillow of the three of us holding hands. Under the drawing she wrote: 'My family – Mommy, me, and Alex.' I made up my mind on the Big Island trip that I wanted to pursue a serious relationship with you, but held back, afraid to reveal my real feelings. It was hard to put down my protective shield for fear of being hurt again. When I saw you with that woman, I knew it required desperate measures."

"Nicolette was no threat. But increasingly, I thought our relationship was stalled at the friendship level. When do you want to tell Nadia?"

"As soon as we eat some of the breakfast *our* daughter prepared." Kelsey sipped her coffee and grimaced. "Alex, you'll need to teach Nadia how to make coffee."

Alex tasted his and coughed, shaking his head. "I'm only doing this for Nadia," he said, and gulped down the bitter brew.

After a bite of the burnt toast, Kelsey flushed the rest down the toilet. "It's our secret."

When they opened the door, Nadia was sitting in front of the TV holding her Ken and Barbie dolls together, then quickly pulled them apart. "Mommy, I want to get matching outfits for my two dolls."

"Nadia, turn off the TV and come and sit with us on the couch. We have something exciting to tell you." She flicked off the TV, ran across the room, and leaped in between them. Kelsey held both of Nadia's hands. "Alex and I are going to get married."

"For real?" Nadia's eyes opened wide.

"Yes," Alex said as he leaned in and kissed the top of her head.

"Oh, wow! I wanted Alex to be my daddy since he helped me build a sandcastle at Hanauma Bay." She paused. "And that means you're going to have a baby." She bounded from the couch screaming and waving her hands wildly in the air.

"Nadia, we'll discuss a baby later after we're married. What would you like to do today to celebrate?"

She put her finger to her chin and tilted her head. "Hmm, I want to go with *just* Alex to Starbucks."

Kelsey frowned. "Why not me?"

"On Saturday mornings, my friends from school go to Starbucks with their daddies while the mommies sleep in."

Kelsey pushed Nadia into Alex's lap. "What a splendid idea! I'm going back to bed." She paused to kiss Nadia on the cheek, then winked at Alex before shuffling to the bedroom.

Nadia brought her favorite Magic Treehouse mystery, *Mummies in the Morning*. The Starbucks was three blocks from her school and noisy with children, mostly with their fathers. One father balanced a toddler on his knee as he tried to read the sports section of the *Honolulu Star-Advertiser*, while another held a storybook with his daughter snuggled against him. Nadia waited in the only available stuffed chair while Alex ordered.

He sat the warm blueberry scone on the tiny table, handed Nadia her kid-sized hot chocolate, and, coffee in hand, squeezed into the seat. She licked the whipped-cream topping, then leaned her head against Alex and whispered, "The coffee I made this morning wasn't so good, huh?"

He chuckled. "Dreadful! But I drank it anyway because you made it." Then he wiped the whipped cream from her nose.

She snuggled closer and handed him her novel and listened attentively as he read a chapter, then put her hand on the page he was reading. "Daddy, that's enough for today. We'll read more next Saturday." She didn't mention that Kelsey had already read it to her. As they left, holding hands, she stopped momentarily to cheerfully say hi to a friend.

Chapter 11

A flurry of changes took place over the next month as they planned for a future together. Kelsey gave notice to her landlord that she would move out at the end of August. Nadia got the cozy attic bedroom with the best view down Manoa Valley to the ocean, and Alex enrolled her in the private Mid-Pacific Institute next to the University of Hawaii.

Evenings were giggle time with family games and Nadia jumping around excitedly whenever she beat her father, unaware that he purposely let her win every second or third game. Nadia quickly discovered that Alex was not as strict as her mother, and sweet talk would get the rules bent.

Nadia was thrilled to be included in the wedding planning but didn't understand why she couldn't go on their honeymoon trip to Italy. All agreed that a beach wedding was preferred, and they explored Oahu's beaches to find the perfect location. Their June wedding would take place a week after Kelsey's hoped-for graduation with a PhD.

A Honolulu lawyer was contacted to expedite the adoption process, and Kelsey traced Nadia's biological father to Costa Rica for his approval. He was married and relieved to learn that signing away his parental rights to Nadia absolved him of past and future child support obligations.

With a secure home and extra space, Nadia began asking girlfriends for sleepovers. Alex and Kelsey would lie in bed listening to the muffled chatter and laughter upstairs. At 10:00 p.m., Kelsey would go upstairs and quiet the girls and turn out the lights. When she would return to cuddle with Alex, she would whisper that it brought back fuzzy-warm memories of her sleepovers as a child.

In addition to finalizing her research and writing the dissertation, she was invited back to present a paper at the Pacific Islands Development Program at the East-West Center when three Pacific Islands leaders were expected to be present. This added extra hours to the fifty hours a week she was spending to complete her dissertation. She promised Alex she wouldn't take on any more obligations after the October conference, and both agreed Nadia needed a brother or sister, and she would try to conceive during their honeymoon in Italy the following summer.

It was late morning in early October when Kelsey arrived unexpectedly at Alex's office door, finding him peering through a microscope at a thin section of basalt. "Dr. Silverton, do you have time to see a graduate student?"

He looked up and smirked. "Depends on what's being offered."

She sashayed over and kissed him on the lips—a solicitous flick of her tongue between his lips. "I thought the three of us would go to lunch."

"But Nadia's in school today."

"She is, but I'm hungry enough for two."

"Then we better go to Annie's Korean Barbeque for their big plate lunch."

"Boy, are geologists thickheaded." She pulled the plastic pregnancy stick from her purse and held it in front of his eyes. "What do you see?"

"Um . . . two red lines . . . So, you're pregnant?"

"Bingo! And you're the guilty party."

Alex jumped up, knocking a pile of papers onto the floor as he grabbed Kelsey and swung her around. "We're having a baby." He kissed her several times, then dropped to his knees, lifted her blouse, and kissed her stomach.

"We have a twelve forty-five appointment with an OB-GYN at Queen's Medical Center to confirm the pregnancy and set up a schedule for the months ahead. Our planned honeymoon to Italy next summer will have to be delayed, as we have a more important engagement."

They were met by Dr. Kintara, who had been delivering babies for more than a quarter century. He had a bounce to his steps as he rushed into the exam room with a warm smile. His rotund head was topped with sparse gray hair swept across his bald dome, and thick spectacles rested precariously low on his nose. He reviewed Kelsey's health, jotting down notes as she described her increasing tiredness in recent months.

A nurse prepared Kelsey for the ultrasound, and Dr. Kintara studied the monitor during the procedure, pausing several times to write on a pad. "Yes, you're pregnant." He pointed to a cashew shape on the ultrasound monitor. "That's the fetus."

Alex squeezed Kelsey's hand and gave her a broad smile.

Dr. Kintara leaned closer to the monitor, his demeanor contemplative.

"Something wrong?" Kelsey asked.

"Nothing unusual about your pregnancy, but there's something of concern." He scribbled cryptic notes. Finally, he pushed back from the screen and took off his glasses and sighed. "You need further tests right away."

"What's wrong?"

"There's something that shouldn't be there, and I don't want to speculate until there are tests and they've been reviewed by our specialists."

"What kind of specialists?"

"Mrs. O'Connor, it's important not to jump to conclusions before the tests are completed and evaluated. Growths are usually not malignant. We have excellent oncologists on staff that will be able to determine your situation and the course of action."

Over the next week of tests, Alex stayed at Kelsey's side, trying to remain upbeat, yet his anxiety showed in his face and eyes. They said nothing to Nadia, even though she detected something was wrong. Finally, at dinner, Nadia asked what she had done to make them sad.

Kelsey caressed Nadia's arm. "Nothing. We love you more than anything. It's just that mommy's been tired lately, and the doctors are doing tests to see what medicine will make me better."

"Maybe you need to eat more vegetables, like you always tell me."

Thursday evening, they were about to sit down for dinner when the phone rang. Kelsey tensed. "Alex, will you take the call?" Her hand shook as she put barbequed chicken wings on Nadia's plate.

"Alex speaking . . . uh-huh . . . uh-huh." He took a pen and wrote on his palm. "We'll be there, Dr. Kintara. Thank you for calling." He hung up and paused, then turned to face Kelsey and Nadia. "Honey, we have an eight-thirty appointment tomorrow morning." His voice was flat—his face expressionless—eyes glassy.

Nadia looked back and forth between the two, searching for signs of what was going on. Alex took a deep breath and tried to soothe her. "Nadia, it's just a doctor's appointment. Nothing for my sweet pea to worry about."

Kelsey reached for Alex's hand, turned it over, and silently read what he had written: "8:30 Dr. Shepard Oncologist."

Dr. Shepard greeted them with a warm, compassionate smile, his eyes enlarged by his thick glasses. He explained that the test results had been double-checked by two other oncologists, then looked into Kelsey's eyes. "I'm sorry to tell you that the tumors are malignant and have metastasized to several organs. I have arranged for you to meet our team of specialists to agree on a treatment program on Monday."

"Am I going to die?"

Even after nearly two decades and hundreds of patients, Dr. Shepard struggled to find an appropriate answer to this question. "Every case is different, and younger people like you generally do better with treatment."

"Do I have months or years? I don't want platitudes."

"I recommend that you take care of important personal and legal matters as soon as possible."

"Will the treatment hurt my baby?"

"The treatment will be detrimental to the development of a healthy fetus. But treatment will extend your life."

"How much more time will it give me? . . . Months or years?"

"For most patients, months, but—"

She cut him off. "I'm not doing anything that will hurt my baby!" She jerked her hand away from Alex and bolted from the room. Alex hurriedly apologized to the doctor, then dashed from the room, catching up with her wandering aimlessly in the parking lot.

"Why me?" she sobbed. "I wait so long to find love and a complete family. Then it's taken away."

He wrapped his arms around her, pulling her tightly against him. "I'll be at your side, holding your hand at every step of the way, and will do everything in my power to raise Nadia to make you proud."

Kelsey wasn't ready to go home, so they drove to Magic Island across from the Ala Moana Shopping Center, once the largest mall in the Pacific. The low, coconut palm–studded peninsula was manmade and the best spot for sunset views of Waikiki Beach and Diamond Head. They walked to the rocky point that enclosed a small lagoon, stepped down to a thumb-nail patch of sand, and sat, backs against a boulder.

"Alex, I don't want to get married. What's the use?"

"Kelsey, that wouldn't be fair to Nadia and me. I don't want to go through life regretting not marrying the love of my life, even if it's for a month, a day, an hour, or a minute. Nadia's so excited to be part of our wedding ceremony, and we can't deny her the most important memory of the three of us together."

Kelsey gazed into his eyes, then touched a finger to his cheek to catch a tear. "Okay, but we must try to save our baby at any cost. It's our gift to each other."

Alex turned to face her, kneeling in the wet sand as he took her hands. "Will you marry me today?"

"But we promised Nadia that we'd be married on the beach, the three of us together, and have a big wedding cake."

"That, too, but I can't bear another day not being married to you."

They rushed home to shower and change into their nicest aloha wear and get their birth certificates. The woman behind the counter in the Honolulu State Marriage License Bureau appeared to be in her sixties, with perfectly coiffured black hair and a bright floral aloha dress and white orchid lei. Clearly a special occasion for her, too—perhaps a birthday.

"I can provide you with the legal forms today, but the office is closing early, and you'll have to come back next week for the official ceremony."

Kelsey began sobbing.

"Dearie, you have a lifetime together. Surely you can wait until Monday."

"I'm dying."

Their eyes locked for several seconds. "Cancer?"

"Is it that obvious?"

"You're beautiful. You see, this is my last day after thirty-four years and seeing thousands of couples, hopeful about their futures. I have made many exceptions and can't think of a better way to end my career than to officiate over your marriage."

The woman took off her lei and draped it over Kelsey along with a warm hug and kiss on the cheek. Then they completed the forms and the simple ceremony. As they prepared to leave, both Alex and Kelsey wished the woman many happy years of retirement.

The woman took a deep breath and said, "I'm also dying of cancer and am thankful for so many good years." The two women embraced, sharing tears of love, sadness, and understanding.

They were waiting at the roundabout at the Mid-Pacific Institute when Nadia appeared with her girlfriend. She waved and dashed to their car, tossed her heavy school bag into the backseat and hopped in.

"Mommy, what's the pretty lei for? It's not your birthday."

"The woman that married us today gave it to me."

"But . . . but you promised we would all be together and have a wedding on the beach, and there would be a big chocolate cake, and we would wear matching dresses."

"That's still coming, but we need to be legally married and sign papers first."

"Getting married is complicated."

"Now, Alex can legally adopt you as your father."

"So does that mean it's okay to tell everyone that Alex is my daddy?"

"Yes, and to celebrate, we're going to the Moana Hotel for high tea, but first we must go home so you can change into the party dress your grandmother sent."

"What's high tea?"

"It's a British tradition to dress up on special occasions and have tea in fancy cups. You'll love it. With the tea, we are served finger-sized scrumptious sandwiches, fresh scones with strawberry jam, and yummy pastries with lots of fruit and whipped cream."

Opened in 1901, the majestic Moana Hotel had long catered to affluent travelers who reached the islands on ocean liners, then gradually adjusted to mostly middle-class Americans and Japanese visitors that arrived by air. Fronting the white multistory plantation-style hotel was an eight-pillared colonnade, flanked by an inviting veranda lined with koa rocking chairs.

The valet opened the car doors for Kelsey and Nadia. "Welcome to the Moana Surfrider Hotel."

They strolled through the lobby of richly-embroidered couches to the high tea veranda in the rear overlooking an enchanting courtyard with a fairy-tale-like banyan tree—its massive branches embracing the courtyard.

Their table had white linen tablecloths aglitter with silverware and gold-edged porcelain cups and saucers. Alex assisted Kelsey with her seat while the smartly dressed waiter seated Nadia. Nadia sat up straight, elbows off the table, as the waiter placed a linen napkin on her lap with a touch of panache.

"My name's Kalani. I'll be your waiter today. Are you here for the high tea?"

Kelsey squeezed Alex's hand. "Yes, and we were married today."

His smile turned more radiant. "I'm honored to serve you and will do my best to make everything perfect. And for the young lady, if you don't prefer tea, we can prepare any special drink you like."

"I'll be having tea today," Nadia said with her most grown-up voice.

The waiter nodded. "Of course. May I suggest our Hawaii Tropical Blend with a dollop of North Shore honey."

"Yes, that's what I want."

They were presented with a black-lacquered box containing a choice of teas ranging from mild to bold, plus Nadia's fruity blend, and a decaffeinated tea that Kelsey chose, as she was pregnant.

Nadia gushed when Kalani appeared with the three-tiered silver tray set with a dozen different choices. "Can I choose any one I like?"

Kalani replied tactfully, "That's up to your parents. The British start with the bottom tray of wedge sandwiches, then move up to the warm scones on the middle tray, and finish with the fruit and chocolate tarts on top. Keikis usually prefer the reverse order."

Kelsey said, "Nadia, as this is a special day, you can eat whatever you want."

Nadia reached for the top tray of sweet pastries, while Kelsey and Alex started with the salmon and cream cheese sandwiches. They met Nadia on the middle tray, sharing scones. Nadia smothered hers with strawberry preserves that turned her lips red, while Kelsey and Alex fed each other morsels brushed with whipped honey butter.

Alex reached under the table and caressed the palm of Kelsey's hand. "Do you know why I wanted to bring you here today?"

"Because it captures the essence of romantic Hawaii?"

"Yes. Here all the senses are piqued in a most satisfying way. The three-sided courtyard is open to the sea to catch the melodic sounds of the surf and gentle breezes, laced with the fragrance of tropical flowers and the scent of the ocean. And the branches of the magnificent banyan encompass the courtyard like a grand umbrella to filter out the harsh sun."

"I never imagined I'd meet a poetic volcanologist."

"I've been thinking about bringing you here from the day we met."

"How about me?" Nadia chirped.

Alex grinned at Nadia with her pouty jam-smeared lips. "Of course, it's a package deal."

Long after Nadia had gone to sleep, they sat together on the love seat swing in their garden, sharing happy moments of their past. Alex wanted to know everything he could about Kelsey's early years—unsaid was his desire for stories that he could tell Nadia when she was older and asked about her mother.

Kelsey leaned her head on Alex's shoulder as she reminisced. "One of my earliest memories is camping near the Merced River in Yosemite National Park. I was a little younger than Nadia. I can still smell the oily fragrance of our heavy green tent, and by morning my air mattress was out of air, and the ground was so hard. The rattle of pans would wake me, and I'd quietly slip from the tent, leaving mom asleep. I remember sitting on a log so big my feet didn't touch the ground as I watched my dad prepare breakfast on a two-burner Coleman stove. Without a word, he would hand me a cup of hot cocoa with lots of little marshmallows floating on top. He would prepare bacon and scrambled eggs and give me a crispy piece after blowing on it to cool it. I don't remember my dad saying he loved me, but the love that came with the hot cocoa and crispy bacon didn't need words.

"I was a late bloomer and didn't have a boyfriend until my senior year in high school. I spent a lot of time wandering through fields of grass and wildflowers down to a brook where I'd sit for hours reading teen romance novels. I had many silly thoughts about my future. Would I meet a charming prince or become famous or become a housewife like my mother? I entered college hoping it would reveal my future, and it did when I took an elective on Pacific Island economies.

"There were countless little events that I remember, but like showing family movies, they are only of interest to the family. I remember building a dollhouse with my dad—opening presents together at Christmas, and my father saying how much he liked the socks I gave him every year—learning to ride a bike and my mother kissing my skinned knee, and it really did feel better. There are so many little things that I wanted to share with Nadia, and now it will be up to you."

Drops of rain sprinkled on the porch as Alex carried Kelsey into the house and set her gently on their bed. She raised her arms as he slipped her shirt over her head. As each piece of skin was exposed, his kisses replaced the touch of fabric. He laid her back on their bed and reached to turn out the bedside light.

"Leave the light on. I have nothing to hide from you. Remember when you rubbed suntan lotion all over my body and between my toes at Hanauma Bay and I screamed at you?"

"How could I forget?"

"Do it again."

Chapter 12

Kelsey and Alex dropped Nadia off for a playdate in Kahala, then drove a few blocks to the upscale Kahala Hotel & Resort for a buffet breakfast on their beachside terrace. There was little time for carefree chatter as their future together was compressed to months.

"Alex, it's difficult to discuss my final wishes, but I want to die knowing my loved ones are okay, especially Nadia and you. I'm grateful that you're adopting her and will be the best father she could ever have. I don't have much in the way of physical assets—a few pieces of jewelry, books, a few antiques, and a small 529 college fund for Nadia. Next week I want to update my will to transfer everything to you. On Nadia's sixteenth birthday, I want you to give her the emerald ring I received on my sixteenth birthday. We're both Geminis, and emerald is our birthstone. Most important is that you give her all the love she needs."

He lifted her hand to his lips. "I promise."

"Alex, a June church wedding is out of the question. My life really started when I met you at last year's East-West Center Christmas party, so I want to celebrate our wedding on

Christmas Day. We can have the ceremony next to the beach, then walk in the surf, letting the ocean that I love so much bless us. Maybe we could have it here at the Kahala Hotel, as it has beautiful tropical gardens, a dolphin pool, and green sea turtles."

After breakfast they watched the dolphins in the hotel's small lagoon, then strolled along the beach as far as Wai'alae Beach Park. Kelsey picked up a fragment of a shell and put it in Alex's palm and closed his fingers. "I want my grave to be on a hill overlooking the sea, and from time to time, you can bring Nadia and her sister or brother for a picnic so I can listen to our children's chatter."

"Kelsey, I want you to fight the cancer and not give up, but I'll follow your wishes. I promise to bring Nadia and hopefully her sister or brother to your gravesite. You'll never be forgotten."

"Alex, I want to live, too, but I must think about our baby first. Imagine our genes shared in our baby and passed on to future generations. Isn't saving our baby's life worth giving up chemotherapy that only will give me two to four extra months of life?"

After a long pause, he nodded weakly, then kissed the shell and handed it back to Kelsey.

Kelsey's parents were delighted to hear that she was pregnant and the wedding plans had been advanced from June to December. She didn't mention it was because of her cancer, letting them assume it was because she was pregnant. Kelsey didn't want to tell others about the cancer until she needed help, giving her more time to live a semi-normal life with Alex and Nadia.

It was difficult finding a pastor to perform the wedding ceremony on Christmas Day, plus a trio to sing the "Hawaiian Wedding Song." Finally, Alex was referred to a Hawaiian pastor in Hale'iwa who, after Alex explained the situation with Kelsey, said he would be pleased to perform the ceremony and would bring a Hawaiian trio to sing their special song.

A large wedding was out of the question, and the ceremony would be subdued, with only relatives and close friends present. Kelsey's father walked with a cane but was adamant that he would escort his daughter down the aisle. Kelsey convinced Nadia that she would like a macadamia nut cake with white frosting, decorated with pink plumeria blossoms. Nadia would be the flower girl and sprinkle plumeria petals behind Kelsey and her father as they walked to the altar.

As Halloween neared, Alex suggested they dress in costumes and go trick-or-treating in Waikiki. Kelsey was less enthusiastic than Nadia, who had visions of lots of candy from the stores along Kalakaua Avenue. As a parody about Wall Street executives, Alex planned to wear his pin-striped business suit along with a gorilla mask that covered his entire head, plus hairy gorilla hands, and carry a leather briefcase. At first Kelsey and Nadia were going to dress as princesses, but when Nadia needed a mouse outfit for a Halloween play at school, Kelsey decided to go as a cat and chase Nadia.

Alex worked for three nights on a cardboard trick-or-treat box in the shape of a wedge of Swiss cheese with a lid that, when lifted, played a short recording: "Trick-or-squeak."

Early Halloween evening, Alex parked next to the Honolulu Zoo, and they walked north on Kalakaua Avenue toward
the center of Waikiki. Alex swayed his arms, hunched over to
mimic a gorilla, while Kelsey in her cat costume chased after
Nadia as she scampered about in her mouse outfit. Young female Japanese tourists squealed with delight and crowded
around Alex, clinging to his arms to pose for photos. They
made slow progress on the congested sidewalk as tourists
stopped them to snap pictures.

"Daddy! Come help. Mommy fell down."

Alex dashed to Kelsey, who was sitting on the sidewalk,
head in her hands. "Honey, what happened?"

"I got dizzy and couldn't stand. I need to go home."

Alex handed his briefcase to Nadia and scooped Kelsey up,
pulling her against his chest as he turned back. Tourists, thinking it was part of the performance, snapped pictures. In the car,
Kelsey told Nadia she was just tired and needed to go home
and rest, and she should go out with Alex to do trick-or-treating in the neighborhood.

At first, Nadia didn't want to go out, but Alex and Kelsey
insisted. After taking off his gorilla outfit and making sure
Kelsey was okay, he took Nadia trick or treating. Within a few
minutes, she met two girlfriends, and he followed at a distance
with the girls' parents. After half an hour, Nadia said she was
tired and wanted to return home.

Nadia sorted her candy on the kitchen table as Alex
watched. "Did you have a good time with your friends?"

"Uh-huh." She didn't look up from the piles of sweets.
"What's really wrong with Mommy?"

Alex struggled to find an answer, not wanting to lie or tell
too much. "In the morning we can discuss it when we're all
together."

Nadia looked up into Alex's eyes. "I'm going to give the best candy to Mommy to make her happy."

"She'll like that."

The next morning, Nadia was playing with her tiny Polly Pocket dolls when Kelsey and Alex entered the kitchen. On the table was a neat stack of Kelsey's favorite Kit-Kat candies in front of a homemade card with three stick figures labeled, "Mommy CAT, little MOUSE, and big GORILLO." Printed at the bottom—"LOVE, Nadia."

"Nadia, thank you for the candy and beautiful card. I'll keep it forever." She turned away and hurried back to the bedroom.

"Why did my gift make Mommy cry?"

"Sometimes really thoughtful things can make parents cry even when they're happy."

"I don't understand."

"Nadia, your mom and I will explain."

When Alex entered their bedroom, Kelsey was standing at the window, her body shaking as she sobbed. He wrapped his arms around her and kissed the nape of her neck. "We need to tell Nadia."

"I know, but it's so hard. She's so innocent and too young to face death."

"Kelsey, she knows something's wrong, and she'll be more resentful if we hide the truth too long."

They returned holding hands and asked Nadia to join them on the couch. Nadia walked slowly to the couch and squeezed in between them. Kelsey pulled her close and gently lifted stray hairs from her face.

"Honey, I know you're worried about me. Um . . . I'm sick, and I can't get better."

Nadia twisted and stared into her mother's face. "You can get some medicine from the doctor and get well."

"Honey, remember when your friend's grandfather died of cancer?"

"Yes, but he was very old, and you said he smoked too much. But you're young and don't smoke or eat too much candy."

"Some people that are healthy get cancer, and I have cancer."

"It's not fair," she screamed as tears burst from her eyes. "I just got a whole family after waiting for years and years."

"Nadia, I want this holiday season to be full of happiness, and I need your help. We'll have a beautiful wedding with my loved ones around me, especially you and my husband. I need you to help make this Christmas and wedding the best ever."

Nadia wiped her eyes. "Yes, Mommy, I'll try my best."

Chapter 13

*K*elsey was insistent that they maintain a normal schedule and shield Nadia from the daily stresses associated with her cancer. Kelsey turned to eating only healthy food and gave up wine and even coffee to stay as healthy as possible. She stopped working on her dissertation to conserve her energy and devote more time to Nadia and Alex.

Planning for Thanksgiving and their Christmas Day wedding dominated family discussions around the dinner table. Most evenings after Nadia went to sleep, Alex and Kelsey discussed alternatives, in case her health declined faster than expected. One evening, after Kelsey had fallen asleep, Alex picked up Kelsey's personal calendar she had left open on their shared desk. He glanced ahead and found a heart-wrenching final entry on March 17: "C-Section." That would be six months from conception and touch and go for the survival of the fetus and for Kelsey. It was an ambitious goal, but Alex didn't reveal his doubts to Kelsey.

Kelsey had hoped to wait until mid-November to inform her parents about the cancer, but her health deteriorated faster than expected, and she made the tearful call on November 7 while Nadia was in school. Two days later, Dora and Don arrived with open tickets back to the mainland. Kelsey appeared to perk up, and Nadia relished the added attention from her grandparents.

The main considerations for the wedding location were that it should be on a beach and away from crowded Waikiki. Elsewhere on Oahu, there were only two church venues for a wedding next to the beach, and neither were available on Christmas Day. Alex was reluctant to call an acquaintance, Lucas Foster, who had a beachside home in Lanikai, but these were not normal times. He had not even finished explaining the reason for his request when Lucas replied, "Jenny and I will be delighted to make our home available for your wedding." Lucas graciously agreed to have a love seat swing placed at the water's edge for the newlyweds.

Nadia was excited to be included in the mother-daughter custom of selecting a wedding dress. While driving along Beretania Street to a Queen's Medical Center appointment, Kelsey had spotted an attractive wedding dress in the window of a bridal store. Returning with her mother and Nadia, they stood on the sidewalk admiring the bridal gown in the window.

"Mom, that's the dress I want."

Dora nodded. "It'll look stunning on you. Let's see if they have your size?"

"Nadia, what do you think?"

"It's the most beautiful dress I've ever seen."

Alex and Don were repairing a leaking pipe under the kitchen sink when Nadia burst into the house ahead of her mother and grandmother. "You won't believe this!" she yelped as she jumped around on tiptoes.

Alex slid out from under the sink. "And what's so unbelievable?

"The funniest thing happened at the wedding dress store. You see, when we arrived, a mother and daughter were looking at wedding dresses. The mother had this disgusted look on her face, like this." Nadia made her angriest frown. "Well, Mommy walked into the store as nonchalant as can be. I'll show you." Nadia flipped her hair back and strutted across the room. "Then Mommy said to the saleswoman, 'The dress in the window is perfect. Do you have my size?' Well, Mommy was gorgeous in the dress, and there was no need to look further, so grandma pulled out her credit card, and that was that! Here's the funniest part. When we were leaving the store, the *exaberated* mother—"

"Exasperated," Dora corrected.

"Whatever. The mother turned to us and said, 'Can you help my daughter decide on a gown?' I'm pretty observant, you know, and pointed to the second dress in the window and said, 'That would look really nice on your daughter,' and the mother agreed." Nadia smirked as she folded her arms across her chest. "The saleslady had told me that they put the best wedding dresses in the window, so I already knew which one to choose. The picky woman looking for her wedding dress wasn't nearly as pretty as my mommy."

Kelsey returned to the living room after reading a bedtime story to Nadia and cuddled against Alex on the couch. Her voice was soft but purposeful. "Tomorrow I want to go to the Valley of the Temples Cemetery to pick a gravesite with a view of the ocean."

There was a long pause, and then without a word, he stroked her hair and leaned in to kiss her softly on her chapped lips. "Okay. Do you want to bring your parents?"

"Yes, but not Nadia. She's too young."

After dropping Nadia at school, they took the Likelike Highway over the Koʻolau Mountains to the Valley of the Temples cemetery located above Kāneʻohe. Kelsey leaned on Alex's arm as they climbed to the top of a grassy knoll. Here, the din of traffic on Kahekili Highway was replaced by the melody of songbirds and the whisper of the wind. They stood in silence, gazing back over Kāneʻohe Bay, mottled in shades of turquoise. "This is where I want to be buried."

Alex, Dora, and Don agreed that it was a beautiful setting. Their smiles were laced with sadness as the reality of the inevitable inched closer. A butterfly landed momentarily on Kelsey's *haku* lei, then fluttered away before Alex could snap a photo. Dora said it was nature's way of blessing the spot, then dabbed her eyes as they turned to walk back to the car.

Of all American holidays, Thanksgiving stood out for family gatherings and being thankful for loved ones near and far. For Kelsey and her family, this last Thanksgiving together had extra meaning. Alex made reservations at the Kahala Hotel & Resort for their lavish buffet but canceled the week before

Thanksgiving when Kelsey's condition deteriorated faster than expected and the venue was shifted back to Alex's home. Her parents wanted to prepare the traditional Thanksgiving dinner Kelsey remembered from her childhood.

On Thanksgiving morning, Dora and Don shooed the others from the house so they could prepare the turkey and side dishes Kelsey loved. Alex, with Kelsey at his side and Nadia in the rear seat, drove along the dry southern coast of stark cliffs and little vegetation, but noted for expansive views across the cobalt-blue ocean, to the island of Moloka'i. Alex bypassed Hanauma Bay and the lookout over its coconut palm–studded crescent beach. Their destination was the Halona Blowhole, known for twenty-five-foot spouts during summer months and a good spot to see migrating humpback whales during the winter. But the reason for the stop at the blowhole was for something more important to Alex and hopefully Kelsey.

In late November, when waves were high on the North Shore of Oahu, the reverse was true on the Southeast shoreline, where gentle waves produced unimpressive waterspouts. "Daddy, what happened to the big spray we saw last summer?"

"The waves are coming in at the wrong angle, but we came here for something better." Kelsey leaned heavily on Alex as he led them to the western end of the parking lot overlooking a tiny cove bounded by sheer cliffs and a small beach, ideal for two. The gentle surf bathed the sand, leaving it glistening golden in the morning sun. "Down there is where the iconic kissing scene in *From Here to Eternity* was filmed. One of the best kissing scenes ever in movies."

Nadia tugged on Alex's arm. "I don't get it. Why would anyone climb all the way down to that itsy-bitsy beach to kiss someone?"

Kelsey ran her fingers through Nadia's hair. "If I could, I'd climb down there any day for a kiss from Alex."

Alex pulled Kelsey against him, brushed her hair back, and kissed her. Nadia folded her arms across her chest and rolled her eyes.

They returned to their home filled with scents of roast turkey and dressing laced with cinnamon spice from the hot apple and pumpkin pies on the counter. Nadia dashed into the kitchen. "Squeak, squeak, a starving mouse needs a treat."

"Only after the hungry mouse wipes her paws," Dora said as she pinched off a piece of pie crust.

Only Nadia sat before Kelsey. Then as they all held hands around the table, Don offered the Thanksgiving prayer Kelsey had heard as a child, but with the following words added at the end: "God, look after our Kelsey until we're reunited in Heaven. Amen."

There was an uncomfortable silence, before Nadia asked, "Can I have a drumstick?"

The conversation livened as Don retold stories of Kelsey's antics in her youth, and Nadia's contagious giggles got everyone laughing. Kelsey complained that her dad was exaggerating and giving Nadia mischievous ideas.

After the meal, Kelsey's parents shooed Kelsey and Alex away, saying they only needed Nadia to help with the dishes. They remained on the love seat swing on the patio for over an hour, gently swinging, as Kelsey reminisced about the events she wanted to share while there was time. Inside, her parents could hear occasional bursts of laughter from Alex and faint gleeful murmurs from Kelsey. Nadia was playing dominos with her grandparents when Alex entered carrying Kelsey, smiled at them, then continued to their bedroom and closed the door with his foot.

"Grandma, is Mommy, okay?"

"She's happy but needs rest. Your dad is giving her all the care she needs, so don't worry."

Every year the shipments of Christmas trees arrived in Hawaii during the first days of December, and within a week, the lots were empty. Kelsey suggested Nadia go with her father to pick out a nice tree and surprise her. The plan was to decorate the eight-foot Douglas fir after attending the Hawaiian-style Christmas performance at the Ala Moana Center, but Kelsey decided to stay home and decorate the tree while Alex took Nadia and her parents to the stage show. As they headed out the door, Kelsey told Nadia to show her father the things she wanted Santa to bring at Christmas.

To Alex's surprise, Nadia didn't ask for the large doll she had mentioned several times in previous months. When he queried why she didn't ask for the special talking doll, she hesitated, then began to cry.

"Nadia, what's wrong?"

"You need the money to buy medicine for Mommy."

Kelsey's parents stayed to do more shopping while Alex and Nadia returned home. The scent of fresh evergreen greeted them as they opened the front door, yet the house was eerily quiet, and Alex's heart pounded as they entered the living room. The Christmas tree had a red bulb on a low branch, and Nadia's homemade gold star was on top, tilted at an angle. An open box of Christmas tree ornaments was on the coffee table, and shards of a gold ornament were on the floor.

Alex rushed into the bedroom and found Kelsey sprawled on the bed, pills scattered over the carpet next to an open bottle of pain pills. He quickly closed the door and rushed to her side. "Kelsey, I'm here," he said as he knelt and lifted her hair from her face.

She moaned, "I got really woozy. I just need a little rest. You and Nadia finish decorating the tree, and I'll come out later."

He kissed her forehead. "Okay." His lips quivered as he put the pain-numbing pills into the bottle. "Kelsey, I love you more than anything." He paused at the door to compose himself, before opening it to find Nadia standing, her arms hanging at her side.

"Mommy's not okay," sobbed Nadia.

"She tried to do too much and is resting. She wants us to finish decorating the tree. Let's make it the prettiest Christmas tree ever."

Nadia decorated the lower branches that she could reach while Alex hung the bulbs on the higher ones and strung the colored lights. He lifted Nadia so she could hang tinsel on the higher branches.

"Daddy, you forgot to straighten the star."

"That's the way your mother put it, and it makes our tree special with touches from all three of us."

Kelsey's parents returned at sunset and added a handmade Hawaiian bulb to the tree, then asked Nadia to help them prepare dinner.

Kelsey smiled as Alex entered the bedroom and lay down beside her. "Alex, I wanted to surprise everyone, but—"

"I know. Nadia helped decorate the tree. She's so proud of our Christmas tree."

When they entered the darkened living room holding hands, the colored tree lights blinked, filling the room with sparkles that reflected from the framed photos on the wall.

"Nadia, this is the most magnificent Christmas tree I've ever seen."

"Mommy, I added extra tinsel to make the tree prettier. Daddy didn't want to straighten the star because you put it on that way."

"Well, with such a perfect tree, we can't have a crooked star on top," she said in a cheerful voice. Alex helped Kelsey balance on a chair next to the tree while she straightened the star, then patted her bottom, making Nadia giggle. Kelsey turned and with a devilish grin, said, "So that's your trick."

Chapter 14

O n the seventh of December, Alex rented a wheelchair that she used when away from home. Kelsey insisted on going grocery shopping to maintain a semblance of normalcy. Increasingly, the focus of everyone's energies was on the Christmas Day wedding. The ceremony and reception were further downsized, and the number of guests reduced to eighteen. Following the reception and traditional cutting of the wedding cake, Kelsey would dip her toes in the ocean—a kind of baptism in her beloved ocean. After the ceremony, only Kelsey's parents and the best man and the maid of honor would join them at home to open presents around the Christmas tree. Everyone put on a positive face yet knew that everything depended on how fast Kelsey's condition deteriorated.

Alex had planned to take off all of December, but Kelsey insisted he go to the university in the mornings and let her sleep in. In the evenings, with the help of Dora, she put on a nice dress, tying a sash around the waist to make it appear less baggy. Dora applied makeup to hide the dark spots and shadows under Kelsey's eyes. Each day, Alex arrived home with a crimson rose for Kelsey.

Dinner was the liveliest part of the day, with conversations about the day that drifted into reminisces about uplifting events in their past. Don kept Nadia giggling with stories about Kelsey's pranks in high school, including when she and two other girls let a jackrabbit loose in the school halls. Alex told about his adventures and mishaps doing research on volcanoes in Papua New Guinea. When Nadia asked what the most dangerous thing that happened was, he talked about being rescued by natives in Papua New Guinea after a flood washed away his camp and boat and his foot became infected with a jungle fungus.

"I stayed in a thatched hut for a week while being treated with smelly herbs the native people said would cure my foot."

"Were you scared?" asked Nadia.

"Only at first, when two natives appeared from the jungle. They looked fearsome with boar tusks through their noses, bows, and arrows with razor-sharp bamboo points. I knew a few words in pidgin, and they carried me to their mountain village."

"Isn't pigeon a bird?"

Alex chucked. "Nadia, there are over eight hundred dialects spoken in Papua New Guinea, and pidgin is an easy language that most understand."

"Say something for Nadia in pidgin," asked Kelsey.

"Easy ones are, *hello*, pronounced *goo-day*; and *thank you*, pronounced *tenk-yoo*. Most important, I knew how to say, *I need your help—mee nee-dim hah-lee-vim bee-long yoo*."

Nadia rolled her eyes. "But why so many languages in a little country? In America, everyone speaks English."

"That's a great question. The thick jungle and steep mountains keep villages isolated even though they may only be a few miles apart. So over a long time, people in isolated villages developed different ways of speaking."

After dinner, they usually played a board game with Nadia, and then Kelsey and Alex tucked Nadia into bed and read a bedtime story. Kelsey read while Alex added scary sound effects, and Nadia grabbed her mother, pretending to be frightened.

They dropped Nadia off at school as usual, but instead of returning home, Kelsey asked Alex to drive to the Ala Moana Shopping Center.

"Kelsey, why don't you rest at home, and I'll do the shopping for presents?"

"I need to go."

Before moving to Hawaii, Alex had assumed *aloha* was an advertising slogan with little more meaning than saying *hello* or *good day*. He had quickly discovered that threads of authentic aloha were woven into the fabric of Hawaiian life. The aloha spirt was particularly evident as he pushed Kelsey into different stores. In Macy's, the woman at the cosmetic counter insisted on applying makeup to Kelsey, and fifteen minutes later, her face was radiant. An older Japanese woman held the elevator door open, then before stepping out, handed Kelsey the bouquet of flowers she had just bought.

Kelsey was most interested in looking at gifts for Nadia, and particularly the special doll they had found in Macy's. "Alex, Nadia told me last night that she didn't want any big presents for Christmas."

"Kelsey, the talking doll is what she really wants, and what I want also."

Unsaid was the real reason.

In mid-December, Alex stopped joining Nadia and her mother at bedtime, to give them more exclusive mother-daughter time. He would return after both were asleep and carry Kelsey to their bed, remove her bathrobe, and slide in beside her. The powerful sedatives put her into a deep sleep, yet he continued to whisper words of love. Although Alex, was not religious in a formal sense, he felt a comforting spiritual presence as he prayed for Kelsey, and that gave him strength.

Like most couples, they had subtle signals to convey interest in intimate *cuddle time*, as Kelsey called it. He was surprised when she ran her fingers through the patch of hair on his chest. He snuggled closer. "Honey, you're too weak."

"Just one more time," she murmured.

He struggled to hold back tears as he turned her over and spread strands of her hair on the pillow. "Kelsey, you're trembling."

"I'm so afraid."

"Me too." His arms engulfed the shell of the woman that had captured his heart. He felt she was an angel sent to earth for a moment to reveal the infiniteness of love. Their slow cadence was measured but purposeful, ending in tears of joy and sadness. Her energy spent, plus the sedatives, put her to sleep. Alex remained awake until the tears stopped—holding her close, not wanting to let go of the feeling.

She awoke with Alex sitting beside her holding a mug of warm honey-sweetened herbal tea. "What does my sweetheart want to do today?"

"Last night was glorious, and I feel stronger today. I want to go to the East-West Center Christmas party where we met a year ago and reenact our first meeting."

A call to the East-West Center, and arrangements were made for guest parking in front of Burns Hall—the main building in the complex. They were met in front by the president's secretary, who placed a parking permit in the car window and accompanied them into the ground-floor party room.

It seemed that the Christmas party was being held to honor Kelsey as people crowded around to greet her, looping their leis over her head and giving her hugs and kisses. Vera from the Pacific Islands Development Program knelt next to her wheelchair and held Kelsey's hand. "We've missed seeing you around the office." Then tears gushed down her radiant Polynesian cheeks, and they embraced.

When the greeters had drifted away, Alex jested, "I put on my best aloha shirt this year, and no one even noticed."

"But I did, and now I want to re-enact meeting across the buffet table."

Alex helped her up from the wheelchair, then circled to the other side of the buffet table. This time when both reached for the broccoli, he didn't pull his hand back, but grasped hers and tried to kiss it.

Pulling her hand away, Kelsey scolded, "My, you're presumptuous."

Those that had gathered around clapped and chanted, "More, more!"

Alex strolled around the table and dropped to one knee. "Kelsey, I've searched the seven seas to find you. Will you marry me?"

"Yes!" she cried, and dropped into his arms. "Now take me away in your magic chariot!"

They said their goodbyes among a teary crowd, then drove to the small coffeehouse in Manoa where they had gone after the party the previous year. It was there over coffee that Kelsey had rebuffed Alex when she discovered he had more than a professional interest in her. The curbside table that they had sat at was occupied, but the couple graciously moved.

Kelsey was pensive when he returned with their drinks and a warm macadamia nut cookie. "And may I ask what's on my ladylove's mind?"

"I'm so happy, I wish I could freeze everything for a few months longer."

Alex slowly stirred his coffee. "I promise that this day, this moment, will be forever frozen in my mind."

"This day never would have happened without your persistence."

He reached across the table and took the cup from her hand, then interwove his fingers into hers. "A year ago, when our fingers touched at the buffet table and I looked up into your emerald eyes, I couldn't breathe. Then, in an instant, you were gone like a mirage. I thought I'd missed my chance. Then Bob Taylor called your name, and you appeared again—a second chance, and I wasn't going to let you escape again."

"You never gave up, even though I fought to keep from falling in love with you. I didn't trust my feelings and pushed back. Thankfully, you persisted."

Alex broke off a piece of the cookie and offered it to Kelsey before popping it into his mouth. "So what made you change your mind?"

"Hmm, it was not like in the movies, that I was swept away by your good looks and awkward charm. My feelings knew on the first Saturday when we went snorkeling in Hanauma Bay, but that frightened me even more, as it was my feelings that got me into trouble in the Galapagos. Both Nadia and my mom went gaga over you, but I thought your charm was to get me in bed. When you rubbed lotion over me, you released emotions that I had suppressed for so long and made me angry that you had penetrated my defenses. That's why I screamed at you. Later, when I walked over to take a picture of you and Nadia building a sandcastle and heard Nadia call you *daddy*, it stabbed at my heart. The seed was planted in my brain, and as the weeks passed, I was slowly drawn closer, and finally succumbed to the love that I had fought to deny. I was frightened because the last time I fell in love, I was abandoned and pregnant. I had built a tall wall to keep love out." Kelsey giggled and squeezed his hand. "But no wall was too high for a geologist that climbs towering volcanoes."

Chapter 15

*O*n December 23, Alex and Nadia greeted Becky Sims, her maid of honor, and Terry Woodburn, Alex's best man, at the airport with traditional flower leis. Alex explained that Kelsey had stayed at home to conserve her energy for the wedding ceremony in two days. He went over the wedding day procedures as he drove them to the Outrigger Reef Hotel in Waikiki Beach.

On December 24, Kelsey only got up for breakfast, and at lunch nibbled on a piece of toast and took a few sips of lukewarm honey tea. At a little after two, Alex heard a glass shatter in the bathroom and rushed in. Kelsey was on the floor, barely conscious. Alex rushed her to Queen's Medical Center, where, an hour later, she lapsed into a coma with Alex and her parents at her side.

Don put his hand on Alex's shoulder. "It's time to call off the wedding."

Alex walked to the window and peered out as he struggled with the decision—tears clouding his vision and feelings clouding his thoughts. "If I call off the wedding, it means I've given up all hope. I'm going to wait until tomorrow morning and pray for a miracle."

They remained at Kelsey's bedside through the night, taking turns talking softly to her, and repeatedly telling her that she needed to wake for her wedding. Dora and Don listened as Alex recounted to Kelsey details of their year together and how hard he had tried to gain her affection, and the wonderful wedding she would have as soon as she woke up in the morning.

Alex was drained of energy and hope as the glow of the morning sun escaped from the edges of the curtains. The nurse entered and pushed aside the drapes to let in the morning sun, then checked Kelsey's vital signs. She appeared perplexed as she called Dr. Dennis Toguchi, Kelsey's attending physician. He rushed into the room two minutes later and repeated the procedures.

"Any change in her condition?" asked Alex.

"Yes. Totally unexpected. Her vital signs are better than when she entered yesterday. But—" he shook his head "—there's only one heartbeat."

Alex leaned over, running his fingers through her tangled hair. "Kelsey, sweetheart, it's Christmas morning, our wedding day, and time to wake up and dress for the wedding ceremony." She didn't stir, and he slowly raised his head. "I better make the calls."

The murmur was barely detectable. He leaned close to her ear. "Darling, it's me . . . Alex. Open your beautiful green eyes. It's Christmas morning—our wedding day."

Alex jerked his head back when her eyes blinked open. Her lips slowly parted to form a gentle smile. Her voice—golden tendrils from heaven. "I had a wonderful dream about angels carrying *me up above the world so high, like a diamond in the sky* . . . just like the melody my mother used to sing to me."

"Kelsey," he sobbed.

"Is our wedding today?" she murmured.

"Yes. Everything's arranged."

"Darling, help me get ready."

Pandemonium quickly changed to resolute determination as everyone jumped into action to achieve what had seemed impossible minutes earlier. Dr. Toguchi had Kelsey repeat twice that she was sure she wanted to be released from the hospital. Her replies were weak yet firm. There were hospital release papers to be signed, including a form expunging any liability to the hospital and staff.

Finally, papers signed, an orderly pushed Kelsey in a wheelchair to the hospital entrance. Alex took the ticket from under the windshield wiper and tossed it in the glove compartment, then drove to the front of the hospital, his hands shaking and perspiration dripping from under his arms. He tried to keep his mind on the road as he raced to their home, then carried Kelsey up the steps and into their bedroom. Dora and Becky helped Kelsey with her wedding gown, hair, and makeup, while Alex dressed in the spare bedroom. No time to shower, he splashed cologne over his body.

Nadia entered and watched Alex adjust his bowtie. "Daddy, you didn't say anything about my new dress and makeup."

"Nadia, you look like a princess, and someday you'll be as beautiful as your mother, and all the boys will be chasing you."

"Really?"

"Yes. And after the wedding, you can be the first one to open the big present from Santa."

There were a dozen cars lining the street on either side of the Foster's beachfront home, plus four cars in the driveway. As a courtesy, Alex had sent an invitation to Dr. Kintara, and to Alex's surprise, he was there.

Alex went inside to make sure everything was in order. The Fosters had set up chairs in the backyard with an aisle down the middle leading to a white gazebo where the ceremony would be performed. Pastor Kakaulani and the trio of Hawaiian singers greeted Alex warmly and went over last-minute details, before Alex hurried back to Nadia at the driveway entrance.

"Daddy, you're squeezing my hand too hard."

"Sorry. I'm just nervous."

Everyone clapped as the white limousine pulled into the driveway. Alex left Nadia to accompany her mother as the flower girl and hurried to the gazebo behind the home. The guests filed into rows of chairs on the lawn and remained standing. Kelsey's father handed his cane to Dora, scooped up his daughter, and proudly limped to the rear of the home. The trio of singers commenced singing the "Hawaiian Wedding Song" as Don walked slowly down the path between the chairs carrying Kelsey, her arms wrapped around his neck. Nadia followed, scattering plumeria petals from her Easter basket. As Kelsey was gently placed in a wheelchair, Pastor Kakaulani spread his arms and gestured for the audience to be seated. The smiles were genuine, yet the glassy eyes and clutched handkerchiefs revealed the juxtaposition of sadness.

Becky smoothed Kelsey's gown and straightened her tiara, then stepped back. Jerry took the ring from his pocket and handed it to the groom. Alex squatted next to Kelsey and held her hand while Dora artfully added touches of makeup to conceal the blotches on her face and the dark shadows under her eyes.

Alex slipped the fragrant *pikake* jasmine lei over Kelsey's head and gently kissed her, defying custom, but time couldn't wait. They were flanked by the bridesmaid on her right and the best man on the groom's left. Alex wore a rented white tuxedo with a crimson rose in his lapel and a strand of maile leaves draped down his front. All eyes were on the bride in her pearl-adorned white gown and pearl-adorned tiara with a wispy veil.

Pastor Kakaulani beamed down at the couple, a worn black-leather Bible in his hands. "Are you ready?"

Alex replied yes, and Kelsey nodded and smiled as she laced her fingers into his. They slowly repeated the vows that had passed through the lips of countless millions. Alex's voice was steady and measured, until he faltered when he got to the part, *until death do us part*. Kelsey's head wobbled, her smile reassuring.

He took a deep breath and continued. When he slipped the ring on—her size a month earlier—it was two sizes too large. She had asked for a simple gold band. Something so important deserved more, and Alex had a ring designed with three strands of gold entwined with three diamonds, representing the unity of Kelsey, Nadia, and Alex.

Pastor Kakaulani closed his Bible and looked fondly at the couple and pronounced them man and wife. "Alex, now you may kiss your lovely bride—" he smiled "—again."

Alex leaned into the wheelchair, wrapping his arms around Kelsey as their lips merged. As seconds passed, a woman in the second row whispered to her husband, "Now that's the way to kiss a woman." When Alex pulled away, his lips were glossy pink, and red rose petals from his boutonniere were stuck to her wedding dress.

Alex carefully lifted his bride, and Becky followed with the wheelchair as he slowly walked to the celebratory wedding cake on a table behind the gazebo. Kelsey gushed weakly and hugged Alex when she saw the three-tiered cake decorated with tropical flowers and crowned with a miniature bride and groom with a child in the middle.

"Mommy, I helped Daddy pick out the cake."

Dora called to her granddaughter, "Nadia, come and stand with me."

Alex positioned Kelsey in the wheelchair next to the table, handed her the silver cake knife, and guided her hand to the cake as she cut two ragged pieces. When her hand shook, dropping the piece, he licked the frosting from her fingers. Her head wobbled as he put a sliver of cake into her mouth, and when most fell on her dress, he kissed her lips.

She smiled weakly and struggled to lean into Alex. "It's time," she whispered, her words as sure as the timeless pulse of the surf.

He nodded and lightly kissed her cheek, then glanced back at the assembled guests standing silently. No words were necessary as he scooped up his bride and took the final steps to *journey's end* and sat her in the loveseat swing at the water's edge. The trio of singers stood on a small berm overlooking the ocean and sang an ancient Hawaiian chant sung to Polynesians as they set off on ocean voyages in catamarans, never to return.

The surf swirled around their loveseat festooned with garlands of pink and white plumeria blossoms interwoven with maile leaves. He positioned her on the cushioned seat and knelt in the surf to remove her satin shoes so her feet could be blessed by her beloved ocean.

Nadia pulled free from Dora's hand and ran to her mother. "Mommy, I'm scared."

Kelsey struggled to lift her hand and touch Nadia's cheek. "Kiss Mommy and run along with your grandmother and find me a pretty seashell."

"Honey, I need a few minutes with your mommy."

Nadia kissed her mother. "Mommy, I won't go far," she said, then turned away.

Kelsey murmured, "I love you," her words lost in the melody of the surf.

She leaned against Alex as he rocked their swing—the squeaks synchronized with the pulse of the surf. He removed her lei and entwined it with his, then released it into the surf. Invisible fingers twirled the leis in a choreographed ballet as they drifted seaward.

Kelsey's head rested on his shoulder; her heavy makeup smeared on his white tuxedo. "Alex, you must let go of what you can't keep," she said, her voice barely audible.

"I will never stop loving you." His voice unsteady, eyes blurry.

"Alex, what will happen to our unborn baby?"

"God has a special place."

They gazed in silence across the shimmering sea that graded from the lightest hue of aquamarine at their feet to cobalt beyond the fringing coral reef. Kelsey had often spoken of the infinite shades of blue that beckoned her back to its shores, like Homer's mythical sirens that lured sailors to their doom in the Odyssey.

"Alex." Her voice was as soft as a heavenly breeze. "What happened to the colors in the sea?" He felt her body quiver, and then her head slumped to his chest, her tiara tumbling into his lap. Alex sobbed as he held her tightly against his chest, unwilling to let go.

Nadia's voice broke the silence as she ambled up the beach, stopping every few steps to pick up a shell fragment and show it to her grandmother. Her voice was full of the innocence that parents try to protect as long as possible from the jagged edges of adult life.

Alex lifted Kelsey's head to his shoulder and positioned the pearl-studded tiara on her head with the veil across her face. He wiped his eyes and looked toward Dora and shook his head. Dora froze, putting her hand to her mouth, then took Nadia's hand and angled her away from the beach back to the congregation.

Alex lifted Kelsey and slowly retraced the steps that their two beating hearts shared minutes earlier. The congregation spread out along the petal-strewn path that had welcomed them, offering sympathy and condolences.

Dora took Nadia back to the limousine and watched her paint Just Married on the back window. As soon as Alex placed Kelsey in the rear of the limousine, Dr. Kintara stepped forward and checked for vital signs, then put his hand on Alex's shoulder.

Alex wiped his eyes as he walked over to Nadia standing between her grandparents. "Nadia, honey, I want you to go home with your grandparents and open the big special gift, and I'll come as soon as I can."

"Daddy, I'll wait for you to open the present." Tears trickled down her cheeks, threading paths through the rouge makeup. "Mommy's not coming home, is she?"

"No, but she'll always be in our hearts." He kissed her on the forehead and quickly turned away.

Alex joined Kelsey in the limousine and waved back at his daughter as they pulled away. He lifted Kelsey's hand to his lips and kissed each finger as he sobbed. The procession of cars followed with lights on, then turned away when the limousine reached the entrance to the mortuary. Alex carried Kelsey inside, then tearfully removed the wedding ring less than two hours after he had slipped it onto her finger. He had promised Kelsey he would give it to Nadia when she was old enough to understand the infinite love between a man and a woman.

Chapter 16

"*W*hite Christmas" wafted from the louvered windows as Alex slowly climbed the steps to his home. He paused at the top of the stairs and stared at the Santa Claus photo Nadia had taped to the door. Flooding his mind were contradictory emotions of deep sadness and Kelsey's wish to make this a happy day for Nadia. Voices were subdued as he opened the door and stepped inside. Dora and Becky were decorating holiday cookies, and Don and Terry were sitting on the couch holding mugs of eggnog and discussing college football to take their minds off the sadness. Spilling out from under the tree were colorful packages—none opened.

Dora smoothed her apron and walked over and embraced Alex. "Thank you for fulfilling Kelsey's final wish. Nadia needs you now. She's in her room."

"I need her too." A trail of wet sock prints followed him up the polished stairs. He paused at Nadia's partially open door to compose the right words when there were none. Nadia was talking in her serious grown-up voice.

"Lucy, Mommy's not coming to our Christmas party because God needs her in heaven. Daddy's really sad, so you need to behave and act cheerful, and no fussing. Do you understand?" She rocked her doll back and forth.

He quietly closed the door, wiped his eyes, and knocked. "Nadia, can I come in?"

"Yes, Daddy."

Nadia was sitting cross-legged on the floor with her arms around Lucy. Alex knelt and brushed back Nadia's hair, then wrapped his arms around Nadia and Lucy. "I love you. Mommy wants us to have a happy Christmas."

"Daddy, it's hard to be happy and sad at the same time."

"I know." He kissed both teary cheeks. "Nadia, Mommy wants us to be happy."

"I know."

Nadia held her father's hand as they descended the stairs to the living room. "It's time for all of us to gather round the tree and open presents," Alex said in a cheery voice. Nadia, I want you to open the first present."

"Nadia, I need a taster for my fresh Christmas cookies," Dora said as she entered with a platter of cookies and a cup of hot chocolate topped with whipped cream.

"I love Christmas cookies," Nadia said as she took one and her drink.

Don handed Alex a mug of eggnog. "It's got two shots of brandy."

"I need that." Alex gulped it down.

"Daddy, which one should I open first?"

"The largest one from Santa."

Nadia picked up the forty-inch box with both hands. She had known there wasn't a Santa Clause since a girl told her in the first grade, but enjoyed pretending. Instead of ripping off the wrapping paper as expected, she slipped off the ribbons and ran her little fingers under the taped edges of the paper and unwrapped it with only one small tear. Nadia squealed when she saw the thirty-six-inch-tall doll through the clear plastic front of the box. She removed the lid and lifted the doll and hugged it. This is what I always wanted."

"Nadia, this is what your mommy wanted for you. She talks. Just squeeze her right hand."

"I know, Daddy." She pressed the red spot on the doll's palm, and it sang a bedtime lullaby.

Somewhere, over the rainbow, way up high
There's a land that I heard of once in a lullaby
Somewhere, over the rainbow, skies are blue
And the dreams that you dare to dream really do come
true
Someday I'll wish upon a star
And wake up where the clouds are far behind me
Where troubles melt like lemon drops
Away above the chimney tops
That's where you'll find me

"It's Mommy's voice!" Nadia cried, then hugged her gift and nuzzled her doll's golden hair.

"Nadia, what do you want to name your doll?" asked Dora.

"Hmm . . . I think I'll call her Rose, Mommy's middle name."

"That's a beautiful name and was my mother's name."

Three-quarters of the packages under the tree were for Nadia. The last package Nadia opened was wrapped in white wedding paper embossed with silver bells. It was a scrapbook chronology of the past year, starting with the photo Kelsey took of Alex helping Nadia build a sandcastle at Hanauma Bay. Each page revealed steps on the journey that culminated with their marriage and Nadia's adoption.

Nadia turned the thick pages, looking at the Hawaiian Airlines ticket stubs from the trip to the Big Island to see the volcano, a picture of the treehouse, pressed plumeria flowers, love notes, movie ticket stubs, the civil marriage certificate, a copy of Nadia's adoption papers, and the wedding announcement. On the last page were tape marks where a photo had been removed.

"Daddy, a picture's missing."

"Uh . . . it was a blurry one," was all he could say, then wiped his eyes. He would let her see the sonogram when she was older.

"You took it out because you only wanted to save the best pictures?"

"Kind of like that. We were going to give the album to you when you were older, but your mom and I decided you're big enough to take care of it now."

"Thanks, Daddy. Don't worry, I'll keep it safe in my room right next to my bed."

After all the gifts were opened, Nadia slid under the tree and retrieved a small package hidden in the boughs, and handed it to her father. "I didn't want you and Mommy to find it. I made it at school." The Christmas tag read: "To Mommy and Daddy, Love, Nadia."

"Thank you, Nadia." Alex carefully opened it as if it contained a delicate piece of china. Inside was a watercolor painting of the three of them holding hands next to the ocean. Nadia had painted Kelsey in the middle with a shiny-gold halo over her head, and at the bottom were the words, "Mommy's Our Angel, Love, Nadia."

Alex leaned over and hugged and kissed Nadia. "This is the most thoughtful gift I have ever received. Nadia, I'm going to frame it and put it on my desk and admire it every day. Where did you get the gold for the halo?"

"My teacher let me use her special gold pen."

"Mommy is really an angel now, isn't she?"

"Yes, and she will always be looking down on us and sending love and kisses."

Becky, Terry, and Nadia picked up the wrapping paper and ribbons while Dora settled on the couch and patted the cushion next to her. "Alex, sit with me. I have something for you." She leaned against Alex and whispered, "Kelsey asked me to give this to you after." She paused and wiped her eyes, then handed an envelope to Alex. "Alex, *it's time*," the same words Kelsey had whispered hours earlier. He opened the envelope and pulled out a photo and folded letter. The picture was of the East-West Center Christmas party where he had met Kelsey the year before. Kelsey was visible at the buffet table, her hand partly blocked by Alex in a drab khaki shirt in contrast to the others dressed in colorful aloha wear.

"Boy, did I look like a nerd."

"Yes, but a promising one. Alex, I knew on the first outing to Hanauma Bay that you two were going to fall in love. It was in your eyes and voice, and in Kelsey's fury when you awakened her suppressed feelings as you rubbed lotion on her. Now read what she wrote while you and Nadia were shopping for the Christmas tree."

On the outside in sketchy letters: "Open on December 25."

My Dearest Husband,

As you are reading this note, you know I have died. I am at peace knowing Nadia is in good hands. You and my parents will ensure that our Nadia has the best Christmas possible under these difficult circumstances.

These past twelve months have been the happiest of my life thanks to meeting you—the love of my life. You are the father Nadia always needed, but our time as a perfect family was too short, yet complete in every way.

For reasons only God knows, Nadia again has one parent when she needs two. Please don't do what I did and put up a wall keeping women out. For Nadia and me, find a caring mother for Nadia and wife for you. I have thought a lot about a perfect mate for you and Nadia, and even secretly looked on a dating site. The woman that would be perfect for Nadia and maybe you is my maid of honor, but Becky's in love with someone else. I pray that you find someone like her, that can love both of you equally.

I hope you will always reserve a spot in your heart for me, but remember, love is also for the living.
Eternally yours,
Kelsey

Alex slipped the photo and letter back into the envelope, and Dora put her hand on his. "I know this isn't the time to think about a romantic relationship, but Don and I can never get our daughter back. Nadia carries Kelsey's genes, and she needs a mother, and only you can make that happen. You need time to grieve. One of the last things Kelsey told me was to tell you not to wait too long."

Over the next three days, Alex rushed around making funeral arrangements while Kelsey's parents and Becky took Nadia on outings to Sea Life Park, the Bishop Museum, and Waikiki Beach. The presence of Nadia kept everyone from openly grieving until after she had gone to bed with Rose at her side. Then the discussion turned to the funeral plans and ended with reminiscing about Kelsey's life—a way of dealing with grief in a positive way.

Kelsey's father rambled on for hours about Kelsey as a child and teen, forgetting he'd told many of the stories before, but it didn't matter. Alex knew that Kelsey loved animals but was unaware that she had a menagerie of animals in her youth, including a boa constrictor named Oscar, two guinea pigs, and a crested society finch that pecked food from her fork and flew freely around the house.

Becky added stories about her two years as Kelsey's roommate and her frustrations as a matchmaker when no man could penetrate her defensive armor. Then Kelsey called to say she had met an irritating and persistent professor from UH, explaining at length why it could never work out. Becky grinned at Alex. "The more Kelsey complained about your faults, the more obvious it was that she was falling in love with you."

Kelsey's funeral was held at 10:00 a.m. on December 29 under a brooding sky. Cars lined the street at the base of the grassy knoll where she was to be buried. Women held their skirts on the breezy hill, and men stood stoically around the shiny white casket that seemed to hover in the air above spindly chrome supports. The gaping rectangular hole would soon be filled and a small plaque added, joining the others neatly spaced in military formation.

Pastor Kakaulani held the same Bible he had used to wed them four days earlier, the gold ribbon bookmark at another page. His long robe flapped in the wind as he gave the eulogy from the crest of the knoll, amplifying the spiritual effect.

When Pastor Kakaulani turned to Alex and asked if he wished to say a few words, he nodded and stepped up to the coffin. "Kelsey, how can I express in words what you mean to me? Funerals are held at the end, not the beginning of a marriage, yet you have left me with memories that will last a lifetime, and more importantly, Nadia, to give me endless joy." His voice cracked, and he placed his hands on the casket. "I will love you forever." He kissed the shiny casket as the wind ruffled his hair.

Nadia ran to his side. "Daddy, I brought the pretty shells I collected on Mommy's wedding day. I want Mommy to have them."

Alex hugged Nadia. "She'll like that."

Nadia unzipped her tiny, plastic purse with a teddy bear print on the side and picked out the shell fragments and placed them on the casket. "Mommy, I hope you like my shells."

As they turned to walk down the hill, the wind paused, and splinters of sun pierced the clouds, producing a rainbow over Kāneʻohe Bay. Nadia pulled on Alex's sleeve. "The rainbow's for Mommy."

Chapter 17

*A*lex struggled with feelings of despair as he drove out of the Valley of the Temples Cemetery. He had felt confident helping Nadia with reading storybooks, doing science projects, and building sandcastles but had depended on Kelsey for girl things, like braiding her hair and choosing the right clothes for school. He wasn't confident that he would be a good father. Dora broke the silence as they approached the Pali Highway. "I think a walk on the beach would do us all some good, and Kelsey would like that."

Nadia piped up. "I can find some more shells for Mommy."

"Good idea, and it's only a few minutes away." Alex switched the car blinker from a right turn onto the Pali Highway to a left turn toward the beach.

Popular with local families, Kailua Beach was over two miles long, providing an abundance of space for people to spread out. Dora and Don remained in the shade of an ironwood tree while Nadia, Alex, and Becky walked along the beach with Nadia scurrying ahead. Alex yelled for her to be careful and not to step on a tiny purple Portuguese man-of-war that would sting her feet. About fifty yards ahead, she stopped next to something dark on the beach, then turned and ran back toward them, waving her hands over her head and hollering, her words muffled by the surf and wind.

"Nadia, what did you discover?"

"There's a smelly dead shark on the beach, and he's this big." She spread her arms wide.

"Well, we better check it out."

They trotted on the sand, dodging the pulses of the surf to the four-foot shark with a swarm of flies around a gash in its head. Alex squatted. "Nadia, it's a white-tipped reef shark. See the white of the dorsal fin?"

"Uh-huh. Does it eat people?"

"No. Both black-tipped and white-tipped sharks are often seen around reefs in near-shore areas, but rarely bite. The more dangerous great white and tiger sharks are usually seen beyond the reefs, far offshore in deeper water. Hawaiians call sharks *mano*, and traditional Hawaiians believe they embody the spirits of family members. This one was probably hooked by a fisherman who killed it, even though it's harmless to humans."

"Then why did the fisherman kill it?"

"A lot are killed because of the image that sharks are dangerous. Only about ten percent of shark species attack people. Now stroke the skin toward the tail and tell me how it feels."

"It's really smooth."

"Now stroke the skin toward the head."

"It's like sandpaper."

"That's because the skin is made of tooth-like scales overlapping toward the tail like the shingles on the roof of our home."

"Cool! I'm never going to kill a shark." Nadia continued walking ahead, with Alex and Becky trailing behind.

"Becky, I'm so anxious. I don't know much about raising a child—particularly a girl. There is lots of girl stuff I don't know. I can't even braid her hair the right way."

"You're off to a pretty good start. Just now, you explained to her about sharks in a way that took away her fear. She trusts you a lot. And remember, what she needs now is *love* more than someone that can braid her hair."

"When her grandparents and you leave tomorrow, it will be just Nadia and me. It's so hard to put on a good face when I hurt so much inside. Um . . . any chance you could remain a few more days to help with Nadia? I'll pay."

A gust of wind blew Becky's hair across her face as she gazed down the beach toward Nadia. "If my fiancé agrees and I can change my flights, I want to stay a little longer to help with Nadia and assist you in sorting through Kelsey's belongings. Kelsey was my closest friend, so I could never take money for helping her at a time like this. I was planning to fly to Boston next week for my future mother-in-law's sixtieth birthday bash, a snobbish affair with lots of Boston blue bloods. I'm trying to get off on the right foot with his parents. But right now, Nadia needs me more."

Becky called three times before Elliott answered. He wasn't pleased that she wanted to stay in Hawaii to babysit when there was such an important party planned in Boston. She fibbed that it was Kelsey's final wish and coyly promised to make it up to him.

"Nadia, it's time to get up," Alex whispered as he gently shook her.

"I'm really sleepy, Daddy."

"I thought you might like to go to story time at the bookstore. There will be authors at a special three-hour children's reading session beginning at ten this morning."

Nadia sat up. "I want to go!"

Becky dressed Nadia in her party dress for the special New Year's Eve event that included three authors taking turns reading stories, followed by book signings, then cookies and punch for the children. As soon as Nadia spotted a friend from her class, she shooed them away.

Alex led Becky to the second-floor coffee shop and ordered two iced caffe lattes. Becky gazed into Alex's eyes, her plastic glass hovering near her lips. "Kelsey used to tell me on the phone that you could turn the simplest outing into something interesting and fun for everyone and that you would make a great tour guide."

He chortled. "Nice to know I have a fallback position if I fail as a professor. The best way to learn to enjoy small things is to grow up poor, because small things are all you get. A big outing was when my parents drove twenty miles to Bodega Bay, where I used a dropline to catch perch from the pier. A special dinner was eating at the Chinese restaurant on Third Street. That's where I learned to use chopsticks. The best part of the Chinese meal was the fortune cookie served at the end that had surprise messages inside. I imagined the messages were meant just for me. One message I will never forget: 'Happiness is not in your wallet.'"

Becky had a pensive look in her eyes as she drew initials on the moist side of her glass.

"A penny for your thoughts?"

"I was thinking how my life will change when I marry Elliot, and that makes me a little apprehensive."

"That's normal. You haven't said much about how you met your knight in shining armor."

"At the end of my second year at UC Davis, I got a summer job as a waitress in an upscale Napa Valley restaurant. One of the regular servers called in sick, and I filled in as a substitute. My heart skipped a beat when I spotted Elliott with an older distinguished couple being seated at a reserved table. I asked the waiter in their section to let me serve them and I'd give him the tip.

"Elliott's father was snooty toward me, and I regretted serving them. At the end of the meal, Elliott followed me into the kitchen and apologized for his father's behavior and asked me out to dinner at the most exclusive restaurant in the area.

"I fell hard, enchanted by his beautiful blue eyes, wavy hair, broad shoulders, and enthralling stories of travel to Africa to see mountain gorillas, and swimming with forty-foot whale sharks in the Maldives. I tried not to be impressed that he was studying for his MD at Harvard, but I was. He had a seductive, sophisticated charm that I'd never encountered. After our first dinner date, a dozen crimson roses were delivered to me at the restaurant, along with a note saying he was awake all night thinking about me. No one had ever done anything like that before.

"We chatted daily on the phone, and a month later he flew out to meet me at UC Davis. We drove into San Francisco for dinner on Fisherman's Wharf, then walked across the Golden Gate Bridge. The cold fog swirled around us, and when Elliott saw me shivering, he took off his suit jack and wrapped it around me. More than the warmth from the wool jacket surged through my body. At Christmas break I visited Elliott and was overwhelmed by their opulent lifestyle that didn't fit me. I told Elliott that it could never work between us, as I came from a blue-collar family and, at that time, was studying viniculture at UC Davis and planned to work in the wine industry. He had a disarming answer, telling me he'd set up his medical practice in the San Francisco Bay area and we'd buy a small vineyard in Sonoma or Napa County. But the main reason I agreed to marry Elliott was, I'd fallen deeply in love with him. Everyone makes sacrifices when they marry."

"Yes, but I can't think of anything I had to give up when I married Kelsey."

"Alex, you made Kelsey the happiest woman in the world. I'll never forget watching you carrying her to the water's edge and holding her close in her final moments."

Nadia skipped across the floor with a balloon emblazoned with the title of a children's book. "Daddy, I had so much fun, and my friend said her parents are letting her stay up tonight to celebrate New Year's. Can I?"

"I don't see why not. We can eat popcorn and watch a movie together, and you can drink sparkling apple cider at midnight."

Nadia picked out the dinner choices—California sushi rolls, spam musubi, and barbequed chicken wings. After dinner, they put on the 1980 remake of the *Parent Trap* and sat together on the couch, passing around a bowl of popcorn mixed with Japanese rice crackers. Nadia's giggling was contagious, and soon everyone was laughing.

Nadia made it until eleven before nodding off to sleep in Becky's arms. At midnight, as fireworks lit up the sky over Manoa Valley, Alex handed Becky a flute of champagne, and they clinked their glasses.

"Becky, I'm deeply grateful that you're here to help with Nadia. You're an angel."

"Thank you for your kind words. Alex, I never expected the year would end with me losing my best friend. But I'm glad I can share it with someone who understands how much I loved her." She raised her glass. "Kelsey, we love you, and you will never be forgotten."

Becky slipped effortlessly into the role of mother to Nadia and took over the task of sorting through Kelsey's clothes that held too many memories for Alex to face. Becky set aside the wedding dress for Nadia and donated most of the rest of her clothes to the Salvation Army, as requested by Kelsey.

Every day after school, Becky and Nadia could be found at an outdoor table in the Manoa Valley Shopping Center sharing an ice cream and talking about whatever was on Nadia's mind—usually something that happened at school that was important in the mind of a eight-year-old. Nadia especially enjoyed planning dinners and helping to prepare meals, but conveniently disappeared when it was time to wash dishes.

Becky wrote tips in a pocked-size notebook on caring for a preteen girl. For clothes and shoes, she advised Alex to let Nadia choose within the price range he was willing to pay, but make sure there was space for her to grow. She drew a sketch with step-by-step instructions on how to fix Nadia's hair and added a footnote to call when he needed help. On discipline, she wrote that showing disappointment in his expression and voice would usually suffice with girls who wanted their father's approval. On playdates, check with the mother of the girl she's going to meet, and make sure there will always be a responsible parent nearby. And most of all, love would patch over his little foibles. In bold, she wrote, "EVERY PARENT MAKES MISTAKES."

Becky faithfully called Elliott daily but frequently failed to connect because of his busy schedule in his hospital residency program. No date had been set for the wedding, but Alex saw doodles of wedding dress designs on her notepad and June circled in red.

She confessed her misgivings about whether Elliott would move to the San Francisco Bay Area to set up his medical practice. His parents wanted him to stay in the Boston area, and they had a strong influence over Elliott's life, and soon—hers. Elliott's parents were anxious to have a grandchild, but Becky feared that having babies before she was professionally established might push her career ambitions out of reach.

On the morning of Becky's departure, Nadia quietly sat cross-legged on the bed brushing her doll's hair as Becky packed her bags. "Are you sure you can't stay just a little longer?"

"Nadia, I wish I could, but I need to return to college, and I have to plan for my wedding. I was thinking we could become pen pals. Would you like that?"

"I'm not good at spelling."

"That's not important, and you can send emails from your dad's computer, and it has spell check. The more you write, the better you'll get at spelling."

"I guess so. But you're going to marry Elliott and have your own children and won't want to come back to Hawaii to see me anymore."

Becky sat beside Nadia and smoothed her hair. "You can pretend that I'm your mommy until your father finds a really nice mother for you."

Nadia clutched Becky's arms. "Why can't you marry my daddy? He would make a really good husband, and he needs your help raising me."

Becky mused, *She asks tough questions.* "I really like your daddy, but I love Elliott and want to marry him. If I had met your father first, I might have fallen in love with him. Nadia,

I'm sure he will have no trouble finding a good mommy for you."

Nadia nodded, then hugged her doll. "Rose, don't worry, I'll never leave you, and I'll be your mommy forever."

Chapter 18

*W*ith Becky's departure, Alex felt the weight of a single parent, trying to fulfill the roles of a father and mother to a preteen girl while maintaining his teaching and research obligations at the university. Even the simplest tasks with Nadia could prove challenging. Becky had shown him how to braid Nadia's hair the way she wanted, but when he tried, Nadia yelled that it wasn't the way her mommy and Becky did it. When a sign appeared on Nadia's door, "Girls Only," it was time to call Becky for advice.

"Hi, Alex, how're things going with you and Nadia?"

"In a word—dreadful! I seem to be doing everything wrong. Kelsey told me how well Nadia had bonded with me, but I'm not so sure anymore. She's snappy and spends most of the time in her room talking to her dolls instead of spending time with me. Last weekend, she didn't even want to go to the beach. She has never done that before."

"Alex, it could be that it reminds her of the three of you going to the beach as a family. You could try taking her away to another island, somewhere where the experience will be just you and her. I bet she'd love to see the whales off of Maui."

"That's a great idea! The humpback whales should be there until mid-April, and many will have had their calves by now."

"I'd love to see the whales someday."

"You're welcome anytime."

"I know. But it would have to be with Elliott."

Nadia was excited about the weekend trip to Maui to see the whales but insisted on bringing Rose with her mother's recorded voice. Alex was aware of the symbolism of Kelsey going with them.

He picked up Nadia at Mid-Pac on Friday after school and drove to the Domestic Terminal in the Honolulu International Airport. The doll was over the limit for cabin luggage, but a short explanation, and the size rule was waived. Fifteen minutes after take-off, Alex pointed to the dark peak poking above a layer of clouds.

"That's Haleakala, Maui's famous volcano where we can go to see the sunrise above the clouds."

"You mean we can drive right through the clouds?"

"Yep! At ten thousand feet, we can look down on the clouds from the crater rim. If you want to go, we'll have to get up really early to drive to the peak to see the sunrise. Haleakala is sacred to Hawaiians, and in ancient times they would trek up the volcano with gifts of ti leaves and leis for the gods."

"I want to go." Nadia had a pensive expression as she stared out of the window. "We'll be closer to Mommy, won't we?"

"Umm . . . uh . . . yes."

"Then we need to bring Mommy a lei just like the Hawaiians did."

Alex bought three plumeria leis at the Kahului Airport—one for Nadia and two to take to the top of Haleakalā. They drove west across the low saddle between Maui's two prominent volcanoes, skirting the historic whaling town of Lahaina, then five minutes north to the Westin Maui Resort & Spa on Kaanapali Beach. Alex's Hawaii driver's license got them a *kama'āina* discount off the normal room rate. Their room overlooked the pool, plus gave a partial view of the ocean.

Alex wasn't surprised that Nadia preferred the hotel's water playland over going to the beach. It had water slides, rope bridges, and a waterfall. He took Nadia's hand and waded under the falls to the swim-through grotto. They sat chest-deep in water, the sound of the waterfalls drowning out the din of civilization.

"Daddy, I like this place."

"I was hoping so."

The young Japanese couple sitting on the other side of the grotto rose and bowed politely, then left.

"Daddy, that man was touching the woman where he shouldn't."

"Ah, well, they're probably newlyweds here on their honeymoon, and when no one is around, it's okay if both agree."

"Well, I saw them."

A girl about Nadia's age appeared from under the falls and sat across from them.

"Nadia, maybe she would like a playmate."

Nadia stared at the girl until she looked their way. "Hi," is all Nadia had to say.

Alex retreated to a poolside lounge chair and watched as the two played together. *Children make friends so easily, so why is it so hard for adults?*

The two played until the girl's mother called, then a hug, and she splashed to the edge of the pool. The mother wrapped her daughter in a towel and gave her a hug.

Nadia swam over and rested her chin on the edge of the pool—eyes fixed on Alex. "Daddy, can we go to the Hula Grill for dinner?"

"How do you know about the Hula Grill?"

"Miki, my new friend, is going there at five with her mother, and she said the tables are right on the sand. And it's only a short walk down the beach."

"Okay, but we need to go to bed by eight tonight because we'll be getting up really early to drive up Haleakala for sunrise."

"No problem." She giggled. "I can sleep while you drive."

As they stood in line at the Hula Grill, Nadia scanned the crowd for her friend, Miki. "She's not here."

"We're a little early, and remember, it's up to her parents where they eat."

"She's in Hawaii with her mother and doesn't have a daddy, so she understands just how I feel."

As they were being seated, Miki arrived holding her mother's hand. "Nadia!" Miki shouted, and ran to her new friend.

"Daddy, can Miki and her mother sit with us?"

"Well, that depends on her mother. Maybe she wants mother-daughter time."

"Please, Daddy . . . just ask?"

"Okay." He walked over to Miki's mother, who had just been seated at a table. "I'm Alex Silverton. My daughter, Nadia, played with your daughter at the pool today, and she was wondering if you would mind joining us at our table."

"Mommy, I want to sit with Nadia."

"Well, I guess we can't disappoint our girls." She offered her hand. "I'm Sonya Hartfield from New Jersey. We've been here for almost a week, and Miki was bored until your daughter showed up."

"Mommy, why don't you sit with Nadia's daddy so I can have Nadia all to myself at our table? That will be much more fun."

She looked inquisitively at Alex. "Sonya, that's fine with me if you don't mind."

"Not at all. Adult conversation will be a refreshing change."

The girls quickly engaged in chatter, but it was a slower start for their parents. Alex said he lived on Oahu and could give her tips on some of the best tourist sites.

"I wish we'd met a week ago, but we're leaving tomorrow morning."

Alex wasn't sure if her disappointment was because she would have liked to see more sights or had an interest in getting to know him. When Sonya mentioned she had a minor role in a couple of movies, he realized she had a faint resemblance to Meryl Streep. Over their meal of fresh island fish in a lemon-butter sauce with Thai basil and ginger rice, they shared courses from the buffet of their lives. Her husband had drowned in a freak scuba diving accident off Cancun, and she'd given up her acting ambitions for a stable job in marketing. The trip to Hawaii was on what would have been their tenth anniversary. Sonya expressed sympathy about Alex's recent loss, but feigned interest in his research on volcanoes.

The conversation was more animated when they turned to the challenges of being a single parent. At the end of the meal, Sonya reached across the table and laid her hand on his. "I wish we'd met earlier in the week, as it would have made our stay more enjoyable."

The girls ran ahead as they walked along the beach back to the Westin Hotel. Parting in the hotel lobby was awkward, with the girls hugging with tears in their eyes. When he leaned in to give Sonya a peck on the cheek, she turned and gave him a meaningful kiss.

"Alex, I'm happy you asked me to join you at your table. Here's my business card. If you're ever in my area, give me a call and we can meet for lunch or dinner."

"I will." He watched as the elevator door closed. Her kiss was unexpected and a nice ending to the evening. Sonya had some of the characteristics he found appealing, and a sister Nadia's age would be a plus. But more importantly, he was grieving Kelsey's death and not ready for a serious romantic relationship.

Nadia's cheery mood evaporated with the departure of her new friend. Later that evening, she yelled from the bathroom, "Daddy, you forgot my bubblegum toothpaste!"

"Well, you'll just have to make do with what I brought. It's only for two nights."

Nadia threw her toothbrush into the sink. "Mommy would know, and you don't know anything about kids!"

"Well, you're not going to bed until you brush your teeth with the toothpaste I brought, and no more back-talk!"

Nadia sniffled and wiped her eyes, then picked up the tube of toothpaste. She ignored him and climbed into bed and turned away.

He leaned over and kissed the back of her head. "Sweet dreams." Her head nodded, and he felt better.

At 3:20 a.m., he gently shook Nadia and whispered, "Honey, it's time to get dressed so we can drive to the top of Haleakala to see the sunrise."

"Okay," she murmured, but didn't budge."

Dressing Nadia was like putting clothes on a ragdoll. The only sign that she was awake was when she put her arms around his neck as he carried her to the car. He laid her in the back seat, loosely strapped the seat belt around her, and propped up her head on his jacket.

The engine of his compact car purred softly until he started up the steep, twenty-one-mile Haleakala Crater Road that zigzagged up the side of the volcano. The small engine whined louder as the road steepened and the air thinned.

A feeling of peace permeated Alex's consciousness as his headlights sliced through the darkness, giving glimpses of the outside world. He carried a precious cargo and thought her anger toward him was more about the loss of her mother than his inexperience as a father.

In the small parking lot just below the crater rim, he unstrapped Nadia and lifted her. "Time to wake up."

She snuggled against him. "Daddy, it's freezing cold."

"At ten thousand feet, it freezes at night. We're just in time to see the sunrise, and with the sun will come warmth."

The eastern sky was letting in blue hues as he sat Nadia on a boulder and wrapped her in his jacket. He filled a cup from his thermos. "Nadia, there was only coffee in the room. I added lots of milk and sugar. It'll warm you up."

She took the cup in two hands and looked up into his eyes. "I'm sorry I misbehaved last night."

"You were tired, and you miss your mother. I'm trying my best to be a father and mother but have a lot to learn."

"Daddy, the coffee warms my tummy." She leaned back against his chest.

The small crowd clapped as the sun peeked above the crater rim, sending beams of light into the dark chasm. Like an invisible painter's brush, shades of orange and yellow replaced the black jagged western edge of the crater.

"Daddy, the sun's super bright."

"Don't look directly at it, even with your sunglasses. The air is much cleaner up here, so the sun's rays are not filtered by pollution. The clean, thinner air makes this an excellent place for telescopes to peer into the heavens."

"Can people see to where Mommy is in heaven?"

"I don't know. But I'm sure she's looking down at us and sending her love."

As the sun rose higher, it illuminated shades of burnt red, brown, and charcoal and the desolate bottom of the crater. They watched several hikers descending into the seven-mile-wide chasm.

"Daddy, why are they going down where there are only rocks and no trees or flowers?"

"It only looks lifeless, as there are hardy plants, including the endangered Haleakala Silversword. The Silversword lives for about fifty years, then in a few weeks grows a six-foot stem with hundreds of purple flowers, and when the flowers die, so does the plant. There's also the Hawaiian goose called a *nene*, and a rare barking owl."

"Does it bark like a dog?"

"I don't know because I've never heard one."

"Nadia, remember in the Hawaii Volcanoes National Park where everything looked desolate, but we found tiny ferns, lizards, and bugs in the cracks in the lava?"

"Uh-huh."

"Nature's adaptable. Plants downsize to survive on little moisture and poor soil. And down there in the seven-mile-long chasm are tiny undiscovered organisms waiting to be discovered by scientists with keen eyes."

"When I grow up, I want to be a scientist and discover things that no one has ever seen."

Before leaving the summit, they knelt and said a prayer for Kelsey, then tossed their wilted plumeria leis into the crater. An updraft caught the leis, twirling them together above their heads before releasing them into the cavernous crater.

It was mid-morning when they reached the restored wooden façades along Historic Lahaina's Front Street. Near the middle of the row of ocean-side seafood restaurants was a narrow wooden stairway down to a funky coffeehouse with four tables. Everything was fashioned from roughly hewn planks—the countertop, the tables and chairs, and even the floorboards with spaces where the surf could splash up from below. Haunting Andean flute music blended with the rhythmic beat of the surf.

Nadia knelt on the floor and peered between the cracks. "I see crabs!" she squealed.

"The tide's exceptionally high today—a treat for your daughter," said the redheaded woman with dangly earrings and a tattoo of a turtle on her shoulder. I'm Jodi, your barista today. I make a pretty mean cappuccino, and for your daughter, I can make a fresh strawberry-banana-guava drink."

"Sounds good, and add two toasted bagels with cream cheese."

"Ouch!" cried Nadia as she shook her finger.

Alex examined the injury. "You've got a splinter."

"I've got tweezers in my purse. It's happened before." Jodi handed them to Alex, and he picked at the tiny piece of wood.

"Ouch!" Nadia yanked her hand away and turned to Jodi. "Will you do it?"

"Of course." Nadia didn't complain as Jodi plucked out the splinter, then kissed her finger.

"Thank you. It didn't hurt at all," Nadia said as she gave a dismissive glance toward her father.

Nadia's comment heightened Alex's feelings of anxiety and incompetence.

Back at their hotel, Nadia stood in front of the mirror admiring the smiley face that Jodi had stuck on her T-shirt. "Daddy, I want a mommy like Jodi. She was so nice to me, and I didn't even feel it when she took out the splinter."

"Someday I'll find you a mommy that's just right for both of us. Now, hop into your bathing suit so we can go snorkeling at Black Rock and maybe see a sea turtle. Then we can stop at one of the beachside restaurants."

"I'm a little hungry."

Halfway along the beach to Black Rock, they stopped for lunch at the Huihui Restaurant in front of the Kāʻanapali Beach Hotel. They had just been seated on the terrace when they were approached by a tall, handsome man wearing a kukui nut lei.

"Excuse me, but are you Dr. Alex Silverton, professor of volcanology at the University of Hawaii?"

"Yes. Have we met before?"

"No. I saw you on a local TV station being interviewed on the sensitive issue of scientific research and Hawaiian culture and beliefs. I'm Mike Walton, the general manager of Kāʻana-pali Beach Hotel. In the interview, you said something that aligns with the philosophy behind our hotel."

"Really? I was wondering if anyone was listening."

"I believe you said that for hundreds of years, Hawaiians have used scientific thinking to ensure the sustainability of their land and ocean resources. Then you added that the Hawaiian welcoming tradition of aloha is the elixir that makes Hawaii unique among the hundreds of tourist destinations. You concluded that Hawaiians must be an integral part of future commercial development planning."

"I'm glad you agree with what I said. Many developers believe Hawaiians are a hinderance to progress."

"Dr. Silverton, if you can spare a few minutes after your meal, I'd like to show you how we're working to preserve the Hawaiian culture in our hotel. My nine-year-old granddaughter is playing in our whale-shaped swimming pool. Maybe your daughter would like to join her while I show you around?"

Alex took up the offer and was shown the dozens of Hawaiian touches and artwork around the hotel, plus the Hawaiian crafts that are taught daily to tourists at their Hale Hoʻokipa Cultural Center. Every hotel guest was invited to attend a brief Hawaiian ceremony at their departure, where they received a Hawaiian chant for their safe travel and a kukui nut lei. The commitment to preserving the Hawaiian culture was reflected among the many staff members with specific training in various areas of Hawaiian culture, crafts, and hula dancing.

Black Rock was a lava peninsula at the north end of Kaʻanapali Beach that provided a sheltered area for snorkelers to see tropical fish and frequently green sea turtles. Alex held Nadia's hand as they snorkeled along the edge of the peninsula, where they saw yellow butterflyfish, a spotted puffer, three Moorish idols, and a green sea turtle grazing on a patch of seagrass. Nadia loved snorkeling, so he was surprised when, after a few minutes, she jerked his hand.

"Daddy, I want to go back to swim in our hotel pool."

He didn't have to ask why. Back at their hotel, Alex found two lounge chairs nearer the shallow end of the pool and ordered snacks and cold drinks. Nadia sat at the edge of the pool sipping lemonade as she scanned the water for children her age.

"Nadia, I'm sure you'll find a playmate."

"You always say that. There's no girl my age."

"How about playing tag with me in the pool?"

"It's not the same."

"Nadia, tomorrow morning will be exciting, as we're going on a boat to see whales."

"Maybe, we won't see any whales."

"Nadia, be optimistic."

Sunday morning, Nadia's mood was still melancholy as they drove to Lahaina Harbor to board the sixty-passenger twin-hauled boat for a two-hour whale-watching cruise. Captain Cory announced that they were sure to see whales, and hopefully a few as close as one hundred yards, the closest the boat could approach whales. They saw more than a dozen spouting whales, but all were too far away for good photos. Most people returned to their seats as they headed back to Lahaina Harbor. Suddenly, the throb of the boat's engines stopped, and Captain Cory announced, "Two whales approaching from nine-o'clock."

For the next half-hour, the whales put on a rarely seen performance. They swam back and forth under the boat, surfacing as if trained to pose for tourist photos. One of the whales repeatedly rose vertically from the ocean, its knobby head eight feet above the surface—an eye on the tourists. Captain Cory announced, "This unusual behavior is called *spyhopping*. These whales haven't been hunted for decades and no longer fear people and, like humans, are curious about us." Several times a whale came within four or five feet of the boat. Captain Cory said, "Whales seem to be attracted to our larger boat for the shade underneath and probably are familiar with the sound of the boat's engine."

Nadia was in a good mood when they left the boat and walked past Banyan Tree Square. "Daddy, look at that humongous tree with kids playing in its branches."

"Nadia, it's the largest banyan tree in the United States."

"Can I climb it?"

"I suppose so, but only on the lowest limbs, and be very careful." Alex knew that if Kelsey were here, she would have been uneasy about letting Nadia climb the tree. But it was a way to build Nadia's confidence, and maybe improve her disposition.

Nadia inched her way out onto a limb that was wider than her body and waved at a girl playing with her younger brother. The girl ignored Nadia as she scrambled after the boy that looked to be no older than six, and too young to be jumping from limb to limb. Alex looked around for a parent, but saw no one, then warned the boy to be careful. The child ignored the warning and jumped for a higher limb and screamed as he lost his grip. Alex lunged underneath, breaking the boy's fall as they tumbled to the ground. A woman ran to them and lifted the frightened boy from Alex's arms. "Donny, my poor baby. Are you alright?"

"I think so," he sobbed, and nuzzled his mother's neck. She turned and walked away.

Nadia jumped to the ground and ran to her dad. "Daddy, are you hurt?"

"No. I just got the wind knocked out of me."

She kissed him. "You saved that boy, and that woman didn't even thank you."

"I'm just glad the boy wasn't hurt."

"Daddy . . . you're a hero." She wrapped her arms tightly around his neck. "Daddy, why do you have tears in your eyes?"

Chapter 19

*T*he trip to Maui was a turning point in Alex's relationship with Nadia. She began helping around the house—picking up toys and clothes, and she complained less about his cooking. Saturday mornings were set aside for the Kahala Mall Starbucks, then up to the Barnes & Noble on the upper level of the mall for the children's book reading hour.

Alex was perusing the travel section on the magazine rack when he heard a familiar voice call his name. Turning, he saw Janice Mitchell walking his way. He hadn't talked to her since she dumped him after a brief romance three years ago. It had been a mismatch from the start—an introvert geologist dating a glamorous blond who thrived on attention and socializing with high society. He doubted the romance would lead to wedding bells, yet was reluctant to end it until she did. She had explained why their relationship had no future, and he'd agreed, even though it hurt. Within a month, Janice was dating a suave real estate developer. Five months later, he saw their wedding photos in the newspaper along with a flattering write-up about the power couple.

"Janice . . . long time no see. I didn't see your name on the list of attendees at the annual governor's ball and assumed you might have left the islands. I read that your husband broadened his real estate interests to the mainland."

She grimaced. "He broadened his interests to more than real estate, if you know what I mean. We had a ghastly divorce, and I've been keeping a low profile. It's taken awhile to get back on my feet and begin socializing again."

"You two seemed a perfect match."

"I thought so when we married, but he was a lying cheat—not like you."

Alex shrugged. "At least I had one good quality."

She smirked. "You also were better between the sheets, because you're a detail person." She giggled.

Alex didn't reply to her solicitous compliment. *She's still as strikingly beautiful as I remember.*

"Alex, I should have known to avoid men that have an insatiable desire to acquire things to sustain their inflated egos. He spent a lot of time in China collecting art pieces for his new hotel in Maui, along with a Chinese girlfriend. I got the Kahala house, but little else. He leveraged all his properties with loans. Then when the real estate market soured, lenders came knocking. I've had to go back to work in healthcare marketing."

"With your personality and experience, you're a natural in sales."

She nodded and paused. "Alex, I was sorry to read about your wife, Kelsey. I heard that you adopted her daughter."

"Yes, Nadia's here at the children's storybook hour. I'm learning the challenges of being a single parent. I've even learned to braid her hair," he jested.

Janice adjusted a gold pin in her coiffured hair as she gazed into Alex's eyes. "Seeing anyone?"

"No. I haven't been up to it yet but know it's important for Nadia to have a mother. I'm the first father she's ever known. Her biological father was only around long enough to impregnate Kelsey."

Janice took a travel magazine from the shelf and flipped through the pages, then put it back. "Alex, I have a nice pool that's rarely used. How about bringing your daughter over for a light lunch and a swim? I have a sociable dalmatian that she'll love."

He hesitated. "Well, I—"

"Daddy," shrieked Nadia as she ran toward them, "I heard the best story ever about a friendship between a whale and a turtle."

"So, this is the little darling you've been telling me about. I'm Janice, an old friend of your father's, and I was just asking him if you two could come over today for a swim in my pool. I have a dalmatian that's lonely and likes to play with children."

"I love dogs. Daddy, can we go?"

It was just after noon when they arrived at Janice's home in exclusive Kahala on the east side of Diamond Head. She met them at the door wearing a green-and-red floral dress, with cleavage that, in a geologist's mind, was like peering into the Grand Canyon. Janice's dalmatian slipped past and licked Nadia's hand. "Her name's Dottie because she's covered in black dots."

Nadia dropped to her knees and got a slobbery lick on her face. "Dottie's so adorable," she said as she stroked his ears.

"Please come in. We'll have a light lunch on the lanai; then you can play with Dottie and enjoy the pool." Janice led them through her immaculate and richly furnished home—a fusion of Asian and Hawaiian art. "Daddy, this is a palace compared to our home."

Alex chuckled. "One thing about children, they tell the unvarnished truth, unless it's who got into the cookie jar."

After jilting Alex once, Janice needed to disarm his defenses, and Nadia was the key. The lunch included hotdogs on a bun, potato chips, barbecued chicken wings, carrot sticks, and for dessert, strawberry ice cream with a chocolate chip cookie. The only deference to adult tastes was a Napa Valley sauvignon blanc.

"Miss Mitchell, this is so much better than lunches Daddy makes."

"So, what does your daddy feed you?"

"Sometimes he tries to make me eat broccoli and gooey spinach, and yesterday he set off the fire alarm when he burned up our toasted cheese sandwiches."

Janice raised her crystal flute. "A toast to less burnt cheese sandwiches."

After lunch, Alex and Nadia played in the pool while Janice watched from her padded lounge chair—her wide-brimmed hat dipping stylishly over her forehead.

Dottie bounded around the edge of the pool, barking until Alex tossed the ball across the lawn for her to retrieve and she brought it back to Nadia. "Well, I know who Dottie prefers." He retreated to a lounge chair next to Janice.

"Janice, this is a special treat for Nadia. She's been asking for a dog, and I'm tempted to get one, but that's a problem when I travel."

"Alex, she can come here anytime to play with Dottie and swim in the pool. That way you don't have to worry about feeding, grooming, and getting shots for a pet and finding someone to care for the dog when you travel."

"Thanks, I might take you up on your offer."

Janice leaned over and put her hand on Alex's thigh. "Alex, I have an invitation to a black-tie charity dinner in two weeks but don't want to go alone. It's a really good cause, raising money for young cancer patients. I would be delighted if you would accompany me. We could make a donation in Kelsey's name?"

Alex turned to face her. "Janice, I'm not up to serious dating yet, and our last go-around ended poorly."

"Alex, leaving you was a foolish mistake on my part. You don't have to think about it as a date, but a way to honor Kelsey with a donation. Okay?"

Alex rented a white tuxedo and went to an upscale salon for a haircut. Janice wore a head-turning body-hugging gown with a one-and-a-half-inch pearl-studded choker, matching bracelet, and earrings. Alex was impressed with how smoothly she navigated through the crowd, greeting by name prominent business and government leaders, and stopping frequently to exchange air kisses with people he had only seen in the newspaper or on TV.

Janice introduced Alex as a professor from the University of Hawaii. Usually, the first question asked was his field of research. He avoided saying volcanology—a sure conversation killer—and said geology. The results were a little better—a polite smile and a nod, and perhaps a superficial comment, before pivoting to current political or economic topics.

After cocktails, Janice accepted her friend Pierre Mairaux's invitation to join him at his table. Immaculately dressed, with an affected French accent, Pierre was the main wine distributor in Hawaii. For twenty minutes, Pierre's attention was focused on Janice, even though she attempted to bring Alex into the conversation. Finally, turning to Alex, he said, "So you're a geologist. I envision geologists deep in mosquito-infested jungles looking for gold and diamonds and scraping blood-sucking leeches from their legs, and at night, hunkered around a campfire drinking warm beers."

Alex smiled weakly at Pierre's attempt at humor. "It's not like in Indiana Jones movies. Most of my time is in the classroom or laboratory, but I've been in leech-infested jungles and climbed active volcanoes. As for beer, a cold one is fine, but I prefer wine in the company of friends."

Pierre grinned; his query had stepped into his area of expertise. "Dr. Silverton, what's your favorite wine for special occasions?"

"Hmm. A few months ago, I shared a bottle of Misty River Vineyards cabernet sauvignon with my wife, and we really liked it. It holds good memories, so I suppose it's my favorite."

Pierre gazed at Alex in disbelief. "You must be confused. Misty River wines are not available in Hawaii. I've been on a waiting list for a case for over a year."

Alex had come to the charity as a favor to Janice, and not to debate wines—something he knew little about. "Perhaps I'm mistaken. As you're the expert, I defer to you to make the wine selection."

Pierre ordered a wine twice as much as anything Alex had ever paid for a bottle. When it was served, Alex feigned interest as Pierre critiqued its delicate bouquet, balance, and structure. Janice reached under the table and squeezed Alex's hand.

After the meal and speeches, Alex excused himself to go to the restroom. As soon as he was out of sight, Pierre said, "I'm sorry for being a little hard on your date, but he was showing off by saying he'd had a bottle of Misty River wine.

If I can't buy a bottle, no one else could possibly buy one in Hawaii. And even if it was available, I can't believe a professor of volcanology is going to pay two hundred bucks for a bottle."

"Pierre, I'm considering making a play for him, but am concerned that he won't be able to support my lifestyle or fit in with my prominent friends. It would soothe my worries if he had connections to the wine industry. Could you do me a little favor and call Misty River Winery and find out if they've ever heard of a Dr. Alex Silverton?"

"Janice, for you, I'll do it, but I'm sure they've never heard of him." He took Janice's hand. "If you want my advice, he'll never fit into our circle or be able to support your tastes."

Janice was in her office on Bishop Street when her cell phone rang. "Hello, Pierre, it was a pleasure to sit at your table at the banquet."

"Janice, the pleasure was all mine. I called Bruce Gortaire, director of marketing at Misty River Vineyards, and asked if he had ever heard of your Dr. Alex Silverton. He'd never heard of him."

"Pierre, I guess it was too much to expect that Alex had connections to the wine industry."

"Janice, Gortaire called back a few minutes later and apologized for his mistake. He said a Dr. Silverton held a few shares in Misty River Vineyards but was not actively involved with the company. The winery periodically sends complimentary bottles to shareholders. So that's how your Dr. Silverton got a bottle. Kind of a waste on someone who doesn't know wines."

"Any idea how much his shares are worth?"

"Gortaire wasn't at liberty to reveal more, as the shares are privately held. But I know from wine industry sources that Misty River Vineyards doesn't make any profits and has never distributed a dime in dividends to shareholders."

"Oh well, at least I can brag that *we* own shares in an exclusive boutique winery."

"Janice, you never miss an angle to enhance your social status. We're too much alike, and that's why it's best for us to remain friends and not lovers."

"Pierre, I'm beginning to like rocks more and more."

While Alex didn't have any hidden wealth, he had a respectable position as a university professor and decent salary. Janice implemented her strategy: inviting Nadia on shopping trips, buying her fashionable preteen clothes, and inviting Nadia to bring friends over for pool parties. She was careful to go slow on the romantic front with Alex, and focused on Nadia, the link to his heart and wedding bells. She talked daily with Alex, always making a point of saying how much she enjoyed doing things with Nadia.

Bonding with Nadia proved difficult as Janice struggled not to reveal her reservations about children. Finally, after Nadia asked several times for help with her math homework, Janice snapped, "Nadia, you need to learn how to solve problems on your own!"

"But Daddy always helps me."

"I'm not your daddy!" Minutes later, Janice apologized and took Nadia out for an ice cream treat.

"Nadia, I thought you liked to go to Janice's home on the weekends to swim and play with Dottie."

"I do, but Janice wants to send me away to a boarding school."

"Nonsense. Where did you get that idea?"

"I heard Janice talking to her girlfriend on the phone. She said she wanted to send me to a boarding school on the East Coast to learn to be a proper lady."

"Don't worry for a single second. You're staying right here in Hawaii with me."

She snuggled against her father, then pulled back and wrinkled her nose. "You're stinky under the arms."

He smiled and pulled her closer.

"Janice, Nadia told me you want to send her to a boarding school. That's not in the cards!"

"Alex, I'm only interested in what is best for Nadia. She's such a pretty, precocious girl, and I thought an exclusive East Coast boarding school would prepare her with skills for life. But Alex, she's your daughter, and you know what's best. I want both of you to be happy. I'm sorry." She stroked his hand and laid her head on his shoulder.

Chapter 20

*T*he funding for Alex's research project in Papua New Guinea was approved in early May, resulting in a scramble to make travel arrangements and get a trusted babysitter for Nadia. He would be away for five weeks, with almost a month in the country's tropical rainforest in the eastern part of New Guinea Island. Taking Nadia was out of the question because of the dangers.

He called Janice and asked if she would care for his daughter, resulting in an uncomfortable silence before she responded. "Alex, I will be delighted to have Nadia stay with me. As I'm working during the day, I'll make sure Nadia gets into a fun summer program, and if necessary, I will take off work early each day to care for her."

"Janice, this means so much to me."

Janice was aware that Alex would be cautious to fully commit to her after she had previously dumped him. Helping care for Nadia was a necessary price to help cement their relationship.

Nadia didn't take the news well. "Daddy, please take me with you. I won't be any trouble. I won't complain a bit, and I'll eat whatever you eat in the jungle—even bugs."

"Nadia, I really would like to take you, and will when you're older. But you're too precious to take the risk. You'll be in good hands with Janice and can swim every day and play with Dottie as much as you want. And don't worry, I told Janice that I would never send you off to a boarding school."

Nadia crossed her arms tightly across her chest. "Janice is not like my mommy!"

"Honey, no one can ever replace Kelsey. Janice is the best that I can do."

"Becky is like Mommy and always makes me happy."

"She has a university degree to finish and is busy planning a summer wedding."

"Pleeaase? Can't you just call and ask her?"

Alex sighed and reached over to wipe a tear from Nadia's cheek. "Okay, I'll call, but if she's not available, I don't want to hear any more fussing about staying with Janice."

She threw her arms around his neck and kissed his nose. "I'm sure she'll come." Then she handed him his cell phone.

Becky answered on the fourth ring. "Hi, Alex, I was just thinking about you and Nadia. How are things going with Nadia?"

"I've got the hang of braiding her hair and making lunches that she'll eat, but there's a *little* problem, and I'm calling because Nadia insisted."

"*Big* problem!" yelled Nadia.

"I hear my favorite girl in the background."

"I'm leaving in nine days on a five-week trip to Papua New Guinea to do research on two volcanoes. It's taken two years to get funding, and I've got to spend the grant money this fiscal year. A woman I've recently begun seeing has agreed to take care of Nadia, but Nadia insists that I ask you. I know you're busy, and fully understand that you're probably unavailable."

"Alex, it's good that you're starting to date again. Is it serious?"

"She's interested in hurrying things along, but I'm not. But it's so soon after Kelsey died, and I don't want to rush into marriage."

"I look forward to meeting her."

"You mean you can come?"

"You should know, I'll do anything for Nadia."

"But what about your research and wedding plans?"

"I'm at the writing stage on my dissertation and can do it anywhere, and the University of Hawaii has a good collection of reports on the Pacific Islands. Elliott's putting twelve-hour days in his residency this summer, so we aren't planning to see each other until September."

"What about the summer wedding?"

"Our wedding plans have been pushed back a year because there's too much going on right now. After the wedding, we want to spend a month traveling around Europe, and that's not possible this year."

Nadia grabbed the phone. "Becky, I'll be the best girl ever, and, and I love you more than anything!"

"Becky, I guess that settles it. I'll buy your tickets and pay you whatever you think is reasonable."

"Just buy me a round-trip economy ticket, and leave enough money for the household and a little extra for our visits to Starbucks, and we'll be fine."

"Janice. I hope you're not upset, but a close friend of Kelsey's has offered to take care of Nadia while I'm away. She'll fly over from the mainland and stay in my home."

Janice's smirk was reflected in the mirror. "Whatever is best for Nadia is fine with me. How well do you know this woman?" She wrote a word on a notepad, then circled it.

"I met Becky at our wedding last December, and she stayed awhile to help with Nadia."

"I assume she's single and has a flexible job to be able to come to Hawaii for five weeks?"

"Becky's engaged to a medical doctor in Boston who's just finishing his residency at Massachusetts General Hospital. She was Kelsey's closest friend and was at Nadia's birth."

Janice crossed out the word *danger* on the notepad. "Alex, I'd like to host a luncheon for Becky when she arrives. I want to assure her that I'm nearby if she encounters any problems."

"That's so kind of you. Sorry about the last-minute change."

"I fully understand."

The flurry of preparations and shots before Alex's departure resulted in delaying the luncheon until the day before his flight. Becky's arrival lifted Nadia's spirits and reduced Alex's anxiety about being away for so long. Alex warned Becky that the casual luncheon might be something quite special.

Janice greeted them at the front door in a tailored muumuu splashed with red hibiscus flowers and a plunging neckline "Becky, how delighted I am that you could come all the way to Hawaii to look after *our* precious Nadia." Janice tucked her hand securely under Alex's arm as she showed Becky her home, then seated them at the antique rosewood Chinese table in her opulent dining room.

For starters, Janice served French wine from the Bordeaux region and canapes topped with Russian caviar. Nadia tasted the caviar and grimaced but said nothing when her father put his finger to his lips. The main entrée was a Maine lobster salad on a bed of local butter lettuce, wedges of vine-ripened tomatoes, and sliced avocado. It was Nadia's first taste of lobster, and she gave a two thumbs up. The crème brûlée dessert was Nadia's favorite, and after finishing hers, she whimpered for some of Alex's.

Alex saw the gracious interactions between the two women, missing Janice's subtle probing. He noticed that Janice frequently used the word *we* as she brushed his hand, and repeatedly commented on how much she enjoyed his company. At the front door, the two women embraced warmly, and Janice whispered in Becky's ear.

That evening, after Becky and Alex tucked in Nadia, they went over the checklist of things Becky would take care of while he was away. Then, as both were about to retire to separate bedrooms, Alex said, "Janice whispered something to you as we left her home today. Is it anything I should be concerned about?"

Becky chuckled. "She warned me that you were taken. I thought it strange, as there's nothing going on between us, and I'm in love with another man. She's jealous about any possible competition."

"I'm flattered. Becky, you've only met Janice over lunch, but do you feel that she might be right for Nadia and me?"

"I don't know you well enough to give that kind of advice. All I can say is it will be difficult to find another Kelsey . . . and Janice is not Kelsey. It may take time for Nadia to bond with Janice. Nadia has you all to herself and will only share you with another woman that she wants for a mommy.

"Janice strikes me as a woman with high-society aspiration, while you're contented as a university professor. But, Alex, high society makes allowances for academics in their midst."

"Does that include volcanologists?"

Becky laughed. "I doubt it. Goodnight."

Janice called as Alex was leaving for the airport to tell him she couldn't come to see him off, because she had forgotten about an invitation to the Hawaii Business Leaders breakfast and hoped it might lead to a better job. "Alex, I'll be thinking of you every day and already miss you. Stay safe."

At the airport, Nadia and Becky gave him the plumeria leis they'd made from flowers in the backyard. Nadia hung on her father's arm until the last minute, then tearfully kissed him. Becky held back until he turned to her, and she stepped forward, and they embraced. Alex whispered, "Your coming means a lot to Nadia and me."

"Daddy, will you be able to call me from Papua New Guinea?"

"I'll try from Port Moresby, but in the jungle, there's no way to call, but I'll be thinking about you."

"That's okay. With Becky here, I won't be lonely."

"You won't even miss me even for a teensy-weensy minute?"

Nadia wrapped her small arms around his waist. "Daddy, I already miss you."

Becky kept an arm around Nadia as they watched his plane taxi onto the runway, then take-off, and wing southwest across the Pacific. They didn't turn away until there was only blue sky.

"Becky, I was wondering if it would be okay to call you Mommy while Daddy's away?"

Becky squatted and brushed Nadia's hair back as she gazed into Nadia's eyes. "Of course, but never around Janice or your daddy after he returns. It must remain our little secret."

Chapter 21

*B*ecky was worried when after four days, Alex hadn't called. When Nadia asked why her daddy didn't call, she soothed her, saying he hadn't been able to get to a phone. "I'm sure we'll get a call soon, so don't worry." On the fifth day, he called, and Nadia excitedly chatted, recounting all the fun things she was doing with Becky.

"Daddy, my Summer Science Lab is right across the street from the university where Becky's using your office. She picks me up every weekday at noon, and we hop on the bus to Waikiki Beach. We know all the best places for tasty ice cream and gelatos. Becky's so much fun; but, Daddy, I miss you. Today we snorkeled in the ocean and built a sandcastle and added pigeon feathers for flags."

"Nadia, I leave tomorrow for the field, so I will be out of touch for a few weeks. You be good and mind Becky. Honey, I need to talk to Becky before I get cut off."

"Alex, we were worried about you."

"I got delayed in Australia when the plane developed mechanical problems. My counterpart in PNG has everything arranged, and we leave Port Moresby early tomorrow morning. I probably won't be able to call you until just before my flight back to Hawaii, so don't worry. How are things going with Nadia?"

"I'm enjoying Nadia immensely, but getting her into bed by nine is a challenge, and in the morning, there's a child-sized lump under my covers."

"I'm so happy you agreed to watch Nadia. I can't tell you how much a relief it is. Um, have you heard from Janice?"

"No. She's probably busy with her work. I'm sure she'll call soon to invite Nadia over for a swim in her pool."

A larger-than-expected crowd showed up at the Honolulu Health Fair where the various medical groups had booths and tents to give free testing for cholesterol, blood pressure, and diabetes. First Medical of Hawaii's three booths included one for health care literature, a second for free testing by two nurses, and a third with refreshments for individuals interested in signing up for their services. Janice stood in front in an eye-catching aloha dress to guide people to the First Medical of Hawaii booths.

"Hello."

The deep baritone voice caught Janice's attention. She turned, almost bumping into a bronze-tanned Adonis with muscles that filled the sleeves of his Reyn Spooner aloha shirt. A splash of gray at his temples enhanced his wavy chestnut hair that swept back over his ears. A stray lock across his brow drew her gaze to hazel eyes that captured the colors of her dress. His large hand took hers, applying the right amount of pressure to be meaningful. "Phillip Wagner, president of Fitness Life Gyms. I hope you're the right person to speak to about becoming a sponsor of next year's health fair."

"Yes. I'm Janice Mitchell, marketing specialist with First Medical of Hawaii. We are always happy to have sponsors. Better that we discuss the matter over a refreshing beverage in our consultation tent."

Inside, Janice pulled out a chair for Wagner. "Call me Janice. Would you like juice, iced tea, or a bottled water?"

"A bottle of water would be fine, and please call me Phil."

She handed him a chilled bottle, then pulled her chair close enough to detect his masculine cologne. "Phil, tell me a little about your company."

"I have a chain of fourteen fitness centers in California and Oregon and am opening my first in Waikiki and plan two more on Oahu and one in Maui. Our interests appear to dovetail with First Medical of Hawaii's goal to promote healthy lifestyles." He presented his gold-embossed card with his color photo.

Phillip R. Wagner–Managing Director–Fitness Life Gyms

She studied the card longer than necessary, contemplating her next move. This was a man worth getting to know. "I'm rather busy with the fair until it closes at five. Then perhaps we could meet and discuss your proposal in detail.

"How about drinks and pupus at the Outrigger Canoe Club at say six?"

Her heart skipped a beat. How did he get into this exclusive club with a ten-year waiting list for new members? Janice pulled out her calendar on the pretense that there might be another obligation. "Looks like my evening's free." She casually mentioned that her home was in the exclusive Kahala area.

As soon as he left, she asked Julie to take over for the remainder of the day, then rushed home to shower and put on a dress that would reveal her best features. She briefly thought about Alex, a sure thing, but it was a package deal with a precocious child that raised doubts. Anyway, it was a business meeting, and no reason to tell Alex. She timed her arrival to be a respectable fifteen minutes late—must not appear too eager. Her name was on the guest list, and she was escorted to an oceanfront table for two on the upper terrace. Phil, now wearing a Thai-silk shirt, rose and gave her a warm hug as his hand brushed her bare back.

"Janice, you look ravishing, and after a day in the hot sun at the health fair. Are you sure you didn't just come from a beauty salon?"

"Just a quick shower and change."

The setting sun silhouetted the surfers beyond the coral reef and added glitter to the wave crests. Their gaze didn't linger on the ocean and setting sun, but on each other as each carefully chose words to impress. In the twilight, tiki torches burnished their faces with a mellow glow and added twinkles to their eyes. The charade of discussing next year's health fair sponsorship was quickly dispensed with, and they turned to more personal matters.

"Janice, I hope you don't think I'm being too forward, but I can't imagine you unattached."

"I was married for a short period to a real estate tycoon that acquired commercial properties, girlfriends, and debts and fled the islands with little more than the shirt on his back. Fortunately, a good lawyer assured me the Kahala home."

"Dating anyone?"

A nervous twitch of her left eye. "Nothing serious. I've had a few dates with a professor of volcanology at UH. He's off stomping around in the jungles of Papua New Guinea for five weeks."

"Sounds adventurous, or perhaps foolhardy."

"He's a nice guy with a secure university position but has little aspiration to climb the financial and social ladder. I can probably adjust, but he has a eight-year-old child that I didn't bargain for, and she could be an expensive liability when she goes to college. He's already sending her to an expensive private school, and university salaries are not great."

He smiled and shook his head. "I hope you don't mind me being frank, but you're a beautiful, interesting woman that has many choices, so why go for bronze when gold is within reach?"

"I was struggling after a nasty divorce, and Alex was a known quantity. You see, I dated him before I left him for the real estate scoundrel. I've only recently started seeing Alex, and no commitments have been made." Her eyes locked on him as she toyed with her dragon earring. "May I ask why you're not attached?"

"My situation's different. I'm divorced with two children in college. An inheritance takes care of their education, plus provides capital to expand my business more rapidly. My grandfather was a business leader in Honolulu, and I always knew I'd return to my roots. Fortunately, my grandfather's active participation in the Outrigger Canoe Club facilitated my acceptance as a member." He reached across the table and touched the back of her hand. "Janice, the moment I saw you, I knew you were the woman of my dreams."

She blushed. "You say that to all the women. Right?"

He gazed into her eyes. "Janice, I meant every word of what I said, and will say it again. When I set my eyes on you, I knew you were the woman of my dreams."

It was almost ten p.m. when he followed her home. The next morning his black Mercedes was still parked in her driveway under a plumeria tree—pink blossoms sprinkled over the hood.

Alex was delayed an hour in customs while his rock specimens were inspected. As soon as he walked out of International Arrivals pushing his heavy luggage cart, Nadia ran and bounded into his arms. She put her homemade lei over his head, then gave him kisses on both cheeks and his nose. "I missed you so much!"

"Nadia, I missed you even more." He swung her around, making her giggle.

As soon as Alex set Nadia down, Becky looped her lei over his head and kissed him on the cheek. "Welcome home."

Nadia clung to her father. "Daddy, I even missed your stinky smell."

He squeezed her tighter. "I hope you and Becky had a good time."

"Super! We had lots of adventures in Waikiki. Everyone is so friendly, and sometimes I get an extra scoop of ice cream for free."

"Well, you'll have to show me your discoveries." He turned to Becky. "I was expecting Janice to be here. Is she okay?"

"I left two messages about your arrival date, time, and flight but didn't hear back from her."

Nadia wrinkled her nose. "Daddy, you need a shower."

Alex was disappointed that Janice hadn't called and wondered if she was having thoughts about the relationship. He was most disappointed that she didn't check to make sure Nadia was okay.

As soon as he entered his home, Nadia presented her father with the special cupcakes she had made with Becky's help. Becky handed Alex a mug of Kona coffee and sat across from him at the kitchen table.

"It's great to be back home again." He wolfed down a cupcake, then opened his knapsack. "I didn't have much opportunity to shop in the jungle but got a couple of gifts for you two." He pulled out a cowrie necklace with a carved mother-of-pearl crocodile pendant. "The native people prize and respect crocodiles for their fierceness and tasty meat. This necklace is supposed to protect the wearer from evil spirits and was worn by a chief's daughter." He carefully put the necklace on Nadia and kissed her cheek.

"Daddy, I'm a native princess." She dashed into the bathroom to admire herself in the mirror.

Alex unwrapped a wooden bowl, inlaid around the edges with carved mother-of-pearl figures—birds, crocodiles, and fish.

"Becky, I want you to have this bowl. It comes with a memorable story. "I was with a local geologist, Johnny Dadae, skirting around a village deep in the rainforest, when a native man came running toward us waving his arms and hollering. I thought we were trespassing and turned away, but Johnny grabbed my arm and said the man's son had been bitten by a poisonous snake and needed help. I had two types of anti-venom, and fortunately, the one I used on the boy worked. The man and his wife gave me their most valuable possession, this bowl. I didn't want to take it, but Johnny told me it would be very rude not to accept the gift."

"I can't take it. It was given to you for saving a boy's life."

"Becky, you came to my aid with Nadia, and that meant so much to me."

Nadia came skipping back. "Daddy, I want to hear all about your jungle adventures. I told my friends at school that you were in the jungle with wild animals and were very brave. Did you see crocodiles and tigers and snakes?"

"There are no tigers in Papua New Guinea, but lots of other critters to worry about, like poisonous snakes, spiders as big as a plate, scorpions, fifteen-foot crocodiles, leeches, and hordes of mosquitoes, some carrying a deadly strain of Malaria that eats away at the brain. Every time we walked through a swampy area, we had to stop and pick off the leeches." He showed the circular red spots where leeches had attached to his legs.

"They look yucky. Did you have to eat bugs and snakes?"

"Villagers offered me live larva and fried monkey brain. I couldn't refuse."

"Daddy, I'm not so sure I want to go into the jungles with you. Maybe Becky can come and stay with me when you go back to the jungle."

"There's also a lot of beauty there. The towering trees form a canopy that blocks out most of the light from the jungle floor. Beams of light slip through and light the heavy mist near the ground. Vines of flame-red orchids are wrapped around tree trunks like strings of Christmas lights. The star attraction was the breathtaking bird-of-paradise that flashed dazzling colors—canary yellow, emerald-green, red and maroon, and aquamarine bluer than the sky. A cacophony of sounds— chirps, caws, buzzing, croaking, and screeches like a human voice filtered through the forest. The lyrebird had melodious songs that varied from mimicking other birds to becoming a one bird ensemble of different tweets and chirrups.

"And above the shadowy jungle floor on the slopes of smoldering volcanoes, the view across the thick treetop canopy was of a world unbounded by the confines of the jungle below. And in the distance, saw-toothed, snow-covered mountains defied gravity, floating above the misty forest canopy."

"Daddy, maybe I'll go with you when I'm bigger and can carry some of your rocks."

"I'd like to go too," added Becky.

"You're both welcome."

When Janice hadn't called by evening, he rang her.

"Hello, Alex, I hope you had a safe trip."

"Yes, it was a success, but exhausting. Um . . . Janice, I expected to see you at the airport or at least receive a call. Has anything changed with us?"

"Yes. Alex, I didn't want to upset you on your first day home. I'm seeing someone."

"Is it serious?"

"I think so. I've done a lot of thinking, and as much as I'm attracted to you, I don't see our relationship working. You love your job teaching and doing research on volcanoes, while I want a lot more out of life. Nadia's a sweet girl, but I'm not ready to take on the role of a mother."

Alex leaned back against the kitchen wall. "Thanks for being honest with me. I hope you've found a man that can give you what you want in life."

"I'm pretty sure this is the one. It was totally unexpected."

"Well, I wish you the best. I guess this is goodbye."

"Yes. I hope you find a woman that can love you and also Nadia. I'm just not that woman."

He hung up. Janice's comment that she couldn't be a mother to Nadia was an instant deal breaker. He was disheartened yet relieved because he wasn't the one that had to break off the relationship.

Becky poured two brandies and handed one to him. "Bad news, huh?"

"She dumped me."

Becky swirled her brandy. "She's a fool."

"Daddy, why do you look sad?"

"Janice doesn't want to see us anymore."

Nadia smiled. "Now I have you all to myself until you find a nice mommy that loves me as much as Becky."

The next morning, Alex was on his knees puking into the toilet with Becky holding him from collapsing on the floor. When he stopped retching, she dragged him to his feet, putting his arm over her shoulder as she struggled to get him back into his bed. She pulled off his sweat- and vomit-soaked T-shirt. Nadia brought a bucket of cool water and a wash cloth.

"Becky. What's wrong with my daddy?"

"I don't know. His temperature is 103, so start wiping him with a cool washcloth while I call Dr. Oshiro, his friend at the UH Medical School."

Thirty minutes later, Jiro Oshiro was at Alex's bedside. "I think he's got a nasty bacterial infection. I've seen two other cases like this from a missionary group that visited Papua New Guinea. I'm prescribing a broad-spectrum antibiotic that you can pick up at Longs. In addition to ibuprofen for his fever, keep as much liquid in him as he can take to rehydrate him, and bathe him in cool towels until his fever comes down. I'll check back this evening after work, but call me immediately if his condition worsens."

Becky delayed her departure and remained at Alex's side, caring for him as he slowly recovered. Nadia was the first one to get her father to sip chicken noodle soup and keep it down. His high temperature broke on the third day, and Becky got him into the bathtub, where he lay back, his head on a rolled towel as she bathed him with a washcloth. When she moved the cloth between his thighs, he stirred, and she pulled her hand away.

"Sorry, I couldn't help it. It's so embarrassing."

"Well, Alex, it's an upright sign you're recovering," she quipped. "Don't worry. You're just a normal male. We'll just forget that it even happened."

Chapter 22

$\mathcal{B}$ ecky extended her stay an additional week after Alex's recovery to be sure he didn't have a relapse. As the departure date neared, Nadia again became more irritable and on the final evening screamed at her father and stormed into her bedroom.

"I don't know what has gotten into Nadia. I just told her to finish her homework before playing with you, and she exploded."

"Alex, it's not you. Let me talk to her." She knocked on Nadia's door. "Nadia, can I come in?"

"Why? You're just going to leave me again."

Nadia was sitting in bed clutching her favorite doll when Becky entered.

"Can I sit beside you?"

Nadia nodded, and Becky sat close. "I love you very much and wish there was a way I could stay longer, but I have another life with Elliot, who misses me, and I need to finish my dissertation. Nadia, you're like a daughter to me, and we can always stay in touch, and maybe you can visit me in Boston."

"You're just saying that to make me feel good. If you really love me and daddy, you will stay here, and you can marry daddy."

"I do love both of you, but in a different way than Elliott, the man I'm going to marry. When you're older, you'll understand."

Nadia took the rubber band from her doll's ponytail and twisted it around her finger. "I know you want to marry Elliott, but you have to finish your *dessert-tation* first. You told me everything you need for your research is here, so why can't you stay and finish your *dessert-tation* here? Daddy's real smart and can help you, and I won't bother you too much. Then go and marry Elliott. But you'll be sorry."

Becky adjusted the ribbons on the doll's braids. "Um, I guess that might be possible. But it's got to be okay with your daddy and my fiancé. No promises."

Nadia jumped into Becky's arms. "I know Daddy will want you to stay, as he needs help with girl stuff."

Becky tickled Nadia, making her squeal.

"What's so funny?" Alex called out.

Nadia handed her doll to Becky and ran to the door. "Daddy, Becky and I have the most brilliant plan ever!"

It took two-dozen calls over three days to make arrangements to stay in Hawaii until the end of the year. Becky's dissertation advisor agreed on the condition that she return to go over the draft. Elliott agreed but clearly wasn't delighted with her staying so long in Hawaii. He reluctantly agreed to come to Hawaii for Thanksgiving, the first time he would miss the gala affair with his parents. She promised romantic nights in

Waikiki and would show him her favorite sights. Alex was pleased to have Becky stay and help with his daughter.

It was in the area of discipline that Alex was often outfoxed by Nadia and most needed Becky's help. Nadia had discovered that producing tears weakened her father's resolve. But when Nadia used her teary-eyed approach on Becky, she'd give Nadia a knowing wry smile and say something like, "Nice try," and shake her head.

Alex preferred to let Becky and Nadia plan weekend outings. Nadia was fascinated with green sea turtles that could be seen swimming off Waikiki Beach, particularly near the concrete jetty behind the Outrigger Reef Hotel and inside the reef directly behind the Hilton Hawaiian Village. But to see sea turtles on the beach, they needed to drive to Laniakea Beach on the North Shore, where three hundred-pound green sea turtles came ashore on most days.

Alex's only request was they go early on Saturday morning to beat the weekend traffic and stop at Coffee Gallery in Hale'iwa for coffee and pastries. Then they'd drive two miles northeast on Kamehameha Highway to Laniakea Beach, locally referred to as Turtle Beach.

Nadia and Becky dozed off in the backseat, leaving Alex to his thoughts on the hour drive to Hale'iwa. Becky had the same qualities that attracted him to Kelsey, yet she was in love with someone else. He was sure that if she was available, he'd pursue her. Their friendship had evolved into a comfortable brother-sister relationship, and he kept his romantic thoughts to himself. If Becky saw him as a threat to her relationship with Elliott, he was sure she would leave. He knew it was time to begin seriously looking for a compatible partner and would start with an eligible faculty woman. A possibility was Jill Haddington, a divorced assistant professor of psychology who had expressed sympathy after Kelsey's death. Jill had suggested she was available if he needed someone to talk to.

Twenty minutes from home, he took the H2 Freeway to Highway 80 that crossed the broad valley between the Ko'olau and Wai'anae Mountains. In a bygone era, the valley hosted a thriving pineapple and sugarcane industry. He bypassed touristy Dole Plantation and drove directly to Hale'iwa, the closest one could get to a historic town on Oahu with its clapboard one-story buildings lining the main street. He pulled into a tree-shaded parking lot next to cafés, gift shops, and the Coffee Gallery.

"Wake up, sleepy heads. Anyone ready for a *loco moco* breakfast?"

Becky sat up and stretched. "Sounds interesting."

Nadia grabbed her arm. "It's a trick. *Loco moco* is a big plate of rice with a hamburger patty on top and smothered in gooey gravy with a fried egg plopped on top. Daddy told me it was bad for me."

"Alex, I smell coffee. A cappuccino and a fresh muffin will be fine."

"Daddy, I want hot chocolate with whipped cream and a macadamia nut muffin."

Rich coffee aromas wafted from the Coffee Gallery across the parking lot, drawing in patrons like an invisible Pied Piper. On the wooden porch, a boy sat next to a cardboard box that meowed. "Free kittens," said the boy as they passed. "You can hold one. They're really soft and cuddly."

A calico furball was in Nadia's arms before Alex could scoot her inside and away from the furry temptation. She nuzzled the kitten. "Daddy, it's soo cute."

"Nadia, we're here for breakfast, not to buy a kitten that requires a lot of care."

"Daddy, it's free, and I'll feed it and clean up its messes and use my allowance for cat food."

"Becky, I need your help."

"I'm here for coffee and a muffin and not to be a referee on whether a darling little girl should have a cute little kitten."

"Whose side are you on?" The sternness drained from his voice. "Okay, Nadia, but you've got to take care of it." He talked to the boy to make sure the kittens were his to give away, then bought a drink and muffin for him. Inside, the barista gave Nadia a cardboard box and newspapers for her new pet.

Even though they were early, there were more than a dozen cars parked on the *mauka* side of the Kamehameha Highway across from Laniakea Beach. Nadia cradled her kitten as she climbed down over volcanic boulders to the sand. On the beach, a teenage girl was laying a thick orange rope in a semicircle around an adult green sea turtle.

"Hi," said the teenage girl. "I'm Tammy, and I will be happy to answer any questions you have about our green sea turtles. The one on the beach is an adult male named Luʻu."

"Um, Tammy, how do you recognize different turtles?"

"The patterns on the neck and head are different. Let me show you the photos in my binder. There aren't that many turtles that come to this beach. Luʻu comes here two or three times a week."

"How do you know it's a boy?"

"Males have a longer tail, and females have short fat ones."

"I would like to do something to protect turtles."

"When you're sixteen, you can volunteer."

"That's way too long to wait."

Alex and Becky sat on the sand—backs against a boulder, sipping cappuccinos as they watched Nadia. "Alex, maybe Nadia will become a marine biologist and stay in Hawaii."

"That's for her to decide."

Minutes later, the teenage girl was holding the kitten, and Nadia was adjusting the rope as Luʻu inched up the beach.

"Alex, I'll miss her a lot. I want to stay in touch but am afraid my life in Boston will be all-consuming."

By mid-morning the beach was crowded with tourists, and they drove a few minutes north to picturesque Waimea Bay. The U-shaped cove had a wide beach, small waves, and beyond, clear water.

"Becky, the water's perfect for swimming in the summer, but during the winter, the bay has dangerously high waves."

They took a short swim with Nadia before returning to their beach chairs and umbrella. Nadia took her boogie board and ran back to play in the ocean. A local girl joined Nadia and showed her how to catch the small nearshore waves.

Alex gently lifted the kitten from the cardboard box. "It's kind of cute."

"Am I hearing the same man that at the coffee shop was telling Nadia she couldn't have a kitten?"

Nadia came running across the beach and tossed her boogie board on the sand. "My friend Tori wants to see my new pet. Daddy, he's licking your hand because he likes you."

He handed the kitten to Nadia. "Maybe your friend can help you choose a Hawaiian name for your pet. Maybe Honu, the Hawaiian name for 'turtle'?"

"Daddy, kittens aren't anything like turtles." She handed her new pet to Tori.

"Nani," said Tori. "That means 'pretty' in Hawaiian."

"I like Nani," said Nadia.

"Nadia, let's take Nani over and show him to my brothers and sisters and give her some fresh milk."

"Daddy, can I?"

"Yes, but don't be a bother to Tori's family."

Tori laughed. "Everyone welcome in Hawaiian family."

They watched as the girls walked across to a family sprawled under a large canvas awning. Nadia was immediately taken into the arms of a rotund Hawaiian woman with big fleshy arms. The kitten was passed among the children while Nadia sat cross-legged on a grass mat eating a heaping plate of food.

"Alex, Nadia has adjusted pretty well after the loss of her mother."

"Thanks to your help. I need to begin seriously looking for someone that will love Nadia as much as Kelsey did."

Becky scooped up a handful of sand and let it sift through her fingers. "You'll never find another Kelsey, and time slips by in the blink of an eye. As Nadia grows older, it will be increasingly difficult to find a woman that loves you and will bond with her."

"Where do I start?"

"You're a handsome, adventurous academic, so you need a smart woman who loves you, the outdoors, and children." She laughed. "But don't expect to find a mate that's into volcanoes."

They took the slow route back to Honolulu following the more scenic side of the island that had yet to experience the over-development on the sunnier western side of Oahu. The two-lane highway hugged the sinuous coast, providing views of crescent coves lined with coconut palms and ironwood trees on the left and lush rainforest sweeping up into the Koʻolau Mountains on the right. Set back in hollows and on hillsides were plantation-style homes—a reminder of the pineapple and sugarcane industries that once dominated the area.

Alex stopped at a roadside fruit-and-vegetable stand but saw no one and was about to drive on when a girl came running down a path from a cottage nestled in a banana and papaya grove. The barefoot teenager had black hair flowing to her waist. She wasn't pushy as she gave prices for the papaya and the bunch of finger bananas he held up. He gave her a ten for the $7.50 price, and she handed him three one-dollar bills in change. She then selected a flower lei from a string of leis and looped it over Nadia's head. "Gift to pretty keiki."

As they drove away, Nadia gushed, "Hawaiians are so friendly and generous.

Alex told her, "*Ohana* means 'family' and is a term I often hear along with *aloha*, that means 'love.' It's the elixir that sets Hawaii apart from other tourist destinations."

"What's *elixir*?"

"Hmm. It's the magic potion that makes Hawaiians especially welcoming to others."

"Like Tori and her family?"

"Yes."

As they neared Kāneʻohe, Nadia asked to stop at the cemetery to show her mother the new kitten. Alex turned into the short drive to the Valley of the Temples Cemetery and past the serene Byodo-In Temple, a giant replica of the 950-year-old Buddhist temple in Japan. As soon as he turned off the engine, Nadia jumped out of the car with her kitten and ran up the grassy knoll.

"Mommy, I got the cutest kitten ever and named him Nani. That means 'pretty' in Hawaiian." She held the kitten over the plaque. He's so pretty with brown, black, and white fur. At first Daddy said no, but he always gives in." She took off her plumeria lei and carefully laid it so it encircled the engraved lava-rock plaque that Alex had cut and polished in his geology lab. "Mommy, I miss you and think about you every day."

Alex and Becky knelt and said prayers, then followed Nadia back to the car. Alex cleared his throat and wiped his eyes when he heard Nadia whispering to her kitten, "Mommy told me not to cry." Becky said nothing as she handed him a tissue and put her arm around his waist.

As they neared the car, Alex paused. "There's Nicole Lamont. Her husband was a colleague of mine and died last year in a car accident. I think I'll go over and see how she's doing."

Becky watched as Alex embraced Nicole as she leaned into him.

Nadia slumped over asleep in the back seat as they drove over the Pali Highway toward Honolulu. Becky put her hand on Alex's shoulder. "Do you find Nicole attractive?"

"Um, yes."

"Maybe you should ask her out and see if there's any chemistry?"

"I wouldn't feel right asking out a friend's wife so soon after he died."

"That so? Any stranger than wanting to ask out Kelsey's best friend, who happens to be engaged?"

"Becky, I haven't asked you out."

"But you want to."

Chapter 23

*A*lex took Becky's advice and asked Nicole to dinner at the Hau Tree in Waikiki. She agreed but told Alex she wasn't up to dating yet.

"Of course," he said with a weak smile.

The dinner and drinks were up to expectations, and the sky filled with stars, yet their conversation was forced with long pauses. Finally, Alex set his half-empty wine glass on the table. "Nicole, I know it's tough moving on after Larry's death. I'm also struggling with the loss of Kelsey and trying to be a good father to Nadia. We both have to move on."

"I know, I know." She looked away. "Alex, my life was so entwined with Larry's, and everything reminds me of him. I'm thinking about leaving Hawaii and traveling around the world to try to find myself again. I might never return to Hawaii, as it holds too many memories. You seem to have recovered better than me."

"I have our daughter Nadia to think about, and that helps. I'm also lucky to have Kelsey's best friend, Becky, helping with Nadia until December."

"Was that the woman with you in the cemetery?"

"Yes."

"I thought she might be your girlfriend."

"She's engaged to a Boston lawyer."

Nicole gazed into Alex's eyes. "So you're not interested in her?"

"I like her, and she loves Nadia. We're just good friends."

"Did she suggest you ask me out?"

"Yes. How did you know?"

"Woman's intuition. Anyway, I enjoyed having dinner with you."

Becky was typing on her laptop when Alex entered. "How was your dinner with Nicole?"

"She wished me luck in finding a wife."

"That's not good."

"She's not ready for dating."

"I bet she contacts you when she's ready to date."

"You're such an optimist."

"There's a large envelope from Misty River Vineyard stamped Proxy. You didn't mention that you owned shares in the exclusive boutique winery."

"You've heard of Misty River Vineyard?"

"Yes. Remember I studied viniculture as an undergrad at UC Davis and worked in a Napa Valley restaurant for two summers."

"Five years ago, I inherited a few shares from my uncle when he died. All I know is the winery doesn't pay any dividends, and with my insignificant number of shares, I just approve management's recommendations. If you're interested, you can read the proxy materials."

"Yes. I'm curious why it doesn't distribute any dividends."

An hour later, she dropped the report in Alex's lap.

"Where do I sign the proxy?"

"Better not. Your measly 32 shares in Misty River Vineyard represent 15.31 percent of the 209 issued shares. In the back of the report are listed the privately held shares in the winery, and the largest shareholder holds 15.31 percent of the company.

"Me?"

"Bingo. Look for yourself." She flipped to the list of shareholders. "If you're Alex Silverton, then you're the top dog."

Alex chucked. "Wow! I'm the largest shareholder in a winery that makes *no* profits."

"True, according to their accounts. Their management costs are high, and production is way below what would be expected from the number of acres in grapes. And listen to this! Armstrong Valley Winery has made an offer to acquire the winery, but management strongly recommends shareholders reject the unsolicited offer. Alex, you need to go to the meeting."

"Becky, I'm unqualified to decide on Misty River's future, plus hobnobbing with a bunch of pretentious wine snobs is something I'm not good at. I'd make a fool of myself."

"Well, if you want, I'll come with you. I'm curious about this little gem of a winery that makes superb wines and no profits. I can give you tips on dealing with pompous wine snobs. I dealt with them while working summers in Napa Valley. Alex, you love new adventures, and here's one we both can enjoy."

The plan was to bring Nadia along and drop her off with Kelsey's parents in San Rafael on the way to the reception and shareholder meeting at the Misty River Winery at the Russian River. Nadia was excited to get out of school and visit her grandparents.

They took the Thursday-morning United flight to the San Francisco International Airport, then drove north on 101 and through the maze of San Francisco city streets to the Golden Gate Bridge. Their compact car was buffeted by the wind as they crossed under the iconic orange towers that disappeared above into the fog.

When Alex turned into Kelsey's parent's driveway, Dora burst from the front door and hurried over to meet them. She scooped Nadia into her arms and smothered her with kisses.

"Nadia, we've missed you so much."

"I've missed you and grandpa too."

The planned brief stop to drop off Nadia wasn't to be, as they had a barbeque planned, and Nadia was treated as the guest of honor.

It was almost 10:00 p.m. when they arrived at the historic Flamingo Hotel in Santa Rosa. After months of living in Alex's home, Becky was comfortable sharing a room as long as they had separate beds. Becky crawled into bed and called to Alex in the bathroom. "Can I trust you to protect me from the big bad wolf?"

"Wolf, wolf."

Alex woke to the lilting sound of singing in the shower. "Becky, will you be long? I really have to pee."

"Yes, I need a long, hot shower. If you can't wait, you can come in, but no peeking."

"Okay." He was distracted by the vaporous shape behind the steamy shower glass.

"You're sure taking a long time."

"I'm just leaving. Mind if I wipe off the steamy glass?"

"Get out!"

The plan was to spend the day visiting wine tasting rooms in the area to give Alex pointers about wines before the reception and shareholder meeting the following day. They also hoped to get comments from competitors about the proposed merger between Armstrong Valley Winery and Misty River Vineyard.

Their first stop was ten minutes north of Santa Rosa at the Kendall-Jackson tasting room set in a fragrant garden of roses. When Alex wavered between the low-cost and higher-cost premium tasting options, Becky handed her credit card to the cashier. "We'll have the premium tasting selection."

"Alex," she whispered, "you need to taste some premium wines and learn how hoity-toity people sip and pontificate about the complexity of aromas in harmony with the wine's balance."

"Just thinking about all the terms and meanings makes me anxious. I wouldn't know a ten-dollar wine from a seventy-five-dollar one."

"Don't worry. At the reception, you'll be served only premium vintages. Just read the descriptions on the medalist wine bottles, then swirl and sip. Next, repeat the words from the bottle, but with the authority and conviction you show when giving a lecture on volcanoes."

"Just parroting what I've read seems like cheating."

"Do you have a better idea?"

"No. I'm a good reader."

Their Kendall-Jackson wine server was knowledgeable and not pretentious. The middle-aged couple next to them flaunted their knowledge of wines for everyone to hear, provoking a duplicitous smile from the server. After tasting a dram of the most expensive reserve cabernet sauvignon, the woman turned to Alex. "Fully developed complexity and balance with notes of blackberry and a hint of oak, don't you agree?"

He tilted his head as he looked at the over-dressed woman wearing a dress that was two sizes too small for her plumpish shape. "The key to the superior bouquet and complexity is the soil near the Russian River—a delicate fusion of minerals extracted over the course of the river through a mélange of Quaternary clays and sandstones with hints of serpentine and weathered Miocene basalt."

A cautious smile and nod as she swirled her flute, then quickly turned away.

Edward, their wine server, leaned over the counter and whispered to Alex, "I don't know what you said, but you sure shut her down."

"I'm a geologist here to learn something about wines and just rambled off random geologic terms."

"You've come on a slow day, and I'll be pleased to give you some pointers." Edward patiently explained the basics of wines and tasting and told him the terms most frequently used. "Our popular cabernet sauvignon has hints of black currants, and it's slight acidity is softened in oak barrels. The zinfandel is a chameleon that can range from light and fruity red, to a rich, hearty wine indistinguishable from a fine cabernet sauvignon."

Alex's head was spinning with wine terms when Becky interceded.

"By any chance have you heard about Misty River Vineyards and their proposed merger with Armstrong Valley Vineyard?"

"Sure. It's the talk of Sonoma County winery people. Misty River Vineyard produces excellent reds, but in such small quantities that it's no threat to other producers. The proposed merger could result in more than doubling production, plus access to Armstrong Valley's national advertising network, so it is being watched with a wary eye by competitors."

The servers at the next two tasting rooms were less helpful about the basics of wines—their voices carrying pretentious notes. The general manager at the last wine tasting room overheard Alex's inquiry about Misty River Vineyard and stepped forward. "You have an interest in the merger?"

"Um, yes, I have a few shares in the Misty River Vineyard."

"Well, if the merger goes through, it will result in a collision of incompatible operating styles and goals. Misty River Vineyard management has recommended that shareholders vote against the proposed merger."

"So what do other producers think about the merger?"

"The proposed merger won't change competition among wineries. If the merger doesn't go through, Misty River Vineyard will remain an insignificant boutique producer. If the merger goes through, it will result in a fractious marriage, so not a near-term threat to other producers."

It was almost three when they arrived at the Korbel Winery for a late-afternoon lunch on their rustic terrace. They shared avocado sandwiches stuffed with alfalfa sprouts, slices of vine-ripened tomato, and their signature tangy, creamy sauce.

"Becky, I'm glad you convinced me to come, but I don't look forward to the vote tomorrow. It sure makes me anxious knowing the fate of Misty River may be in my hands—a total novice."

"But you're smart, and I'm sure you'll vote for what's best for Misty River, and that may not be true of the present management."

"I'll be blamed either way."

"Don't be so sure. You have me as an advisor." She popped a grape in her mouth.

Alex had booked a river-view cabin a five-minute drive from Guerneville. He cautioned Becky not to get her hopes too high about the great Russian River view shown in the brochure. In Guerneville, they picked up a take-out lunch platter of smoked salmon, cheese, grapes, and crackers to eat on the cabin's porch. The rustic cabin was on a low bluff overlooking the river.

Becky laid out the food while Alex opened a bottle of white zinfandel. The sun had dipped below the redwoods when they settled into wooden rocking chairs, the wine and food on the redwood table between them. They exchanged warm smiles as their flutes clinked, then silence as their senses soaked up the tranquility of the setting, the leathery scent of the redwoods, and the lamenting sound of a mourning dove across the river.

"Am I an acceptable stand-in for Elliott?"

Becky put a piece of cheese on a cracker and handed it to Alex. "Maybe too good."

Chapter 24

"*W*ake up."

Alex opened an eye as Becky gently shook his bare shoulder. "What time is it?"

"Almost seven, and the view from the porch is marvelous." Her hand moved to tickle him, and he grabbed her arm, accidently pulling open her pajama top. She jerked away, quickly covering herself. "That wasn't the view I was talking about."

"Just an unintentional but equally marvelous glimpse. Ah, I smell coffee."

"I found a welcoming packet of Folgers coffee and two bagels. Not the vanilla-macadamia nut coffee you're used to."

"Better, as it reminds me of camping with my parents." He slipped on a sweatshirt and followed Becky onto the porch. "You're right, the view is like a Monet painting with the fog softening the details of the river and redwoods."

They watched the tendrils of mist rise from the languid river and seep through the lacy brows of the towering redwoods. In the distance, the sorrowful oowoo-woo-woo-woo of a mourning dove punctuated the silence.

"Becky, sitting here with you is the best part of the trip. I feel perfectly at ease but am dreading today's shareholder meeting."

She laughed. You're probably the only middle-class shareholder, and surely the only professor of volcanology to have a major shareholding in any winery. You should feel honored," she jested. "Those that own privately held stocks in a winery like Misty River Vineyard are high income, and that makes you a rarity."

"Becky, you really know how to build up a guy's confidence."

Becky patted his arm. "I can't think of anyone else I'd rather be with at the shareholder meeting."

Alex stroked the back of her hand. "It's because of you that I came."

The small parking lot was filled with luxury cars, and a smartly dressed young man directed them to the back of the lot. Alex joked, "I guess they don't want our compact car among the shiny Mercedes and Jaguars."

"That's about to change." She tucked her hand under his arm as they strolled over to the short line at the reception desk. "Nothing like a geologist to put some spice into the party."

"Becky, what makes you so confident?"

"Because I know who holds the royal flush."

The sign at the entrance read, "Tasting room closed today. MRV shareholders and invited guests only." Neatly laid out on the table were engraved, shiny-copper badges for shareholders and printed name tags for invited guests. The cheery receptionist greeted people by name and, without checking the list of invitees, handed them their badges along with a crimson rose for the women. There were no unclaimed badges when Alex and Becky stepped up to the table.

"Alex Silverton and my guest, Becky Sims."

The receptionist quickly scanned the list of invited guests, then shook her head. "Mr. Silverton, your name's not on our invitation list. We're closed to the public today, but our tasting room will be open Sunday, two to five."

"Today's reception is for MRV shareholders and guests only. I can give you two complimentary coupons for our wine tasting tomorrow."

Becky reached across the table, flipped the glossy brochure to the last page where the shareholders were listed in order of percentage of stocks owned, and put her finger on the first name. "Does this help?"

The receptionist gasped. "You're Dr. Silverton from Hawaii!"

"Yes, I assumed I was invited when I received the announcement and papers to the special shareholder meeting."

"I'm so sorry about the mix-up. Our managing director, Mr. Corbett, told me the shareholder from Hawaii never attended. I hope you don't mind if I write you and your wife's names on stick-on tags?"

"Ms. Becky Sims is my personal advisor on wines."

"Of course, Miss Sims is most welcome."

The reception was behind the Spanish hacienda-style building, on a vine-shaded patio trimmed with MRV pennants. The view of the Russian River was even better than from their cabin porch. They paused at the edge of the patio and scanned the smartly dressed crowd—women dripping with jewelry and tailored cocktail dresses, and men with sport coats and silk pocket squares. The announcement had said summer causal, and Alex had worn his expensive Tori Richards aloha shirt and tan slacks.

"Becky, I feel like a country bumpkin."

"*Au contriare.* Your fashion statement is about to become *de rigueur.* Now let's enjoy the hors d'oeuvres and wine and meet a few shareholders."

People were in chatty groups, and except for furtive glances their way, the only people to approach them were servers with flutes of wine and appetizers in the shape of grape leaves. Becky giggled as she sipped her wine.

"You're really enjoying this, aren't you?" Alex asked her.

"This is like being on stage in a play when the audience is unaware of the final scene. And where else can we get such tasty appetizers and wine? For a winery that has yet to produce a single dividend, it sure goes all out to impress shareholders."

Alex wasn't as assured as Becky and slipped away to the restroom to make sure he wouldn't have to go during the shareholder meeting. The fixtures were gold-plated, and the linen hand towels were monogrammed MRV in gold. When he returned, Becky was in a lively conversation with a tall, broad-shouldered man with a deep tan and heavy, black-rimmed glasses that reminded Alex of Cary Grant. His equally tanned wife stood out in a stylish safari outfit with epaulets, accented with a necklace of African trading beads.

"Alex, I want you to meet Don and Karen Kingsbury. Mr. Kingsbury is managing director of Armstrong Valley Winery and would like to explain the advantages of their offer to acquire MRV."

Don's smile was genuine and his handshake firm, as was his wife's. "Dr. Silverton, Mr. Corbett told me you weren't coming and always voted in favor of the recommendations of MRV management. But Ms. Sims told me you're undecided on how you will vote."

"Yes, I haven't made a final decision. That's why I'm here. I want to hear both sides before casting my vote."

"Good. Is it okay if we use first names?"

"I prefer it."

"I'm glad you wore an aloha shirt, or I wouldn't have spotted you before the shareholder meeting."

Becky nudged Alex and gave him a smug *I told you so* look.

"Alex, I've talked to every shareholder except you. I was told that you'd already voted by mail, supporting MRV's recommendation. By my count, I have only 43 percent in favor of the merger. So your 15.3 percent of the voting shares will decide whether the merger is approved. Harry Corbett, the managing director of MRV, has vigorously campaigned against the proposed merger, and he personally knows every shareholder but you."

"Why is Corbett so strongly against the merger?"

"In a sentence, he's toast if the acquisition goes through. He's failed to generate value for the shareholders, and he'll lose his cushy job. I give him credit for producing one of the best wines in the region, but MRV uses less than half of the grapes from their vineyard and sells the rest to other wine producers. Their overhead is double ours, and they have almost no national advertising. For a fledgling startup, this would be understandable, but after a decade, shareholders should demand profitability and dividends."

"So what does Armstrong Valley Winery bring to the table that will assure profitability?"

"Our analysis indicates four major changes to MRV are needed. First, we'll double wine production within three years through upgrades to the facilities. Second, we'll overhaul their antiquated financial management system. Third, we'll expand marketing from mainly local to national through Armstrong Valley Winery's marketing network. Finally, there will be changes to MRV's management. Our analysis indicates a 34 percent reduction in costs per bottle and a 2.5 to 3.0 percent dividend to shareholders in the second year, and 4.0 to 4.5 percent in the following years."

Chimes tinkled along with the announcement that shareholders and guests should make their way to the meeting room. Alex and Becky moved to the rear of the line. Corbett stood at the door greeting each person by name—warmly shaking hands along with hugs and air kisses to the women. The line moved slowly as he added personal comments to every shareholder. "How's Amy doing at Stanford? Sorry to hear about your mother's passing," and so on. Here was a man that had mastered the art of schmoozing his financial backers.

As the line dwindled and they neared Corbett, Becky whispered, "Prepare for Corbet's look of astonishment, then gladhanding like you've never experienced."

Corbett paused, a puzzled expression as he read the name-tag stuck to Alex's shirt, then a generous smile as he grasped Alex's hand. "Dr. Silverton, what a pleasant surprise that you were able to come all the way from Hawaii to attend our shareholder meeting." He pumped Alex's hand like the handle of an old-fashioned water pump.

"Mr. Corbett, I apologize for the confusion about my attendance."

"It's all my fault for not calling and inviting you personally. You must use our special guest house during your stay."

"Thank you, but we already have accommodations."

"Dr. Silverton, I hope you're able to spend a few days in the area, so I can show you around and arrange a dinner party for you and your wife."

"Unfortunately, we can only stay for the shareholder meeting. Ms. Sims is my guest and advisor."

Corbett turned to Becky and warmly took her hand. "A pleasure to meet you, Ms. Sims. My wife, Wendy, just loves

Hawaiian clothes, and your dress is stunning. I hope you won't mind sharing with my wife the boutique that carries your fashionable Hawaiian dress."

Becky flashed a Cheshire cat grin. "I'm a grad student on a budget and bought my dress on sale at an ABC Store in Waikiki."

"Well, you sure can teach Wendy a thing or two about getting the *haut couture* look at bargain prices."

Becky fluttered her eyelashes along with a coquettish smile. Her wily subterfuge was missed by Corbett, who viewed these novice outsiders as easily manipulated for his purposes.

"Please come with me so I can ensure you have seats in the front row." Corbett asked a couple if they would mind moving to the second row so their distinguished visitors from Hawaii could have a seat. There were low murmurs and bewildered looks of shareholders as they wondered about these interlopers.

Corbett strolled to the podium, straightened the cuffs of his dress shirt, then opened a leather folder embossed with the MRV logo. He gazed over the people he had carefully cultivated to view owning MRV shares as membership in an exclusive fraternity. Each shareholder received engraved wine glasses and complimentary bottles of MRV wine every Christmas. *One* person in the room could destroy everything.

"It is indeed a pleasure to see that every shareholder was able to attend the most important shareholder meeting in MRV's history. Before we get down to business, I have the esteemed pleasure to introduce Dr. Alex Silverton and Ms. Becky Sims, who flew from Hawaii to attend this meeting. Would you please stand so we can welcome you to the MRV family?"

Corbett led the applause. Alex nervously smiled as he nodded to the audience, while Becky gave a cheerful smile and a reserved queen's wave. There was a rustling of papers as everyone checked the list of shareholders in the back of their glossy brochures.

Corbett launched into a PowerPoint presentation of the financial accounts of the previous twelve months, with optimistic projections for the coming year. The presentation was slick and highlighted the two gold and one silver medalist awards over the past year. Corbett read the write-up in the *California Wine Tasters Magazine*:

Misty River Vineyard is the most under-appreciated producer of premium cabernet sauvignon and zinfandel wines in Sonoma County.

"Ladies and gentlemen, you have been patient shareholders while we invested our profits into building the finest boutique winery in Sonoma County, and I believe, in California. I want to announce today that next year we anticipate issuing our first dividend to our patient shareholders."

Corbett then presented a professionally produced twenty-minute film that included all aspects of the business from planting grapevines to the final product, and the gold and silver medalist awards. Over half of the film was devoted to cameos of shareholders and spouses, plus important county officials espousing the contributions of MRV to Sonoma County. At the end of the film, Corbett lightheartedly said, "Perhaps we should have next year's shareholder meeting in Hawaii."

After the self-congratulatory, feel-good advertising film, Corbett turned to the purpose of the shareholder meeting. "Misty River Vineyard exists today because of the thirty-seven shareholders that recognize the value of a boutique winery producing premium wines among the giant producers that are more concerned with volume than quality. We have purposely avoided competing with larger wineries, such as Armstrong Valley Winery, that target the mass market. The unsolicited offer from Armstrong Valley Winery is at odds with the MRV philosophy and tradition, and management strongly recommends that you vote *no* to the proposed acquisition, so we can continue the tradition of making the finest wines in the area." Corbett paused while his faithful shareholders applauded. "My dear friends, Armstrong Valley Winery does a good job in producing wines for the masses—you know, the people who drive compact cars and pickups that you won't see in our parking lot."

Alex nudged Becky with his elbow.

"Mr. Kingsbury, the managing director of Armstrong Valley Winery, has asked to present the case for acquisition. Mr. Kingsbury, the podium is yours."

Kingsbury stood and walked to the podium, opened a thin folder, and then clasped his hands and rested them on the podium as he gazed over the audience—his smile friendly yet reserved. "Mr. Corbett, thank you for giving me the opportunity to present the case for the proposed acquisition. My wife, Karen, is distributing summaries of the proposed acquisition prepared by a well-known, accredited, independent financial consulting firm. I hope I can convince you in my comments that our proposal will benefit both companies. I want to begin by complimenting Mr. Corbett and his staff for the premium wines MRV consistently produces. We examined seven small wineries in Sonoma and Napa counties, and MRV came out on top as the one with the most upside growth and profit potential over the next decade.

"There are four key reasons to support the acquisition as discussed in detail in the handouts. First, we plan to expand marketing from mainly northern California to the entire United States, including Hawaii." He smiled and nodded toward Alex. "We wouldn't want to disappoint MRV's largest shareholder. Second, production will be doubled in the first three years after acquisition, reducing costs per bottle by 35 to 40 percent. Third, the financial management system will be upgraded to be fully compatible with Armstrong Valley's system. Fourth, there will be changes in senior management. The MRV brand name will be retained, and it will continue to be marketed to buyers willing to pay a substantial premium to Armstrong Valley Winery brands. Our marketing studies show that over half of buyers of Armstrong Valley Winery wines eventually move up to higher-priced wines, and we hope to capture a portion of that market with MRV wine."

"Mr. Kingsbury!" Corbett interrupted. "You're mixing apples and oranges. Buyers view Armstrong Valley Winery as a producer of cheap wines. When they switch to higher-priced premium wines, it will not be wines branded by your company. The acquisition would cheapen the MRV brand and be counter to our philosophy."

"Mr. Corbett, you raised an important question that must be considered in the vote today. As I said, the Misty River Vineyard name will be retained, and our marketing studies show that buyers of premium wines buy wines that produce gold and silver awards. We plan to triple MRV entries in wine tasting contests. Increased sales are meaningless if the results don't show up on the bottom line. The 10.4 percent growth in sales projected by Mr. Corbett is suspect when compared to an average increase of 3.2 percent per year over the past five years. However, under Armstrong Valley Winery management, we believe that in the first year after acquisition that a

28 percent increase in production is realistic by using the grapes MRV has been selling to competitors, plus streamlining operations. We estimate that the 7.3 percent operating profits before taxes can be doubled within three years. During the first year, operating profits will be invested in expanding and modernizing the facilities, and dividends will be paid starting in the second year. Our goal is an annual dividend in the range of 3.5 to 4.5 percent. Armstrong Valley Winery will invest $21 million to upgrade and expand MRV and receive 220 newly issued shares, bringing the total issued shares to 429. This will give Armstrong Valley 51.3 percent of the shares in Misty River Winery and is necessary for us to make the changes needed and achieve the future sales and profitability goals I have outlined. Every shareholder has the option of selling their shares to Alexander Valley Winery for 30 percent above their market value today. Regardless of how you vote today, you are all invited to visit our winery, and I will personally show you why our profits are well above the industry average."

Corbett clenched his fist, then quickly regained his composure. "Are there any comments or questions before we vote on whether to continue MRV's tradition of premium wine production or allow our company to be swallowed up by a company producing cheap and inferior wines?"

Alex raised his hand.

"Dr. Silverton, you have a comment before we vote."

"Yes." He stood, dropping several pages that scattered at his feet. "I drive a compact car." There were no snickers. "Mr. Kingsbury's presentation was compelling. I am new to the wine industry, and Becky Sims is advising me, as she understands the economics of California wine production. It appears that MRV has been run more as a wealthy social club than a commercial business. Mr. Kingsbury is offering both, and that's why I'm going to vote yes in favor of the acquisition."

Mr. Corbett gripped the sides of the podium as he gazed over his carefully cultivated congregation. "Dr. Silverton, I think the shareholders should know what specific qualifications you and Ms. Sims have in the wine industry."

Alex nodded. "Yes, I'm a geologist specializing in volcanology and have no specific expertise in the wine industry, as Mr. Corbett wants you to know. However, I do want my investments to earn money. My associate, Ms. Sims, has a degree from the University of California, Davis, on wine industry economics and has reviewed your financial statements."

Corbett smirked. "Ms. Sims certainly has a good academic education but doesn't have practical experience outside of the classroom. I have over twenty years of commercial experience, and the proof is the excellent wines produced by MRV."

Kingsbury spoke up. "Ms. Sims has no skin in the game and provides an unvarnished objective view of the economic benefits of the proposed acquisition."

Corbett bellowed, "Unvarnished and naïve! My dear shareholders, you have the choice between my extensive experience versus a well-meaning but inexperienced university student's. Keep these facts in mind as you decide our future."

The vote took less than fifteen minutes. The financial manager of MRV and an independent auditor tallied the votes, then handed them to Corbett.

Corbett frowned and shook his head as he stared at the sheet of paper, then looked up, lips pursed. "The majority have spoken with 131 yes votes out of a total of 209 votes or 62.7 percent in favor of the acquisition. With this disappointing result, I'm announcing my immediate resignation as managing director of Misty River Vineyard."

Kingsbury rose from his seat. "Mr. Corbett, we would like you to remain as an advisor to the new MD for the next twelve months, and your compensation package will be tied to the performance of MRV."

Becky whispered to Alex, "Shrewd move to ensure Corbett doesn't sabotage the transition."

As they left the meeting, the receptionist met them with a gift basket of cheeses, Italian salami, caviar, grapes, and two bottles of MRV wine. Several shareholders approached them and said they had been concerned about MRV management practices but were hesitant to challenge Corbett.

Don and Karen Kingsbury walked with them back to their car.

"Becky, we're both alums of UC Davis. Twenty-six years ago, I came from Cape Town, South Africa, to study viticulture at Davis and met Don, the love of my life. I hope you'll accept our invitation to stay with us the next time you two visit the area."

Becky was effervescent as she recounted the cascade of events over the past three hours. "You may be just a volcanologist, but by tomorrow, your name will be known throughout the Northern California wine industry. You might even be featured in a wine industry magazine. Imagine the heading: 'Volcanologist Causes an Eruption at Mistry River Vineyard Shareholder Meeting."

"Ha, ha. I'm not doing any interviews about wines. Seriously, none of this would have happened without your insistence that I come to the meeting."

"Alex, your short speech to the shareholders was convincing." She poked him in the side. "If I were attending UH, I might even sign up for one of your volcanology classes."

Chapter 25

*B*ecky put her hand on Alex's shoulder as they pulled out of MRV's driveway and turned west on River Road. Her fingers stroked the hairs at the nape of his neck. "I haven't had so much fun in years."

"I was really nervous as the votes were counted, as Corbett had made a strong case not to trust my judgment," Alex told her. "If you hadn't read the shareholder materials, I would have blindly voted my shares in favor of management—the biggest mistake of my life."

"Alex, you saved MRV, and by my calculation, your shares are worth about three million, and that could soon double. Not bad for a novice volcanologist."

"A relief, because now I know I have enough to pay for Nadia's university education, something I promised Kelsey before she died."

"Your name will be known all over the wine country when you return to next year's shareholder meeting."

"I hope to know a little more by next year and will bring Nadia and take her on a canoe trip. I suppose there's no chance of you coming with us?"

"Elliott knows a lot about wine and schmoozing with rich people. Would you mind if I brought him?"

"No way I'm sharing a cabin with you and Elliott."

"Ditto." Becky rolled down the window, letting her hair dance in the wind. "The smell of the redwoods is intoxicating. Just imagine that these redwoods were already hundreds of years old when Columbus discovered America. Imagine the secrets they could reveal if they could talk."

"Their growth rings tell stories, recording each year's weather and forest fires."

"Are layers of sandstone analogous?"

"Hmm? Yes and no. Sandstones contain fossil remains of the things that lived when the sand was deposited, and trees don't."

"How about insects in the amber that oozes from certain trees?"

"If I'm ever on a debate team, I want you. There are so many things I need you for."

Becky mused, *I hope Elliott feels the same about me.*

The temperature hovered in the mid-nineties as they pulled up to their cabin. The sultry air carried the leathery scent of the redwoods and buzzing sounds of cicadas. The cabin, even with large, screened windows, was unbearably hot, and they moved to the shaded porch. Below, the jade-green river was stirred by a procession of Burke's canoes. Becky's waves were enthusiastically returned by canoers—some blowing kisses.

"Becky, isn't it strange that the people waving to us would look at us with suspicion if we greeted them in the city?"

"Not so strange. We adapt to our environments. They can easily see that we're not a threat, but there's no filter on a city street, so people must be wary."

"You sound like a psychologist."

"Working summers as a waitress in a Napa Valley restaurant gave me experience in judging people."

"What was the biggest factor?"

"Usually not the specific words, but the tone and facial expressions."

They remained on the wooden rocking chairs until twilight, after the canoes were gone and the river again languid. The only sounds—the occasional splash of trout jumping to catch insects hovering over the water. A pair of doves cooed in the distance, accompanied by the resonance of clinking wine glasses. Their planned meal in Guerneville was pointless after the MRV gift basket and wine.

Alex took the empty glass from Becky's hand and set it next to the empty wine bottle. "There's a chill in the air," he whispered as he put his arm around Becky. She leaned closer, her head resting on his shoulder—hair tickling his neck. His fingers caressed the silky strands as she tilted her head and their lips met.

Becky slowly pulled away. "Alex, it's time for us to go to *separate* beds."

Alex lay in bed long after Becky fell asleep, listening to her purring—aroused.

Becky awoke and looked at her watch—2:17 a.m. The bed next to her was empty, and the bathroom light wasn't on. *Where's Alex at this late hour?* She was drawn toward the moonlight streaming through the door at the rear of the cabin.

From the porch, she heard a familiar sound from her child-hood—the splashes of pebbles being tossed into water. Her gaze homed in on the source—the diminutive shape of a man squatting at the river's edge. This awkward, gentle geologist had stolen Kelsey's and Nadia's hearts, and tugged at Becky's.

Alex turned toward the soft sound of footsteps in the sand. "What are you doing here?"

She shoved a folded blanket into his arms. Her bathrobe slipped from her shoulders, revealing a sinuous figure silhouetted in the moonlight.

"Damn you," she whispered.

Chapter 26

"*O*uch! That hurts!"

"Shush, you big baby. You're lucky I only scratched your back. Now sit still while I rub lotion on your itty-bitty wounds."

"Last night at the river's edge was a fantasy come true."

"Last night never happened. You know I'm in love with Elliott, and I'm going to marry him. He's a perfect gentleman, not someone that will take advantage of a vulnerable woman on the beach."

"I was tossing pebbles in the river when you showed up with a blanket."

"You know the setting was very seductive. Your gallant performance at the MRV shareholder meeting, then a romantic cabin overlooking the Russian River, and too much wine. A romantic dream woke me, then your moonlit silhouette on the beach. You looked so lonely, innocent, and vulnerable. I had a lapse in judgment."

"The romantic dream that woke you—was it Elliott or me?"

"My dreams are private and none of your business. I want you to promise never to mention our little tryst, and from this day forward, you're to treat me strictly as a family friend."

Alex gazed into her eyes, searching for her true feelings, but she didn't blink. "I promise to try my best, and my lips are sealed."

"Good!"

Nadia was baking cookies when they arrived at her grand-parent's home.

"Can't I stay a little longer?" she complained as she stuffed her new clothes and books into her backpack.

"You have school on Monday, but I'll bring you back next summer, and we'll take a canoe trip down the Russian River."

"Can Becky come?"

"Nadia, I'll be in Boston with my husband Elliott, so I won't be able to come. But you and your father are always welcome to visit us."

A week passed before Nadia approached her father on their lanai. "Daddy, I know something is wrong between you and Becky. You two used to laugh and joke with each other, but since we returned from California, you barely speak to each other. You always told me you would tell me the truth when I ask a question. You treat each other like . . . like strangers. What happened?"

Alex stroked his daughter's hair. "Nadia, you're observant. You see, I'm attracted to Becky, and she cares a lot for me but is in love with Elliott and going to marry him. We both agreed that the attraction between us wasn't a good idea, so that's why you have noticed a change. It's for the best."

"Why can't she change her mind and marry you?"

"That's up to her, not me."

"Maybe if I'm really nice to Becky, she'll change her mind."

"Becky loves you, and her decision to marry Elliott has nothing to do with you."

"If she marries you, she gets me, too, and will never have to get fat to have a baby. It's like a two-for-one deal."

Alex laughed and kissed her on the forehead.

Naomi Tanaka, a second-generation Japanese American, was Nadia's best friend at Mid-Pacific Institute. Her grandparents had come to Hawaii to work on a sugarcane plantation and scrimped until they had enough to open a tiny clapboard shack selling cheap imported dry goods that Japanese workers preferred. Seventy years later, Tanaka stores were on three islands.

Nadia picked Naomi as her partner on the school outing to Pearl Harbor. The big-screen documentary of the surprise attack on December 7, 1941, brought Naomi to tears. Following the short movie, the class took the National Park Service launch to the glistening white-marble memorial located over the sunken USS Arizona. The shrine in the shape of a futuristic ship was positioned at right angles to the USS Arizona, forming a cross when seen from the air.

Naomi pulled Nadia along as she maneuvered through the crowd to the marble wall containing the engraved names of the 1,177 men that died in the surprise attack on Pearl Harbor. They squeezed between the tourists to the front.

Next to them stood a paunchy man with plaid shorts and a confederate flag pin on his baseball cap. "Marge, look at all those names of our boys killed by the sneaky Japs. I'll never trust one of those Japs as long as I live."

Naomi pointed to the wall of names. "Nadia, Kenichi Tanaka was my grandfather and proud to wear a navy uniform. He died defending America."

The woman standing next to her loudmouthed husband, snapped, "Burt. You're a big fool and don't know when to keep your mouth shut!"

Several people clapped, and a woman stepped from the crowd and gave Naomi a flower lei.

As Halloween approached, Alex asked Nadia what kind of costume she wanted. "I don't want to dress up this year. I'll just hand out candy to trick-or-treaters."

Alex suspected Nadia's reluctance to dress up was because it was at last year's Halloween celebrations that she discovered her mother was sick. "Nadia, your mother wouldn't want you to stay home because of her."

"I know."

Alex's anxiety about Nadia staying home on Halloween ended when her best friend invited the whole class to a Halloween party at her house. Nadia wanted to buy a princess outfit at a particular store, and the reason became evident when Alex dropped her off at the party, and Naomi ran out to meet her in an identical dress.

Alex took Becky to Restaurant Row, a complex of restaurants a few blocks from the central Honolulu business district. It was a popular gathering place for adults in costumes on Halloween and a nice place to dine away from Waikiki. When the sashimi was served, Becky swirled a morsel in soy and wasabi and offered it to Alex.

"I was harsh with you after the California trip because I was angry with myself for letting my emotions get carried away. It scares me that I love two men. If I'd met you first, I'd have married you. But I fell in love with Elliott first and have made my choice. That's how life is."

"Becky, I was making a mess caring for Nadia after Kelsey died, and you stepped in to make my family whole again. I didn't plan on falling in love with anyone so soon after Kelsey died, but I did. I know it can never be, but I'm thankful you have remained to give your love to Nadia and help me heal from the loneliness. I want to do something special for you before you leave—something memorable."

"Not necessary. You already did."

"The Russian River?"

"Yes and no. I was in love with you before our tryst at the Russian River, when my *feelings* took control over my *brain*. It's a memory I'll never forget, but did not alter my commitment to Elliott. Alex, when Elliott comes for Thanksgiving, I want you to treat him with warmth and civility."

"I promise, and I'll give you two the master bedroom in my home."

"That's taking civility too far. I'm not going to make love with Elliott in your home, and definitely not in your bed. We'll stay at a nice hotel in Waikiki. I want Elliott to like Hawaii so he'll want to return in the future."

Elliott had preferred that Becky fly to Boston to have Thanksgiving dinner with his parents and two sisters and their spouses and four children but had acquiesced when Becky agreed to have future holiday meals with his family in Boston.

Alex was waiting with Becky and Nadia in the arrivals area as Elliott strolled off his flight with the first-class passengers, his blue blazer slung over his shoulder. He had a relaxed yet confident swagger that enhanced his good looks.

Becky sashayed across to her beau in a tight-fitting dress and slipped a fragrant lei over his head, followed by a passionate kiss as he pulled her against his chest.

"Elliott, I want you to meet Alex and his darling daughter, Nadia, that you've heard so much about. Elliott shook Alex's hand as they eyed each other, then turned to Nadia and patted her on the head. "So you're the girl that's keeping Becky away from me."

Nadia smiled briefly, then looked away. Alex quickly filled in the uncomfortable silence. "Becky's been of immense help caring for Nadia. I feel guilty for keeping Becky away from you for so long."

Becky rolled her eyes. *No you don't.*

Becky and Elliott walked behind Alex and Nadia down to the baggage claim area. While Nadia ran over to collect tourist brochures, Alex stayed by the baggage carousel to pick up Elliott's oversized suitcase. He pulled the suitcase ahead so he wouldn't see the lovebirds and kept his eyes fixed on the highway during the drive into Waikiki beach. He turned on Hawaiian music to drown out the murmurs from the rear seat. At the Halekulani Hotel, he remained just long enough for Elliott's bag to be taken by the porter, then waved and drove away.

"Daddy, I don't care much for Becky's boyfriend. He patted me on the head like I'm a puppy dog."

"Honey, he's probably not used to being around children, and his mind was on Becky. I want you to treat him nicely when he comes to our home for Thanksgiving."

"I know, Daddy." She kicked off her flip-flops and put her feet on the dashboard. "She's making a big mistake."

"Nadia, it's best not to judge people before you get to know them. He's smart and handsome and working very hard to complete his medical degree at Harvard, and Becky can look forward to a comfortable life with Elliott."

Nadia crossed her arms over her chest and frowned. "Becky told me that girls are way better at figuring out men than the other way around. So tell me why she would choose Elliott instead of us? She told me a hundred times she loves me, and when I asked her if she loved you, she said yes, but in a different way than Elliott. And she told me she likes Hawaii way more than Boston. So she can change her mind and marry you."

"Whatever her reasons, it's her life, and we must respect her choice. And, Nadia, I see your toes wiggling, and that usually means you're thinking about something mischievous. I'm warning you to behave when Elliott comes over."

The three of them had spent the week before Elliott's arrival planning every detail of the traditional Thanksgiving dinner. The refrigerator was crammed with dishes ready to go into the oven or on the stovetop. The only exception to the traditional meal was the ahi sashimi that Nadia insisted on having as the appetizer.

Elliott and Becky arrived an hour late, and Alex was going to skip the appetizer, fearing the turkey and vegetables would be overcooked.

"Daddy, you can't leave out sashimi, my favorite part of the meal."

"Alex," Becky said, "I like sashimi, too, and it will be a new experience for Elliott."

Nadia's delicacy was served along with a pinot grigio in the living room. The coffee table was covered with the embroidered tablecloth Alex had brought back from Vietnam. He poured three glasses of wine while Nadia brought the platter of sliced, bright-pink sashimi from the kitchen.

"Elliott, you'll love this," Becky said as she mixed green wasabi with soy sauce in a tiny dish. Using chopsticks, she plucked a sliver of tuna from the plate and swished it around in the sauce. "As the honored guest, you get the first tasty piece."

He jerked his head back as she moved the pink morsel toward his lips. "Becky, I don't eat raw fish! The slippery texture makes me gag."

The sharpness of his rebuke caused an awkward pause before he regained his composure. "I appreciate the thoughtful offer, but I'm not used to island delicacies."

Becky turned to Nadia. "I know who will really love the first bite."

"Elliott, how about cheese and crackers?" Alex interjected.

"The wine is sufficient." He warily watched as Nadia, Becky, and Alex ate the sashimi with chopsticks, with Nadia and Becky playfully fighting over the last piece.

Elliott was in his element at the dinner with a thoughtful toast about the meaning of Thanksgiving and lively conversation about lives he had pulled back from the edge of death in the emergency room. He deftly wove a few lines of Robert Frost's poetry into the conversation as he looked into Becky's eyes. Becky maintained an enigmatic smile through most of the dinner, laughing politely at Elliott's polished jokes. While Alex was reserved, Nadia added her version of her father's adventures that seemed to bewilder Elliott. Her chin smeared with the glazing from a turkey leg, she cut into Elliott's discourse. "My daddy goes into dangerous jungles where there are poisonous snakes that can kill you like that—" she snapped her fingers "—and crocodiles that swallow people whole in one bite, and natives that eat people, and boiling lava from volcanoes, and—"

"Nadia, honey, you're exaggerating the dangers. The native people don't eat people anymore."

"Daddy, remember your friend working there said his Indonesian guide was captured and eaten?"

"Yes, but that was a long time ago."

"I'm not so sure. Who's going to talk if they've been eaten . . . huh?"

Elliott forced a smile as he looked across the table at the petulant child that was trying to outdo him with stories about her dad. "Alex, your daughter will make a good debater when she grows up. What do you want her to become?"

"My job is to give her a safe and happy home and encourage her curiosity. The rest is up to Nadia."

After dropping off Elliott and Becky at their hotel, Alex drove two miles to the Diamond Head end of Waikiki Beach to build a sandcastle with Nadia. He scooped sand with a plastic beach bucket, and Nadia patted it with her hands, then added bits of coral and feathers to the top.

Later, Nadia snuggled against Alex as they watched the sunset. "Nadia, I know you like sashimi, but it isn't your favorite food, so why were you so insistent on having sashimi as an appetizer?"

"You'll be angry if I tell you."

"Nadia, you know the truth is best, and I won't be mad."

"Becky told me that Elliott had never had raw fish, so I wanted to make him look silly, so Becky could see you're better."

"You're a stinker to try and embarrass Elliott. You stole the show with your exaggerated story about the dangers I faced in the jungle." They both laughed, and every time Elliott's name was mentioned, Nadia giggled and covered her mouth.

They remained after the sunset watching the glittering lights on a dinner cruise ship. "Nadia, I want to do something special for Becky before she leaves in January. I was thinking we could all go to the Big Island to see the volcano. Remember how much you enjoyed the trip with Kelsey?"

"Bad idea. If you really want to impress Becky, take her to Thailand to ride on an elephant."

"Nadia, that's impossible! She's leaving in a little more than a month, and I couldn't make the arrangements on such short notice. Why Thailand?"

"Remember when you were in Papua New Guinea? Becky and I went to the Honolulu Zoo. Well, when we saw the Asian elephants, she said her dream was to go to Thailand and ride an elephant, but she said Elliott would never do something like that. I'm sure if you take Becky and me to Thailand to ride elephants, she'll change her mind and marry you."

"Nadia, I'm not trying to get Becky to change her mind about marrying Elliott."

"Why not?"

Chapter 27

Nadia's suggestion about a trip to Thailand was impractical at every level. December was the holiday season, and flights were heavily booked and expensive. Nadia wasn't aware of the tryst at the Russian River and Becky's determination to avoid another romantic situation with Alex. Then there was Elliott, who surely wouldn't want his fiancée traveling to exotic Thailand with another man.

After a restless night, Alex paced the kitchen floor, a mug of coffee in his hand. He had pushed Thailand from his mind and was thinking about a trip to Kauai rather than the Big Island. They could take a boat tour to the craggy Na Pali Coast and probably see dolphins along the way. He was kneeling to wipe up spots of coffee on the floor when Nadia opened her bedroom door.

"Nadia, you're up early. What are you doing with your Menehune bank?"

"Daddy, you can have all the money I've saved for a trip to Thailand, and I'll clean my room every week without being told, and—"

"Nadia, honey, it's not about money." He struggled to hold back tears as he looked into the innocent eyes of his daughter. "It takes time to arrange a trip like that, and Becky will only be with us for a little more than a month."

"Have you even tried?"

"Um, no."

"Then you don't know. You always tell me not to give up without even trying."

Alex nodded. "Nadia, you're impossible. Okay, I'll check with my travel agent, but when she says the flights are fully booked, I don't want any complaints from you."

"Deal!" and she gave him a wet kiss on his neck. Before he could stop her, she ran into Becky's room, and a minute later, they appeared, Becky still in her pajamas.

"What's this about a trip to Thailand to ride elephants? Didn't you think about asking me first?"

"It was just ten minutes ago that Nadia pestered me into checking on flights. Last-minute flights to Asia in December are almost impossible to get, particularly for three. I wanted to know if it was possible before asking you. Anyway, would you go if seats were available?"

Hands on her hips, she locked her gaze on Alex. "You know why it's a bad idea."

"Then the answer's no," Alex said.

"Becky, pleeaase?" Nadia begged.

Becky bit her lip as she gazed into Alex's eyes. "I'll have to ask my fiancé, and he probably will nix the idea."

Nadia jumped up and down, hanging on Becky's arm. "We can ride an elephant together."

She was surprised that Elliott answered on the first ring. "Becky, I'm just about to start my shift in the ER, so we'll have to make the call short."

"Alex and Nadia are planning a short trip to Thailand in December and have asked me to join them. I would like to go if it's okay with you. You know I've always wanted to go there to ride an elephant."

"Becky, I expected you to fly back to Boston and spend Christmas with my family."

"I know, and I miss you so much. But I'll be there in January, and this may be my only chance to go to Asia, as I know you prefer European and Caribbean trips."

"Well, okay. You better get Asia out of your system, because I'm not going there. I don't like Thai cuisine or getting dysentery from unsanitary food. Are you sure you're safe to travel with Alex?"

What does Elliott mean? she nervously thought. "He's been there before and has contacts to look after us, so I'll be safe."

"Okay. But, Becky, I don't want you running off into some snake-infested jungle with this Indiana Jones guy."

"Don't worry. Nadia will be along, so everything will be kid-friendly."

"One last thing. Make sure Alex doesn't get any romantic ideas about you."

"Elliott, he's still getting over Kelsey's death and knows how much we're in love. I worry more about some enchanting blond nurse sinking her talons into my handsome Harvard doctor."

Alex doubted that American Express would be open at 8:00 a.m. on Saturday. But if there was an available seat, Anne would find it. She answered on the second ring. "Anne Umeda speaking."

"Hi, Anne, it's Alex Silverton. I didn't expect you to be open today."

"We're not, but I have a difficult client that needs a last-minute reservation to Tokyo."

"I was wondering if there might be three round-trip economy seats available to Thailand?"

"What month?"

"This December. I know it's nearly impossible to get a seat on such short notice."

"Alex, you're impossible! One seat is possible with last-minute cancelations, but three seats is a real stretch on such short notice and during the holiday season. Only chance is a cancelation, and it will have to be an instant purchase with no changes or refunds. And forget about discounts. Do you still want me to try?"

"Yes. A two-week trip would be ideal, with a week on the beach in Phuket, and if possible, a stopover in Bangkok and maybe three days in Siem Reap to see Angkor Wat."

"And I suppose you want white-gloved limousine service at every stop?"

He chuckled at her sarcasm. "Anne, I promise I'll make it up to you."

"Not on your salary. Now, if you'll stop using up my time with your sweet talk, I'll check out flight options."

Anne called back twenty minutes later. "Alex, five seats just opened up for instant purchase for a two-week package that includes two nights in the deluxe Oriental Hotel, three nights in Siem Reap, Cambodia, in a French-style guest house, and five nights in a beach-side resort in Phuket that has two elephants to ride. The package price is $7,865. Can a struggling professor handle that, because it's an instant-purchase deal? Oops, two seats just sold."

"I'll take it!"

"Hold on a moment." He could hear the chatter of keys. "Do I use your credit card information on file?"

"Yes."

"Got it! You only have flexibility on the flights from Bangkok to Phuket, as there are many daily flights. I'll email you the itinerary."

"Thanks, Anne. You're a miracle worker. What can I bring you from Thailand?"

"A nice one-carat ruby set in gold would be nice," she jested. "Enough chatter. I've got another impossible client to take care of."

Alex hung up and turned to Becky and Nadia. "We're going to Bangkok, then Siem Reap to see the ancient ruins around Angkor Wat. And just for Nadia, a resort on the beach in Phuket that has elephants to ride."

Nadia jumped into her father's arms. "You're the best dad ever!"

Becky rubbed her hand across Alex's shoulders. "Thank you. I never expected such a generous going-away present." She turned away and walked into the bathroom and locked the door. Standing in front of the mirror, she was the only one to see her doubts. A trip to exotic Thailand came with risks. She had failed to contain her romantic feelings at the Russian River. At least with Nadia along, there wouldn't be a resurgence of uncontrolled romantic feelings.

None of them could have known that a far greater danger awaited them.

The days prior to their departure were packed with both holiday and trip planning activities—buying and decorating a Christmas tree, shopping for holiday gifts, attending a play at Nadia's school, and trips to Barnes & Noble to peruse travel guides.

Their flight itinerary included a transfer from United to Thai International in Narita International Airport. Fifteen minutes out of Honolulu Airport, the seatbelt sign was turned off, and Nadia sprawled out between them, her head in Becky's arms and feet in her dad's lap.

Becky gently stroked the hair of the sleeping child. "Nadia's so angelic when she's asleep."

"That's because you didn't get her stinky feet."

Moments later, a sock-covered foot levitated toward his nose, and a faint smile appeared on his sleeping daughter's face. He tickled the innersole of Nadia's foot, and she jerked her foot away and giggled.

On the two-hour stopover at Narita in Japan, they were given complimentary passes to the Thai International lounge. Throughout most of the flight across China to Thailand, Nadia occupied herself with games and reading one of her Magic Treehouse novels.

Bangkok's massive Suvarnabhumi International Airport was the bustling hub for connecting flights throughout Southeast Asia, with a cacophony of sights, sounds, and fragrances as Buddhists, Muslims, Hindus and Hill Tribe people surged through customs. As they stepped out of air-conditioned customs, they were assaulted by sweltering humidity laden with ginger and the spice-scented smoke of cigarettes. Their fixed price, flamingo-pink airport taxi careened in and out of traffic to their hotel, where they were greeted by the doorman in a ceremonial starched-white military-style uniform festooned with shiny brass buttons.

A Thai woman in a shimmering Thai silk dress greeted them with the traditional *wai* (hands together in a prayer-like gesture) and escorted them to the check-in counter.

The historic Oriental Hotel oozed with elegance, from the fifteen-foot-high flower display and marble elephants inlaid with mother-of-pearl in the lobby, to the eye-catching Thai prints in the hallways and rooms.

"Alex, when I saw the movie *The King and I,* I fell in love with the fictionized version of the king of Siam and an English schoolteacher. I wrote a report in my history class about Siam and always wanted to come and see if it feels anything like the movie."

"So, Becky, what are your first impressions?"

"Hmm. The noise and traffic in Bangkok are a little off-putting, but the exotic essence is infused in the city. The ubiquitous presence of Buddhists in saffron robes adds a touch of tranquility to the apparent chaos."

Their fourth-floor room was decorated with the art and styles of Thailand, plus two queen-sized beds with Thai silk bedspreads. In Nadia's eyes, the four oversized pillows on each bed demanded a pillow fight, and she jumped on a bed and was about to launch a pillow when her dad shook his head. "No pillow fights or using the beds as trampolines."

Becky stood at the window taking in the view of the Chao Phraya River and the hotel's pool. "Nadia, I see two children playing in the pool. How about all of us go down for a dip and iced Thai tea?"

Nadia raced ahead as they followed in the hotel's monogrammed robes over their swimsuits. After a dip in the lukewarm water, Alex and Becky moved to a bed-sized canopied lounge next to the pool, leaving Nadia to play with two British children. They ordered Thai iced tea (spiced black tea with sweetened condensed milk) and fishcakes with a sweet dipping sauce.

Becky lay back on a log-shaped silken pillow, her head inches from Alex's. "This is right out of Somerset Maugham and Joseph Conrad novels."

Alex nudged closer, her wet hair against his cheek. "Becky, during the days of steamships, three hotels stood out as the premier destinations in Asia. Hong Kong's Peninsula, Singapore's Raffles, and the Oriental of Bangkok. Famous writers, including Somerset Maugham, Noel Conrad, Joseph Conrad, and James Michener stayed in the Oriental Hotel. There's even a Somerset Maugham suite."

"How do you know such details?"

"I've been to the reading room off of the Author's Lounge where the books of famous writers are on the shelves."

"When we were riding through the noisy, congested streets, I was a little disappointed. But the Oriental Hotel lives up to my fantasy image of Thailand."

"It's a city of six million people trying to hold on to the past while embracing the future. That distant rumble, like a continuous thunderstorm, comes from over a million vehicles—tuk-tuks, motor scooters, trucks, and buses entangled in a road system built for a tenth of today's traffic. Remember, Bangkok was once a city of canals like Venice—now filled and replaced with roads. The Chao Phraya River that snakes through Bangkok has been the lifeblood of commerce for over six hundred years and is still important for goods and water taxis that are faster and cheaper than car transport."

"Have you spent much time in Bangkok?"

"Between my junior and senior years as an undergrad, I spent two months backpacking around Southeast Asia, but the Oriental Hotel was out of my ten-dollar-a-day budget."

Becky kissed his cheek. "There are so many things I like about you. It's best that we didn't meet earlier, or you might not have met and married Kelsey, and Nadia wouldn't have come into your life."

"Then you wouldn't have met and fallen in love with Elliott."

"I'm here because of you, not Elliott, who's a half world away."

Is she thinking what I'm thinking?

"I'm hungry and thirsty," squealed Nadia as she jumped on the lounge bed and shook her head, sprinkling water over them, then climbed over her father for his iced tea.

Becky sat up and laughed. "I couldn't ask for a better chaperone."

The six-hour time difference between Hawaii and Thailand defeated their evening plans to dine on the terrace restaurant and watch the fireworks display and procession of riverboats adorned in festive lights. Nadia had fallen asleep on Becky's bed while Alex and Becky were dressing for dinner.

"Alex, our dinner plans are kaput, unless we can get a hotel babysitter for Nadia."

Alex shrugged. "I don't want Nadia to wake up with a stranger in the room, so how about ordering room service and watching the fireworks from our window?"

"Good idea, as I'm kind of tired too."

They ordered the popular pad Thai, a spicy blend of noodles, prawns, peanuts, eggs, bean sprouts, and pad Thai sauce, plus green papaya salad and two Singha beers. Alex added his favorite dessert—fresh mango over sticky rice, drizzled with coconut milk.

Alex toasted to a memorable first night in Bangkok, and Becky asked why he didn't toast to a memorable trip.

"I don't want to use up all my toasts on the first night." He paused, then reached for Becky's hand. "What made you decide to come on this trip, knowing my feelings about you?"

She turned her hand and laced her fingers into his. "As I said, it's a chance of a lifetime, as Elliott is unlikely to come here with me. And even if he agreed to come, the experience would be different because his feelings about Asia are so different from mine."

"Anything else?"

She pulled her hand away and twisted her fork in the noodles, then took a bite, slurping up a long noodle.

Alex reached across and wiped sauce from her chin, then moved to her pink lips.

"Ouch! You bit me for no reason."

"A warning. At times, I feel like I'm the luckiest woman in the world when I'm at Elliott's side, and he's the charming center of attention at parties. But I need him more than he needs me, and that worries me. Can our relationship ever be equal?"

Alex spiked a piece of ripe mango and raised it to her lips. "You'll always be equal in my eyes."

The whistling sound of fireworks drew them to the window. Alex stood behind Becky, his arms cozily around her waist as they watched the dazzling spectacle. Riverboats slowly filed past adorned with strings of colored lights, as fireworks lit the sky, mirrored on the river and in their eyes.

Becky leaned into Alex—his fingers snugly around her waist. She didn't resist as his fingers slid under her blouse, ever so gently caressing her belly button as he nibbled her earlobes and whispered words only Elliott was supposed to say. Flashes from exploding fireworks revealed one silhouette within an ornate window frame. The fireworks came to an end, leaving the room dark and quiet, except for murmurs.

Chapter 28

"*D*addy, I'm starved."

Alex rolled away from Becky and opened his right eye. Nadia stood next to the bed, fully dressed with hands on her hips. "What time is it?" he whispered.

"Almost six, and I've been awake for hours. I'll die if I don't get something to eat right away."

"Well, I better not let that happen. Go brush your teeth while I dress."

"I already brushed my teeth."

"Do it again."

"Humph." She marched off to the bathroom.

Alex quickly rolled out of bed and gathered the trail of clothing from the window to the bed and stuffed it in a suitcase. Then gently shook Becky's shoulder. "Ready for breakfast?"

"No. You two go."

He kissed her shoulder then covered her.

A waiter was wiping moisture from the tables and chairs when they entered the riverside terrace restaurant. He paused and gave the *wai* greeting with his hands and said, "*Sawasdee krup*," (hello greeting to a man). Then in English added, "So sorry, restaurant not open yet."

"Is there somewhere nearby where I can get a pastry and hot chocolate for a hungry girl?"

The waiter smiled at Nadia. "Cannot disappoint such a pretty young lady." He seated them at the table next to the river and scurried away.

A muffled rumble drew their attention to the fog-shrouded river as a ponderous barge materialized like a mythical beast, followed by another and another. The sound of water lapping against the low terrace wall assured them that the strange shapes were real.

"Nadia, what do you think of Thailand so far?"

"I like the pool and bed with big fluffy pillows. But you said I'd see jungle and ride an elephant."

"You'll see that soon enough, but today we're going to see the Grand Palace where the king of Thailand and the royal family once lived. And you'll see a Buddha with toes as big as you."

"Will I see a real king?"

"No. But you'll be walking in the footsteps of kings and can pretend to be a princess."

"Daddy, you can be my king."

Alex mused, *She already knows how to twist me around her finger.*

A basket of danish pastries and miniature croissants were served with hot chocolate and strong coffee. Nadia licked the icing off a pastry then gazed at her father with a quizzical expression.

"Okay, Nadia, what's going through that mischievous mind of yours?"

"Well, you always tell me not to throw clothes on the floor, but you and Becky left your clothes scattered all over the place."

He cleared his throat. "It was late, and we were tired, and ah—"

"Hi, early birds," Becky said as she strolled across the marble terrace, a purple orchid behind her ear. She leaned in and kissed both on their cheeks, then settled into a chair and reached for Alex's cup.

"Becky, I trust you slept well?"

"Yes, I had an amazing dream."

Nadia frowned. "I only get to sleep with Daddy when I have a bad dream."

"Nadia, you don't need to worry about nightmares, because I'm sleeping with you every night for the rest of the trip."

"Did you sleep in Daddy's bed because you had a bad dream?"

Becky adjusted the orchid over her ear. "You were sprawled across the bed, and I didn't want to disturb you."

The waiter returned with a basket of stale bread for Nadia to feed the catfish. Becky avoided eye contact with Alex as she watched Nadia toss pieces of bread to the melee of fish churning the water, just feet from the edge of the terrace. Nadia scolded the larger fish that crowded out the smaller fish.

"Becky, you arrived just in time to halt Nadia's inquisition about last night. I don't like lying to her. I think she knows more than she's letting on."

"Alex, from now on, we'll allay her suspicions and my guilt by sleeping in our own beds."

"You regret last night?"

She ran her fingers through her hair. "When I'm old and no man wants to sleep with me, I can think back about the night

261

I spent in Thailand's most romantic hotel with one of the two men that I once loved."

"Why do you say love in the past tense?"

"Because, I can't give myself completely to Elliott if I still love you, so last night was *lag gorn na,* meaning goodbye in the sense of loving you. This time, I really mean it when I tell you we're just good friends."

With only one full day in Bangkok with its stifling humidity, they decided to limit their sightseeing to the Grand Palace and nearby Wat Pho, home to the 150-foot-long reclining golden Buddha. Their waiter suggested they take the River Express and avoid the congested city streets.

Alex held Nadia's hand as they boarded the packed river ferry. A Thai man gave his seat to Becky, and she pulled Nadia onto her lap, while Alex stood. By eight thirty, the languid Chao Phraya had molted into a bustling serpentine thoroughfare through the heart of Bangkok. The River Express pulled into the stream of boats, the sound of its throbbing engine drowned out by the deafening roar of long-tailed boats skittering over the water. Their wakes rocked other boats and splashed against the pilings under flimsy shops and homes perched at the river's edge.

The structures edging the Chao Phraya were an eclectic blend of shacks, old colonial buildings, and glitzy skyscrapers. Their view from the river ferry added depth to the city—impossible to appreciate from the narrow, crowded streets. As the Chao Phraya swung in a wide arc to the left, Wat Arun appeared with its twenty-five-story central prang (spire) piercing the sky, surrounded by four smaller spires.

"Daddy, what makes it so shiny?"

"The gleaming spires are from millions of shards of broken porcelain and tiles left behind by Chinese ships that no longer needed it as ballast. And Wat Arun was once home to the sacred Emerald Buddha."

Their attention quickly turned to the opulent Grand Palace on the right side of the river. The royal complex contained a complex of ornate buildings, prangs, and chedis enclosed by more than a mile of walls. The dominant features were the Royal Pantheon with its steeply pitched reddish-orange roofs, edged in green and gold, and the adjacent Phra Si Ratana Chedi, with its golden prang gleaming in the morning sun. They followed the stream of tourists onto the Tha Chang Pier and past flimsy stalls bulging with tourist trinkets, postcards, guidebooks, and tubs of ice and bottled water.

Inside the Grand Palace gate was a dizzying labyrinth of gilded structures that overwhelmed their senses. The walled complex of tightly spaced buildings kept out the gentle breeze, heightening the oppressive effect of the heat and humidity. Nadia was the first to complain. "Daddy, I'm melting. I want to go back to the hotel pool."

"Nadia, I saved the best for last. Wat Phra Kaeo contains the Emerald Buddha, the most revered image of Buddha in Thailand. We won't stay long, and we'll get a cold drink as soon as we leave the Grand Palace grounds."

"Okay, but I can't walk very far. You know I have little legs."

Nadia posed for photos next to the fearsome stone guards guarding the entrance to the Emerald Buddha. Shoes off, they shuffled quietly inside—the air thick with incense. Atop a thirty-four-foot golden throne sat the Emerald Buddha, only slightly more than two feet tall, but strategic lighting added a divine halo glow.

As soon as they stepped outside, Nadia grumbled, "Daddy, the Emerald Buddha is so small."

"Size doesn't mean greatness. The Emerald Buddha has a fairy-tale history. For hundreds of years, it was hidden in plain sight, covered in plaster in a *wat* (small temple) in Chiang Rai in the far north of Thailand. Then, about five hundred years ago, lightning struck it and cracked the plaster to reveal the Emerald Buddha. The king of Chiang Mai, Thailand, sent an army and elephants to bring the Emerald Buddha to him. According to legend, the elephants refused to take the sacred buddha to Chiang Mai and instead took it across to Lampang, Laos. Later it was moved to Laos; then about two hundred years ago, the Thais brought the Emerald Buddha to Bangkok. It's so sacred that only the king of Thailand has the authority to change the gilded robes worn by the Emerald Buddha."

"But it's still just a pretty piece of carved rock?"

"Yes, it's a symbol of the belief in Buddha's teachings—kind of like we have statues of Jesus on the cross that people worship."

"Is it really made of emerald?"

"No. As scientists are not allowed to examine it, we can only speculate. Most believe it's semiprecious jasper. When it was carved, there were no modern carving tools, so it's a remarkable piece of sculpture in addition to its religious importance."

"Daddy, do you think there are other Emerald Buddhas that haven't been discovered?"

"That's the kind of question archeologists ask. Since green jasper was available, I would be surprised if there aren't other ones, but maybe not as big."

In front of the Grand Palace, Alex pulled out a Bangkok tourist map, and immediately a three-wheeled tuk-tuk swerved to the curbside. The driver—a generous smile on his face—motioned for them to get in.

Alex shook his head. "We're walking."

"Daddy, it feels like a thousand degrees."

"Honey, it's just a five- or ten-minute walk."

"That's pure torture in this heat."

"Alex, I'm with Nadia, and a tuk-tuk ride will be fun."

Alex turned to the grinning tuk-tuk driver. "How much to go to Wat Pho?"

The driver's gold tooth glinted in the morning sun. "So sorry, meester, Wat Pho closed today, but take you to special jewelry shop where you get best discounts in Bangkok. So nice for rubies, jade, and gold necklaces, then go to famous Jim Thompson House for Thai silk." He handed Alex a glossy card—Thai Gem Emporium.

Alex smiled. "But I want to know the price to go to Wat Pho."

"Okay, okay. One hundred fifty baht." His expansive smile frozen as he gazed into Alex's face.

Alex grinned at the driver. "You take us to Wat Pho, and I pay you one hundred and fifty baht if it's closed, but the ride is free if it's open."

The driver squinted and his smile wavered. "You been Bangkok before."

Alex nodded. "Fifty baht."

"Seventy-five baht. Hop in."

"Have a nice day." Alex took Nadia's hand and turned away.

"Okay, okay."

In four minutes they pulled up in front of Wat Pho, and the driver asked for sixty baht but got the agreed fifty—both exchanged knowing smiles.

Sixteenth-century Wat Pho was both the oldest and largest statue of Buddha in Bangkok. The stark, unappealing building belied the auspicious statue under its corrugated metal roof. As they stepped inside, their senses were overwhelmed by the immensity of the reclining golden Buddha that if standing could peer into the windows of the fifteenth floor of a building.

"Daddy, why is the Buddha so humongous?"

"Perhaps to leave us in awe."

"What's awe mean?"

"Something that makes your mouth drop open when you see it. For Buddhists, it gives hope that there is something higher than everyday toil and demands their respect."

"But, Daddy, you told me the Emerald Buddha was the most sacred thing in Thailand."

Becky laughed. "She's boxed you in."

They followed the slow-moving crowd around to the Buddha's car-sized feet. Inlaid in the feet were 108 mother-of-pearl images, intricately carved with *lakshanas* (auspicious) signs of the true Buddha. Nadia wanted a photo taken of her standing next to the toes that were as big as her. Behind the Buddha, a row of one-hundred bronze prayer wheels was kept in perpetual motion by the line of faithful and tourists—the sounds of tinkling coins in the hundred dishes were reminiscent of the sounds of slot machines in Las Vegas casinos.

Before Nadia could ask, Alex handed her his small baht coins. "Say a prayer when you spin the prayer wheels; then give an offering."

Alex took Becky's suggestion of an air-conditioned taxi back to their hotel. After a swim in the pool, Alex and Becky retired to a double lounge bed and ordered grilled chicken satay and deep-fried spring rolls. Like a trained seal, Nadia jumped from the water as soon as the food arrived and ate the braised chicken cubes as fast as Becky stripped them from the bamboo skewer. Her cheeks bulging like a squirrel's, she attempted to escape back to the pool.

"No you don't!" Alex said as he grabbed her foot. "Swallow your food and let me wipe the peanut sauce off your face."

Nadia paused until he let go, then screamed as she cannonballed into the pool, splashing water over them.

Alex threw up his hands. "Only eight, and she already has me beat."

Becky grinned as she stirred the Thai iced tea, commingling the thick milky layer with the black tea. "You love it."

"How will I ever control her when she's a teen if she gets everything she wants as a preteen?"

"It's more important that you love her than rules that every teen will test. But then, you'll have a partner to share the responsibility."

"What makes you so sure I'll find someone?"

"I'm a woman."

They all needed a rest in their room before going to the Author's Wing for late-afternoon tea. The airy, sunbathed room had white rattan chairs with tropical cushions and potted leafy palms and orchids. Elegant stairs led to a small balcony where a violinist played haunting melodies. On the back of their gilded menu was a history of the fabled hotel built by two Dutch sea captains in the 1870s. It had hosted kings, presidents, prime ministers, adventurers, and countless writers and actors. The author's library off to the side contained shelves of autographed novels from famous writers and a writer's desk.

Nadia's eyes were on her dad, feigning interest in his words, while her fingers stealthily moved to the dish of powdered cookies. The astute waiter poured the tea for Alex and

Becky and shifted the cookie plate closer to the little hands. Over cups of fragrant tea, they perused the Angkor Wat travel guide until the glow of the sun's rays disappeared and Nadia slumped in her seat. He scooped his sleeping daughter into his arms and carried her back to their room. Becky wiped the powdered sugar from her lips and Alex's shoulder as he tucked her into bed.

"Becky, looks like dinner for two in our room again."

Becky smiled. "But no special dessert."

Chapter 29

D addy, you're kidding. We're leaving this really nice hotel to go somewhere hotter and with no pool."

Becky chuckled. "Alex, you've spoiled Nadia by starting off in the deluxe Oriental Hotel."

"Nadia, where we're going, you'll be riding elephants in the jungle and visiting ancient ruins."

"Will I see tigers and elephants?"

"Elephants for sure, and maybe even a king cobra."

"Really?"

"Unlikely, but cobras are common in this region. You'll see legendary Angkor Wat that was lost in the jungle until the explorer Henri Mouhot discovered it in 1860. It's the largest set of temples in the world, and new discoveries are made every year. Anthropologists have estimated that Angkor Wat once had a population of a million people—making it the largest city in the world at that time."

"Maybe I can discover something."

"Anything's possible if you keep your eyes open for details that others miss. You can be a real-life Indiana Jones."

"Are there secret passages?"

"Well, we'll have to go to find out."

Their one-hour flight landed at Siem Reap International Airport mid-morning. Most passengers filed off to the Visa on Arrival or the Cambodian Residents window. Only one other couple was in the line for Foreigners with Visas.

"Alex, you were smart to get our visas in advance."

Alex calmly placed their passports on the counter. The emaciated official took them, sized up Alex, then waved Becky and Nadia through. Alex was familiar with the ritual as he studied the officer in his pressed but frayed uniform, waiting for the hand gesture or hushed request.

The officer flipped through the passports, then looked up, eyes momentarily engaged. "Tip," his voice so low and indistinct that a novice traveler would miss it.

Alex maintained a poker face as his hand slid across the counter, polished by thousands before him. The transaction completed; three bangs of the entry stamp, and a wry smile as the passports were placed on the well-greased surface.

"Was there a problem?" Becky asked as they headed for the exit.

"Nothing unexpected, and easily solved."

Outside arrivals stood neatly dressed tour group greeters with glossy signs, and a few holding placards with handprinted names. A neatly dressed, slim man waved a placard with his name misspelled: Doctor Silveron.

Alex waved. "I'm Alex Silverton."

"So happy to meet you. I'm Pong, your guide and interpreter." After shaking hands, he insisted on carrying both Becky's and Nadia's bags to their car. The rotund, middle-aged driver put the bags in the trunk before being introduced by Pong.

"Kep is our driver. He only knows a few words in English, but he's an excellent driver, and the AC in the Honda works superbly."

As they rode into Siem Reap, Pong pointed out remnants of the French colonial period—wide tree-shaded boulevards, the picturesque tree-lined Siem Reap River, and ochre French colonial homes with wide verandas overlooking flower gardens. Like other Southeast Asia tourist meccas, modern hotels were erasing the colonial past.

Set back from the road was the Angkor Sunrise Guesthouse overlooking the river. They were met on the steps by the manager and invited for refreshments on the veranda while their room was readied. The squawking of a parrot drew Nadia to the rear of the house.

A few minutes later, Nadia came skipping back and gulped down an iced tea. "I love this place."

"What changed your mind?"

"I made friends with a talking parrot."

Alex smirked. "Did he say, 'Polly wants a cracker'?"

Nadia put her hands on her hips. "He doesn't speak English. He hopped over to me and said, '*Johm riab sua.*' That means 'hello' in Khmer."

"And smarty-pants, where did you learn Khmer?"

Nadia giggled. "It's on the sign on the cage."

They dined on the terrace on fish cakes and *laap*—a spicy Laotian salad of fish cubes marinated in lime juice, mint, spring onions, and chilies, while Pong reviewed the proposed itinerary. The afternoon would be spent at the Banyan temple complex with its enigmatic Buddha faces, then to the hilltop Phnom Bakheng temple to view the sunset over Angkor Wat. Day two would include the Ta Prohm temple ruins that were held in the clutches of the massive roots of strangler fig trees, then Angkor Thom. The grand finale was on the morning of the last day when they'd watch the sun rise over Angkor Wat.

"Dr. Silverton, you can modify the itinerary to fit your preferences. Maybe a little extra charge for faraway sites."

"Daddy, I want to explore secret passages and look for treasures."

Pong looked bewildered. "All the places around Angkor Wat are major tourist attractions. Sadly, during the treacherous Khmer Rouge regime from 1975 to 1979, thousands of priceless artifacts were looted or destroyed."

Nadia frowned. "Will we see any cobras?"

He shook his head. "They're here, but rarely seen in tourist areas."

"I really would like to see a cobra."

Pong leaned back in his rattan chair and stared at the ceiling fan. "There's a place an hour and a half drive from here that's not open to the public. It was discovered two years ago, and the government has been waiting for international funding to explore and restore the site. To get in, you'll have to crawl through a narrow, muddy passage."

"Daddy, can we go?"

"Becky, what do you think?"

"I'm in, but I'll walk behind you, so the cobra bites you first."

"Pong, how do we get permission?"

"I know the guard, but . . ." he rubbed his thumb and index fingers together.

"How much?"

"Hmm. Sixty dollars split three ways between the guard, driver, and me. I can't guarantee my friend will be there. Even if we can't get in, you'll need to pay our driver twenty dollars to drive there and back. As it's off limits to tourists, you can't take pictures or post any information online about the visit. Also, it's a very dusty one-lane road."

"Nadia, are you up for a long drive on a dusty road?"

"Yes! I won't complain a single bit."

Alex swirled his iced tea. "Okay, but first we'll visit the temples around Angkor Wat."

The entrance to the various temple complexes was through the main entrance to Angkor Wat. The mysterious Bayon Temple was situated within the ten-square-kilometer Angkor Thom complex. At its peak, it had a larger population than any city in Europe. Regardless of the approach to the Bayon Temples, massive Buddha heads with beguiling smiles were looking down at you. In total, there were 216 identical stone faces thought to resemble its thirteenth-century Khmer ruler—Jaya-varman VII, who directed the construction of the complex.

"Daddy, can I explore?"

"Yes, but don't go far, and be careful not to slip on rocks, and watch out for scorpions and snakes."

"Daddy, I need your hat and flashlight."

"Sure, Indiana Jones." His fedora was too large and kept slipping over her eyes. An hour passed as Nadia roamed through the temple ruins, popping out from behind Buddha heads three times her height and around porticoes and window openings. Nadia stood in the larger window openings, taking off her hat and making sweeping bows, before vanishing inside.

They were only able to see a fraction of the more than ten thousand bas-reliefs of figures before Pong signaled that it was time to go. As they emerged sweating from the bushes, Kep popped open his trunk and handed everyone cold washcloths and bottles of ice water from a Styrofoam cooler—a nice gesture that ensured happy clients and generous tips.

It was almost twilight when they arrived at the base of the jungle-clad hill crowned with the Phnom Bakheng temple. The broad path up to the temple was packed with tourists, and off to the right was a shack selling tickets for elephant rides.

"Nadia, I'm sure you'd rather walk than ride an elephant up to the temple."

"No way! I want to ride an elephant!"

To Alex, forty-five dollars was expensive for a fifteen-minute ride on an elephant, but he couldn't refuse his daughter. From an elevated rickety platform, they climbed onto the rectangular, wooden seat balanced on the back of an elephant. The seat was designed for two adults, but wide enough for Nadia to squeeze between them. The mahout sat in front on the neck of the elephant. Alex had been on elephant rides when he visited Chiang Mai and didn't expect this one to be much different, but he was wrong. The jungle quickly closed in around them, muffling the sounds of civilization, replaced by the prodding footsteps of their five-ton pachyderm and whiffs of vegetation—a musty fusion of unfamiliar aromatic scents. The hypnotic swaying of their perch as they zigzagged up the narrow trail added to the Zen feeling of tranquility.

They emerged from the forest cocoon into a circus-like setting. The temple was crowded with hundreds of noisy tourists waiting for the sunset. The sun was brushing the treetops as they climbed the nearly vertical steps to the temple's fifth-tier terrace. People were packed tightly together, preventing Alex and Becky from a view of the sunset over Angkor Wat, but Nadia was able to worm her way to the front.

"Becky, this didn't work out. We climbed to the top of the mythical Mt. Meru to view tourist heads."

"Alex, the ride was an unforgettable magical experience. When I was a little girl, I was always in a hurry, and my daddy would say 'Slow down, the journey's most important.' I didn't understand what he meant."

Darkness set in quickly as clouds filtered out the stars and moon. They waited as the crowd slowly descended the steeply dipping stairs that barely provided a foothold. Flashlight beams crisscrossed the temple giving it the appearance of a light show. Alex and Becky went first so they could catch Nadia if she slipped.

"Nadia, be careful," Alex warned as he lit the nearby steps with his flashlight. Nadia was helping a petite woman down, positioning her feet in the small niches. When they touched the ground, the frail woman turned to Nadia and grinned, her mouth nearly toothless, and gave a *wai* with her boney fingers. Someone said, "I wish I had a daughter like that," and Alex pulled Nadia closer.

A tray of warm croissants, fresh papaya, coffee, and juice was served as soon as they entered the lobby at seven in the morning. Pong appeared anxious as he puffed on a cigarette and paced the lobby floor.

"Pong, anything wrong?" Alex asked.

"No." He snuffed out his cigarette and pulled up a chair. He glanced around the lobby, then unrolled a sketch map and pointed to a red dot marked 436. "The temple doesn't have a formal name yet. We have to be careful when we visit the temple today."

Nadia was still nibbling on a croissant when they turned onto the paved highway in front of their guesthouse. Ten minutes later, the road narrowed to one lane with churning dust, reducing visibility to three or four car links. It was as if they had suddenly lost the color in a travel movie. The tan dust rose from the road in plumes, spreading a layer over everything, masking the colors—the monotony broken by the occasional bamboo house on stilts, accompanied by a ragtag assemblage of children, chickens, and mangy dogs. Barefoot children ran toward them, excitedly waving their hands, then faded into a cloud of dust.

They saw mostly bicycles and motor scooters on this road, and the occasional car was usually a tourist. Pong said, "The houses are on stilts as the area is under three to four feet of water during the monsoon season."

"Mr. Pong, why do some homes have round poles holding them up and others square ones?"

"Nadia, you're very observant. Poisonous snakes can't coil around and slither up square poles."

The turnoff was poorly marked by a dust-caked, hand-painted sign in Khmer and English—No Trespassing. As soon as they turned down the track, a second red sign needed no translation. It had a skull and crossbones symbol and warnings in Khmer and English: Preah Khan (Danger Mines). Underneath it read, "Access strictly forbidden beyond this point."

Pong motioned to the driver, and they continued along the overgrown track to a flimsy bamboo gate. A guard in a faded military uniform stood, shouldered his rifle, and sauntered to the car. Pong stepped out of the car and offered the guard a cigarette. They chatted in Khmer—occasionally a chuckle—

until the smokes reached their fingertips, and an envelope exchanged hands. The guard glanced inside, nodded, then
slipped it under his shirt.

He lifted the bamboo gate and waved them through. They
stopped several times to slash away the branches blocking the
narrow road. There were elephant footprints but no visible tire
tracks.

Pong said his friend, Bodhi, told him it had been four
months since a team of government anthropologists had briefly
visited the site. The team leader had told Bodhi they hoped to
begin work on the ruins the following year with Swedish aid,
but priority was on restoration of the extensive ruins around
Angkor Wat that generated most of Cambodia's tourist income.

The road ended abruptly at a stone wall overgrown with
ferns and shrubs and strangler fig tree roots. "This is the outer
wall of the temple. The survey team walled off the main entrance to prevent looting. But there's another way in." Pong
took out a small bamboo cage from the trunk of the car.

Nadia peeked in the cage. "What's the mouse for?"

"Patience and you'll see. Now, follow me, and don't put
your hands into cracks in the wall, or you might get a nasty
sting from a scorpion. Don't worry about the big spiders.
They're not poisonous and will scurry away."

About thirty steps to the right, Pong used a machete to chop
away the overgrowth that concealed a twenty-five by thirty-
inch square opening in the stone wall. "This is our only way
in."

Alex boosted Pong up to the opening, then handed him the
three-cell flashlight. Becky followed, then Nadia and Alex. Inside, the three-foot thick wall was an eight-by-ten-foot room

with two walls covered in bas-reliefs of warriors riding elephants. As the flashlight beam moved across the wall, saucer-sized spiders scurried into cervices.

"Daddy, I'm scared of spiders."

"Nadia, remember, they just want to get away from us."

They followed Pong down a passageway built for people several inches shorter than Alex. A right turn brought them into a more spacious corridor that opened into a courtyard overgrown with jungle vegetation.

In the center of the courtyard was a massive strangler fig tree, its octopus-like roots wrapped around a semitransparent pinkish Buddha. The walls of the courtyard were covered in intricate bas-reliefs partially hidden by moss and ferns. On the wall touched by sunlight, patches of gleaming gold could be seen, indicating the bas-reliefs had been covered in gold leaf. Like Christmas tree lights, tiny yellow and white orchids sprouted from the trunk and limbs of the tree. The chatter of monkeys broke the silence as several monkeys scrambled up a wall and disappeared.

"Pong, this is beyond anything I could have imagined," gushed Becky.

When she reached for her camera, Pong again warned that no photos were allowed, as it could bring treasure hunters and land his friend in prison.

"Daddy, what kind of rock is the Buddha made from?"

Alex ran his fingers over the Buddha. "It's rose quartz, but I've never seen a piece large enough to be carved into a six-foot-tall statue. It belongs in a museum."

Becky was standing, hands on her hips, in front of the largest bas-relief on the back wall. "Alex, this is totally different from any of the bas-reliefs I've seen or read about. There are no warriors or armies fighting. It looks like a paradise with a Buddha image on top of a tall mountain looking down into a valley of people and animals. There are children sitting next to what appears to be a leopard, and a woman sitting on a deer with a single straight horn."

"Daddy, the woman's riding a unicorn."

"Sure looks like a unicorn. Maybe a deer that lost one of its antlers."

Nadia shook her head. "Daddy, who would spend a lot of time carving a picture of a deer with a broken antler?"

"Nadia, you have a point. It's a bas-relief of nature in harmony, and including a deer with one antler broken does seem odd."

"If it looks like a unicorn, then it's a unicorn," insisted Nadia.

Their attention turned to Pong, who was squatting next to the base of the statue, positioning the cage near a hole between the roots of the strangler fig tree. He attached a string to the door and stepped back, beckoning Nadia with his hand. The caged rat was scratching to escape from the rear of the cage. First, they saw the reflected light of its eyes, then a flowing movement, both sensuous and frightening as the gray serpent slithered from the dark hole between the roots.

Nadia jumped behind Pong as the king cobra rose and flared its hood. Pong pulled the string, flipping open the cage door—the only escape route—certain death. The rat paused at the back of the cage, its tiny brain weighing impossible odds of escape, then dashed through the door. A squeal as the cobra struck, then muffled sounds as it slithered back into its dark hole, then silence.

"Why did the rat have to die?" Nadia moaned.

Pong nodded. "We Buddhists don't like to kill any creatures, but rodents are a big problem in our villages. They eat our rice and bring diseases. This cobra is special, as it is a guardian of a special Buddha and must eat to live."

Alex put his arm around Nadia's shoulders. "Nadia, Mr. Pong went through a lot of trouble so you could see a cobra. You should thank him."

"Yes, Daddy." Pong appeared surprised when Nadia said thank you and jumped up and gave him a hug and kiss on his cheek.

Chapter 30

The guard raised the bamboo gate as soon as they appeared. They stopped to give him another pack of cigarettes, then turned on the road toward Siem Reap. Pong recommended having lunch at a roadside restaurant a few miles before reaching the Angkor Wat tourist area. He explained that the food was authentic and tasty but too far from the tourist area to get much business.

The crudely painted sign read, Welcom Cambodian Kichen. Set back from the road was a thatched awning over a long table that could seat a minivan full of tourists. Behind, smoke seeped from the cook shack with a rusty corrugated roof.

Before the dust settled from their vehicle, a young girl dashed from the shack. "You most welcome to vely excellent lunch," she said in fractured English. "Wait moment. I wipe table." She hurriedly cleaned the bamboo table and chairs, then helped seat Becky.

"Thank you," Becky replied. "Do you have a lunch special to recommend?"

The girl pointed to the printed menu. "*Trei kor* most excellent today."

Pong added, "I recommend it. The steamed freshwater fish with sugar palm and rice is delicious."

Everyone except Nadia ordered the special. She asked if they had roasted chicken satay with peanut sauce like she had in Bangkok. The girl didn't understand, so Pong explained in Khmer.

"Yes, yes, she cheerfully replied. I ask cook to make vely excellent roasted chicken so nice with peanut sauce."

The girl hovered close to their table, refilling glasses after every sip. Pong asked how the business was doing.

The girl twisted a napkin around a finger. "No so good. Only two tourists come this morning. Buy Cokes. No tip." She was quiet for a couple minutes, then asked Nadia where she was from.

"America. My name's Nadia. What's your name?"

"Sari. I'm twelve."

Soon they were chatting and giggling. When Alex asked for the bill, Sari said, "I give you best desert if you have time. Not cost anything."

"Yes, but I want to pay."

Nadia yelped with excitement when Sari returned with a platter of sticky rice covered in slices of ripe mango drizzled with coconut milk. The bill for five, including drinks, was sixteen dollars. Alex paid with a twenty and told Sari to keep the change. The man and woman in the kitchen waved as they headed back to their car. Sari walked beside Nadia.

"Daddy, Sari needs a ride to Siem Reap."

"Honey, there's only room for five in the car."

"Sari can sit on my lap."

Alex gazed into his daughter's expectant face. "I suppose we can squeeze in a sixth passenger."

Nadia hugged him. "Thanks, Dad!"

"Pushover," Becky added.

Becky pulled Nadia onto her lap, giving a space for Sari, and the two girls chatted nonstop on the trip to Siem Reap. Sari gave directions in Khmer to her uncle's street stall located next to the Angkor Night Market. When Sari got out of the car, her uncle gave her a hug, then insisted everyone, including the driver, have a free cold soft drink and a snack from his small cart.

Nadia was the last to get in the car as they were about to leave. "Daddy, our hotel doesn't have a pool or anyone to play with. Can Sari come and play with me? Then I can go with her to the puppet show tonight. It's in Khmer, but Sari can translate for me."

"Okay with me, but Sari needs to get permission from her uncle."

Her uncle agreed and gave Sari 1,500 riel (US$0.35).

The girls spent the afternoon playing on the rear terrace and trying to teach the parrot to say "Nadia" and "Sari." After showers, Alex and Becky relaxed on the front terrace where they could hear the girls playing.

"I'm so glad that I came on this trip with you and Nadia."

"Including the evening at the Oriental Hotel?"

Becky spun a large rubber band on her finger. "Men have such fragile egos about their prowess between the sheets. I don't love you more or less for screwing me. Any man can do that. I love you because you make the littlest things interesting and you're such a good father to Nadia."

"That's all?"

"Elliott has most of the qualities I'm looking for in a man. We have three years of history together. Alex, I've seen the results of girlfriends that fall in and out of love too quickly—

always looking for something better, then regretting what slipped through their fingers."

He shrugged. "Um, I've been thinking about asking you and Elliott to become Nadia's godparents. I know it's something you'll have to discuss with him, but I can't think of anyone else I trust more than you."

"I've been thinking the same thing. I'll have to ask Elliott first." She leaned over and gave him a kiss on his cheek.

There were no taxis available, and Sari negotiated a cheap fare in a three-wheeled *remorque* (tuk-tuk) to the puppet show next to the lively Psar Chaa shopping bazaar. It was a tight squeeze with Nadia on her father's lap and Sari on Becky's. A crowd of Cambodian children was sitting on the ground in a half circle in front of a simple outdoor puppet stage. Sari pulled Nadia along as she weaved through the children to a small space near the middle. In the rear stood Cambodian parents.

The cacophony of happy voices dwindled to a murmur as the curtain opened to the lilliputian stage. A puppet resembling a colorful court jester welcomed the children in Khmer, then vanished in a puff of smoke. For almost an hour, puppets in colorful costumes battled and chased each other across the stage, accompanied by drums, cymbals, and recorded gunshots in sync with the puppet's guns. The children screamed warnings, sometimes jumping up and pointing when villains lurked, and cheered when they were vanquished by the hero. As the performance neared the end, two women worked their way among the adults, collecting donations. Alex added a five-dollar bill to the pile of Khmer notes and coins in the basket.

At the end of the performance, Alex asked Sari if she would join them at a nearby restaurant, but she shook her head.

Nadia whispered to her dad, "Sari doesn't have much money, and we would rather buy snacks from a street vendor."

"Sari, why don't you take Nadia to eat where you go?"

"So good street food near here. Vely cheap."

"Let's go," yelped Nadia.

Alex and Becky followed a few yards behind the girls as Sari pulled Nadia down an alleyway filled with carts belching steam and smoke infused with sweet and spicy smells. Observant sellers tripled the price once they saw Sari was with foreigners, but she bartered hard to get a reasonable price. They sat on child-sized red plastic stools with their one-dollar plates heaped with spicy shredded meat and vegetables over rice. Sari was surprised that they could use chopsticks.

For dessert, Sari led them to a stall selling her favorite treat—toasted tarantulas.

Nadia grimaced. "Sari, I never ate a spider before."

Without asking the price, Alex handed the seller two one-dollar bills. Sari picked two-four-inch-wide spiders and handed one to Nadia, who gingerly bit off a tiny piece of a leg.

"Um, it tastes like a crunchy, meat-flavored potato chip."

As they walked by the entrance to the bustling Psar Chaa shopping bazaar, a family of tourists paused to gawk at Nadia and Sari. A blond girl wearing a University of Iowa T-shirt sneered and said, "Eating spiders is totally gross!"

Nadia shoved her tarantula in the girl's face. "Want a bite?"

The girl recoiled, almost tripping over her younger brother. "Nooo way!"

Nadia beamed. "You're missing a scrumptious treat that you won't get back in Iowa." Nadia bit off a leg.

Becky elbowed Alex. "You're not raising a sugar and spice and everything nice girl."

"I'm glad she's open to trying new things and isn't intimidated by snooty Americans."

It was a tearful departing for the girls at her uncle's. Sari took off her woven bracelet and put it on Nadia's wrist. "This keep you safe."

Pong was pacing back and forth in the lobby when Alex and Becky came down the stairs, trailed by Nadia leaning on the banister.

"Why do we have to go so early? It's dark and we can't see anything."

Pong nodded. "Daybreak won't wait, even for a pretty little girl. You're going to see the most spectacular sunrise in all of Cambodia. Of the more than one hundred temples in the area, Angkor Wat is the largest and most famous. It's on our national flag, and Cambodians call Angkor Wat 'Heaven on Earth.'"

They arrived to find throngs of tourists streaming across the marble causeway. The best spots to view the sunrise over the temple were filled, but Pong said not to worry and led them left to a sparsely crowded location next to a broad pond with a silvery sheen.

"Daddy, what makes the water shine with no light?"

"Good question. The water's smooth surface is a good reflector of the small amount of light from the sky."

The silhouette of Angkor Wat gradually took shape, first framed in indigo, then shades of blue, until the dazzling rays of the sun appeared between two majestic spires. Murmurs swept through the crowd as cameras clicked to catch the double image; the inverse reflected on the pond. Pong explained that the central tower represented Mt. Meru, and below were

courtyards representing continents enclosed by a moat, and beyond, oceans.

As the sun rose higher, they merged with the crowd and
crossed the wide stone bridge to the main Angkor Wat complex bordered by a half mile of bas-reliefs. Pong told them that
hundreds of artisans with crude tools took more than a million
man-hours to carve the history and legends of Khmer civilization in intricate bas-reliefs.

Pong said the hundreds of bas-reliefs were too extensive to
see in the short time they had and led them to the more important ones. The most stunning was a bas-relief called the
Churning of the Ocean of Milk. "Nadia, what do you see?"
Pong asked.

"Um, it looks like scary demons pulling one end of a giant
serpent and an army pulling the other end, causing a big storm
in the sea."

"You're a very observant girl. On one end, demons are tug-
ging on the massive serpent, and helmeted gods are pulling on
the other end."

"But why are they fighting over the serpent?"

"The churning of the sea is to extract the *elixir of immortality.*"

"Daddy, what's *immortality*?"

"For centuries people have searched for special herbs, por-
tents, and spring waters that can make people live forever. But
they have all failed. Nadia, what's most important is how you
use the years you have on earth and not how long you live."

"Daddy, are you saying that so I'll be good?"

"You're already a good girl most of the time."

They were unable to see all the bas-reliefs before they had to return to pick up their luggage and depart for the airport. Pong helped them with check-in, then Becky and Nadia gave Pong hugs, and Alex shook his hand and gave him an envelope with a generous tip for Pong and the driver.

While waiting for their flight, each shared what was most memorable about the trip to Angkor Wat. Becky liked the intricate bas-reliefs that gave insights into the culture and beliefs of the ancient Khmer empire. Alex was awed by the rose quartz Buddha. Nadia said she would remember her friend Sari the most and would write her.

"Why are you two squeezing my hands?" protested Nadia.

Chapter 31

*T*he flight from Siem Reap to Phuket International Airport took three and a half hours including the transfer in Bangkok. Phuket Island was located along the southwestern coast of Thailand at the edge of the Andaman Sea. It was late afternoon when they emerged from the modest airport and were greeted by their smartly dressed driver, holding a Laguna Palms Resort's sign with Alex's name. The hotel pickup service was much more expensive, but reliable. Their Mercedes whisked them in air-conditioned comfort past a seemingly haphazard collection of ramshackle stores, eateries, and homes that varied from shacks to mansions.

The entrance to the Laguna Palms Resort was a quarter-mile paved road bordered by hedges of red, yellow, and white hibiscus flowers, and beyond, manicured lawns and coconut palm trees.

The open-sided, A-frame teak roof of the check-in pavilion appeared to float above the palms and orchids that concealed its pillars. A floral-patterned golf cart carried them to the stairs to their second-floor room overlooking a lagoon—an artfully landscaped remnant of the era of mining the tin-rich sands. Their room was furnished with honey-colored rattan furniture and tropical patterned cushions matching the bedspreads.

"Daddy, there's a big bowl of fruit for us." Nadia skipped across and took a banana, then hopped onto the bed nearest the balcony. "I want this bed so I can see Santa when he brings me a present." Nadia enjoyed keeping the myth alive—a piece of her make-believe world that held memories she wasn't ready to release.

"Nadia, what makes you so sure Santa Claus can find you here?"

"He just knows," she said with a grin. While Alex and Becky unpacked their suitcases, Nadia explored the room. "Daddy, there's a bunch of shells in the bathroom wall."

Alex examined the wall around the shower. "You're right. They're fossil shells preserved in limestone. I'm not sure, but they appear to be from the Eocene Period, so are more than forty million years old."

"Hey, you geologists, if you want to catch the sunset, we better head for the beach now."

They hurried to the wide beach at the rear of their resort and only caught a couple minutes of the sun before it slipped behind a layer of clouds on the horizon. The salty breeze was laced with spices wafting from the row of beachfront shacks, with tables and chairs in the sand under palm-leaf umbrellas.

They walked no further than the first Sea Gypsies Restaurant before a Thai woman appeared in an ankle-length silk skirt and gave a purple orchid to Becky and Nadia, then motioned them to be seated. They took her recommendations and ordered *kung mangkon phat phrik phao* (barbecued local lobster with chili sauce), *dom yam gung* (a prawn and lemongrass soup), and *som tam* (shredded green papaya vegetable mix with lime juice and fish sauce).

Nadia scooted down in her chair. "I like to wiggle my toes in the sand."

Becky adjusted the orchid behind Nadia's ear and kissed her forehead. "I like the feel of my toes in the sand too. It makes the food taste better."

As darkness closed in, candles were lit on the tables, pulling couples and families closer, each in their private orb of flickering light. Thai children emerged from the shacks to play tag on the beach.

"Daddy, I'm too full to eat another bite. Can I play?"

"I suppose so. But stay where we can see you."

Becky swirled her Singha beer as she studied Alex. "I don't think I've ever heard you say no to your daughter."

"She knows my weak spots. I'm doing everything I can to make her happy."

Becky dug her toes deeper into the sand, and she studied his face. *It's not only Nadia that you're eager to please.*

Their room rate included a buffet breakfast in the ground-floor terrace restaurant and a surprise for the children. They arrived early so Nadia would have something to eat before being distracted by the special guest. The five buffet tables had lavish spreads of Thai, Indian, Japanese, and Western food, plus a table of fresh fruit, puddings, and assorted tarts. Nadia veered off toward the dessert table.

"Nadia. Don't even think about dessert before you've had a healthy breakfast."

Nadia frowned at her father, then turned to the Western buffet table of scrambled eggs, fried potatoes, crispy bacon, and pancakes.

The terrace air was saturated with spicy fragrances, Asian languages, and the universal squeals of children. Nadia's whipped-cream-topped hot chocolate had just arrived when screams came from the terrace entrance, then pandemonium as children abandoned their meals and ran toward the two juvenile elephants.

Alex didn't try to stop Nadia as she jumped up, almost knocking over her chair, and bolted toward the elephants. A waiter brought a basket of over-ripe bananas for the children to feed their half-ton playmates. When Nadia approached the one called Lucky, it snatched one of her flip-flops with its trunk and held it over her head, waiting for the ransom price— a banana. Nadia stood in line, hopping from one foot to the other, impatiently waiting for her turn to ride Lucky.

When Nadia's turn came, Lucky used his trunk to boost her onto his back. Becky handed Nadia a bunch of bananas as Lucky turned to plod down to the lagoon. "Lucky, want a banana?" No response.

"Tap head," the mahout said. A simple tap on his head of prickly hairs produced the desired results. Lucky's trunk curled back over his bulbous head and, as if his trunk had eyes, took the banana from Nadia's hand.

The mahout turned to Alex. "Does girl want ride to beach?"

"Daddy, can I? Please?"

"Okay, but be careful not to fall off."

She leaned over and took his fedora. Visitors snapped photos of the young Indiana Jones riding an elephant through the resort. A potbellied man in a gaudy shirt and baggy shorts stepped in front of Lucky, holding his camera in one hand and a cocktail glass in the other. Lucky deftly moved his nimble trunk to the glass and drained it in one noisy slurp.

Lucky lumbered across the beach, past startled sunbathers, and plunged into the ocean. Nadia was joined by a handful of Thai children that raced down to the mobile diving platform. Lucky repeatedly curled his trunk over his head, then catapulted squealing children into the ocean.

A few Thai words from the mahout, and Lucky shook off his screaming charges and waded back onto the beach. When Alex took out a hundred-baht note for the trainer, Lucky snatched it from his hand and stuffed it into the mahout's shirt pocket.

The afternoon was spent between the shaded lounge chairs on the beach and dips in the resort's one-of-a-kind pool. From the swim-up bar, the pool narrowed to a sinuous four-foot-deep channel that snaked a quarter mile through the resort, ending at a low waterfall.

Becky thought it curious that Alex insisted that they wear shorts to dinner and not their colorful sarongs they'd bought at a beach shack. The reason became clear when Alex led them to the two elephants on the beach. Nadia ran to Lucky, while Alex and Becky climbed onto the cushioned teak-framed seat of the adult elephant. Behind their seat was a woven basket of chilled wine and glasses. As the embers of the day were extinguished, turning them to silhouettes against the Andaman Sea, the only sounds were of the surf and the clinking of crystal flutes.

"Alex, this is almost like a honeymoon."

He raised his glass. "Practice run."

"You're impossible."

The stars had found their place in the sky by the time they returned. Standing in front of the Sea Gypsies Restaurant was the same woman, now holding a handful of bananas for the elephants. Lucky waited patiently, as if he understood the woman's words, before taking the banana she offered. Their table was waiting, with a Reserved sign, and orchid blossoms for Becky and Nadia.

"Alex, she knows how to guarantee repeat business."

"Daddy, can I sit at that table?" No explanation was needed. The waitress moved them to the table next to a girl speaking English to her parents. Both girls glanced at each other, and then Becky whispered, "Nadia, say hello to the girl."

"Maybe she doesn't want to talk to me."

As if she overheard Becky, the girl at the adjacent table chirped, "Hi, my name's Elsa. I'm from Bethesda, Maryland."

"I'm Nadia. I live in Hawaii."

"We're going to stop in Honolulu for a few days on our way home. Can you tell me some things to see?"

"Oh, yes, I know all the neat places for kids."

The girls talked throughout dinner. Elsa wanted to ride an elephant but was afraid of falling off as had happened to her when she was riding a pony.

"Elsa, maybe tomorrow, we can ride Lucky together. You'll be really safe."

Elsa's mother, Angela, turned to Becky. "We've been here for five days, and Elsa is starved for a playmate. Would you mind if we arrange a playdate for the girls?"

Before Becky could reply, Nadia blurted out, "We're having a playdate, and we can both ride Lucky."

Elsa's father, Norman Joma, was a doctor at the National Institutes of Health, and Angela was a pediatric nurse. Norman had come from Nigeria as a premed student and met his wife, a second-generation African American from Liberia. They were celebrating their tenth wedding anniversary in Thailand.

Toward the end of the meal, Angela said, "With tomorrow being Christmas, you probably have plans, but if not, we would be pleased if you would join us on a charter boat to Ko Phi Phi to snorkel, then lunch on a private island. If conditions are right, we'll kayak into a sea cave."

"Alex, what do you think?" Becky asked.

"Daddy!" Nadia shouted. "Elsa and I can have so much fun together, and you can have grown-up time without me pestering you."

Alex laughed. "Seems the decision is already made."

Chapter 32

*B*efore going to bed, Nadia checked their sliding balcony door. "Daddy, I'm leaving the door unlocked so Santa can deliver maybe just one teensy-weensy present. I know he'll leave the bigger gifts at our home in Hawaii."

"And what makes you so sure Santa will go to all the trouble to bring you a present in Thailand?"

She studied her father's face until a wry smile appeared. "I love you, Daddy," then turned over, facing the unlocked sliding glass door.

They waited a half hour to be sure Nadia wasn't pretending to be asleep, before unrolling and taping a cutout Christmas tree on the sliding-glass door. The three gifts hidden in his suitcase were put on the floor under the cutout Christmas tree.

"Becky, I'm anxious because Kelsey died last year on Christmas Day and don't want Nadia to feel sad."

"Alex, children are resilient when they're loved and nurtured, and the exciting boat trip with her new playmate will make it a fun day." She stroked Alex's arm. "How about you?"

"I miss Kelsey." He took a deep breath. "But being here with our daughter and her closest friend eases the pain."

"Santa came!" Nadia shrieked as she jumped onto his bed. Alex opened an eye—signaling she had his attention. She giggled as she straddled him and kissed his nose.

"Amazing that Santa would come all the way to Thailand for one little girl."

"Santa thinks I'm special."

Alex nodded. "Where's Becky?"

"She went to get breakfast so we can eat in our room while I'm opening presents."

Alex was brushing his teeth when Becky returned with a waiter pushing their breakfast cart.

After a hurried breakfast, Alex and Becky sat next to Nadia as she opened her gifts. She felt the first present. "Hmm, maybe a book in the Magic Treehouse series." It was the one she had asked for in the letter to Santa Claus. "Just what I need for the long trip home on the plane." The second was a makeup set that Becky had picked out over Alex's feeble objections.

"Daddy, can I put on lipstick to show Elsa?"

He shrugged, then grinned. "You can thank Becky for convincing Santa. I still think my little girl is too young to wear lipstick."

"All the girls at school wear lipstick, and Santa thought it's okay because he gave me a makeup set."

The third gift was a stuffed elephant with "Lucky" embroidered on its side. She hugged her cuddly soft gift. "Daddy, now I'll always remember Lucky."

"Becky, I think Santa might have left both of you something under your pillow."

Becky sat her coffee aside, reached under her pillow, and retrieved a tiny box with a red bow.

Nadia leaned against Becky. "Open it."

Inside were two gold necklaces with jade elephant pendants—one for an adult and the other for a child. "Alex, you've already given me so much with this trip to Asia."

"I want you two to have matching mementos of our trip."

Alex's reward . . . a meaningful kiss from Becky and wet kisses from Nadia on both cheeks.

They met Elsa and her parents in their resort lobby and shared a minivan on the drive across the island to the Phuket Town Harbor. Both girls were excited about their Christmas gifts. Elsa wanted to be a doctor like her father and had received a Girl Scout first aid kit, plus a necklace with a heart-shaped pendant of tiny rubies.

They were met at the pier by Craig West, owner and operator of a twenty-five-foot boat named *Wave Skipper*. The six-foot, sandy-haired Australian towered over his five-foot Thai wife, Chennai. He was quick to recount how he met Chennai during a scuba diving trip to Thailand—boasting that he went into a shop to rent scuba gear and came out with Chennai.

Chennai smirked. "He big talker, but Aussie men just puppy dogs." She pointed to the photos of their two boys on the wall. "They just like their father."

As they boarded the boat, Craig went over the day's activities. "There are few tours on Christmas Day, so beaches won't be as crowded. Also, the tide will be exceptionally low this afternoon, so we'll probably be able to explore a hidden world reached only by kayaks through a sea cave."

"Will we see sharks?" asked Elsa.

"Maybe a reef shark or two, but they're not allowed to eat tourists."

The girls giggled.

"If you agree, this is our itinerary. We'll dash across to Ko Phi Phi, about forty kilometers from here, and spend one to two hours in Maya Bay on the beach. It was the stunningly beautiful setting for the movie *The Beach*, staring Leo Di-Caprio. Because it's Christmas Day and we're early, we might have the beach all to ourselves. Our second stop will be a small, private coral cay for snorkeling and lunch. Our last stop is an hour and a half north in Phang Nga Bay, where, if conditions are right, we'll enter a sea cave that leads to a hidden water sanctuary only accessible when the tide is exceptionally low."

The girls were required to wear lifejackets before Craig would let them ride on the bumpy bow. The adults sat on cushioned seats on both sides in the rear. As soon as they cleared the harbor, Craig jammed the throttle forward, and the two Yamaha 120 hp engines sprung to life. The *Wave Skipper* lived up to its name as it skipped across the wave crests, the front half of the hull lifting out of the water then slamming down, sending spray over the girls. Their shrieks were muffled by the waves crashing over the deck and the throaty roar of the outboards.

A half hour from the harbor, Craig pointed to surreal limestone shapes thrusting up from the sea. "The one on the right is Ko Phi Phi island," he yelled, his voice barely audible above the roar of the outboard engines. "The karst limestone islands are remnants of coral reef deposits laid down 130 million years ago. Then 75 million years ago, geologic forces pushed the limestone beds hundreds of meters above sea level."

The entrance to Maya Bay remained hidden until they were directly in front of the fiord-like bay, bounded by 150-meter-high cliffs. The limestone was mottled with green shrubs and stunted trees in bizarre shapes. At the back of the bay was a white crescent beach bounded by dense tropical foliage. The deep azure at the bay's entrance transitioned to ever lighter shades as they neared the beach. Craig cut the engines, and they glided to within a few meters of the beach.

"We're in luck. This is the first morning in months that there aren't people already on the beach. On most days, by noon, there isn't enough space to spread out a beach towel, and the roar of long-tail boats reverberating off the limestone cliffs is deafening."

Nadia and Elsa were the first over the side, splashing onto the sand and racing to the far end of the beach, where a hammock hung from a limestone overhang. The couples separated, so only the whispers of the surf and distant squeals of Nadia and Elsa could be heard.

Becky pulled the green scrunchie from her ponytail and shook her head, fanning hair over her shoulders. Resting back on her elbows, she gazed across the water, embraced by cliffs. "I wonder if heaven is like this?"

"Do you wish Elliott was here?"

She turned on her side and raked her fingers through the sand. "Not really."

Alex reached over and ran his fingers through her hair.

"Time to cool off." She jumped up and ran into the surf.

Alex charged after her, but a toot from the boat's horn ended their frolic in the ocean. "Becky, you're saved by the bell."

A second double toot, and two heads popped up from the hammock. The girls waved, then tumbled out and ran back to the boat. "Why do we have to go so soon?" they clamored.

Craig helped the children aboard. "There's a triple-deck tour boat just entering the bay. If we leave now, we'll miss the gaggle of tourists that will be hitting the beach in a few minutes. This will give us more time at our private island to snorkel and have a delicious lunch prepared by Chennai."

As they pulled away from the beach, tourists were climbing into small boats that could navigate through the shallow water to the beach. Craig lamented, "Before *The Beach* was filmed here, this was truly a hidden treasure." He motored slowly past the small boats heading for shore, then jammed the throttle forward, the roar of the throaty engines echoing off the cliffs.

Fifteen minutes from Maya Bay, Craig pointed to a dozen coconut palms that appeared to be sprouting from the sea. "That's our coral cay." As they neared, a patch of porcelain sand appeared under the coconut palms. Chennai joined the girls on the bow and guided the craft through the narrow channel in the coral reef.

Alex and Norman assisted Craig and Chennai with the ice chests, mats, and folding tables, then shooed them away so she could prepare the meal.

Alex and Becky swam behind the girls as they snorkeled over the shallow coral garden, at places only a foot below them. The corals embraced a kaleidoscope of shapes and colors. There were aptly named brain corals, staghorn ones as large as elk antlers, and umbrella-sized mushroom corals. The subtle hues seen in Hawaiian corals were enhanced with vivid yellow, orange, red, and purple colors. In the clutches of the corals were eight-to-ten-inch-wide tridacna clams that can reach four feet in diameter in the South Pacific—their wonderous iridescent blue-green mantles shimmering like the veins of fire opal Alex had seen at Australia's Lightning Ridge.

The girls paused, treading water at the outer edge of the reef, then abruptly turned and swam back toward their parents. Elsa yanked her father's hand and yelled, "Shark!" and all four turned toward the beach. As they waded ashore, Norman asked Elsa about the shark's size.

"It was big enough to eat me."

Nadia added, "The shark was so close I could see his beady eyes and sharp teeth."

Alex laughed, "I've never seen you swim so fast."

"Daddy, he wanted us for lunch."

When they told Craig of the shark encounter, he shrugged. "No worries. They're just curious."

Each couple was seated on the beach at a low Japanese-style table, while the girls sat on woven grass mats in the shade of a coconut palm. Chennai served the appetizer of marinated cubes of raw reef fish in freshly split young coconuts. "Eat sashimi with chopsticks, then scrape out soft coconut meat with spoon."

The main course of grilled king prawns on a bed of jasmine rice was accompanied by chilled Lindeman's sauvignon blanc. Craig quipped. "It's good for you Americans to learn to appreciate our Aussie wines."

Chennai shook her head. "Craig thinks everything Australian is best."

After lunch, the wives and girls collected shells from the beach while Alex and Norman helped pack. Before leaving, Craig carefully raked the sand above the high-water mark, leaving it smooth for their next group of tourists.

As they headed north to the sea cave, the azure water gradually lost its transparency, replaced by a milky jade color. Karst monolithic islands, called *stacks*, grew in number until they saturated the horizon.

"That's the island," Craig shouted above the roar of outboards, and pointed to a fortress-like island. Add a pennant flag and a crenellated top to the vertical cliffs, and at a distance it was a medieval castle. There were undercut cliffs from wave action, but no visible entrance until they rounded the east side and spotted a Chinese junk next to a low grotto opening.

"The inflatable kayaks on the side of the junk are what you'll ride into the sea cave. The two guides speak little English but know how to navigate to the center of the island that's open to the sky. It's pitch black inside the twisting tunnels, but the guides will be wearing lamps on their heads, plus I have two small waterproof flashlights for you. If any of you are claustrophobic, I suggest not entering the caves."

"Daddy, what's claustrophobic?"

"Nadia, it's fear of dark places."

Nadia and Elsa huddled for a couple of minutes, and then Elsa spoke. "We're a little afraid of the dark but still want to go."

One of the guides spoke to Chennai in Thai. Then she told the others that they needed to go right away because the tide was rising.

Each kayak carried a family with a child in the middle and father in the rear. The guides swam in front, pulling the kayaks—Alex, Becky, and Nadia were in the lead. The opening had jagged stalactites up to four feet long. Beyond the wide entrance, they entered a narrow labyrinth of winding passageways. The beams of light revealed glistening stalactites that in places came within inches of their heads as they lay back, almost flat, in the kayaks.

The lead guide said, "May be problem for long-nose foreigner." Moments later, a scratching sound like fingernails dragged across a large balloon, then silence.

"Daddy, we're not moving. I'm scared."

"We'll be okay," Alex whispered as he gently rubbed Nadia's forehead. Then, a hissing sound, and their kayak settled lower in the water.

"Daddy, we're sinking!"

The kayak began to move again. Then a dim light led to the interior of the island. They emerged from the cave into a circular lake about 150 feet wide, surrounded by sheer walls draped in vines, ferns, and orchids. Mist hung in the air, penned in by the ten-story-high walls.

"Nadia, what do you think of this hidden paradise?"

"It's like going into another world, but I'm a little afraid that we won't be able to get out."

Their guide pointed to a cave opening about ten feet above the water level. The guides pulled the kayaks across the lake, then after saying a few Thai words, tossed a rock into the cave. A few bats fluttered from the cave, then came a whooshing sound as hundreds streamed from the opening.

"Daddy, this place is spooky."

"Nadia, do you want to explore the cave for treasure?"

Nadia turned to Elsa. "I'll only go in if Elsa comes too."

"Nadia, I want to go back before the water rises and traps us."

Even though the water had only risen a couple of inches, that was enough to force Alex to turn his head to the side to pass under the lowest hanging stalactites. They all cheered as they emerged into the sunlight.

Chennai told them that there were many stories and myths about the donut-shaped island and the bat-filled cave. She said the cave originally contained a human skeleton and several jade amulets, and there were stories about a pirate treasure.

Craig reduced speed to give them a more comfortable ride back to Phuket Harbor. While the parents slumbered, the girls made plans for the day after Christmas, not realizing that it would be the most consequential day of their lives.

Chapter 33

*A*t first Elsa's parents weren't keen on the idea of the girls going on an elephant ride alone, but Alex convinced them that the mahouts were well trained, and it would be a memorable adventure for the two girls. The hotel activities director confirmed that the elephant ride was safe, and Jitaree, their most experienced mahout, would be with the girls.

"Nadia, are you sure you don't want us to come along?"

"Daddy, we're sure. We have it all planned out. We're shipwrecked on an uninhabited island and are exploring it on a wild elephant we tamed . . . and Elsa's bringing her first aid kit, two bottles of water, pastries from breakfast, and bananas for our elephant. What else could we possibly need?"

Becky and Angela snapped photos of the girls sitting together in the teak-framed seat atop the nine-foot back of their adult elephant, Khao, meaning "mountain" in Thai. Jitaree sat in front of the girls, behind Khao's head, his bare feet behind the elephant's ears. Khao plodded away as Jitaree gave soft commands in Thai and nudged the back of Khao's ear.

Angela turned to Becky. "Seems only yesterday I was afraid Elsa would fall off her little tricycle, and now she's riding off on an elephant."

Norman slipped his arm around Angela's waist. "Now we have two hours to poke around in the beach shops without our little daughter pestering us." They strolled north past the row of beachfront restaurants while Alex and Becky settled onto the resort's lounge chairs facing the ocean and ordered Thai iced tea.

The languid, humid air demanded little of the people on the beach, with only small children and sandpipers scurrying about. In the distance, the Andaman Sea merged seamlessly with the sky, freeing distant yachts from the confines of the ocean's surface.

Becky had just lay back, eyes closed and a contented smile, when hundreds of seagulls suddenly took flight. Alex sat up. *What frightened the birds?* His eyes focused on the receding surf that exposed the shallow seafloor. Children and adults ran toward the sea to catch the fish flapping on the exposed seafloor. It was a scene he'd seen a dozen times in the grainy, black-and-white clip of the ocean moments before a tsunami struck Hilo, Hawaii, in May 1946 and killed ninety-six people.

Alex bolted to his feet, knocking over their glasses of iced tea, and yanked Becky from her lounge chair. "Tsunami! Run and climb that banyan!" he screamed in her face. He spun around, waving his arms as he shouted *tsunami* toward the people on the beach. Most families either didn't hear him or didn't understand what he was saying—the critical seconds between life and death, lost. The white line across the horizon morphed into a wall of water moving faster than a speeding train toward shore. The distant sound of a waterfall grew into a thunderous roar as the tsunami raced ashore, drowning out the screams of people as they turned, too late to escape.

Alex spun and dashed to the banyan tree and shoved Becky to higher branches. A blond woman was close behind, lifting her toddler toward Alex as the wave roared across the beach.

"Save my baby!" she shrieked.

He leaned down, yanking the toddler from her arms, then swung the child up into Becky's arms. He leaned back to grab the woman's outstretched hand. Their fingers touched, and then she was gone. Becky held the child tightly to her chest as the screams and the splintering sounds of destruction saturated the air. Helpless, they watched as the raging sea obliterated all but the concrete buildings and large banyan and hardwood trees.

Within minutes, the roar of the ocean subsided as the surge reached its zenith and paused for an eerie few minutes, as the water swirled aimlessly around their tree. Then it reversed direction, gaining speed back toward the sea. Helpless, Alex and Becky watched people clinging to anything that floated, and bodies flowing past among the debris. Leaning low to the water, Alex cried out as he tried to grab outstretched hands that swept past.

As the waters receded, Alex struggled between immobilizing fear of Nadia lost in the tsunami and survival instincts. To have any chance of saving Nadia, he had to stay focused—logical. As soon as they could stand in the subsiding water, they waded to the concrete resort buildings. The glass doors and windows on the lower floor were gaping holes of jagged glass. At the front of the resort, people were assembling, many sobbing, as they prepared to respond to the crisis.

Becky said she'd stay and help with the injured here while Alex searched the beach for Nadia and Elsa. She joined others with first aid training at the triage station in the lobby, and Alex plunged back into knee-deep water to search for the girls. He didn't get far, as there were so many cries for help—recognizable in any language. His conscience wouldn't let him pass an outstretched hand or cry without giving aide. The first victim was a Thai woman pinned under a tree branch. He scooped her up in his arms. As he stumbled back toward the resort, a tender smile appeared on her face, enhanced by radiating wrinkles. When he handed her over to a nurse in the triage section, she felt for a pulse. He turned away, not wanting to hear the words he already knew.

His progress was slow, as there were so many people needing help—a hand reaching out or moan. By nightfall, he had searched only a half mile of beach. He stopped just before reaching their resort and scanned the beach, hoping to see the silhouette of an elephant.

Becky staggered away from the nurse station and threw her arms around Alex. "Anything?"

"Nothing. Maybe that's good and they escaped to higher ground in time. I'll start looking at daybreak."

There was no water or electricity in their second-floor room. The beds had been stripped of blankets and sheets for the injured. Alex brought a bucket of saltwater from the pool so they could bathe. In the light of their flashlight, they dined on snacks and drinks from the mini-fridge. Overwhelmed by the misery and death of the day, they ate in silence, leaning against each other.

They covered themselves with beach towels and clung together. Their voices halting as they made plans for the following day. Alex would continue his search further down the beach, while Becky would contact local hospitals and clinics. She would try to find a working photocopy machine to make copies of Nadia's passport photo and post details and contact information. Finally, Alex whispered, his voice faltering, "We need to check for information about recovered bodies." Then he collapsed into Becky's arms, sobbing.

It was a night of fitful sleep and frightening nightmares—ending with one of pounding on their room door that wouldn't stop, even when Alex opened his eyes. "Nadia, is that you?"

"Alex, it's me, Norman."

Alex staggered to his feet as Becky sat up. "I'm coming," and he flung open the door. Elsa's parents were spattered in blood—their faces haggard. "You're hurt?"

Norman shook his head. "Are our girls safe?"

"I don't know. I searched all day but found no signs of the girls or their elephant. Where have you been?"

"We escaped the tsunami and have been working in a make-shift clinic in a hotel a few hundred yards up the beach. Norman was the only doctor available. A Thai doctor and several Thai nurses arrived during the night, freeing us to search for our girls."

"How did you avoid the tsunami?"

"Angela saved our lives by having to go to the bathroom. We were on the second floor of a hotel when the tsunami struck. We had to stay to help the injured."

Alex went over the plan as the four of them spooned peanut butter from the jar Becky had in her suitcase and sipped warm Cokes. Alex and Norman would head further down the beach, while Becky and Angela would search hospitals and anywhere that refugees gathered. Unsaid was that they would check the lists of information on bodies recovered.

They waited until there was enough light to navigate through the debris before stepping outside to begin the search. A dark, hazy mist softened the harshness of the devastation, but not the stench in the warm, humid air. As they rounded the corner of the building, they heard excited Thai voices on the beach.

"What's the commotion about?" asked Becky.

Alex climbed onto an overturned boat. "I think it's an elephant! I can't see if anyone's ridding it." As the pachyderm plodded toward them, blurry figures could be made out. Alex, Becky, Norman, and Angela waved and shouted their daughters' names.

"Daddy . . . Elsa and I are okay."

Becky jumped on Alex sobbing and laughing as Norman swung his wife around. Then they knelt on the ground, holding hands as Norman said a prayer.

Khao appeared larger-than-life as he ambled toward them, debris snapping under his feet. Nadia was sitting behind Khao's head in the mahout's position, and Elsa was in the wood-framed chair cradling an adult. Clinging to the back of the chair were three children.

"Anyone hurt?" called Norman.

"Jitaree. I think his leg is broken! Elsa's taking care of him."

Elsa waved to her parents.

"Nadia, can you guide the elephant to the front lobby of the resort?"

"Sure." She nudged Khao's left ear with her bare foot and gave a command in Thai.

The parents followed alongside Khao as people poured out of the lobby to greet the elephant and his cargo of children. At the lobby entrance, Nadia tapped Khao's head and gave a command, and he slowly knelt as a dozen hands reached for Jitaree and the children.

"I don't need help," Nadia said, then swung over Khao's head and slid down his trunk. People brought bananas and a bucket of precious freshwater for Khao and stroked his head. Norman and Alex carried Jitaree to the makeshift medical examination area.

The three extra passengers were taken to a roped-off area for children without parents. A Thai and a British woman took down names and contact information of the children. Each child was photographed, and a nametag was penned on the child's shirt. After putting a proper splint on Jitaree's leg, Norman hurried back to his daughter.

The girls were served tepid rice soup with a few bits of chicken. The waiter in a dirty uniform shook his head. "So sorry. Congee not so good, but all we have."

"It's delicious," the two girls replied, then put the plastic spoons aside and slurped the soup from the bowl.

Angela wiped tears from her eyes. "I never thought I'd be so happy seeing my daughter eat like a pig."

"Oink, oink," replied Elsa.

"How did you two survive the tsunami?" asked Alex. "Weren't you riding on the beach when the thirty-foot-high tsunami wave came ashore? Even an adult elephant would be swept away by the wave surge."

Nadia set her bowl aside and wiped her mouth on her dad's sleeve. "We rode a long way down the beach past three hotels. Then Khao turned away from the beach and ran past a row of shacks to a fruit stand with a painting of an elephant on the side. A gray-haired woman with a cane limped outside and greeted Khao, and he put his trunk around her neck like he was greeting a dear friend. Jitaree climbed down and sat on a stool smoking a stinky cigarette while the woman chatted with Khoa as she fed him ripe bananas from a basket. Khoa seemed to understand her words as he kept giving her little kisses on her neck with his trunk.

Elsa jumped in. "Suddenly, Khoa's ears stood out, and he raised his trunk way up over our heads, like he was sniffing the air, then took off running so fast we almost fell off."

"Elsa grabbed my arm, or I would have fallen off. Khoa seemed crazy as he ran straight up a small hill with a Buddhist statue on top."

"Nadia, remember how we screamed when we saw the whole ocean crashing over the land and breaking up everything. It was horrible to see the little shack washed away by the gigantic wave."

"Daddy, we heard so many people screaming and saw people carried past in the rushing water, but we couldn't help them." She teared up as she grabbed both her father's and Becky's hands. "You were going to stay on the beach with Becky, and I was so afraid the big wave would come too fast for you to escape."

"Nadia, your smart father knew a tsunami was coming when the ocean receded from the beach, and we both escaped up a banyan tree. How did Jitaree survive?"

"Well, as soon as the water went back to the sea, Khoa raced back down to where the shack had been, and we heard Jitaree calling out for Khoa from under a jumble of tree branches. Elsa took care of Jitaree's leg just like a real nurse, and the two of us, with Khoa's help, lifted him up to the *howdah*."

"Elsa, what's a *howdah*?"

"Dad, it's the wooden seat on Khoa's back."

Norman pulled his daughter closer. "You're so smart. You did a great job with the splints. Where did you pick up the three children?"

"They were on top of a big tank. The ladder had washed away. Khoa walked over, and they just jumped onto our elephant taxi. We decided not to try to come back last night because Khoa might step on something sharp and hurt his foot. Jitaree taught Nadia some Thai words so she could guide Khoa."

Nadia spoke up. "You know, elephants are really smart." Her smile faded. "Daddy, what made the ocean flood the land and hurt so many people?"

"Honey, there was a massive earthquake under the sea in Indonesia that made a big wave that spread out all over the Indian Ocean causing widespread destruction, and a lot of people died."

"Daddy, you're a geologist. Why can't geologists predict earthquakes?"

"We've been working on that problem for a century and still can't predict when and where big earthquakes will occur. Think about it as bending a branch. We know it will snap at some point but don't know when. Just before an earthquake, sensors in the ground can detect tiny movements of the earth, but that gives only a few minutes' warning, and there's no warning system in this region."

"Daddy, when I grow up, I want to find a way to predict earthquakes so no more people will be killed by tsunamis."

Norman and his wife decided to remain in Thailand to help in a local hospital. Becky helped with children waiting for parents that, for many, would never come. Alex joined search parties combing through the debris for survivors, and Elsa and Nadia helped by reading stories to the younger children.

A week after the tsunami, Norman, Angela, and Elsa saw them off at the airport—bonds made that would last a lifetime. Elsa and Nadia exchanged their necklaces and promised to wear them forever. Alex wasn't sure Nadia should accept such a valuable gift, but Norman and Angela were adamant. "Our girls went through an experience they'll remember forever and might not have survived if they weren't together. No one can put a price on what they bravely faced together."

The long flight back to Hawaii gave Alex and Becky time to decompress and reflect on the events of their Asia trip. The solace that Alex found in Becky's arms the night after the tsunami eclipsed the rapture of making love in the Oriental Hotel. They had shared the highs and lows of a lifetime in eight days. He struggled with how to return to just being friends, yet that was the only way.

In Becky's mind, the trysts with Alex were about passion in romantic places and didn't change her commitment to marry Elliott. Her girlfriend, Janet, had a fling weeks before saying her wedding vows, and it didn't affect their marriage. Yet surviving a life-and-death situation wasn't comparable to a romantic tryst. Alex's quick reaction had saved her life. Would Elliott have reacted the same way? She pushed the thought from her mind as she laid her head on Alex's shoulder.

Chapter 34

*A*lex nudged Nadia as their flight descended toward the Honolulu International Airport. "Nadia, we're almost home."

Nadia leaned over Becky to peer out of the window. "I can't wait to see the presents Santa left under our tree."

Alex had sent an email to Don and Dora telling them they were all safe and their flight details. As expected, they were waiting with leis as they stepped out of arrivals, along with a reporter and cameraman. After the hugs and kisses, the reporter stepped forward.

"Excuse me. Do you mind if I interview your daughter, Nadia, about her experiences during the tsunami?"

"How do you know about Nadia?" Alex asked.

"Her photo on an elephant is all over the news. I'm hoping you'll let us interview her for the local news."

"Nadia, do you want to talk to the newswoman about your experience during the tsunami."

"Umm, yes, if I can talk about Khoa and Elsa?"

"Of course."

Alex, Becky, and her grandparents stood aside while Nadia gave an animated account of her survival story, then wiped tears from her eyes as she described the people she had seen being carried away in the tsunami.

Becky brushed her hand over Alex's back. "She's the kind of daughter I hope to have someday."

Don and Dora had stocked Alex's refrigerator and added presents under the Christmas tree. While Alex and Becky took separate showers, Nadia checked the packages to see how many were for her.

"Daddy, there are so many packages it will take all day to open them."

"Well, we better get started."

Dora passed around mugs of coffee as Nadia sorted the gifts into piles. They waited for Becky to finish her call to Elliott.

"Elliott, I'm safely back in Honolulu."

"Becky, I was so worried about you when I heard about the tsunami. I tried several times to call your hotel but got only out-of-service messages, and the US embassy in Bangkok was of little help. A desk officer just took down your name and hotel information. He told me they'd contact me if they got any information about you. I wanted to fly to Thailand, but I wouldn't be of much use, as I don't speak the language and would arrive too late to help save any lives. There are no words to say how happy I was to receive your call. Darling, can I call back after seeing my patients?"

"Yes. Of course."

"Becky, I love you so much."

Becky had a pensive expression as she joined the others around the tree.

"Everything okay?" asked Alex.

"Yes. Elliott was in the middle of his rounds with patients. He'll call back as soon as he's free."

"Daddy, I can't wait another second."

"Well, then we better get started."

Nadia's squeals as she opened gifts brought smiles and temporarily suppressed memories of the tsunami. Nadia tore through the gifts—her pile dwarfing the others. Alex shook his head as he gazed at the books, diary with a lock, children's jewelry, Polly Pocket toys, and clothes.

"Nadia, where are you going to put all your new clothes?"

She put her finger to her chin. "Daddy, I'll need just a teensy bit of your closet space."

"We'll discuss that later."

"Daddy, you and Becky haven't opened the gifts I made for you."

Nadia chewed on a fingernail as the two calendar-sized gifts were unwrapped. Becky grinned and held up her painting of a woman and young girl in bed with a book. The caption: "Happiest Part of the Day."

"I'll frame your beautiful gift and hang it over my desk."

Alex gazed at his painting for a few moments before turning it for the others to see. Nadia had drawn a man, woman, and girl sitting at a table with drinks. White pigeon feathers were glued onto the woman. Above was a crudely painted green Starbucks logo, and below the caption in red letters: "Mommy's Our Angel." Alex's eyes turned glassy, and his lips quivered as he thanked Nadia.

"Why is everyone looking so sad? I wanted my paintings to make people happy."

Becky knelt beside Nadia and kissed her forehead. "Your dad's tears are the happy kind."

While Alex and Nadia cleaned up the wrapping paper, ribbons, and boxes, Dora discreetly slipped a sealed envelope into Becky's hand. "Kelsey wrote this a week before she died and asked me to give it to you, one year after she died if you weren't married. I've struggled with whether and when to give you the letter."

Becky ran her fingers over the envelope, then retreated to the lanai.

December 18, 2003

Dear Becky,

If you're reading this letter, you didn't marry Elliott in June as planned. If you're still single, I'm hoping you can think of Alex as more than a good friend. He's shy when it comes to dating and can be awkward at parties. I don't know if there's any chemistry between you two, but you'll have to take the initiative, or nothing will happen.

I have a selfish reason for this letter. Nadia means the world to me, and she needs a mother that truly loves her. You've known Nadia since she was a toddler, and I've seen the love in both of your eyes when you're together.

Alex is a wonderful man—smart, funny, and quite romantic. I hope you'll give him a chance, but the first move will have to be yours. Whatever you decide, I want you to know you're the best friend I ever had.

Love always,
Kelsey

Becky, folded the letter and walked to the edge of the lanai. Like the tinsel on the Christmas tree, a silvery ribbon waterfall plunged down the cliff at the back of Manoa Valley, and above, a double rainbow arched over the valley. So much felt right about Alex, Nadia, and Hawaii—except for one piece.

Why did I let this happen—falling in love with two men? For the umpteenth time, she had to remind herself of the reasons why Elliott was the best choice. In her third year at UC Davis, she had written her mother asking for advice on two equally desirable suitors. Her mother had replied: "The choice isn't important, as true love is built or not over time. Once you select a mate, remember, the green grass on the other side of the fence is only greener as long as it remains out of reach."

The shrill ring of the telephone snapped Becky back to the present, and she rushed inside. It wasn't Elliott, but Nadia's girlfriend calling for a playdate the following day. Alex said she should spend the time with her grandparents, but Dora sided with Nadia. "Don and I want to do some shopping at the Ala Moana Shopping Center, and Nadia will have more fun with girls her age."

After dropping Nadia off at her girlfriend's home, and Don and Dora at the Ala Moana Shopping Center, Alex parked at the Ala Wai Yacht Harbor. Sandals in hand, Alex and Becky strolled along the beach, skirting around a six-foot-long monk seal on Ft. DeRussy Beach.

They stopped at the Sheraton Waikiki for croissants and iced lattes on the terrace overlooking the infinity pool and ocean. Becky took a long draw on the straw, draining a third of her drink, then licked her lips. "Alex, how can I ever repay you for saving my life?"

"You already have." For a moment, his gaze locked on her eyes, before both looked away. "Becky, it's time to go to Elliott. That's how life works."

Becky put down her drink and took Alex's hand. "But I'll never forget what we shared together."

Alex reached across and dabbed a tear from the corner of her eye.

Nadia's grandparents left two days before Becky's flight to Boston. Nadia seemed to block out the fact that Becky was leaving, until the morning when they were about to leave for the airport. She was playing with her favorite doll when Alex called her. "Nadia, we've got to go so Becky doesn't miss her flight."

"I'm not going!" she yelled.

"Don't be stubborn. I don't have time to argue. Get in the car now!"

The bedroom door slammed before Alex reached the door. "Nadia, unlock the door now! I'm not leaving you home alone."

"Alex, let me talk to Nadia."

"Be my guest!" He turned away—his frustration from more than just Nadia acting up.

"Nadia, sweety, I can call a taxi if you don't feel like going to the airport to see me off. I understand you're unhappy. So am I."

The lock clicked, and the door opened, and a teary-eyed Nadia slowly emerged, her arms around Rose. Nadia leaned against Becky as they rode to the airport, their whispers too low for Alex to hear.

Nadia stood stoically as Becky checked in and got her boarding ticket. Then, when her flight was called, Nadia broke into tears. "Please don't go. Daddy can marry you, and I promise to do everything you ask."

Becky put down her carry-on bag and swept Nadia up into her arms. "I must go. Your daddy will find a wonderful mommy. I promise."

Nadia struggled and pulled away as tears streamed down her face. "I'm not going to come to your wedding! I hate Elliott!" She spun and ran past Alex, and by the time he caught Nadia and brought her back to the departure lounge, the plane was taxiing onto the runway.

The Hawaiian woman sitting next to Becky handed her a tissue. "Missy . . . maybe you found the real meaning of *aloha*."

Becky nodded. "But why does it have to hurt so much?"

"Honey. Because whatever it is, it's intertwined with love."

Chapter 35

*N*adia's outburst had unnerved Becky, leaving her unsettled during her flight to Boston and her new life. She watched a movie before finally falling asleep.

"Excuse me, are you okay?"

Becky opened her eyes. The woman seated next to her was patting her shoulder.

"Sorry. I was having a nightmare about the tsunami in Thailand."

"You kept crying out, 'Alex, save me.'"

That led to a long conversation with a stranger she would never see again. Becky recounted the terror of the tsunami and the miracle when Nadia reappeared on an elephant. But discussing Alex caused her to repeatedly falter and rephrase what she'd said—unsure of her words—her conviction. The stranger listened without judgment or advice—just what Becky needed.

As their flight descended toward Boston's Logan International Airport, the woman reached for Becky's hand. "Long ago, I was in love with two men and chose Barry, who gave me security and the proverbial *home with a white picket fence.* I was at Barry's side when he died last November. Eric, the man not chosen, joined Doctors Without Borders and recently died in a plane crash in the Democratic Republic of the Congo. I'm on my way to meet the executor of his estate. He never married and willed me his personal items, including eighteen diaries. I gave forty-three years of my life to Barry. I'm giving the rest to Eric—walking in his footsteps through his diaries— starting with a visit to the coffeehouse he frequented when he was in medical school at Penn State University."

The woman's story unnerved Becky. She didn't want romantic memories of Alex to linger into her marriage with Elliott. She exited the flight, her heart pounding in anticipation of Elliott's arms. She stood for several minutes searching as arriving passengers merged with friends and relatives. Then as the crowd thinned, she headed to the baggage area. Doubts surfaced. *Maybe I was wrong and I've made a colossal mistake?*

She reached for her cell, then Elliott appeared with a bouquet of red roses. She broke into tears as they embraced—his familiar cologne, intoxicating; his kisses, magical.

"Darling, there was a last-minute emergency at the hospital. A patient went into cardiac arrest, and I jumped in and saved his life."

"Where did you get the beautiful roses?"

"I wanted to get them from my favorite florist but was running late and bought these at the hospital gift shop. Sorry."

"That's okay. I was so afraid when you weren't waiting for me."

"Becky, you don't need to worry ever again. I'm here for you and always will be." He signaled a porter to carry her bags to his gold Lexus. He drove with one hand on the steering wheel and the other inching up her thigh.

"Honey, wait until I shower."

Elliott's artsy two-bedroom condo overlooked the Charles River. Becky took a long shower, then liberally dabbed perfume in the right places. Elliott was gazing at the Harvard sculling team when she emerged wrapped in a fluffy white towel. "Any chance you can take your eyes off the river?" she purred.

He rose and planted a kiss on her lips, then moved to her chin and down her slender neck, pausing to admire her as the towel fell to the floor.

It was almost midnight when Becky whispered, "I'm famished." Minutes later, Elliott returned with a silver tray of imported cheeses, grapes, sliced french bread, and a bottle of California sauvignon blanc. She mused, *Elliott leaves little to chance.*

The following morning, they were off to the Faneuil Hall Marketplace for breakfast in a red brick building dating back to the American Revolution, then to Boston's Museum of Fine Arts with sculptures from ancient Egypt, Rome, and Greece. Elliott brought the art and sculptures alive with his vivid descriptions.

Discussions about their April wedding were put off until the second day when they had dinner with his parents. Becky knew that the affair was more to please his parents than their choice and had given up any attempt to keep it small and intimate. Elliott was the intermediary, explaining to Becky that after the wedding they would have a month honeymoon in Europe. Elliott had been there several times and promised Becky outdoor cafés on Paris's Left Bank, romantic gondola rides in Venice, and a honeymoon suite overlooking the Acropolis in Athens.

Most difficult was adjusting to the fact that her PhD research on Pacific Island economies would be of limited value living in Boston with the social demands that went with marrying into a prominent Boston family. She hoped to get a part-time teaching job at a university and publish her dissertation. Then there would be children, something Elliott and his family frequently mentioned. She hoped for a girl like Nadia, but not right away.

They were having iced coffee at one of Elliott's hangouts in Harvard Square when he leaned over and touched the small scar above her right eye. "I can't get over how beautiful you are. A little dab of makeup will cover that blemish."

"Does it bother you?"

"Darling, I didn't mean it that way. If I was there, I could have stitched up the cut so there would be no visible scar."

"But you weren't there!" she snapped. "I was lucky. Two hundred thousand people perished, and thousands that survived will have scars that will never heal. The few available doctors had more important things to worry about than my insignificant cut."

"Becky, you know I wanted to jump on a flight to come, but I would've arrived too late to help." He leaned over and kissed the scar. "Sorry that I upset you."

Becky's eyes narrowed, and she mused as she moved her finger over the moist side of her glass. *I was blessed to be there with Alex when the tsunami struck.* She quickly rubbed out the initials.

Elliot gave Becky what she needed to assuage her doubts. He was at his best in his environment—sophisticated Boston, where he wined and dined her. They ate in the finest seafood restaurants on the North End, accompanied by fine French wines with names she couldn't pronounce. He took her to funky eateries known for their food, not décor—Mike's Bakery for delectable Italian pastries fresh from the oven, and Boston's best clam chowder at the no-name restaurant on Fisherman's Wharf. At twilight, they skated on the Boston Common as he whisked her around like a ballerina. It seemed that everywhere they went, someone knew Elliott.

On their final evening, Elliott took her on a dinner cruise around Boston Harbor, with the lights of the city twinkling across the water. Becky maintained a demure smile as the sommelier exchanged pompous banter with Elliott about the best wine pairing with their rare prime ribs—a reminder of the chatter at the Misty River Vineyard reception.

Elliott turned to Becky. "Darling, do you have a preference?"

"Yes, but I doubt they have it."

The sommelier stiffened. "Madame, we carry the best selection of fine wines in Boston and have at least one bottle of every medalist California and French wine over the past five years. We only carry premium wines and not those intended for the mass market."

"Well then, I would love to share a bottle of Misty River Vineyard cabernet sauvignon with my fiancé." Her decorous smile confused Elliott.

"Honey, are you sure about the name?"

"The sommelier can correct me if I'm wrong."

"Madam, you're correct. It's a superb wine from a boutique winery that's causing a buzz in the wine industry. It was recently acquired by Armstrong Valley Wines, and we're told there's a twelve-month wait before the next vintage. Madam, would you happen to know a distributor that might have a few bottles?"

Becky reached into her purse and took out her cell. "May I borrow your pen?"

The sommelier handed her his Montblanc and card, then stood back, hands clasped in front like a schoolboy waiting for a teacher to tell him his grade.

She handed him the pen and card, the name and telephone number written on the back. "You can give him my name—Becky Sims. Maybe he'll be able to get you a few bottles."

As soon as he walked away, Elliott shook his head. "You continue to amaze me. Is he a family friend?"

"No. I only met him once."

At the end of the meal when Elliott waved his hand for the bill, the maître d' hurried to their table. "I called the private number you gave our sommelier. He's managing director of Armstrong Valley Wines and said the total stock of Misty River Wines was sold out. Then he said for Miss Sims, exceptions could be made, and a case would be shipped immediately. For your most generous help, your meal and drinks are complimentary."

Becky didn't bring up the matter of becoming godparents to Nadia until the last day before her flight back to California. "Elliott, you know I've grown quite fond of Nadia. She's almost a daughter to me. I was thinking we could become Nadia's godparents."

Elliott pursed his lips. "Darling, you've become too attached to Nadia. She needs a mother, and that's up to Alex, not you. You'll have your own family soon enough and will make a great mother for our children."

"Elliott, I don't think becoming godparents is such a big thing."

Elliott shook his head. "Alex is a single parent and runs around in jungles full of deadly snakes and malaria and climbs into active volcanoes that can erupt at any moment. That's fine for an Indiana Jones movie fantasy, but not real life. It's a wonder that anyone would insure him. The bottom line is, our chances of ending up raising Nadia are high, and I don't want to raise someone else's kid. I'm only thinking of what's best for our future."

"I understand." She didn't want to leave on a sour note. Elliott had given her a memorable week in Boston, and in three months she'd be walking down the aisle at their wedding. But Nadia would have a godmother. Now there was a second secret she'd keep from her fiancé.

Chapter 36

*B*ecky's departure had brought a disturbing change in Nadia's behavior. She became increasingly confrontational with her father. Her volatile and angry responses to simple requests were exasperating, causing Alex to snap back at her.

Work at the university provided little respite from his melancholy mood—the Hawaii legislature had cut the university budget, his NSF grant was delayed, and he had to teach a double load after a colleague unexpectedly resigned. He hired a university student to care for Nadia after school and made a point of being home for dinner, frequently picking up take-out meals from the Manoa Market Place.

He wasn't in the mood for dating, yet that was the necessary path forward for Nadia and himself. Nadia had a knowing expression when Alex appeared from his bedroom wearing an ironed aloha shirt, tan slacks, and a strong scent of musk cologne.

"Daddy, do you have a date?"

"No. I'm just going out for a drink."

"There's beer and wine in the refrigerator," Nadia said with a wily smile.

The multistory parking garage at Ward Center was nearly full—a good sign. He walked over to the second-floor bar and restaurant that catered to the singles crowd and paused to see if there was an open seat next to an unaccompanied woman. Seeing none, he spotted three empty seats and took the middle one at the raised bar at the window overlooking Ala Moana Beach Park. He ordered a glass of pinot grigio and gazed out of the open window trying to appear relaxed.

"Mind if I take a seat?"

Alex looked into the engaging eyes of a muscular man with short-cropped hair and a sleeveless tank-top. *This wasn't what I was expecting.* "Not at all. I was just leaving." He gulped his wine, nodded to his unexpected guest, and walked briskly out of the door.

"Daddy, you're home early."

"I missed you. I picked up some pot stickers that you like."

Nadia scrunched her nose as she studied her father's face. "The date fizzled."

He shrugged. "Worse. There was no date."

"Daddy, I love you."

Nadia was on a playdate, giving Alex time to clean his daughter's messy room without her getting in the way and telling him not to touch her stuff. A trail of cookie crumbs led him under her bed to a stash of chocolate chip cookies, a small flashlight, a mirror, and a marking pen. As he brushed crumbs into a pile, a reflection in the mirror caught his eye. He slid out and rolled onto his back, then pulled himself back under her bed. His hand shook as the flashlight beam passed over the wooden slats revealing Nadia's secrets, written with a black marker.

I only had a mommy as long as I can remember
Everyone else had a daddy and a mommy
Then mommy met Alex and I had a family
Then mommy got cancer and died
That's not fair
Then mommy's best friend Becky came to live with us
We had so much fun together
Daddy and Becky liked each other a lot
Then Becky left to marry Elliott
It's Alex's fault for letting Becky go
I'm lonely and want to run away

Alex's immediate thought was to call Lora Daniels, the twice-married psychiatrist that he had briefly dated. But he wasn't up to listening to her outrageous and seductive comments. Then there was Becky, who understood Nadia and cared. But a call to Becky would be an admission of defeat. He needed to put more time into strengthening the frayed bonds with his daughter. He didn't tell his daughter that he had read her secret writings. He decided to take off for the coming summer to rebuild his relationship with his daughter.

He was at his desk grading papers when his office phone rang. It was an 808 area code, so a local call. Probably an anxious student about their final exam grade. "Alex Silverton speaking."

"Alex, it's me, Becky."

"Becky! What are you doing in Hawaii? You're supposed to be on the mainland planning your wedding and finishing your dissertation."

"I'm across the street at the East-West Center. My advisor sent me back to Hawaii to get help from Dr. Richard Sheldon on a chapter dealing with environmental damage from phosphate mining on the island of Nauru in the South Pacific."

"Why didn't you call me so I could pick you up at the airport? You can always stay at my place, and Nadia would love to see you."

"Alex. You know why. It's over between us."

"So why are you calling?"

"I don't know why. I feel guilty being five minutes away and not even calling after all we've been through together. I thought we might have a cup of coffee at the Campus Center, and you can update me on Nadia."

"Nadia's been impossible since you left. She blames me for you leaving."

"She's a child and doesn't understand. You can fill me in over a coffee. But, Alex, there's little I can do but listen."

"I know. It's noisy in the campus cafeteria. How about grabbing cappuccinos from Nelson's espresso cart at the entrance to the East-West Center and drinking them in the Japanese garden behind Jefferson Hall?"

"That's fine. See you in ten minutes."

Alex met Becky on the steps of the East-West Center and gave her an awkward hug. They strolled past the thicket of four-inch-thick bamboo, down to the manicured lawn edging a koi pond. Across the pond, a Japanese tea house added to the tranquil setting. Becky slipped off her shoes and dipped her feet in the water, scattering the orange-and-white mottled koi.

"Alex, such a beautiful setting, and we're the only ones here."

"Japanese couples sometimes come here for wedding photos, but otherwise, I rarely see anyone. How're your wedding plans going?"

Becky stirred the water with her toes. "I'm mostly a bystander, as Elliott's mom has taken over everything for the coronation of Prince Elliott. We'll have a short honeymoon in the Bahamas. After Elliott completes his residency next year, we'll take a month-long honeymoon trip to Europe."

"Sounds a lot better than our disastrous trip to Thailand and almost losing our lives in a tsunami."

Becky cocked her head and pulled her scrunchie from her ponytail, letting her hair fall across her shoulders. "I'd never wish anyone to live through what we experienced with the tsunami, yet I know your character more than I'll ever know Elliott's." She looked away. "It's better if we talk about Nadia."

"It hurts me that she's so angry at me. There's little I can do to make her understand I'm doing the best I can to be a good father."

"It's safe for her to blame you because she knows you won't abandon her. If you think it will help, I'll have a talk with Nadia and explain that my decision to marry Elliott has nothing to do with you."

"I'd like that, but first there's something I want you to see at my house."

"Alex, I can't go to your place."

"Nadia wrote something important on the wooden slats under her bed. You need to read her words. I promise to stay six feet away from you."

Becky laughed. "You know it's not how far you stand from me. It's that your home brings back memories." She twisted her hair and slipped on the scrunchie. "Okay, I'll come, but I can only stay for a few minutes."

Becky lay back in the car's passenger seat, eyes closed and window down as Alex drove up Manoa Valley. "I can tell where we are by the sounds and scents in the air. There's nothing comparable in Boston, yet Boston is steeped in America's rich history."

Alex gripped the steering wheel, his pulse racing in Becky's intoxicating presence.

Becky slipped off her shoes at the front door and took the flashlight from Alex's hand. Inside Nadia's room, Becky lay on her back and scooted under the bed. Alex stood nervously at the bedroom door. When Becky began sobbing, the tears sprung from his eyes.

Nadia appeared bewildered when she entered the admissions office and saw her father waiting.

"Daddy, why are you coming to get me in the middle of the school day?"

"You'll see."

Nadia screamed when she spotted Becky, and ran into her arms. "Becky, I told my doll, Rose, you'd came back! I have so much girl stuff to tell you."

Becky held Nadia until they got home, letting Nadia do the talking.

"Becky, I'll make sandwiches while you two chat."

Becky took Nadia's hand. "I need to explain why I left."

"You came back to stay. Right?"

"Please just listen to me. I can't stay, but it has nothing to do with your wonderful father."

Tears burst from Nadia's eyes as she pulled away. "You shouldn't have come back! I never want to see you again." She ran to her room and slammed the door and kicked it.

Alex rushed to the door. "Nadia, unlock the door right now and apologize to Becky!"

"Alex, please don't yell at Nadia. She's just a little girl with a broken heart. She needs time to calm down." Becky stood next to the door and talked softly, coaching Nadia to come out, but she didn't.

While Alex and Becky waited in the kitchen, Alex admitted that he hadn't started dating but was thinking of asking out a woman in the geography department. Every few minutes, Becky went to the door and cajoled Nadia to open the door. But there was only silence.

They waited two hours before Alex walked to her door. "Nadia, honey, open the door, or I'll pop it open with a nail." Silence. It took seconds to open the locked door. "She's gone." They looked under her bed and in the closet. "She must have climbed out of her window."

They searched the bushes around the house and his car, then Alex called her friends parents. No one had seen Nadia.

"I better call the police," Alex said.

"I think I know where she's gone."

"Where?"

"She wants her mother more than anything. I bet she's gone to the cemetery to be near Kelsey."

"It's on the other side of the island, but she has a bus pass." Alex sped up the Pali Highway and over the Koʻolaus. As they zigzagged down the steep Windward side, Becky's cell chimed.

"Maybe it's Nadia."

"No, it's the Boston area code. Hello, Elliott, Nadia's lost, and I can't talk now."

"You told me you weren't going to contact Nadia on your Hawaii trip."

"Honey, I'll explain later. Got to go." She ended the call and turned off her phone.

"You better leave your phone on in case Nadia calls," Alex told her.

The sun had dipped behind the Koʻolaus by the time they entered the main gate of the Valley of the Temple's Cemetery. In the twilight, the sky straddled blue and purple, and the breeze seemed to pause. Becky jumped from the car before Alex turned off the engine, kicked off her shoes, and ran up the grassy knoll toward Kelsey's gravesite. Alex lost sight of her until he neared the top of the hill and saw her silhouette kneeling on the grass. *Where's Nadia?*

As he closed the distance, a whiff of wind brought the lilting sounds of Becky singing a nursery lullaby. She was cradling Nadia in her arms. He knelt on the grass and wrapped his arms around them. "I love you two with all my heart."

The shrill ring of Becky's cell shattered the serenity. She stiffened and snatched up her phone. "Elliott, I told you I can't talk right now. Nadia needs me."

"Becky! I'm your fiancé . . . the man you're going to marry in six weeks. I'm not going to play second fiddle to someone else's precocious, spoiled brat! You're not Nadia's mother! Now listen to me. The printer fucked up the printing of our wedding announcements, and my mother's mad as hell!"

Becky kissed Nadia's forehead, clicked off her cell phone, and handed it to Alex.

Nadia snuggled closer. "Who was that saying those bad words?"

Becky leaned into Alex's comforting arms as she laced her fingers through Nadia's tangled hair. "My ex-fiancé."

Made in USA - Kendallville, IN
28937_9781649535276
11.08.2023 1459